KU-674-411

PENGUIN BOOKS

A BOUQUET OF BARBED WIRE

Andrea Newman was born in Dover in 1938 and brought up
in Shropshire and Cheshire. In 1960 she graduated from London
University, where she married while still a student, and then
worked as a civil servant and a teacher before becoming a full-
time writer.

Her publications include *A Share of the World* (1964), *Mirage*
(1965) *The Cage* (1966) *Three Into Two Won't Go* (1967) and
Alexa (1968), of which the last two were published simultane-
ously in Penguins with *A Bouquet of Barbed Wire*. *A Bouquet of
Barbed Wire* was recently dramatized by her as a seven part series
for London Weekend Television. She also has contributed to
other television series such as *Tales of Unease*, *The Frighteners*,
Love Story, *Seven Faces of Woman*, *Intimate Strangers* and *Helen*,
A Woman of Today.

Andrea Newman is divorced and lives in London.

ANDREA NEWMAN

A BOUQUET
OF BARBED WIRE

PENGUIN BOOKS

Penguin Books Ltd, Harmondsworth, Middlesex, England
Penguin Books, 625 Madison Avenue, New York, New York 10022, U.S.A.
Penguin Books Australia Ltd, Ringwood, Victoria, Australia
Penguin Books Canada Ltd, 41 Steelcase Road West, Markham, Ontario, Canada
Penguin Books (N.Z.) Ltd,
182–190 Wairau Road, Auckland 10, New Zealand

—

First published by Triton Books 1969
Published in Penguin Books 1976
Reprinted 1976 (five times)

—

Copyright © Andrea Newman, 1969

—

Made and printed in Great Britain
by Richard Clay (The Chaucer Press) Ltd,
Bungay, Suffolk
set in Linotype Juliana

Except in the United States of America,
this book is sold subject to the condition
that it shall not, by way of trade or otherwise,
be lent, re-sold, hired out, or otherwise circulated
without the publisher's prior consent in any form of
binding or cover other than that in which it is
published and without a similar condition
including this condition being imposed
on the subsequent purchaser

To my parents
with love

I

It began to rain as he entered the park, but not hard enough to make him look round for a taxi. Emerging from the station, he had been tempted by a pale gleam of sunshine, sufficient to convince him of the physical benefits of walking. He needed exercise, he had decided, just as he needed fewer cigarettes and less alcohol: it was pathetic how the habits of sloth and self-indulgence crept up unnoticed, along with middle age, that unbecoming state which you did not even recognize until events brought it sharply and unkindly home to you. And now the fine spring rain, for her first day back. He pictured her with painful tenderness, suntanned and shivering, getting ready for college in the unfamiliar flat. Was he too late? Would she still be there by the time he was able to phone? He had left home an hour ahead, under Cassie's indulgent eyes, to catch an earlier train, feeling he could only telephone properly from the office, yet not knowing what he could possibly find to say that would be sufficiently casual when he finally heard her voice.

In the office Monica was laying mail on his desk as he arrived. They greeted each other with the easy friendship of people who have worked together harmoniously for years. He was fond of Monica: he would miss her.

'How was your weekend?' he asked her, not really wanting to know but wanting to let her tell him. Her plain face lit up: it really did become glowing and pink as if illumined from inside by a rose-tinted bulb. He hoped life would always seem as good to her as it did now. She was, in his view, a deserving case, but perhaps for that reason all the less likely to be rewarded. Once in a while he had instincts about people and Monica was one of them: he had never felt her to be endowed with luck. In the circumstances he was even surprised that the wedding was still on. He wished, with sudden fervour and the conviction of disaster ahead, that he could give her some luck as a present. That was all she needed, all anyone needed. All the rest was superfluous rubbish. That fairytale about all the various gifts – quite unnecessary. In fact even fatal: for the over-endowed, like Prue, the gods meted out special punishment.

'Well, we went to see the house again,' Monica said, blushing happily, 'and d'you know, the decorators have nearly finished. Isn't that amazing? I thought they'd be *weeks* overdue – everyone always says how slow they are.'

Of course. They were her first set of decorators. Her own personal decorators working on her own first house. No wonder the poor child was red-faced with pride, dazzled by novelty. 'That's marvellous,' he said.

'Isn't it?' she beamed at him. 'And it really looks good. I mean they've done a good job, they haven't been slapdash. Harry was so pleased. Well, we both were.'

How tenderly she said his name. Lingering over it, caressing it with her tongue, then rushing on, embarrassed, trying to be casual. It was all so familiar. Wasn't that how Prue spoke of Gavin?

'That's splendid, Monica,' he said heartily, but she stopped, hesitated, a little uncertain, looking at him like a dog trying to gauge its master's mood. Had the shadow of his thoughts reached her already?

Something had to be done. He could not bear her to suffer for his state of mind, to go away thinking she had made a fool of herself, or bored him. He sat down at his desk, smiled up at her and said with a deliberate and whole-hearted effort of charm, 'Monica, d'you think you could do me a favour?'

She brightened instantly, her smile becoming at once more confident. 'Yes, of course.'

'Could you rustle up some coffee – now? And maybe a couple of aspirin. I've got the devil of a head – it started on the train.'

She was happy again. He had made her happy by needing her help. If only it were always so simple. He glanced at his watch: there must still be time. 'Oh, and Monica—'

'Yes?' She paused at the door, on her way to the coffee.

'Could you get Mrs Sorenson on the line for me first?' He pronounced the name reluctantly, with irony, forcing himself to use it because he ought not to resent it so much, and because Monica, he knew, would have methodically and automatically reclassified Prue with her new name and number. Prue would now occupy a different page in Monica's office address book. And if Gavin should happen to answer, Monica would say with slight emphasis, 'Is Mrs Sorenson there? Mr Manson would like to speak to her.' But that should not happen, for Gavin had further to travel than Prue: Manson had seen to that when he helped them with the flat.

He went through his mail. Monica had pencilled in suggested answers for him to accept or amend. In the middle of it, the phone. Prue.

'Hullo.' How faint she sounded.

'Hullo, darling. I'm so glad I've caught you. I was afraid you might have left for college.'

'Well, I would've done, only I'm cutting the first lecture.'

'Oh. No good?'

'It's not that, it's me. I'm no good. I've been so terribly sick.'

Monica put coffee on his desk, smiled, and went out. Two aspirins lay in the saucer.

'Are you all right now?' How hard it was not to betray insane anxiety.

'Oh yes.' She sounded very tired. 'Well, better, anyway. Just terribly limp. I went back to sleep actually.'

'And I woke you up.'

'Oh, no. Well, sort of, but it's just as well. I've only got an hour to spare.'

He hesitated. 'Why not take the whole morning off? May be what you need – do you good. After all your health's more important ...' She should be laughing, going to parties, studying for fun; shopping and spending his money and

11

ringing up to tell him about it. Not being sick in that flat.

'Oh, I can't. We've got Partridge at eleven and I mustn't miss him. What were you phoning about before I started telling you my troubles?'

He couldn't ask about the honeymoon. Not yet. He knew he ought to but the words just refused to come. 'Well, it seems a little inappropriate in the circumstances.' He drank some of the coffee and threw the aspirins in the waste bin. 'I was going to invite you to lunch.'

There was a pause. Then: 'Oh.' The old familiar sound, a cross between 'oh' and 'ooh', full of childish excitement and adult mystery. It was a very feminine sound to him, his reward for offering her a treat. 'Would you think me a terrible pig if I accept?'

'Not at all, I'd be delighted. But will you feel up to it?' He was obliged to ask and yet if she said no it would be another twenty-four hours at least before he could see her. He held his breath.

'Well, that's just it. Right now, no, the very thought makes me shudder, but by one o'clock I just *know* I'll be ravenous. That's the way it goes.' She laughed apologetically. 'I'm getting to know the new me.'

He brushed that aside: it was too much for him. 'Then I'll pick you up at one, outside the main entrance. Will that do?'

'Lovely. You *are* sweet. Where are we going?'

He shook his head, forgetting she could not see him, drunk with the pleasure in her voice. 'Surprise.' When he put the phone down he buzzed Monica and asked her to book a table for two at the Mirabelle for one-fifteen. He added, as an afterthought, that the coffee was excellent and the aspirins had worked wonders already: his headache was nearly gone.

2

'Taxi, no less,' she said, impressed and disapproving, as she stepped into it. 'You *are* extravagant. I thought you must have brought the car when you said you'd pick me up.'

They kissed. He searched her face for signs of illness and recovery but the suntan masked it. Otherwise she looked the same, dark and thin. It did not show yet. She was wearing a pretty grey dress at the latest fashionable length – he thought it was new but could not be sure – and her hair was scraped back and tied with a red ribbon. She wore no make-up, except for stuff round her eyes. She was absurdly young and it hurt him to see her.

'Well,' she said under his scrutiny, 'how do I look?'

He had to make an effort. 'Fine. Perfectly fine. I think you were shamming.'

She laughed triumphantly. 'There you are. In the morning the Dying Swan, by lunchtime the Hungry Horse. Where are we going, by the way?'

He smiled. 'You'll see. How was Partridge? Worth getting up for?'

She glowed. 'Oh yes, he always is. But Judson wasn't. He came afterwards. I nearly went to sleep. People had to keep nudging me. That's the other awful thing: apart from being sick in the mornings, I keep falling asleep all over the place. D'you know, I actually fell asleep in the bus queue this morning. Yes, really. Or very nearly. You know the sort of sleep you have in church, when you let your head sink lower and lower and your eyes close and maybe you sleep for ten seconds or so, I don't know, and then your head jerks up with a terrible jolt and you wonder if anyone's noticed. Well,

I did that, sort of, only in a bus queue. I just started drooping and drooping until I finally keeled over on the man in front and then of course I woke up and he was holding me and people were crowding round saying are you all right and other people were pretending not to notice. And I said yes of course I was all right, just pregnant and liable to go to sleep anywhere, and they all said oh well, and hum, and that's different then, and they all got back in their places and we pretended it hadn't happened, only the bus was ages coming and I had to make a real effort to make sure it didn't happen again.' She giggled. 'That would have been *really* embarrassing.'

He said soberly, 'You shouldn't have been in a bus queue.'

'Oh now *really*.' She was unconcerned, even teasing. 'I can't take taxis everywhere, like some people.'

'You could. I'd be happy to pay.'

'I know.'

'But you wouldn't use the money for taxis if I gave it to you. Would you?'

'No.'

'Why not?'

'Oh—' She shrugged, cornered. 'I just couldn't. It would seem so extravagant when we need so many other things more.'

'Such as?'

'Well—' She paused, suddenly alert. 'Now this isn't one of your – I mean, you promise you aren't pumping me so you can rush off and do something silly.'

'Me?'

'Yes, you. I know you.'

'Come on, Prue. Out of purely academic interest. What is it you need more than taxis right now?'

She shrugged. 'Oh, I don't know. Nothing important. Nothing we can't do without. But Gavin needs a new suit, you know, and some shoes, and if I had taxi money I'd rather buy things for him, or half a pound of steak instead of half a pound of cheese—'

14

He said sharply, 'You mean you're not getting enough to eat?' and she laughed.

'Oh, of course we are, it's all protein. I just mean fun things like Horlicks.'

'Horlicks?' he repeated stupidly.

'Yes. It's very expensive, didn't you know?' She was proud of her knowledge: a month ago, he reflected, she would not have known the price of such things any more than he did. 'Oh, and flowers and theatre tickets and all sorts of silly little extravagances. Because that's what taxis are, after all. Anyway, it's not going to arise because we're going to manage as we are, that's all agreed, and we *are* managing, too. Heaven knows we should do after all you did to help us over the flat.'

'Wedding present,' he said automatically. They had had conversations on this theme many times. 'That's allowed, after all.'

'When I think what that lease must have cost you,' she said, serious, 'I go cold with horror, I really do. I mean, I've looked around and I know, well, it just can't have been less than a thousand pounds.'

Her eyes searched his face for confirmation and he saw genuine horror and guilt. He did not understand it. How did it happen that a girl, not rich but not poor, all her life accustomed to the best that ordinary professional middle-class standards (if you cared to be technical about it) could provide, how did it happen that this girl had never learnt to spend money with abandon or to take any of these things for granted? He made his face a blank and said firmly, 'Now, Prue, presents are presents. You do like the flat, don't you?'

To his amazement her eyes went misty. 'You know I do. I adore it. It's the most lovely flat in the whole of London.'

'Well then, that's fine. Just enjoy it. That's what presents are for. Tell you what, I'll make a bargain with you. I won't mention taxis again if you don't mention the lease. How's that?'

'It's a deal.' She held out her hand and he shook it. A cold hand, even on a warm day, but a firm handshake. There was a lot of decision in her, he thought. Not always for the good, but *there*.

'Anyway,' she went on cheerfully, 'lots of pregnant women walk about and take buses. It doesn't do them any harm.'

And what if it did? he thought. They could all choke on their varicose veins or miscarry on the pavement and I would only think what a pity, and maybe donate a little money to some appropriate charity, or increase my subscription to Oxfam, but they would not wring my heart, because they are not you.

'That's not the point,' he said lightly.

'What is then?'

He smiled at her as they reached their destination. 'The point is, you're my daughter.'

Prue said, getting out of the taxi, 'I should have known we were coming here. Oh, you *are* lovely to bring me. I know you think it's vulgar but I can't help loving it.'

Manson glanced over his shoulder at the doorman. 'I think he heard you.'

'Oh dear. Will he mind?'

'He'll be pleased.'

They went down into the bar and were given the full treatment. Manson had been there often enough on business. Prue had tomato juice while she studied the menu : this was a new development. There had been a time, he reflected, when she could drink him under the table, when she was about seventeen, before she went away to college, and he remembered thinking smugly that no man would ever be able to take advantage of her through drink.

'I don't know what I want,' she said rapturously. 'I could eat it all.'

'If you really could,' he said, 'I would let you and I'm sure they wouldn't charge. It would be such excellent publicity.'

She smiled up at him and he saw a great vista of meals stretching back into the past. Prue with a bib being fed in her high chair (he had never been squeamish about doing things for her, though less helpful later with the twins), Prue with

16

braces on her teeth being taken out to tea from school, Prue an adolescent with the largest appetite he had ever seen. 'What are you going to have?' she asked.

'Avocado, steak and salad. A man of simple tastes.' He sipped the Scotch he had not meant to order : the drink before lunch that he had thought to cut out.

'Mm, avocado.' She actually licked her lips. 'There's always that, of course. But how do I decide between that and prawn cocktail?'

'If you choose the prawn cocktail I might just let you share my avocado. Or you could have avocado with prawns.'

'Oh, that's a lovely solution. But there's still the smoked salmon, isn't there?'

'Now there I can't help you.'

The waiter smiled tolerantly and moved away. Prue crammed her mouth full of nuts and olives. 'Oh, it's so difficult. Maybe I don't need to eat. Maybe I should just pin a menu on the wall at home and read it three times a day.'

At home. She meant the flat. He said with an edge to his voice, scarcely perceptible but there, 'If you could decide on your main course I could order the wine.'

Her head jerked up from the menu. 'You're cross. I'm wasting your time.'

'Not at all. But it would be something for them to be getting on with, that's all. I've got all the time in the world till three.' Had he ruined everything?

'I'll have smoked salmon, and the lamb to follow with peas and celery, no spuds.' She closed the menu. 'There. Will that do?'

'That's fine, if that's what you really want.' He gave the order to the waiter who had magically appeared at the precise moment. 'And the wine list.'

Her eyes were troubled. 'I've done something, haven't I? Or said something.'

'No.'

'What is it? Tell me.'

'You haven't, Prue.'

'Yes, I have. You're cross. You were all right before so it

17

must be me. I ought to know but I don't so you must tell me. That's only fair.'

How direct she was. Much too direct and logical. Coming right out with it. Like that other time. 'Daddy, I've got something to tell you. I'm going to have a baby.') 'Gevrey Chambertin,' he said to the waiter. Prue did not care for rosé. Always an extremist, my daughter, he thought.

'Well,' he said, 'I'm ashamed to admit it, but it hurts me when you mention the flat as home. There now. My secret is out, and I know it's quite indefensible, that's why I didn't tell you. Because you are quite in the right, the flat *is* your home and I am being absurd and sentimental and I know it.'

She was staring at him, both hands clasped over her mouth. She looked shocked. He thought, this gets worse and worse. Now I've disgusted her as well. Finally she moved her hands and said, 'Oh God, I said it. It slipped out. I've been so careful – I knew you'd feel like that, you and Mummy. I've really made an effort not to use the word at all. Oh, I *am* sorry.'

His eyes stung. 'Prue,' he said, 'you're an idiot.'

'Am I?'

'And I love you.' How seldom this was said after childhood: what curtain of restraint descended?

'I love you too.'

They clinked glasses.

'Strong stuff, this tomato juice,' said Prue.

3

Rupert lounged back in Manson's chair, tipping it so that it rested on two legs instead of four and made deeper dents in the carpet. He was wearing a check jacket in two shades of mustard, pale and dark, and a shirt in the pale shade with pants in the dark shade. He wore suède mustard shoes and no tie and was smoking a cigar, giving it occasional quite unnecessary taps on the ashtray in front of him, and in between these dropping ash in generous amounts on Manson's carpet. It made Manson laugh just to look at him: not at him but simply out of sheer exhilaration that characters like Rupert existed outside fiction, that he could be there and all of a piece, perfectly assembled with a sense of design and symmetry rarely found beyond the bounds of art. It was refreshing, if you spent much of your time dealing in fiction, to find that your editor was a man who might well have stepped out of it: it reaffirmed your faith in the validity of what you were doing. I choose my staff well, he thought.

'So,' Rupert said, 'you're even later back from lunch than I am. That takes some doing.'

'I had a very special date,' said Manson, just for the hell of it, and watched Rupert's eyebrows lift. Even these seemed mustard-coloured today: could it be that he dyed them to match each ensemble? Surely that would be too much, even for Rupert. 'Prue,' he added, to let Rupert down.

Rupert smiled, as if to show that he had not for a moment thought otherwise. I am well known, Manson reflected, for not being That Kind of Man. And Rupert – what kind is he? All kinds to all men. And women, come to that. 'Ah yes,' Rupert said. 'Dear Prue. How is she? Gently burgeoning?'

Despite his affection for Rupert, Manson felt himself bristle. 'Not yet,' he said. 'Give the girl a chance.'

Rupert took the rebuke with good humour. 'Oh well,' he said, 'I suppose it's early days yet. I hope she still regards me as a secular godfather.'

'I don't know,' Manson said. 'I expect so. We didn't talk about you.' He had not meant to be so late, to find Rupert waiting for him, but instead of sending Prue back in the taxi he had gone with her, just for the ride, and then had to travel back again to the office, adding about half an hour to his journey. 'So how did your lunch go?' he asked, feeling

19

they had been personal long enough. Lunch with Prue had made him forget the appointment with Rupert at three-thirty. Monica should have reminded me, he thought irritably; she's getting too starry-eyed if it makes her forget things like that. Then at once he blamed himself for being so quick to blame her.

'Oh,' said Rupert, leaning back even farther so that the chair actually touched the wall, 'it verged on the disastrous, I think one could say.'

'Oh really,' Manson said conversationally, sitting down in the visitor's chair and lighting a cigarette. 'Care to tell me why?' So that was how those marks on the wall were made, those curious scratches. It must have been Rupert all along. I'm sure I don't lean back like that, he thought; I'm sure I'd notice if I did. He was not unduly worried by Rupert's description of the lunch, knowing Rupert's penchant for melodrama.

'Well, she'd actually read the contract,' Rupert said. 'I mean right down to the small print. I assumed she'd acquired an agent but she said no, she'd merely taken what she described as "a crash course", I suppose that was just a macabre joke – what do you think?'

'I don't know,' Manson said. 'Was there anything wrong with the small print? I didn't actually see the contract before you sent it to her but I assumed it was standard. Wasn't it?'

He had never come so close to seeing Rupert shame-faced. 'Well—' Rupert said slowly, dragging the word out, 'just a shade on the mean side.'

'One hundred and fifty pounds and ten per cent to two thousand, five hundred?' Manson asked.

Rupert jiggled his fingers so that more ash fell on the floor. 'One hundred pounds and ten per cent to three thousand, five hundred,' he said, almost inaudibly.

Manson said, 'Rupert, you've been up to your old tricks again. Let me see.'

Abruptly, now that the truth was out, Rupert ceased to be shamefaced and became almost belligerent. 'Well, it worked with Lucy.'

'Yes, it did. Once. But she was forty years younger and green as grass. Let me see.' He held out his hand.

'Well, it was worth a try,' Rupert said sulkily, handing the contract over.

Manson skimmed through it with the thorough speed of familiarity. 'Oh, Rupert. *Twenty* per cent of the film rights.'

Rupert shrugged. 'First novel, publisher's risk,' he remarked in mock-Jewish tones.

Manson said, 'But there won't *be* any film rights, will there?'

'There you are,' Rupert exclaimed in triumph. 'That's what I told her.'

'Meaning there will be? I thought you told me it was dry as dust but clever and good for our intellectual image, especially now with a lawsuit pending.'

Rupert looked sly. 'That's what I thought, at first. But when I looked at it again I began to see Distinct Possibilities. A sort of *mélange* of Jane Austen, God rest her soul, and Ivy Compton-Burnett, and Iris Murdoch. What more could anyone ask? Good intellectual stuff but with a nicely bubbling cauldron of evil beneath its voluminous skirts.' He gave a maniacal laugh, almost a cackle, like a stage witch, that quite startled Manson.

'Well, I only read it once,' he said, 'and I agreed with your first impressions. Anyway, this plainly won't do. Fifty per cent of the foreign, twenty-*five* per cent of America – Christ Almighty, Rupert, you'll never swing that.'

'I did with Lucy,' said Rupert with complacent nostalgia, 'and it paid off.'

'Yes, it did,' Manson agreed, 'and where is Lucy now?'

Rupert threw up his hands, scattering ash. 'I know, I know. You don't have to remind me. Gone over to the enemy. Alas, the fickleness of women. Mozart was right.'

Manson actually feared that Rupert, in his present mood, might be going to burst into song. He said hurriedly, 'So the little old lady has rumbled you. She knows she can take it anywhere and get better terms than these.'

'Yes,' said Rupert calmly. 'But she won't.'

21

'Why won't she?'

'A reason so simple it may not have occurred to you. She likes me.'

'Oh, really,' Manson said. 'That's nice. How did you bring that about?'

'You may not have noticed,' said Rupert smugly, 'but I am really very likeable. Underneath, as you might say. Fundamentally. When you get past the unnerving artificiality of my veneer.'

'I had noticed,' Manson said, smiling, 'but I didn't expect this to be instantly apparent to little old ladies who write like a cross between Jane Austen and Ivy Compton-Burnett.'

'And Iris Murdoch,' said Rupert. 'Don't forget Iris Murdoch.'

'I am hardly likely to. Ah, thank God—' as Monica entered with a cup in her hand. 'Tea, Rupert? I'm sure Monica can find an extra cup.'

Rupert flashed a dazzling smile in Monica's direction. 'Coffee?'

She beamed back. 'I'll see what I can do for you, Mr Warner.'

'But, Monica, you know what you can do for me. We've discussed it often. I can't imagine what's holding you back.'

'I'll get your coffee.' Monica, scarlet-faced but still smiling, left the room. Rupert shouted after her. 'Tell whats-is-name I shall claim *Droit de Seigneur*.' He turned to Manson. 'What is his name?'

'Harry?'

'Oh yes, Harry. Girl blushes easily these days, doesn't she? What made old Harry finally pop the question then?'

'He got a decree nisi,' said Manson drily.

'Oh really,' said Rupert. 'I didn't think Monica was that kind of girl. She certainly doesn't look like that kind of girl, more's the pity. If ever I saw a real example of clean living, a healthy mind in a healthy body – oh, thank you, lovey, that's marvellous—' as Monica reappeared with a cup. 'Made with your own fair hands, is it? Bless you. And when's the happy day?'

Monica said in a faint, little-girl voice, 'Three weeks on Saturday.'

Rupert took hold of her hand. 'You know I don't mean to be offensive. You know I wish you every happiness, don't you?'

Monica's eyes sparkled. 'Of course.'

Rupert released her. 'There's a good girl,' he said, as the door closed behind her.

'You're quite right, as it happens,' Manson said, drinking his tea. 'It's desertion, all quite above board. Monica's not involved at all.'

'I knew it,' said Rupert with satisfaction. 'Funny thing about names – have you noticed that? They're more potent than we realize. Now *Monica* . . . what image does that conjure up? The hockey field. The swimming bath. The gymnasium. Tennis courts and netball and lacrosse.'

'All right, you've made your point.'

'Well, I'm just trying to cover all possibilities. After all I don't know what kind of school she went to. Might have been croquet. But the principle's the same, I agree. The poor girl simply couldn't fight the image of her name. Society imposed it on her and she had no choice but to live up to it. Her thighs waxed muscular through no fault of her own. Her cheeks grew red without her willing them to do so. Poor child. No wonder she's so innocent. And Rupert,' said Rupert, warming to his theme, 'now am I not the perfect example of the genre? If Monica had to be Monica, am I not the quintessence of Rupert? No Rupert-seeker could possibly be disappointed in me, for I combine in glorious disarray every quality that is implicit in the name of Rupert. Shall I go on?'

'No,' said Manson, amused but satiated. 'Please don't.'

Rupert affected to look hurt. 'After all, it *is* the tea-break. It's not my fault that in your case it comes hard upon the heels of lunch. Has Monica nominated her successor yet?'

'Not yet. I gather she's having trouble finding one. She's interviewed them by the score, but there's always something wrong. I suspect any one of them would be perfectly adequate but Monica's standards are far higher than mine so the search goes on. Anyway. How did you charm your old lady?'

Rupert quenched his cigar. 'All right. I give in. You're the boss. Well, first of all I conceded defeat with good grace – that's always appealing – and lopped off five per cent all round. Then I discovered she was what your son-in-law would probably call a health-food nut. Now this was something in the nature of a tragedy, since I'd taken her to L'Escargot, but I rose above it and turned it to our best advantage. We had a strictly vegetarian lunch while she lectured me on vitamins and I admitted most touchingly that for years I had been poisoning my system with dead animals and toxic fertilizer and that at last someone had put me back on the road to health. She went away quite convinced it was an honour to pay some small percentage for this privilege.'

Manson said, 'I always knew there was a special reason why I hired you.'

Rupert looked inquiring.

'You're a con man.'

Rupert looked gratified. 'Of course I shall have to phone the manager before I dare use the place again. They must have thought I'd gone clean out of my mind. She's a wee bit deaf as well, so the whole discussion was conducted *fortissimo*, just to drive the point home, as if it wasn't enough that they'd never seen me eat an omelet before. And of course no alcohol. That's highly toxic. That was the really gruesome part.'

'Good God,' said Manson, impressed. 'I'd no idea your devotion to duty was so great. Are you sure we're paying you enough?'

Rupert smiled modestly. 'Well, now you mention it, perhaps the time has come for a small revision. But far be it from a teetotal vegetarian to take advantage of a man in his cups, burdened with toxic juices. Anyway you haven't heard the bad news yet. Joe still hasn't come through with the re-write. Says he's not convinced the passages *are* obscene and anyway they're essential and integral, etcetera, etcetera. The correspondence continues and it's all *rather* dreary.'

'Get Lloyd to write to him. Maybe he'll take more notice if he gets it straight from the legal boys.'

'I doubt it, but it's worth a try.' Rupert uncurled himself and stood up, a long mustard streak. 'Eric wants to know why we don't want *Indigo* and I thought I'd already explained.'

'You could show him the readers' reports.'

'Yes. I'd just rather not be *quite* so callous, if I can avoid it. Well, I'm off. Oh, is that the Delmer rough?'

'Yes. What d'you think?'

'Hmm.' Rupert held it at arm's length. 'Not sure about that orange.'

'Neither am I. But Morris has gone to Ibiza for a month so there's not much we can do about it.'

'We're not in a hurry, are we?'

'No. It's just annoying.'

'Quite. Well, Peter, these things are sent to try us, as my old nanny used to say. Have you ever stopped to wonder why one's old nanny should be a repository for so much corny folklore?'

'Not exactly.'

'Ah well, there you are.' Rupert wagged a finger at him. 'Now perhaps you see the error of your ways. The secret lies in the nanny, or Whatever Happened to Bette Davis?'

Manson smiled at him with the fondness he could afford to indulge because the calibre of Rupert's actual work, on paper and with people, was so unfailingly high, and his judgement so unerring. In seven years, Manson thought, I have never known him back a loser, and the winners I have lost count of. He may talk like an idiot but it's all there. God knows what instinct guided me to him at one interview, with no background, no experience. Just occasionally he overreaches himself, that's all. But that's a fault of youth.

'Rupert,' he said affectionately, 'you're impossible.'

Rupert appeared pleasantly surprised. 'Do you know,' he said, 'that may be the secret of my success.'

4

Prue, putting the phone down, thought: I exploit him, I know I do. Or victimize him even. Now Mummy's different: hearing her voice just now there was no tug of war. Perhaps she prefers the boys, always did; or maybe she just accepts me as another grown-up woman. But Daddy I take advantage of, even more than I used to. I simply can't avoid it: an irresistible impulse to play the little girl, to see how far I can go, to what length of self-indulgence he will allow me to sink. Gavin won't. Gavin won't put up with my nonsense. It simply doesn't appeal to him. He's tough.

It's extraordinary how quickly Daddy's forgiven me. Amazing, when I remember how angry he was. But he hasn't forgiven Gavin. Not at all. He can't even mention his name. I'm rather glad. That's wrong of me, I know. I should want them to like each other, but I don't, not if I'm really honest, and I always am, to myself. They both love me: that's enough. I don't need them to love each other as well. And if they did it might somehow diminish their love for me. I might not be quite such a special person for either of them if they drew together over me. They might see me too clearly. Or they might like each other too much, and where would I be then? Squeezed out by all those things men like to talk about, whatever they are, when they're alone. It's bad enough when Gavin's friends come round.

I wonder who would have won if they'd had that fight. I'll never forget it: how they looked and how grim they sounded. (Daddy: I'd like to break your neck. And Gavin: That's understandable, sir, but I don't advise you to try.) And Daddy didn't try. I was disappointed. There now,

there's honesty. What a nasty thing it is too. I w[...]
a fight, a fight over me, a fight between *them*, my [...]
But I wanted Daddy to win, because that would have [...]
something up to him, if he had beaten Gavin. In a way [...]
should have beaten Gavin, he *needed* to beat him. And I
could have comforted Gavin for losing, whereas I could never
have comforted Daddy. But if Gavin had beaten him I could
never have touched Gavin again. It would have shown such
greed, with everything else on his side. No one deserves that
much victory. It's immoral. Sometimes I think there's something immoral about how I feel over Gavin. It's just too
much. It takes up all my energy. I feel I'm plugged in to a
generator that's pumping out love for Gavin all day and I
have to absorb and consume it, or make good use of it, because there's always more on the way. Sometimes I think it's
going to do me actual damage.

No, I wouldn't have liked to see them fight, not really. Of
course I wouldn't. I was appalled by the very thought of
them taking off their jackets, lashing out at each other.
Would they have done it then and there, in the house, or
would they have gone into the garden? It's comic. And what
would Mummy and I have done: stood by and watched or
rushed in to separate them like mad dogs – with buckets of
water perhaps? Oh, it doesn't bear thinking about. But if
part of me was relieved that they didn't, part of me was
disappointed too. I don't know what that proves – that I'm a
bitch I suppose. I wonder if my baby will like having a bitch
for a mother.

Funny how Daddy went on as if it was all Gavin's fault.
And now still: forgiving me but not him. I suppose he can't
bear to think what his daughter's like. It would have been
positively alarming if it hadn't clicked with Gavin, the way
we were doing it all the time, all over the place, with nothing.
Even then it took months. So much for teenage fertility.

She paused in front of the mirror, catching sight of herself,
and patted her stomach. Oh, come on, baby, hurry up and
grow so I can feel you. Hurry up and come out of there so I
can see you.

5

The afternoon stretched into the early evening and Manson
missed his usual train. He had been involved in a long discussion with Hargreaves, the accountant, who wisely lived just
around the corner and so had no train to miss. A man of
more decision, Manson thought, would have said, 'Now, look
here, Bill, this won't do. I must be off,' and would have *been*
off, regardless. Or he would have said, 'Well, I've got a home
to go to if you haven't,' and gone to it, promptly. Instead he
had let the discussion grind to its conclusion, and watched
Hargreaves leave, and then, having just missed his train,
stayed at his desk in the new empty office and phoned Cassie,
to warn her, so that dinner would not spoil. Her voice betrayed no irritation, merely concern for him; she was, he
thought, the calmest and kindest human being he had ever
known, if it was possible to say that without making her
sound dull. For she was anything but dull; to him she even
had certain earthy qualities that he himself lacked. I should
have been an academic, he reflected, not for the first time.
Someone had told him this once, he forgot who, and it had
stuck. At Cambridge he had not thought of anything else:
while others wrestled with the shock of claustrophobic isolation, to him it was like coming home. He had never wanted
to leave such a place. The peace of it alone seemed to make
his brain expand, like grass growing invisibly in the night.
Sometimes he felt himself on the edge of some important
discovery, some revelation about the world or the nature of
man. It was nearly there, but it eluded him, finally. The
whole place made his nerves tingle, like a delicate tooth
exposed too abruptly to the extremes of hot and cold. But

with Father dying and Uncle Bernard ever with an eye to the main chance, there had not been much choice, and he did not exactly regret it. He had been happy enough.

Mindful of Bernard, now, he sat at his desk for a little while longer and wrote him a memo. Sometimes he felt the whole place existed on memos. But it was simpler, in the long run, than bellowing the firm's affairs into a hearing aid that seemed even feebler than Bernard's ears. He hoped Bernard would not attend the sales conference on Friday but he expected he would. If he did, everything would have to be said three times and the meeting would be unbearably protracted. Moreover, any policy decisions, however brilliant, were apt to lose some of their lustre after so much repetition. It brought an aura of ridicule to the proceedings and Bernard should have been the last person to encourage that. But it would be fatal not to inform him about the meeting. He would be sure to find out and he would come and make a scene. Manson did not relish the spectacle of the old man making himself ridiculous in public. Why could he not see that his innings was over? At almost eighty, for God's sake, it should not be so difficult to let the power pass, officially, into other hands. Or was he not aware that the deference accorded him was mere courtesy and it was years since he had actually been allowed to make a decision? Yet it was Bernard, incredibly, who on reading *The Forsyte Saga*, had muttered 'People don't behave like that.' Now that his deafness was advanced Manson wickedly lived in hope of hearing him say 'Nobody ever tells me anything.' Meanwhile he went on doggedly writing memos: Peter Eliot Manson to Bernard Eliot, and praying as never before that when *his* time came he would go quickly, under a bus.

He liked the peace of the office at night: he was almost reluctant to leave. Perhaps it was the resemblance to his rooms at Cambridge, if you could forget the traffic outside. The noise doubled as he reached the street and looked round for a taxi. He did not feel like walking now. In fact he was surprised how tired he was. He stood on the pavement searching for the comfortable black shape and welcoming light, and the crowds scurried past him on either side like a column of ants parting when they encounter an obstacle. A taxi appeared and he got into it, giving the name of the station. It occurred to him, as they began the long, slow crawl through traffic, that he had been doing this journey, one way or another, for half his life.

6

'I saw Prue today,' he said to Cassie, after they had greeted each other. She always kissed him when he got home, not a conventional peck on the cheek but a light kiss full on the mouth : she had moist, wide lips and usually forgot to wear lipstick. There was always a smell that he liked at this time of day, faded perfume not yet renewed, so that it had the aura of powder or soap rather than scent. Blindfolded, he would have said, 'That's Cassie.'

'I know,' she said. 'She rang me later.'

'She wasn't sick again?' he asked in sudden panic.

Cassie laughed, but gently, and said in a soothing voice, 'Of course she wasn't. It *is* called *morning* sickness, you know.'

Manson said, 'Yes, she had a bad bout of it *this* morning.'

'I know. But she enjoyed her lunch enormously. That should put your mind at rest.'

'Was that what she rang up to say?'

'More or less. She just wanted to chat. I invited them both for the weekend – was that all right?'

'Of course. Are they coming?' He held his breath, hoping without hope to hear that Prue was coming, yes, but Gavin was unfortunately prevented.

'Yes, but not till Saturday. Apparently Gavin has to see somebody on Saturday morning.'

'He could go up by train from here. Or I could bring Prue back with me on Friday night and he could follow.' It was so nearly what he wanted.

'I know, I suggested that. But they don't want to be separated.'

'Good God, for twenty-four hours?'

'I know, I know.' She was smiling. 'But we used to be like that, don't you remember?

'That's hardly the point.'

'What is the point?'

'Oh, I don't know. I need a drink, I expect.'

She was already mixing one. 'Well, they're coming on Saturday. In time for lunch, Prue said. She still has a very healthy appetite, your daughter.'

'Yes, she put away the soufflé today like nobody's business.'

'I know. She gave me a fork by fork account of the whole meal. She said how Gavin would envy her when she told him.'

'Well, I'm not going to start feeding Gavin as well, if that's what she's thinking. Thanks.' He took the glass and drank slowly, closing his eyes.

'You're tired,' said Cassie, studying him. 'Shall I leave you alone for a bit? I've got dinner to see to anyway.'

'No. Stay awhile. Talk to me. The hell with dinner – we've got nobody coming, have we?'

'No. Just us.'

'That's all right then. It can wait.' He took another gulp of Scotch. 'Do *you* think I should start feeding Gavin as well?'

'Did I say so?'

'No.'

'I don't think you *should* do anything. But it would please Prue, that's all.'

'Well, it wouldn't please me.'

Cassie shrugged. She began to pour gin for herself. 'I saw

Marjorie today. She and Alec want us to go over for dinner one day next week. I said I'd have to ask you.'

'Damn Marjorie and Alec.'

'Why?'

'That's not a proper invitation. One day next week. How can we possibly get out of that?'

Cassie poured tonic into her gin. 'Why do you want to get out of it? You like Marjorie and Alec.'

'Yes, of course I like bloody Marjorie and bloody Alec. Cass, haven't we done enough to please Prue, too much maybe?'

'Meaning we've spoilt her?'

'No – but – oh, I don't know, maybe we have at that. She's never had to do without anything, I don't mean she's unappreciative, quite the reverse, but when it came to the point she couldn't do without Gavin either.'

Cassie sat down opposite him, turning her glass in her hands. 'Darling, you're going to have to get over this. We all had a lot to say at the time, we were upset and quite rightly, and we said what we thought and they took it. That's enough. It has to be enough. They're married now and Prue's having a baby and it hardly matters any more when she started it. A few people will gossip but that's all. It's over. It's settled. It's not an issue any more.'

'Is that how you think of it?'

'How else can I think of it? Darling, look, I was as upset as you were when it happened but—'

He interrupted her. 'No. No, I don't think you were.'

'Well, nearly. It's always worse for fathers of daughters.'

'How calm you are. Putting it all into neat little categories. It's *Prue* you're talking about, you know.'

'Yes, I know. But it's *over*.'

They stared at each other for a long moment. Finally Cassie got up and went over to the window. Manson closed his eyes again. She sounded very distant when she said, 'You do have other children, you know.'

'What on earth does that mean?'

'Just that. Prue doesn't have to be your sole preoccupation, especially now.' An apologetic note crept into her voice. 'After all, she is officially off our hands.'

'Yes.'

Cassie turned from the window and walked back to him. He noticed that her new middle-aged roundness of which he had only recently become aware was emphasized by a dirndl skirt and blouse in the same shade, giving her two main curves above and below a wide waist. The outfit was green, almost as grass, and had a homespun quality about it, as if she had made it herself – though he knew she had not. She had a peasant air, which intellectual women often acquire, perhaps in compensation, as if hiding a brain behind the earth-mother image, wide child-bearing hips, freckled skin. He remembered a holiday in France when the children were small and Cassie had worn her then honey-coloured hair in plaits round her head. They had eaten bread and cheese by the roadside, drunk rough red wine and camped in a tent, and she had seemed the personification of unthinking sensuality. I seek refuge in her, he thought, but she is not like me, she does not see things as I see them.

Cassie said, 'You haven't accepted it yet, have you? But you must. They're married. She doesn't live here any more.' Her voice was tender but she spoke slowly, as if to a foreigner unfamiliar with the language.

'I know that,' he said, brushing away the tenderness. 'It's the future I'm worried about. What sort of life will she have with him? What are they going to live on?'

'If he gets his degree,' said Cassie placidly, 'they should be all right. It won't do them any harm to struggle for a bit. Look, darling, I hate to be so unoriginal, but what's done is done. You know?'

'Yes. And we let it happen.'

'Well, we discussed it very thoroughly. But we didn't have a lot of choice, did we?'

'We could have stopped them.'

'And had them go to court?'

'They might have been bluffing. We should have called their bluff.'

33

He was not aware how grim he sounded. Cassie sat down again, saying, 'Just a minute, are you telling me now that we made a mistake?'

'I'm saying that they made a mistake and we helped them perpetuate it.'

Cassie looked at him thoughtfully for a long moment. 'Do you really think he's so bad?'

'Well, he's hardly what I would have chosen for Prue.'

'No. But Prue chose him for herself.'

'Did she? Do you call that a free choice? After what he did.'

She said mildly, 'It does take two, you know.'

'Cass, you know I hold him entirely responsible.'

'Then you're just not being realistic. Prue isn't a child and she isn't a fool. She knew what she was doing.'

'That's ridiculous.'

'Peter, he wasn't the first.'

Manson was suddenly aware of the empty glass in his hand and the longing to break it. He put it down. 'How do you know?'

'She told me.'

'When?' He heard his own voice, quite calm and chill.

'Before the wedding. She was trying to reassure me, I think, that she was really in love and not trapped. She said, "Mummy, I wanted this to happen. I really did".'

Manson felt sick.

'I wasn't going to tell you but now you seem so worried maybe it's better you should know. There was more than one before Gavin. She said she was curious and she thought she was in love, all that, but she never wanted to be pregnant till she met Gavin.'

Manson said, 'I don't think I want to hear any more.'

'I'm only trying to show you that she really loves him. Can he be so bad if she loves him that much? Do you credit your daughter with so little judgement?'

Manson got up abruptly and poured a fresh drink. 'I don't know what I credit her with. I'm not sure I know her any more. For you?'

'Thanks.' Cassie gave him her glass. She was frowning. 'Darling, this has blown up awfully suddenly, hasn't it? What was it . . . seeing her for the first time since the wedding that did it?'

He answered reluctantly. 'I suppose so. Oh, I don't know, she's been on my mind all day, that's all. Did she tell you she fell asleep in a bus queue this morning?'

'No.'

'Well, that's pretty alarming, isn't it?'

'I don't know, is it? Did she hurt herself?'

'No, some man caught her, she said.'

'Well, then.'

'Now you're not going to tell me that falling asleep in a bus queue is a normal symptom of pregnancy.'

Cassie smiled. 'Oh, she's probably exaggerating a bit. I used to get pretty sleepy when I was pregnant, don't you remember?'

'No.'

'Well, I did. That's quite normal. I expect she just built up the bus queue story to make it entertaining.' She sipped the fresh drink he had given her. 'Or to get attention.'

'What?'

'Don't be so shocked, we all do it. It's nice to get attention. Like saying "I nearly got run over" when what we really mean is a bus passed a bit close. God knows there's little enough drama in life.'

He said with sudden feeling, 'Yes, that's horribly true.'

She looked at him steadily. 'Do you wish there was more?'

'I don't know. I just feel – oh Cass, I just feel so old.'

7

Prue said, 'Well, we needn't go if you don't want to.' She was lying on her back with her arms behind her head. The curtains had not been drawn and a small amount of moonlight shone across the bed. She stretched and made a purring sound. 'I'm quite happy to stay here, you know that.'

'Yeah, I notice you wait till my defences are down before you spill the good news.'

'Oh, Gavin.' She raised herself on one elbow to look at him. 'Are you mad at me?'

'No, I'm not mad at you, honey. It's just not my idea of a crazy weekend, that's all.'

'I'll cancel it.'

'No.'

'Yes, I will. I'll ring up first thing in the morning and say we can't come.'

'No. Hell, we can't do that.'

'Why not?'

'Think how sore they'd be. Your old man'd blow his top.'

Prue lay down again. She said firmly, 'If you don't want to go, I don't want to go.'

'Now that's just ridiculous.'

'Why is it ridiculous?'

'Because they're *your* folks, that's why. Naturally they want to see you and naturally you want to see them. What we really should do is sleep in a hotel round the corner, then you could spend all day and all evening with them and I could take in a movie or something.'

'Oh, Gavin, now *you're* being ridiculous.'

'Honey, you know I don't dig this family scene.'

Prue said in a small voice, 'I hope you're going to dig *our* family scene.'

'That's different.'

'Is it really?'

'Sure it is. I can't wait to feel the little bastard kick.'

Prue curled herself round him. 'Oh, Gavin, I do love you.'

'That's good, baby, that's good.'

'Do you love me?'

'Now what do you think?'

'Do you?'

'Honey, you know I don't like you asking me questions like that. Sure I love you. Just don't keep on asking.'

'What shall we do about the weekend?'

'That's another question.'

'Yes.'

'Do nothing, is all. We're going. I'll just have to mind my manners and keep out of your dad's way.'

Prue said confidently, 'It'll be better when the baby's here.'

'Yeah, so long as it looks like you.'

'No, that won't matter. Nothing will matter then. They'll be so thrilled to be grandparents they'll forget there was ever a time when they didn't like you. You'll see. The baby will make everything all right with them.'

'Poor kid. That's some job it's got on.'

8

The week crawled by. He did not know whether he was dreading the weekend or longing for it to arrive. He read interminable manuscripts and readers' reports, either ahead of Rupert or to supplement his judgement. He was perfectly aware that this was the job he resented giving up and he still made an effort to retain at least some part of it for himself. Rupert pretended not to notice the encroachment. Manson thought back to the days when he had been young and each manuscript, before he opened it, looked as if it might be the one. If you could not stay at Cambridge, not produce anything of your own, you might at least discover a rare talent and nurture it: that would be worth doing. And not sourly, with envy, as a writer-manqué, like so many publishers, but generously, with a sense of importance in the role of guardian.

There had been relatively few worth nurturing, however, and the sympathetic sorrow he felt at composing letters of rejection had faded as fast as his eager anticipation on facing a new title. He had been truly amazed. If people played the piano like this, he said, they surely would not look for work in a nightclub. If they danced like this, they would surely not even attempt to join the chorus in a provincial show. Nobody bricklaying at such a standard would ever dream of trying to get a job as a bricklayer. What was it about the written word that made it fair game? He began to have fresh respect for the masters, few as they were, and most of them dead, and though he looked in a sense harder, with more need and appreciation, for new live ones, he looked also with less actual hope of success.

But the job at least was a real job. Of all the aspects of the business in which he had been forced to dabble with an appearance of humility, the boss' son learning the trade, it was the most congenial and, he felt, the one for which he had the most genuine aptitude. His mind did not run much on advertising: he had never thought to display himself to the best advantage so could not do it for books either, though they were pointed out to him. The legal and accounting departments spoke a language of their own of which he learnt only the rudiments. Impossible to infiltrate there. The art department attracted him more, but everyone was so expert that he was no use to them except as an interested observer and independent voice. The public relations side was easy, publicity and so forth, because people tended to like him, or, at the very least, not dislike him : he did not put their backs up, and this quality, he discovered, was highly prized. Among all the agents and authors and reviewers and publicists and columnists and other publishers he saw, he never made an enemy. He himself did not think in terms of enemies, so this achievement had to be pointed out to him. It was only later, when he was older and had more experience of others' failure in this direction, that he realized quite what an achievement it was. At first he merely took it for granted. He was young and had pleasant manners. He had not had any enemies at Cambridge; he did not expect to have any here. He passed from this, with discreet encouragement, to satisfaction at evading what others appeared to find so difficult to evade, and then, finally, to a feeling of futility and anticlimax. A man who made no enemies, he began to think, must be a colourless sort of man, perhaps with few friendships or at least no deep ones, the sort of man about whom nobody cared much one way or the other. He did not wish to be that sort of man.

He remembered one time, long ago, hearing two typists discussing him, and one saying, 'What I like about Mr Manson, he's such a *gentle* man,' and the other agreeing. He had looked in the mirror and said to himself 'Hear that?' and pulled a face, for it was at a time when Prue was small and he was on the way to becoming an expert at face-pulling to entertain her. He would practise new faces in secret, the way other men might buy toys or make model aircraft. But even then, in his thirties, he had felt that gentleness, though undoubtedly an asset, was not a glamorous quality, would not stir up any man's life into wild excesses of vice. Not that he wished for such things, as it happened, but it would have been nice to feel that they were immediately accessible, had he so wished : that his very nature and aspect did not preclude them without an element of choice. If he looked in the mirror again he would see the same conventional reflection – a gentle, cultured Englishman, with dark, greying hair and a face that managed to be aesthetically pleasing without being remarkable in any way. A quiet, attractive family man, well groomed and well dressed, to whom no one could take exception, but who had given up making faces to amuse his daughter now because he, and she, were both fifteen years older.

'I think I've found you a secretary,' Monica said. He did not hear her. There seemed to be a faint buzzing in the room; he went on reading the same paragraph over and over again. She cleared her throat sharply and he looked up.

'I think I've found you a secretary.' She smiled. 'I'm sorry to interrupt you when you're so busy but I think I've really found one who might do. If you like the sound of her I thought we could interview her next week. She's in publishing already, she has three years' experience with Farrer, but she wants a change and promotion. She's only twenty-three, that's the snag, but at least she won't be set in her ways, and she'd probably stay till she gets married at least.' The unspoken 'like me' hung coyly in the air. 'Here's her letter.'

'Well, I've no objection to poaching from Farrer,' said Manson. 'They're probably paying her the minimum anyway.' He read the letter. Nothing much emerged in the way of personality: a list of facts, concisely presented, a carefully worded paragraph on her reasons for moving as if to stress proper ambition without a shadow of disloyalty. She might as well have written 'I am not a fly-by-night but I do want to get on'. Perhaps if anything the letter sounded just a shade smug to him. He could imagine her being very pleased with herself when she had completed it; it read as though it was the outcome of several drafts and had wound up as the perfect paradigm of a business letter, fit for use in schools. Not a word, not a comma out of place. He looked at the signature, in its neat, sharp handwriting. Well done, Sarah Francis, he thought. 'She seems very efficient,' he said.

'Yes.' Monica beamed as if personally responsible. 'That's what I thought. And that's unusual in such a young girl.'

He felt suddenly that this applicant was going to be his secretary, had been divinely chosen by Monica, and there was nothing he could do about it; the whole matter had been taken out of his hands and the interview she was proposing was a mere formality or, at most, a chance for Monica to make sure *she* approved.

'Shorthand one hundred and twenty, typing one hundred,' he read out. 'Is that really necessary? I'm sure I don't dictate as fast as that, and there aren't *that* many letters per day.'

'She's no faster than I am,' said Monica, a trifle sharply.

'No, I'm sure she isn't. But I'm equally sure I've never used your – er – speeds to the full either. Have I?'

'Well, not very often. But it doesn't do any harm to have them, all the same. It leaves a good safety margin.'

It sounded to him as though they were discussing dangerous machinery rather than secretarial work: he had a vision of cogs and wheels and hair tied back in a net. 'Monica,' he said, 'I wish you weren't going.' He meant that too many things in his life were changing at once. He nearly added 'I'm used to you,' but realized in time that this might sound unflattering so changed it into the time-honoured words 'I shall miss you.'

Monica to his horror burst into tears.

'Oh, Monica,' he said aghast, 'what's the matter? I didn't mean to upset you.'

Monica stood in the middle of the room, her hands over her face and sobbed. He felt impelled to greater efforts of consolation.

'Now come on, my dear, sit down.' He got up from his chair and began fussing round her. 'You're overwrought. It's pre-wedding nerves, that's all it is. Better have a drink.' He managed to get her seated, still weeping, and rooted in the cupboard of drinks kept for visitors. There being no brandy, he poured her a large glass of sherry instead. 'Now then, you drink this and you'll soon feel better.'

Monica took a large gulp. He heard her teeth trembling on the glass. She swallowed and sniffed. Inevitably her first words were, 'I'm sorry.'

'Now there's nothing to be sorry for.'

41

A fresh wail of grief. Choking sounds interspersed with words. 'Didn't mean – not fair – burden – sorry – always been so kind—'

He put his hand on her shoulder. 'Monica,' he said, 'calm down. Take your time. Is it more than pre-wedding nerves? Do you want to tell me about it?'

Monica nodded vigorously. She produced a packet of tissues from her handbag and blew her nose and wiped her eyes on three of them in quick succession. He waited, wishing he had poured himself a drink, but it was too late now: it would break the moment if he got up.

'It's Harry,' Monica eventually said.

He prompted her. 'You had a row.'

She nodded.

'A serious one?'

'I don't know.'

He waited.

'It's just that – well, I get so tense with all the waiting. I keep thinking, suppose something goes wrong and he doesn't get the decree absolute and we can't get married.'

Manson said in his most soothing voice, 'Now, why should anything go wrong?'

'I don't know.'

Manson wished he didn't feel so sure that something would indeed go wrong, only not until later, when it would be too late.

'You haven't moved in together or done anything that might complicate the divorce?'

She shook her head. He wondered if he had shocked her. One way and another, he thought, I don't understand the younger generation. My own daughter, at nineteen, carries on little better than a whore, and my secretary at thirty-plus behaves like the Virgin Mary. I need a holiday.

'Well then, there's nothing to worry about, is there? It's all going to go quite smoothly and you'll get married just as planned and move into your nice new house. You'll see.'

Monica raised a ravaged face from the tissues. 'But suppose Harry changes his mind?'

'After all this time? Now you're being silly. Why should he change his mind?'

'I'm being so moody. It's enough to put him off. I wouldn't blame him—' A new howl of misery as full realization sank in, of the horror that Harry's change of mind would entail.

'Well, I would. I'm sure he understands how you feel. Waiting is always the worst part of anything, particularly at the very end. It's bound to get you down. I expect he's feeling tense himself and that's why you quarrelled.' He went on and on in this vein – it was like talking to a frightened horse; any moment he might give her a reassuring pat – and watched her grow calmer. Finally she said as if to reward him for his efforts, 'I really am trying to find you the best possible secretary.'

'I know you are. And I appreciate it.'

'Well, that's what you deserve. Oh—'

God, she was starting again.

'I've been so happy working for you.'

'I don't know what I would have done without you, Monica.' Somehow the conversation served to remind him that he had not yet bought her present. She would have to have a personal present from him, as well as the one from the office. What on earth could he give her? He had not the remotest idea. But Cassie would know. Or perhaps he would ask Rupert, though Rupert's suggestions might be obscene.

Monica sniffed and said, 'It's been a wonderful nine years.'

'Has it really been as long as that?'

'Yes.' She looked at him with bright, shiny eyes. The end of her nose was pink. Monica, he thought, I am very, very fond of you, and you are without doubt the plainest girl I have ever seen.

He walked in the park at lunchtime. It was sunny and he did not want to eat, beyond beer and a sandwich in a pub. As usual it was full of people and because he had been reading for most of the morning he saw them as characters, each

43

waiting to be chosen by an author. Where did they all go? He remembered being a child, shopping with his mother the week before Christmas, holding tight to her hand, his bright woollen mitten in her sober leather glove, and looking round at the lights and the shops and the people scurrying round Oxford Street and Knightsbridge like rabbits. He liked rabbits: he had just acquired one for his birthday and was hoping to be given another for Christmas, then they could have babies. He saw himself selling them at school, becoming a rabbit tycoon and amassing vast wealth in shillings and sixpences, and he knew at the same time that he would never want to part with any of them, although people told him that rabbits produced babies very fast and in great numbers. He had watched the rabbit closely since it was given to him and he thought that the people in the street moved in very much the same way, with small, urgent steps and sudden changes of direction.

'Where do all the people go at night?' he asked his mother, and she said, 'They go home, of course,' in her don't-bother-me-now voice. Her face had the same expression, when he looked up at it: all busy and preoccupied and somehow shut in upon itself, as if it could actually grow smaller. He thought of it as her folded-up face.

But it wasn't a satisfactory answer; though he knew he wouldn't do better while she was in her shopping mood. Shopping ought to be fun; he wished she would make it fun. But he no longer expected her to. He knew now that she always got very grim before Christmas and said that she had too much to do. He never actually found out what.

He had tried to picture the people in the street all going home but he couldn't; it was impossible to imagine enough houses to contain them all. He didn't know about flats. So he pictured them going into burrows instead, vanishing one by one into holes in the ground in a wood like the one he played in. And when he got tired of that he pictured them in cages, like *his* rabbit's cage, being fed with lettuce and carrot by other rabbit-people, and he laughed because it was funny, because he was still seeing them with their hats and coats and shoes on. It was like *Alice in Wonderland*, only better.

His mother looked down at him and said, 'What's the matter with you, what are you laughing at?' and he said 'Nothing,' because it was always safer, and because he knew that she did not really want to be told, not now, and because even if she had it would have been too difficult to explain, in the street with the noise of the traffic. He would have had to shout and he wanted to whisper.

There was a December smell in the street, a city smell, full of chestnuts and petrol and frost and soot; he liked it very much. There was a rawness about the air, so that when he breathed it in he was not entirely comfortable, but he didn't mind. It was always like that and it was very important that things should go on being the same. He was not even sure that he would have liked – *really* liked – his mother suddenly to forget about all the things she had to do and decide that shopping was fun. It would have been nice but alarming, as if she had turned into someone else.

In the park he sat on a bench for a while, before resuming his stroll, and watched the ducks and the people feeding them. He thought he had not developed very far from the boy he remembered in the Christmas street forty years ago: he still resented change. And yet in a sense he craved for it. Perhaps it was that if certain changes were forced upon you, you were obliged to long for others, even to create them, in order to prove that you still had some control over events. What did he have to look forward to? Prue's baby – a mixed blessing – another fifteen or twenty years in the firm and the hope that either David or Andrew, if not both, would care to follow him there in due course. Retirement: would he become a mellow old man in the garden, sniffing Cassie's roses and sleeping in the afternoons? Christ! It was unbearable. He was not yet fifty and he was practically burying himself. They did not *have* to live in the country after all; they could take a small place in town and lead a gay life seeing lots of people, as they had when they were first married. He wondered if Cassie would like that again. He was

45

not even sure that *he* would, but at least it would be a change. Or he could retire early and really do some academic work, maybe even carve out a new career for himself. That was more like it; but would he have the initiative when it came to the point? And it would mean leaving David (or Andrew) to cope at a relatively early age – as he had been left. He knew how tough that could be. And suppose neither of them cared to take it on, what then? He would have worked all these years very largely for nothing. It would not be a family firm any more.

He looked at the people around him, at the cross-section attracted by the park. Only the young ones showed some emotion, wrapping themselves round each other as he had seen Prue and Gavin do when they thought he was out of the room. He couldn't bear to watch them. It was so long ago since he and Cassie had done that, but he had not thought to be reminded so abruptly that he was well and truly middle-aged. Past it, he thought bitterly; now there was a nasty expression, full of cruelty and patronage. It could only have been invented by the young. He looked at the faces of the older people, at the ones his age and older, and he thought he detected resignation, in faces and movements, as if they knew that the young condemned them and they accepted the verdict: it was indeed all over for them, and they hid their anxieties and preoccupations behind a mask of indifference. He wondered if he looked the same to them.

9

'Mummy, please may I have some more?' Like a child.

'Yes, if there is any more.' Cassie scraping the remains on to her plate.

The boy, silent, as if by non-participation he could at least be sure of not giving offence. Long hair. A flowered sleeveless jacket and tie on a black lace shirt. Flowered trousers. Maroon suède shoes. And Prue in some long shapeless thing not at all like the nice grey dress she wore for lunch the other day.

'Gavin?'

'No, thank you, Mrs Manson.'

'You ought to call her Mother.'

'Don't be silly, Prue, it doesn't matter. Let him do it when he's ready.'

'You should call them Mother and Father.'

'Prue. Leave him alone.'

'I was only teasing him.'

Prue in a bikini. Was he the only one to feel his eyes riveted on her stomach? Nothing to see. Gavin rubbed oil all over her, very slowly and conscientiously, then she turned over so he could do her back. Cassie read a library book; Manson sheltered behind dark glasses. Why in God's name did it have to be hot so they were all forced together into the garden? Not that it wasn't big enough for separation but somehow while it was all right to use different rooms in the house because of their allotted functions, in the garden it would have seemed pointed not to sit together in a close little group on the lawn. If only the boys had been home from school: at least they would have made a decent noise. It seemed to him that he could hear every bee that buzzed as a separate entity. A distant plane droned overhead. Someone nearby started up a motor-mower. A dog barked.

'Are you asleep, Daddy?'

He didn't answer her.

'Mummy, what's up with Daddy?'

'Darling, he'll hear you.'

'No, he won't, he's asleep.'

'He's not asleep and the window's open.'

'How do you know?'

'I just opened it.'

'No, about him not being asleep.'

'Oh, I just know.' Cassie filled the kettle.

Prue sighed. 'Do you think I'll ever know Gavin that well – to know when he's only pretending to be asleep?'

'I expect so. But it's not vital – just convenient.'

'Hm. But why is he pretending?'

'I expect he doesn't want to talk.'

'Oh. I left him alone with Gavin in case he woke up and they wanted to talk.'

'Never mind. You can't force it, you know, Prue. They've both got a lot to forget. Now if you really want to help you can butter some bread.'

'You're awfully tolerant, aren't you?'

'Am I? Hovis and raisin bread, it's on the table in front of you. Well, it's just no good trying to force people. I remember when I was at school being introduced to some child and the teacher saying, "Now I want you and Josephine to be very good friends." Who knows, we might have been, but for that. That started the biggest feud in the history of the school. People were still talking about it years after we left.'

'Why didn't you tell me that before?'

'I don't know. I suppose I didn't think of it. Is it important?'

'I like hearing about you when you were young.'

'Darling, don't use the butter straight out of the fridge, it's much too hard. There's some more in the larder.'

'Sir, do you and Mrs Manson have any plans for the summer?'

'Why?'

'I merely wondered.'

Is he trying to be pompous or polite? Or am I supposed to respond with a question?

'Why, do you?'

'Oh, Prue and I thought we'd go to the South of France

48

for a month or two. I've got a friend over there with a cottage we could use.'

A month or two. So casual. Meaning I won't see her all that time.

'You and Mrs Manson could join us if you'd care to.'

Incredible. He can't mean it. A grand gesture. Anyway, quite out of the question. 'Thank you, Gavin, but I'm afraid that's not possible.'

'Oh, that's too bad.' Never any expression in his voice, even when I threatened to hit him. Wish to God I had. 'We wouldn't be going till August; we're going to work all through July to make the fare.'

'Both of you?'

'Yeah.'

'Are you sure that's a good idea?'

'Well, we can't make enough otherwise.'

'I'm talking about Prue's health.'

'Prue's perfectly healthy, sir.'

'I think that's a question for her doctor to answer. Being sick and fainting in the street—'

'She's okay, sir.'

'I'm delighted you think so. But you're hardly an expert, are you?'

'No, sir, I'm not an expert.'

'And you don't think it would be advisable to consult an expert?' Christ, what is it about him? He always makes me sound so pompous I hate myself but can't stop. Does he do it deliberately or is it just our mutual chemistry?

'I don't think Prue needs her doctor's permission to put in four weeks in an office.'

Now I'm making him pompous. If I wasn't so angry I would find it funny. A great human limitation, to realize something is laughable and yet not be able to laugh at it.

'You must realize I'd be more than happy to pay Prue's fare.'

'I do realize that, sir, but we couldn't accept.'

He enjoyed using that 'we'. Damn him. I realize I actually,

49

actively hate every bone in his body. He's going to ruin my daughter's life and he's made a good start already.

'Well, of course, if your pride is more important than Prue's welfare . . .'

'That's not how I look at it, sir.'

This exaggerated, phony respect makes me choke. 'How do you look at it?'

Shrugs. Really those clothes of his are detestable. 'We need the money and it won't do Prue any harm to work. It's no harder than studying.'

'Tea-up.' Prue shrieking across the lawn. We both turn and wave. Cassie with a tray coming nearer and nearer, white linen cloth and the best china. Different kinds of bread, pots of honey and jam, biscuits and chocolate cake already starting to melt in the sun. He gets in first, leaping up to take the tray from her. 'Gee, that looks good.' Prue, a little behind, looks from one of us to the other.

'What's the matter? What have you two got such long faces about?'

Cassie : 'Prue, darling, do hush. Have a little tact.'

'But they look so *grim*.' Quite unabashed, my daughter.

'Your dad can't join us in France, hon, that's all.'

'France?' says Cassie inquiringly.

'Mrs Manson, can I give you a hand?' Gavin's sudden appearance in the kitchen gave Cassie quite a shock.

'Oh. No, thank you, Gavin. I think everything's under control.'

'Oh, pity.' He hovered by the sink. 'I guess I wanted an excuse to talk to you.'

'Do you need one? All right, then, you can peel the mushrooms.'

'Great.' He perched on a stool and began. 'I thought – well, I thought maybe I should leave Prue and her father alone for a bit, I thought maybe they'd have things to say.'

'That was very tactful of you.'

'Well, I thought we might too. I . . . don't know quite

50

how to put this but ... well, I sure hope our being here isn't going to create any kind of discord.'

Cassie frowned. 'Between whom?'

'Well, you and Mr Manson. And look, I'm sorry about that Mother and Father bit but I just can't manage it yet.'

'That's all right,' Cassie said easily. 'Nobody expects you to. Nobody but Prue, that is.'

'Oh, she likes playing. That's nothing.'

The remark struck a chill into Cassie. How well you know her, she thought, my daughter. Is this what she wanted, this absolute knowledge and acceptance? 'Well, I shouldn't worry about discord,' she said. 'We've been married a long time and we understand each other.'

'Yeah.' He brooded, peeling a mushroom with extreme care. 'Well, I sure hope Prue and her dad are going to get over this thing.'

Cassie said with feeling, 'Yes, so do I,' and wondered if she was being disloyal.

'Because – to be quite honest with you – it makes me uncomfortable to be around it. Look ... I wouldn't have come. I mean it's okay with me if Prue wants to visit on her own. But she wouldn't come without me. So I said I'd try to keep out of her dad's way.' Another pause. 'I guess I haven't been too successful.'

Cassie sighed. 'Gavin, it's going to take time, that's all. It's – very difficult.'

'But not for you. You've accepted it. I mean you don't treat me like I'd crawled out from under a stone.'

Cassie said lightly, 'Well, you haven't, why should I? Anyway, it's easier for me.' She felt he deserved an explanation but that was as close as she could get.

'Is it? Oh, I guess it must be harder for fathers of girls.' He pondered, the mushroom stalk pale in his hands. 'I sure hope our baby's a boy, that's all.'

'Well, we had a super honeymoon, thank you for asking,' Prue said sharply.

'Good. I'm delighted to hear it.'

51

'It was nice of you to pay.'

'Your mother paid. It was her present.'

Prue shrugged. 'Same thing. Anyway, I think honeymoons are a *great* idea.'

Goaded, he said, 'Is honeymoon quite the word?'

'Why not?' She opened her eyes wide: he could almost believe her surprise was genuine.

'In the circumstances,' he said tightly.

' "Honeymoon," ' Prue recited, ' "the first month after marriage, the interval spent by a newly married pair before settling down in a home of their own." That's the dictionary definition. I looked it up.'

'You know quite well what I mean.'

She shook her head. 'No, I don't. It doesn't say anything about pregnancy, if *that's* what you mean. And anyway, why is that such a dirty word? After all I am *married* now, it's all *respectable*. Don't you want to be a grandfather?'

'In normal circumstances, yes of course.' But he had never considered it. It had always seemed such a long way off.

'So you haven't forgiven me.' She came nearer, eyeing him curiously. 'Funny, on Monday I thought you had.'

'Prue, you know my views. I just don't want to discuss it any more.'

She turned away. 'No, you really don't, do you?' She shrugged, and picked up the paper. 'Which room have you put us in, by the way?'

'What? Oh, the spare room.' The question took him by surprise.

'Oh. Not my old room.'

'No. We – thought you'd be more comfortable in the spare room.'

She turned back, wearing the disappointed face of childhood. He had seen it often (No, you can't have another meringue, Yes, you must clean your teeth after meals) and knew well the sulk that followed it.

'Oh, what a pity. I love my old room. We could perfectly well have managed in a three-quarter bed. No trouble at all.'

He flinched from the picture she was conjuring up. 'Well, your mother thought the spare room would be better.'

'Oh, *Mummy*.' A tiny smile, just this side of mockery. 'I bet she didn't. I'm not big yet or anything. In fact it doesn't show at all yet, does it?'

'No.'

'Can't we swap? I hate twin beds.'

'Prue, it's all arranged ...'

'Oh, I see. You're putting your foot down. Well, the spare room it is then. I *guess* we can manage in one of the beds if we try.'

In the evening a concert on television. Submerged by the music, trying to pretend that the undercurrents simply don't exist. My daughter quiet and tense, withdrawn in her chair, curled up with her feet under her. Somewhere inside her, beneath the absurd heap of clothes, that baby floats. His baby. Little arrogant go-getting runt in the chair next to her, impregnating her, marrying her, holding a gun to our heads, when she should have had the best and all the time in the world to find it. For what else was she born, for what else did we make her, Cassie and I?

He's holding her hand. If I didn't love her I wouldn't care that she's lowered herself to this. But what a solution. Is this the answer, to stop loving your children so that whatever they do it cannot hurt you, because you don't care? Her choices are over, and they'd hardly begun. She's only nineteen and her life is fixed, a long corridor, interminable, with no doors opening off it. Whither he goeth, she goes. He'll drag her down and down, to whatever level he chooses, and I am powerless to help. There is nothing more I can do for her. I am reduced to buying her lunch at the Mirabelle and paying for a lease on her flat so that she can live in comfort with *him*. I can no longer guide her, advise her or help her : she is out of my sphere of influence. All her potential, all that bright shiny talent we nurtured so happily, the ponies and the music and the fun, all sunk into cooking his meals and

53

bringing up his child. She could have had anyone and she chose to have him.

Prue said to Gavin, 'Isn't it lovely?'

'Yeah, great.'

'They put us in here on purpose.'

'What?' Gavin was pulling his shirt over his head.

'They wouldn't let us have my old room. Don't you think that was mean?'

'I don't see that it matters.' Gavin unbuckled his belt and slid out of his trousers.

'But I love my old room.'

'So? You've slept in it often enough. What's one night more or less?'

Prue looked at him. 'But I wanted to sleep there with *you*.' She put her arms round him. 'Oh, aren't you delicious, all dark and hairy in your pants. Take them off.'

'Well, that is what I had in mind, just give me some space.' He tugged them off and threw them in a corner. 'Which bed do you want?'

'Whichever you're having.'

'Oh, honey, come on, not again.'

'What d'you mean, not again?'

'Like this morning we nearly missed the train.'

'I know, wasn't it fun?'

'Yeah, it was great. And tomorrow maybe. Only right now I'm pooped.'

She switched on mock-misery. 'You're bored with me already. Oh! How shall I bear it? My lord and master wearies of me. Oh!'

'Cut it out, honey. I'm tired.'

'But you've done nothing all day.'

'Yeah, I know. But doing nothing down here beats a whole week at school.' He got into bed. 'Put the light out, huh?'

Prue stood at the window in the dark. She said presently, 'Even the garden doesn't look right from here. I hate this room. It's for guests.'

'We *are* guests. Go to bed.'

Pale moonlight gleamed on her newly-brown skin as she crossed the room. 'All right, since you insist. Move over.'

'Oh, Christ.'

'Well, that's a nice welcome.' But her fingers had reached him. 'Oh ho. Who said he was tired?'

'Reflex action.'

'Oh yes. That's quite a reflex you've got.'

They grappled in silence. Presently he said, 'Well, you asked for it.'

'Oh yes. Please yes.'

'Slave?'

'Yes. Anything you say.' And much later, drowning, gasping for breath, 'Oh please more. Really hurt me this time.'

'There, that wasn't so bad, was it?' Cassie said when they were undressing.

'What?' He despised himself for affecting not to understand but the pretence was automatic.

'Our day *en famille*.' She spoke tolerantly, humouring him, he felt, which enraged him.

'No, it was *great*.' (In the spare room, two walls away, Prue slept with Gavin.)

Cassie began to laugh, then, seeing his face, stopped. 'Oh, darling, it doesn't *matter* how he talks, does it? Really? He can't help it.'

'And the clothes. And the hair. He can't help that either?' (It would have been intolerable to have them next door.)

Cassie shrugged helplessly. 'He's just young. They're all like that now. It's just a fad. Part of being young. We all did it once, more or less. We had our funny fashions and our special slang.'

'Oh yes?' He got into his pyjamas, unpleasantly conscious of looking and sounding sulky. If they had been next door, in Prue's old room, he would have been listening, and trying not to hear.

'Well, didn't we? Don't you remember?'

What did she mean, that he was too old to remember? Was she taking sides with them against him? His last citadel fallen and the world upside down. That was bad enough, but it was the sense of ridicule that was hardest of all to bear, and that came as much from within him as from those around him. I am making myself a laughing-stock, he thought, behaving like a jealous old man because it's all over for me and for them it's still *happening* or whatever they call it. The world belongs to the young and you're a fool if you resent it. They're the new *élite*. You're a narrow-minded sentimental old fool if you object to your daughter being knocked up by a long-haired layabout.

'Anyway,' Cassie went on, 'what was all that about France?'

'Oh.' He got into bed and looked defensively round for a book. 'We were cordially invited to spend our summer holidays with them in the South of France.'

'And you said we couldn't go.'

'Well, naturally.'

'Why?'

He was truly taken aback. Perhaps the passages in books he had summarily rejected in which people said 'What do you mean, why?' and 'Are you seriously suggesting ...' in outraged tones, were not so wide of the mark. The highbrow novel might endeavour to reject cliché, but cliché was the humiliating stuff of real life. He surrendered to it and allowed himself to say, 'I should have thought that was obvious.'

Cassie sat on the edge of the bed in her nightdress and said seriously, 'I don't see why. It might have been very nice.'

'Nice!' He could not prevent himself from echoing her. (Were they asleep?)

'Well, we won't get anywhere by ignoring them, will we? We might all have got along quite well in the sun. You *like* the South of France, you might even get to like Gavin in a holiday atmosphere.'

Out it came, too much, too bitter, but unstoppable. 'Why should I, when you obviously like him enough for both of us?'

Cassie gave him a long, thoughtful look which he very

56

much resented. 'Not particularly. I mean I don't like him or dislike him. I just accept him and I think it would be a lot better for you, as well as everyone else, if you could too. There's simply no point in keeping up a feud when he's one of the family. If he was ... Dracula we'd have to accept him now or risk alienating Prue. And neither of us wants to do that.' She got into bed. 'At least if he asked us to join them on holiday *he's* making an effort, isn't he? It can hardly be his idea of fun. When did we ever ask my parents to go away with us?'

Manson lay down and switched out the light on his side of the bed. 'Now you're saying he wanted us to refuse. So what would have been the point of accepting?'

Cassie sighed. 'I'm simply pointing out that he was making a peace move which I think was rather nice of him.'

'Only he didn't want to be taken up on it.'

'Well, probably not, but—'

'Then I did him a favour. He had all the kudos of making the offer and none of the inconvenience of having it accepted. Ideal.'

Cassie switched out her light. 'All right, we won't talk about it any more. Prue looks very well, don't you think?'

This was too much for Manson. 'She won't much longer if he has his way.'

'Whatever do you mean?'

'He wants her to work in an office all through July to earn the fare for the holiday.'

'Well?'

'You find that quite acceptable, do you?'

'Why, won't he be working too?'

'Yes.'

'Well, then.'

'You don't see any difference?'

'Darling, do try to be rational. She's only three months pregnant. Lots of women work up to six or seven months. It's perfectly all right so long as she takes it easy and gets enough rest.'

'You never worked when you were pregnant.'

57

She squeezed his shoulder. 'I was lucky, I didn't have to. But I would have done if we'd needed the money.'

'Well, I wouldn't have let you.'

'I do love it when you sound masterful. It makes me feel young again.'

'Now you're changing the subject.' He hated himself for not being able to respond to the warmth in her voice. He would have liked nothing better than to make love to her and by so doing forget the whole ghastly mess, but he was prevented as surely as if they were in different rooms.

'Oh.' He heard her registering the rebuff. 'Well, times have changed, I suppose. The working wife is taken for granted now, even the pregnant working wife. When we were young it was rather unusual.'

Everything went back to age. It was as if he was on some hideous roundabout, perpetually passing the same point, unable to jump off. He lay in the dark and let the words revolve in his mind: too old, times have changed, they're young, accept the inevitable, things are different now, on and on, digging an endless division. Not a family any more but two generations at war. How abruptly it happened.

Cassie said gently, 'I'm sorry you're taking it so hard.'

'Yes, I'm making a fool of myself, aren't I?' The bitterness shocked him, yet he could not control it.

'No, I don't mean that and you know I don't. It's just sad.'

'Yes, it's pathetic that I haven't come to terms with it.'

She didn't rise to that. Instead she said slowly and distantly as if to herself, 'It's different for men, I suppose. There's no dividing line. Once I accepted that I could never have another baby, that all that was over for me, I also accepted that nothing would be so sad ever again. In a way Prue's doing it for me, having the baby. It does make me envious, up to a point, but happy as well. I don't feel so much a grandmother as a sort of proxy mother-to-be.'

He said, wondering, 'Why did you never tell me you felt like that?'

'There wasn't much point. You can't fight the menopause.' It was like her to use the correct term. 'You didn't want any more children after the boys were born, and it wouldn't have mattered how many we'd had, I'd still have felt the same, I think. It isn't the actual child you want, in the end, just the knowledge that you're capable of having one.'

He put his arm around her. Presently, more out of proximity and tenderness than actual desire, they began to make love.

10

'Now is there anything you'd like to ask me?'

Manson always gave them this opportunity after he finished his dissertation on publishing in general and the firm of Eliot and Manson in particular. Sarah Francis had listened attentively with a polite expression, not a smile, not a blank. Her eyes were dark though he could not tell what colour, and heavily made-up, her hair blonde; dyed, he presumed. She had very golden skin, either from a holiday or make-up, and pale lips, and her hair was tied back severely, like Prue's. Although it was June she wore, instead of a summer dress, a grey linen suit and white blouse – to look the part, he supposed. The only concessions to summer were the open neck and the short sleeves. She wore black patent sling-back shoes and carried a huge black patent handbag.

He did not normally study anyone in such detail but he had been talking for about twenty minutes and had nowhere else to look. Against his will he found himself contrasting the girl's neat appearance with the clothes Prue had worn at the weekend – to keep Gavin company, he assumed. The weekend still rankled: on Sunday morning he had been forced to play chess with Gavin, while Prue and her mother prepared lunch, and Gavin had let him win. He was sure it had not been a genuine victory : Gavin, whatever else, was not stupid and not a beginner, and he had made the kind of mistakes that only a very stupid beginner could make. The condescension had been harder to take than defeat. Then after lunch, while they were still browsing through the Sunday papers, Prue had come up with some thin story, some reason for returning to London which she thought she had mentioned already, hadn't she? and they left before tea.

'Yes,' Sarah Francis said. 'I'd like to ask you when I can start.'

He laughed, pleasantly jolted out of his reverie. He had not expected such a direct approach.

She went on quickly, 'Oh, I know you can't answer that, you haven't even offered me the job yet, and you've probably got dozens of other people to interview. But that's really all I want to know. It all sounds super and I had a long chat with Miss Bradley after she gave me my test and she's been so happy here, I'm sure I would be too.'

He could not see, apart from surface diplomacy and technical competence, that they had enough in common to ensure that what pleased one would please the other, in fact quite the reverse, but of course he could not say that. He asked instead why she wanted to go on working in publishing, expecting her either to profess a love of books which from a secretarial point of view would be largely irrelevant, or to mention glamour and excitement which after three years she must know hardly existed.

Sarah Francis said, 'I like to feel I'm doing something useful.'

'I'm glad you think publishing is useful.' Manson smiled. 'I sometimes have doubts about that myself.'

Sarah Francis smiled back as if to say that they both knew these doubts were not serious and could be dismissed. 'I think what I mean is, I could work in, say, advertising, but I'd have to admit I was wasting my time. On the other hand, I really ought to work in something medical, only I'm a bit squeamish.' She looked apologetic. 'So here I am. Compromising.'

It was a curious voice: rather pretty but completely accentless, and neither too high nor too low. It went with her looks and her clothes as if she had chosen it, picked it off a rack to complete her outfit and create a good impression.

He said, 'And what do you do in your spare time, Miss Francis?'

She hesitated for what he now felt was the prescribed length of thinking time, and said, 'Oh, I like going to the theatre and playing tennis and . . . having dinner with people. And I make clothes sometimes. That's about all really.'

'Do you live at home?' He knew she would not but it seemed better than asking her if she lived alone.

'No.' She concealed any hint that the idea was absurd. 'I share a flat with three other girls.' She grinned, letting some of the poise slip. 'It's a bit chaotic at times but it's fun and very cheap.'

'I have a daughter about your age.'

For the life of him he did not know why he'd said that. He had had no idea he was going to: the first he knew was when the words were actually spoken. And yet he was not sorry because it seemed somehow important.

Sarah Francis said, 'That's nice. What does she do?'

'She's a student.'

Her eyes were serious, as if she knew more than she could possibly know about what they were discussing.

'My parents wanted me to go to university but I couldn't wait to start earning money. I'm not sure I was clever enough to get in, anyway. Is your daughter very clever, Mr Manson?'

'Not very.'

'Still, she must be quite clever or they wouldn't have taken her. It's getting very competitive now, isn't it?'

'Yes.' It occurred to him that she had trained herself to hold a conversation regardless of subject; if he had asked her to talk for one minute on any given topic she could have done so.

'People keep telling me I'll regret not going. I don't know. I haven't had time to find out yet.' She smiled at him as

61

if – to his newly sensitized perceptions – asking forgiveness for her youth. He stood up to indicate that the interview was over, and held out his hand.

'Well, Miss Francis, I've enjoyed talking to you. You'll hear from us very soon. I promise not to keep you in suspense.'

They shook hands. She had a very firm grip, but knew when to let go.

'I'll cross my fingers.' Again the grin, which was positively mischievous compared with the smile, which was prim and polite. Somewhere under the cool façade Miss Francis had a sense of humour.

She walked to the door, the grey linen very neat and uncreased as if she had never sat down. She went out without looking back or fumbling with her bag and the door handle. No bungled exits for her. He heard her exchanging pleasantries with Monica in the outer office, then another door closed neatly. She had gone.

Monica knocked and bounced in. 'Well, what do you think?' Her eyes shone with pride and satisfaction, as if she had created the *soignée* Miss Francis out of papier mâché and genius. Manson flopped in his chair.

'All right, Monica, she's the winner. Especially as there aren't any other contestants.'

Monica looked crestfallen. 'You didn't like her.'

'Yes, of course I did. How could I dislike her? I just can't believe that out of the whole of London you could only find one girl worthy of interview, even at your exacting standards.'

Monica's expression grew more and more perturbed. 'We had about thirty-one applicants,' she said, 'but I weeded them out.'

'Evidently. That's not weeding, that's more like savage pruning.' He was surprised to find himself with an urge to needle Monica. Unusual.

'I'm sorry if I did the wrong thing. I was only trying to save you the trouble as you're so busy.' Her shut-down face. He had offended her.

'I know and I appreciate it. Of course you didn't do the wrong thing.' Climb down; make it all right. He didn't want to conduct dozens of interviews, anyway, and they would all be the same if Monica vetted them first, all perfectly charming and efficient. He would not be able to tell one from the other, let alone *choose*, so what was the point? But still something in him resented that he had not been given at least an illusion of choice.

Monica said doubtfully, 'Of course you could still interview them all if you want to. Although there were only five or at the most seven who were even worth considering. This kind of job attracts a lot of the wrong types.'

Did he want to interview seven little girls? Of course he didn't. He would probably end up with Sarah Francis, anyway. And Monica was leaving in a fortnight, come what may. He said, 'Write and tell her she's got the job.'

II

Cassie said hesitantly, 'Do you think all fathers feel so – possessive about their daughters?' She watched Marjorie position the cigarette in its holder, light it, and inhale while considering her answer. I shouldn't be talking to her at all, she thought, only there is no one else to talk to, and I'm tired of thinking and I've had too much wine.

'I dunno.' Marjorie said, exhaling. 'I suppose it's quite common. I'll ask Alec if you like. I'm not sure how he feels about Judy.'

'Oh no, no,' said Cassie automatically, now feeling disloyal; then, reflecting that Marjorie would almost certainly discuss it with him, anyway, in the curious non-privacy of marriage, 'Oh well, all right. It might be a good idea.' It was at times like these that she should have either more friends or none at all, close to hand; it hardly mattered which. But to be stuck with Marjorie alone, bless her, was absurd.

She had lost the habit of girl-friends and confidence; confessions were hard to arrive at and stuck in her throat. Friendships, intense at Cambridge, during the war, had vanished, surprisingly, with marriage and children. She had expected to keep up with her friends but she had not. The hectic years in London meeting mostly new people and entertaining business contacts for Manson, then the move to the country when Prue was born. It had all, to her surprise, been fully absorbing, and in what time she had, she read books, propping them against the high chair while she fed Prue, beside the bath when she washed her, above the cooker while she cooked. She read books, after motherhood, as if she had never seen a book in her life before, voraciously, one after the other and often two or three at once, as if she had never obtained two degrees (to Manson's feigned chagrin at having only one) which she still thought vaguely she might use one day. It was as if Prue's birth released a kind of intellectual hunger that she had only glimpsed before. But with the twins it waned: gone into the sheer physical and nervous strain of coping with two energetic small boys and Prue as a moody adolescent. It had not returned – instead she found herself making jam and gardening, occupations she would once have scorned – and it seemed to have taken her capacity for friendship with it, or to have replaced it at a time when both could not be fitted in. She had chosen books because her life then had seemed so full of people she had hardly needed any more; she had needed a refuge from them instead.

'Of course, mothers feel a bit funny about their sons,' said Marjorie chattily. It occurred to Cassie that she might actually be pleased to be having a fairly intimate conversation for a change. 'Don't you think? I know I do.' She giggled. 'I wouldn't admit it to anyone else but it's quite different from how I feel about Judy.'

Oh dear, Cassie thought, that means she regards me as a special friend. Oh dear. How can I possibly reciprocate that or deserve it? And how extraordinary. Unless of course she, like me, is stuck with no other choice so I am, *faute de mieux*, a friend. I must not flatter myself without cause.

'I suppose there is a difference,' she said vaguely. 'I've never really thought about it.' *Was* she more maternal, more possessive, over the boys? Was there a sexual element in her love for them? Thinking about it she immediately pictured them in the bath and wondered if that was significant.

Marjorie laughed in rather an embarrassed and adolescent way. 'Well, I wouldn't like to go into it too closely but I'm sure it's there. It must be quite normal. Nothing to worry about. So I shouldn't get in a state about Peter being a bit funny over Prue.'

'No, you're right,' said Cassie at once, wanting to end the conversation and wishing she had never started it. She could not think what had possessed her to do such a thing. 'It's all very trivial,' she said, to convince herself as much as Marjorie. 'Just a bit tiresome when we're all together, the four of us. It makes such an atmosphere, his disliking Gavin so much. That's all that bothers me really.'

But Marjorie was not so easily deflected. 'They like to think their little girls are pure as the driven snow, you know. Now mothers are more realistic. I'm perfectly sure Judy must be – what do they call it now? – heavy petting all over the place, if nothing worse, but I've never said so to Alec. Even in his profession I'm sure he's not broad-minded about his own daughter. If she actually got pregnant he'd hit the roof.'

Cassie began to wonder if she had been right to inform certain neighbours and friends of Prue's pregnancy. At the time of the wedding, with all its talk-provoking suddenness, it had seemed much more sensible to be open with a selected few and avoid the inevitable speculation and sidelong glances. She was always, where possible, in favour of honesty, and it was at best a difficult situation to carry off with dignity, but if Marjorie was going to keep *on* about it ...

'So he has to blame the boy,' Marjorie went on triumphantly. 'His daughter has to be pure so it must be all the boy's fault. But let me see now, how would it go? ... If he also *envies* the boy he has to be twice as angry because the boy's done what *he'd* have liked to do and—'

'Yes, Marjorie, I do understand.' Cassie did not even care now if she sounded rude. But she blamed herself very much for letting Marjorie get the scent of blood in the first place. A nasty disloyal feeling of 'Have I betrayed Peter?' crept over her like fog swirling up from the ground.

Marjorie was immediately repentant, though not on the right wavelength. 'Oh, I'm sorry, I always state the obvious, I know I do. No wonder Alec gets so impatient with me.'

'Sure your dad wants to screw you, baby. Sticks out a mile.' Gavin punctured a Coke and began to drink it from the tin.

Prue felt herself starting to blush. She had not blushed with Gavin since the first time she took her clothes off in his presence. She was not good at undressing, being unconvinced that she looked better naked than dressed, and had needed a lot of reassurance on the subject, which Gavin had been happy to provide. Now she protested, 'Oh, Gavin, *really*,' and Gavin stopped drinking to laugh.

'I don't mean he's aware of it. He's got it all buried way down. But it's there all right. That's why he'd like to cut my balls off.'

Prue dug in the refrigerator to cool her face and find a Coke for herself. She said, 'I thought he was horrid to you. I was very cross. You were falling over backwards to be nice to him.'

'Yeah, but what good is that when it's you he'd like to have fall over backwards.'

'Oh, don't, Gavin.' The trouble was that she got vivid mental pictures of everything Gavin said.

'What's the matter? You were happy enough screwing me all over town, what's wrong with your dad? He's a well-preserved man for his age.'

'Gavin, he's my *father*.' She pressed her cheek against the cold cloudy tin of Coke.

'So what's wrong with incest? At least it's all in the family.'

Manson sat alone in the office after Monica had gone. The farewells, accompanied by the inevitable drinks and tears, had got a little out of hand, and now in the ensuing silence he could still hear them ringing in his head. He had no urge to go home. He had not phoned Prue since the weekend visit and when Cassie reported non-committal conversations on the phone he did not comment. As far as possible he was excluding her from his thoughts and, totally, from his speech. It was all part of his new policy of training himself not to care. Let her ruin her life. Why should he knock himself senseless trying to stop her? Let her get on with it. If seeing her worried him, it was better not to see her, avoid all contact. Once he found something else to do in the void, it might not be so painful. It should not be too difficult: after all he had quite enough work to occupy his mind and his home life was harmonious – well, fairly harmonious, at least; he thought Cassie had been untypically moody of late, but perhaps he was merely projecting his own *malaise* on to her.

It occurred to him that he would like to go out and get very drunk, something he had not done in years.

Rupert, resplendent in various shades of purple, adorned with a golden tie, said to him on Monday, 'Is that your new secretary-bird? *Really?*'

12

Sarah settled in quickly. He had expected to have to train her and be patient with her mistakes, but for the first week even, there were surprisingly few. He noticed that she was often to be seen clutching or thumbing through several sheets of closely-typed paper: on inquiry he was told that it was the office routine, as set down by Monica for her enlightenment. He was impressed and asked to see it, and there, down to the tiniest detail, was the customary procedure for every eventuality. Everything was listed: the location of spare stationery, pencils, indiarubbers, stencils, carbon ... There was a detailed guide to the filing system. An outline of an average day, which he could even recognize as such, with the times for tea and coffee underlined in red, and his preferences in sugar, milk and biscuits minutely described. There was even a rundown on staff: who they were, what they did and in which offices they could be found. Under Bernard's entry his deafness was allowed for; under Rupert's he read 'Mr Warner may seem a little eccentric in manner but as a person he is really perfectly charming'. Even the office wolf was pinpointed: 'Mr Cowan, once firmly rebuffed, will not try again'.

He began to laugh, it seemed for the first time in weeks. 'Dear Monica.' He felt very fond of her and hoped very much that Harry would make her happy.

Sarah said, 'Yes, isn't she fantastic? She simply couldn't have done more to help me.'

Manson said, 'Well, she's succeeded. I think you've made a very good start.'

'There's just one thing. Do you think you – I mean everyone – could call me Sarah, instead of Miss Francis? Only I got so used to it at Farrer's and I think I'd feel less of a new girl if you could.'

He said, 'I should think we could manage that. After all you work as if you'd been here for years.'

She smiled. 'Thank you.'

He wandered along to Rupert's office at coffee time. Rupert was fixing his current motto for the week on the pin board above his desk. This one read 'Thought costs nothing and is instantly eradicable'. Manson stood in the doorway regarding it.

68

'True,' he said. 'Very true.'

'Well, someone has to state the obvious occasionally,' said Rupert, 'and it may as well be me.' He jabbed in the last drawing-pin and stood back to admire the effect. 'How's your Miss Thing, why aren't you having coffee with her?'

'I came to see you.' Manson installed himself in Rupert's chair. 'And she's not Miss Thing any more. As of now, we are all formally requested to call her Sarah.'

'Are we indeed?' Rupert made a whistling sound through his teeth. 'Well, that shouldn't be too difficult, should it? Nice little thing. Not very like our beloved Monica, though, is she? *Quite* a different kettle of fish. She's got the whole office eyeing you with ill-concealed envy at last.'

'Rubbish,' said Manson uneasily, and went on to tell Rupert his entry on Monica's information sheet.

'Bless her,' said Rupert, pleased, 'I could hardly have done better myself. She was a dear child. I hope Whatsisname will gratify her every whim. But I can't say I'm sorry she's gone. Miss Thing is so much prettier and she seems just as efficient. I'm told she's arrived early every morning so far, and hasn't cheated on her lunch hour once, as yet.'

'You're told?'

'Oh, my spies are out, you know,' said Rupert airily. 'I have my sources. But like most of their kind they wish to remain undisclosed. How's Prue?'

'Quite well,' said Manson shortly. 'I haven't seen her lately; they're both working now that term's over, and next month they're off to the South of France.'

Rupert sighed. 'What it is to be an impoverished student. I suppose they get all kinds of ridiculous concessions. No currency *crise* for them. Ah well. The penalties of success. The moment you pass an exam in this country or win a prize or earn some money, you're victimized. I sometimes think that if our dearly beloved Government that *some* of us were misguided enough to vote for doesn't move over soon and let us breathe just a *little* fresh air, I for one will have to find a bolt-hole somewhere else.'

They discussed politics with idle enthusiasm for some time.

Rupert was fond of baiting Manson for his share of the responsibility for the mess they were now all in. 'It's people like you who put them there,' he would say. 'Lucky for you that *we* are merciful. The penalty for treason is normally death, after all.' When Manson went back to his desk he felt restless. He applied himself to a backlog of paper work, but his heart wasn't in it and he was conscious all the time of a nagging desire to telephone Prue. He stuck it out till lunchtime, then went to his club, a place he liked to maintain, for no particular reason, and then forgot to visit for long periods of time. Today he found it restful and soothing: the older members made him feel young again by contrast, and the leather-mahogany atmosphere created the illusion of a time when the generation gap either did not exist or was firmly ignored. He did not telephone from there.

But how was she? Had she specially given Cassie her office number so that he *could* telephone? It was impossible now to get her at home without Gavin being there too. Did she *want* him to phone? Why had she not contacted him since that weekend? What if she actually *went away* without contacting him?

It was this final thought that made him act. At teatime, after Sarah had brought in his cup, he dialled the number and asked for Prue's extension. He could not bring himself to get Sarah to do it. Prue came on the line sounding very cool and brisk.

'Hullo, yes?'

He said, 'Hullo, stranger.'

There was a pause, of the peculiarly intense variety that only the telephone can produce.

'Oh, Daddy. It's you.'

'Yes.'

She permitted another silence. He could not think how to go on. He said foolishly, 'How are you?'

'Oh, I'm fine.'

'Good.'

'And you?'

'Yes, yes, I'm quite well.'

'Oh, good.' Yet another pause. Then: 'Look, Daddy, I am awfully busy and they don't really like me to have calls here . . .'

Somehow this made him find words. 'Prue, what are we fighting about?'

A very cold little voice. 'We're not.'

'Yes, we are. Are you still sulking about the weekend?' He noticed he had chosen a word to suggest her behaviour was childish and she picked it up at once.

'I'm not sulking. I think you were very nasty to Gavin, that's all, and I'm upset. It hurt me very much that you wouldn't meet him halfway.'

He noticed that she was using equally loaded words to suggest that he was completely in the wrong. 'I see,' he said evenly, considering his next move.

Lack of retaliation made Prue gather strength. 'I was very disappointed. I thought he was trying so hard that you'd be sure to respond.'

'It's no good, Prue,' he said, stung. 'You get your own way more than most people but even you can't expect to win one hundred per cent.'

'That's not what I'm talking about. Look, I'll have to go. I can't talk any more now.'

He said goodbye wearily, with a sense of defeat, to the purring receiver. Prue had already rung off.

Sarah came in with some letters for him to sign. 'Sarah,' he said, 'you're a young girl. What makes a young girl of nineteen want to get married and have a baby before she's even finished her education?' He went on signing the letters without looking up.

'I can't imagine.' She did not sound surprised at the question. 'But then I'm not sure I shall ever want to.'

'Oh. Why is that?' Careful, now; it was early days to get personal. The relationship with Monica which had worked so well had been built up very slowly. But today he felt vulnerable and in need of comfort.

'Well, I'm very independent. And there are so many other things I want to do.'

71

'Such as?' He glanced up briefly from the letters and found her watching him, seriously, thoughtfully, almost with sympathy. She might not have been talking about herself at all. The eyes that he had found merely dark turned out to be grey like slate, like city roof-tops, edged with thick, dark-pointed lashes, and shadowed and outlined in the manner of the day. They dwarfed the rest of her face, making it seem more bony and fragile than ever: they were like two huge flowers with drooping petals. He wondered how they looked without make-up.

Good God, he thought, what's the matter with me?

Sarah said, 'I'd like to travel and meet people. Just see the world and try lots of different things.' He wondered if she meant men. She added, neither proudly nor apologetically, 'I think I have a horror of settling down. My sister married young – well, she was seventeen and she's only twenty-four now. She has three kids and she's bored to death. There's nothing wrong with her husband but everything's *fixed*. Do you know what I mean?'

He said, 'Yes. I do.'

She held out her hand for the letters. A small, square hand, with short nails, shiny but not coloured. A practical hand. 'Thank you.'

He said, without meaning to, 'I was talking about my daughter.'

'Yes.'

'Did you guess?'

'No.'

'I'm very worried about her.'

'I'm sorry.'

This exchange, though on the surface casual and meaningless, seemed very important to him. He went on, 'I think she's ruined her life.' Sarah said nothing; she just stood there holding the signed letters. 'And there's nothing I can do about it. That's very hard to bear when you're a parent.'

Sarah said unexpectedly, 'Perhaps she can get a divorce later on.' He must have shown his surprise at this for she added, 'Don't be shocked, I don't mean to sound cynical.

72

Only my parents did that and they've both been much happier since.'

'Pull up a chair and tell me about it.'

She glanced at her watch.

'Never mind the time. Perhaps Monica forgot to include cheering me up among your many duties.'

She laughed and sat down. 'Well, it was very simple really. They waited till we were grown up, which I call a mistake but it made them feel better, then they simply split up. They'd never liked domesticity, you see. My mother went off and married a very rich man and she travels everywhere with him and has a lovely time, and my father has turned into a sort of elderly beatnik and just drifts around doing odd jobs and drinking and smoking pot. They're both much happier. When you meet them now you can't imagine how they ever lived together for a day let alone twenty years.'

Manson said grimly, 'I shouldn't be surprised if my daughter and her husband are smoking pot already.' He had no reason to suppose so, but it went with the general image, he thought bitterly.

Sarah said, 'I shouldn't worry. They probably aren't, and anyway some people think it's harmless.'

'Is it?'

'Well, I don't know, I've never tried it.' She smiled. 'I'm a bit square, you see, I prefer alcohol. I should think it's safer than nicotine, if it doesn't lead to anything else. But then I don't smoke at all so I can afford to be smug.'

How assured they all were: Prue at nineteen, Sarah at twenty-three, the unidentified masses he saw in the street, in the park, on the train. He remembered himself at their age, all hands and feet and blushes and spots, with a way of being rude when he most wished to impress, out of sheer terror.

'Yours is a very confident generation, isn't it?' he said to her.

'Is it?' She shrugged. 'I don't know, I can't really judge.'

'No, of course not. Tell me, when you're with your parents, do you feel very conscious of the generation gap? Is there a gulf between you?'

73

She hesitated; he could see her thinking. 'Well, there always was, actually. I mean we never really had much in common. I think they got on better with Barbara. But – it's probably better now, now they're divorced. I don't see them so often and they don't have the same jurisdiction – you know?'

'In other words they don't interfere.'

'Well, they never did, much, to be fair to them.'

'But now they don't even get the chance. Is that what you mean?' He was thinking of Prue. What chance did he have to influence her life?

'I suppose so. But it's more than that. They're more – just people. They don't have to worry about appearances.' She smiled ironically. 'I mean they're not worried about the parent image any more. That all stopped when they got divorced.'

'So divorce paves the way to happy parenthood.'

'No. But it does cut out a lot of – what shall I call it? – role-playing, and there's quite enough of that going on as it is.'

He was interested; she spoke so feelingly while trying to sound detached. It was the first glimpse he had had of a possibly real person beneath the secretarial façade. Intrigued, he asked, 'How do you mean exactly? Give me an example.'

'Well.' She was concentrating; she seemed to have forgotten about the office relationship. 'I suppose it's unavoidable really. If – well, if I have two boyfriends, say, for the sake of argument, and one is very kind and reliable and the other is rather erratic but exciting, I'll put up with much worse treatment from him than the first one because it's in character. It's part of his role to behave like that. But if the first one steps out of line I probably won't put up with it. I'll react quite differently to the same behaviour from two people, which is illogical, and it's all because of what I *expect* from each of them. I've given them each a role to play, or they've chosen their own, and I expect them to stick to that image.'

Manson said, 'And what role do you choose for yourself?'

'Well, that all depends who I'm with.'

74

'So you have no central persona at all.'

'I don't know.'

'I mean is there a real Sarah Francis or just a series of roles?'

'Yes, I know what you mean but I can't answer you. Sometimes I think there isn't a real me at all, and other times I'm sure there is, only it's right in the middle and terribly small, like a walnut, and I can't get at it. So I don't really know if it's there or not.'

He smiled. 'That's a good description.'

She smiled back. 'English was always my best subject.'

'Thank you for cheering me up.'

She took this as a departure signal and stood up at once. 'Did I really? It was a pleasure. You know, I shouldn't worry too much if I were you. Things have a habit of working out.'

'I rather doubt that.'

'Do you?' She looked surprised. 'I take it for granted.'

Manson smiled. 'If you and I were both looking at a bottle that was neither full nor empty, you'd call it half-full and I'd call it half-empty.'

'Why?'

'Because you're an optimist and I'm a pessimist, that's all.'

13

The boys came home from school and the house reverberated with them. Manson loved their noise: he felt it might have a healing effect, just as fire can cauterize a wound. He looked at them playing, and shouting, and eating, and consciously forced himself to think, over and over again, these are my sons. After all, Cassie had reminded him that he did have other children, and he loved them. But he did not see them as vulnerable; they did not tug at his heart in the half-sick, half-enchanted way that he welcomed and dreaded. The spell of the first-born remained, as potent as ever.

Cassie sensed a withdrawal of spirit in Manson, though superficially they were as close as ever. They did not discuss Prue at all : a tacit armistice. Cassie took the phone calls and Prue and her father exchanged guarded messages of affection through her. She regretted her conversation with Marjorie and made sure it could not recur, by never being alone with her. She made small, domestic efforts to please Manson, feeling that she must make amends to him for the offence he did not know she had committed, be 'a better wife' in textbook terms to compensate for a moment's disloyalty.

She longed to speak of holidays, and could not. She yearned silently for Scotland, where they had spent their honeymoon, and to comfort herself pictured them returning there, perhaps when the heather was out, driving and stopping as the fancy took them, and growing close again through nostalgia. And she saw them both younger, as they had been before there was anything to worry about or any tension between them, and she was happy, and she wanted to cry. Intellectually she knew it was impossible to turn back the clock, but she longed for a miracle nevertheless. Perhaps she had been wrong, seeming to take Prue's side against Manson, but she had only meant to belittle the conflict and so re-create family peace. Instead she seemed to have driven him into some lonely interior place where the conviction of being right was sufficient to sustain him. He had shut her out. She went about the house in a daze, her mind constantly reviewing the situation, each move, each tactical error, like a game of chess, and the boys had to repeat things they said to her and then she was profusely apologetic. But they, being twins, did not mind too much and went on playing together : even at ten they were largely independent of her at home, and the school life they shared so closely made a further bond. She wondered if it was in fact their twinhood which made her love for them so casual, easy and undemanding. She had examined her feelings closely after lunch with Marjorie and she did not honestly think that the intense, possessive element was there. But then, how to focus such emotion on a dual object? And she had always been fearful of loving one more than the other, of discriminating between them. Since they were so close to each other, irrespective of normal, healthy violence and argument, they seemed to set her an example of unadulterated love. The purity of their feeling for each other, their instinctive empathy, was something she had to emulate. Now she wondered if in her efforts not to love one or the other too much, she had failed to love either enough. And she thought that perhaps, if so, it was a good thing, she had done them a favour, for they would all be spared the situation that Prue and her father were now in. But it struck her as sad that too much love should be as damaging as too little.

Sarah, making love with Geoff, wished she could stay in bed for ever. It was the only place she felt safe, and sure of her talent to please. The rest was manufactured and artificial, not instinctive: the effort to be smart and amusing and invulnerable. He wanted a glossy girl with no problems, she thought: at least she did not feel she could burden him with any without spoiling her image as an entertaining companion with other men in her life. She was not his responsibility. She was not Simon's, either, but Geoff did not know that. He had found out about Simon by accident but had shown no jealousy; she interpreted this as relief that he need not take her too seriously. He had presented himself superficially, as a playboy, mocking the family firm ('But where else could I get such a salary at my age?') and teasing her ('You're after my car and my cock, in that order; I know you.') and she had accepted him at his own valuation. His conversation was less interesting than Simon's but he made love better and took her to more exciting places in the Jaguar, for which she felt disproportionate affection. It was the height of some adolescent ambition to be driven about in a red E-type by someone who looked at least like the men in advertisements,

77

though he was in fact an engineer with a rich and indulgent father. His family tolerated her. She thought it would be a good thing if she could get the Jaguar phase, as she called it, out of her system : but it showed no sign of abating. The two men complemented each other : dates with Geoff made it easier to enjoy cooking on Simon's gas ring, standing in the rain for buses, paying for herself at the cinema and listening to his post-graduate study problems. He was gentle and serious and showed a sort of tenderness for her that moved her very much, though she had never put it to the test. He did not know about Geoff and she hoped he would never find out : he would not, she felt, understand how reassuring she found it to move from one to the other. She did not see it as cheating. With Simon she was gentle and serious, like him, and reciprocated his tenderness : there was a sibling warmth between them. Whereas with Geoff she was tough and sexy, appreciative of luxury but offhand and casual, because she felt this was what he expected and she did not want to disappoint him. But each role seemed equally valid. Geoff had been hard to find, and in the end she had had to steal him from one of the girls in the flat she then shared. Subsequently, having broken a basic law, she of course had to leave the flat, and in her hurry to escape from the atmosphere she had created, she had plunged too fast into the new flat, without sufficiently vetting the other three girls. Connie was recovering from a broken engagement at a leisurely pace and ostentatiously not bothering with men. The others picked their way through her sharp remarks as through splinters of broken glass. Ann was probably a soul-mate, Sarah decided, as she was out a lot and the telephone constantly rang for her. But it was with Annabel that she had made her mistake, for the lease was in Annabel's name and though all were theoretically equal it was Annabel who made final decisions on who came and went, by virtue of her original tenancy. She had accepted Sarah readily but then both she and Sarah had been on their best behaviour, instinctively compensating for their deficiencies by each appearing respectively more broad-minded and more conventional than they really were. It was only later that Sarah discovered there were house rules (no doubt Annabel felt such a nice girl would not need to be told) and men could not stay overnight. The reasons given were inconvenience to the other girls, use of the bathroom, and fear of the landlord, for even Annabel did not dare to raise moral objections, but Sarah got the message and a very unpleasant one it was. Not that it really mattered, at least at the moment, for both Geoff and Simon had somewhere they could take her, but it was the principle of the thing: she did not feel her room was her home if she could not behave as she wished. Her previous flat where there had been no taboos, apart from the one she had violated to get Geoff, seemed a paradise of freedom by comparison, and she began to miss it keenly, and to wonder, with her new job and her increase in salary, how long it would be before she could afford to live by herself. She had known all along, from the day she left school, that this was what she wanted to do, but she was not prepared to do it in a slum.

Geoff asked, 'What's your new boss like?' as he was driving her home.

'Great fun. And very easy-going.' Simon had asked the same question and to him she had said, 'Oh, sweet. Rather a sad man,' because Simon liked feeling sorry for people and would devote his surplus pity to dogs, cats and newsvendors, as well as the starving millions, if she did not keep him supplied with other worthy objects. Besides, she liked to create different images for Manson as well as for herself: it seemed to make them more equal.

Prue found now that when Gavin made love to her she could not shut her eyes for a second without seeing her father's face. It was unnerving and made her blush. Gavin had planted such a vivid image of Manson in her brain that even to talk to her father on the telephone now embarrassed her. It was in fact more embarrassment than indignation which had caused her long silence and eventual rudeness. Now she did not know what to do: she seemed to have got into a self-perpetuating situation. And she hated the job, though she dared not admit to Gavin that her father had been right. Only the prospect of France served to sustain her. Her back ached and she was bored, working with one eye on the clock and spinning out her lunch-hour as long as she dared. She had never behaved like this at college. If this was what working life was like, in the ordinary world, she would have to do post-graduate work as soon as she qualified, or stay at home with the baby. For long, arid portions of the day she sat at her desk with the appearance of working and let her mind drift. She recalled her courtship and marriage, in long passages of sexual fantasy, but eventually, by whatever route, her thoughts always came back to what she now regarded as the feud. Much as she might genuinely regret and deplore it, it also gave her a certain keen satisfaction because it demonstrated her power over her father. She had never had such power over another person before. It was like teasing an animal. She was ashamed of herself but she could not stop because she found it fun.

14

Manson found himself becoming fascinated by Sarah. She was so genuinely keen on her job, asking him questions without being intrusive, and thinking up ways of streamlining the office routine. Rupert assured him that she was still arriving early and taking minutely accurate lunch-hours. But it was more than that. He took active pleasure in seeing her there in the outer office as he came and went: she was so clean, so tidy, so suitably dressed, so discreetly scented. She was any man's dream of a girl with whom to confront the world: this is my secretary. He could be proud of her at

80

meetings. He felt mildly ashamed of not missing Monica –
dear Monica – but Rupert was quite right, as usual : it was
pleasant to have a secretary who was elegant as well as capable. When he thought of Monica's sturdy arms and legs it
seemed to him by contrast that Sarah's bones might break if
she bumped into anything. She was tiny and angular under
the golden skin, which had little golden hairs on it when you
looked more closely, over a letter or something – perhaps she
was really blonde after all – and the back of her neck was soft
and somehow vulnerable, like a child's. Like Prue's. He had
spent many years looking at the back of Prue's neck with
delight. Now he realized that he still thought of her as a
child. A child with child, confused, despoiled, led away.
Whereas Sarah – what a difference those four years made.
She was so out-going, so forward-looking. He saw at least two
different young men calling for her after work or sometimes
at lunchtime, so she was clearly not making the same mistake
as Prue and going steady with one with a view to falling in
love. She had talked of travel : she wanted to see the world.
She would like her own car, she said, when she could afford
it; she had passed the test already and sometimes friends
would lend her a car so she could keep in practice. He pictured her in a white sports car, very much a status symbol,
hair blowing in the breeze, as in the petrol ads, only sometimes the hair was dark when he pictured it. He had always
planned to buy Prue a white sports car when she was twenty-
one; he did not know if he still would. As things were, Gavin
would benefit. Prue was so soft, she would be sure to lend it
to him. Manson did not know whether he could stand the
sight of Gavin roaring up to his front door in the white sports
car, Prue's birthday present, with her sitting meekly by his
side. And he did not trust Gavin not to kill Prue (and himself, please God) on the road; he was sure Gavin would drive
too fast.

So Prue might not get her present; and he might not get
the pleasure of giving it to her. Jewellery, perhaps that was
the answer. Gavin could hardly wear her jewellery, although
these days one could not be too sure, anything seemed

81

possible. But it would be satisfying to give Prue the jewellery that Gavin could not afford to buy her. Maybe he should not wait for her twenty-first but start now with the coming birthday, and of course Christmas. He began to feel excited at the idea. A really beautiful piece, something so stunning that she would forget they had ever quarrelled. And she would have to wear it whenever she saw him, at least, and each time she put it on she would think, she would have to think, my father gave me this.

'Sarah,' he said. She was typing but the door between their offices was open for ventilation as it was late July and remarkably warm. People were beginning to remark on the summer.

'Yes?' She stopped typing and turned her head with a half-smile.

'It's my daughter's birthday in October and I'd like to give her some jewellery. What do you suggest? She's about your age.'

Sarah said, 'What does she look like?'

'Small, dark, pretty.'

'And what sort of clothes does she wear?'

Manson flinched. 'Sometimes perfectly normal and sometimes rather ... hippy or whatever it's called nowadays.'

Sarah said doubtfully, 'Maybe long ropes of pearls, if she wears beads. If she likes pearls, that is. I don't myself but a lot of people do.'

He couldn't see Prue in pearls. He said, 'No, I don't think so.'

'Of course,' Sarah said, 'the point is, do you want to give her what you think she wants or what you'd like her to have?'

He was momentarily chilled. 'How very perspicacious of you. Both, I suppose.' A dishonest answer, he thought with disgust.

Sarah said, 'Then how about a gold bracelet. You can spend whatever you like and it's classic and never goes out of fashion and she can wear it all the time, with everything.'

He thought about it. He liked the picture. 'Yes, that's a

good idea.' But he was not sure if it was the bracelet itself that he liked or Sarah's description of it. She had seemed so sure that Prue would wear it all the time. How had she known that was just what he wanted?

'Or a watch,' Sarah said. 'Has she got a watch?'

'Yes. That was her eighteenth birthday present—' laughing apologetically. His eyes lighted on Sarah's own watch, very slim and gold and unobtrusive. Easily a hundred pounds. 'Rather like yours,' he added. Again by suggesting a watch she had hit on something that Prue would seldom remove. He found it uncanny.

Sarah said lightly, 'She's a lucky girl. My father never bought me anything like that. Oh, not that I blame him, he couldn't afford it. But it must be fun if you can. I love my watch.'

'Boyfriend?' Manson kept his tone casual. He was surprised to find that it mattered to know who had given Sarah the watch. Perhaps he had been wrong about her.

She laughed. 'Good heavens, no. Stepfather. It was a piece of bribery and corruption, you see; supposed to make me love him.' She spoke very flippantly but Manson thought he detected real bitterness underneath: the first hint that her parents' rearrangements were perhaps not as ideal as she had painted them.

'And did it?' he asked. Conversations with Sarah were like trips on an escalator: it always seemed impossible to get off halfway but the end when it came was abrupt.

'No. But he bought my sister a washing machine and a fridge at the same time and she loves him.' She started typing again.

The phone rang. It was Prue.

'Daddy.'

He was startled into saying, 'Darling, are you all right?'

'Yes, yes of course I am.' But she did not seem to be laughing at him. 'I just called to say goodbye.'

Called? *Called*. She had picked up the beastly word from *him* of course. 'Goodbye? But you're not off till next week.'

'No, we're going tomorrow. The cottage is empty so we

may as well be there – and I hate my job.' Pause. 'You were quite right.'

He couldn't say anything.

Prue went on, 'I don't think work suits me.'

'Oh, what nonsense. It just wasn't the right job, that's all.'

'I don't think anything suits me.'

'Prue, whatever do you mean?'

Choking sound. 'Oh, Daddy, I'm so miserable.' She was actually crying.

'Darling, what *is* the matter?' He had a tight, hard sensation in his chest, a pain like a lump of apple lodged against his rib-cage – the way he ignorantly imagined heart-cases would feel.

'Oh, nothing.'

'It can't be nothing. You don't make a fuss over nothing, you never have.' As a child, her courage had astonished him : she had always been much braver than the twins. Falling out of a tree, burning herself, being bitten by a dog, she always, after the age of nine, tended to turn white with shock rather than cry. He remembered in particular one hideous cut, right to the bone, on a spike, and her ashen, incredulous face at the pain and the blood and the damage she had done herself. But no tears.

She said, almost inaudibly, 'I'm sorry we had that fight.'

'Oh, darling, you're not crying about *that*.'

She didn't answer.

'Look, Prue, we were both sticking up for ourselves, that's all. Two pig-headed old characters locking horns.' He was too moved to disentangle the metaphor. 'That's all forgotten.'

She sniffed, and he heard her blowing her nose. 'Was that all you were crying about?' He wondered (hoped?) that she had quarrelled with Gavin and wanted his comfort and advice.

She said faintly, 'I 'spect so', and the childishness caught at his heart. 'I'm crying a lot these days, it must be my hormones. Well, I must go. Take care of yourself, Daddy.'

He found himself clutching the phone with both hands.

84

'Have you got enough money?' Was that *all* he could do for her from now on, for ever?

She said gently, 'Oh yes, yes. You spoil me.'

'Well, have a lovely time, darling.'

'Yes, I will. I'll get brown and send you postcards.'

'Yes.'

'All right then.'

'Well, have fun.'

'Yes. Oh, Daddy—'

'What?'

'Nothing. I'm just being silly. Take care of yourself. 'Bye.' She blew a kiss down the phone and hung up.

He put down the receiver slowly, unaware how his face looked. He said, 'That was my daughter.'

The atmosphere was so highly charged that Sarah judged she could say, 'You love her very much, don't you?'

'Yes.' He spoke like a man in a trance.

Sarah said, 'She's lucky.'

15

Prue was scared. She had actually made the phone call while crouching on the floor in what she now noticed was very nearly a foetal position. She replaced the receiver reluctantly: even dead in her hand it was some small link with her father, with the outside world. She did not know what she had expected: magic words, a healing spell, absolution? Her eye looked dreadful in the mirror; she flinched from looking at it with the other one. She had worn dark glasses to the shops but even so had imagined everyone could see behind them and would know why she was buying meat. She felt silly, too, for she had no way of knowing if this really was an effective cure: she had only heard about it. Like buying gin for abortion (not that she had ever wished to do *that*), it was the classic remedy of folklore to which the mind automatically sprang, but without any factual knowledge.

When she got home she had applied the meat, feeling totally ridiculous. She did not know how long to leave it on for or how bloody it ought to be. It made a terrible mess of her face and she kept thinking how everyone would laugh if they could see her all alone in a darkened room lying on the bed with a piece of meat on her eye. So presently she took it off and laid it carefully on the plate she had brought from the kitchen for the purpose. This, too, made her feel hysterical. Then she had to get up and go to the bathroom to wash off the blood and inspect her injury for signs of instant improvement.

But why had he hit her? What was so terrible about wanting to give up her job after only three weeks instead of four? She was temporary staff and no notice was required; people were coming and going all the time. Financially, it would not make all *that* much difference: they had their fares and their pocket money was dictated by the Government. But if they got really short she could no doubt arrange with her father that friends of his in France could help them out and he would repay them. It could be a sort of advance birthday present. Gavin had said, 'God, you're a spoiled brat', and she had become indignant. 'Why? Why am I? I hate the job, it gives me backache. You don't know what it's like being pregnant—' using the one unfair and irrefutable argument she had, and he had said furiously, 'Oh yes, the great out. Now you've got to get away with everything instead of just nearly everything, you can't even sit at a desk for four weeks and get paid for it, well *that's* how impressed I am,' and he had slapped her across the face.

She still trembled when she remembered the shock of it. It was neither a heavy blow nor a light one but it took all the breath from her body with shock. It was not the pain, such as it was, that she minded: there was even a faint sense of pleasure in the stinging sensation and the knowledge that

Gavin had caused it. He had always been very rough with her in bed, which she liked and had come to take for granted. But her dignity was hurt, and she could not have been more affronted if Gavin had spat on the floor. She said incredulously, 'You hit me. You hit me.'

'Sure I hit you.' He had no sense of the ridiculous. He was talking and behaving like some third-rate gangster in a very old B picture and it did not seem to strike him as the least absurd. The independent bit of her mind, the bit that provided the running commentaries on her life, wondered if Americans as a nation had been fed so much on their own movie culture that they were now spewing it out in the naïve belief that this was how everyone talked. 'I'll hit you again if I like. If I think you need it. I want you back at your desk, that's all.'

She shouted at him, 'But I feel ill, I told you', backing away from him.

'Balls. You're fitter than I am.' He came nearer: with every step she drew away he came closer to her, till she felt herself sweating with fright. 'So you're going to work. Is that clear? I'm not having you prove your old man was right.'

So that was it. She was out of her depth now. It had started so casually, innocently, waking up with a headache (the sickness had stopped so no excuse there) and thinking how nice to stay at home. The idle thought of a day off had turned pretty swiftly, as she lay curled up against Gavin's sleeping warmth, into not being back at all but going instead on holiday just a week early. The more Gavin, when he woke up, opposed this plan, the more set on it she became, and the more she had exaggerated (with conviction) her pains and aches, her boredom. She had never dreamt he would make such an issue of it.

'I shall please myself,' she said to him when backed (now literally) into a corner. She had to be brave now. But it was exciting to be so frightened. He looked like a stranger.

'But I want you back at work,' he said as if there was no argument about it, almost pleasantly.

'I'm not going.'

87

'Then you need an excuse.' Still no sign of temper.

'I've got one. A real one.'

'Well, now you have,' he said, a second after he punched her.

It really hurt. She saw all the stars in the firmament on a clear night, and the fireworks on Guy Fawkes night for good measure. It was a stabbing pain that went through to the back of her head and somehow made her feel sick. She clutched her face and screamed.

Gavin did not attempt to comfort her. Nor, to give him his due, did he say anything about disturbing the neighbours or keeping her voice down. He said nothing at all and poured himself a drink out of their emergency bottle. When she had stopped screaming and started crying he gave her a drink too. Bourbon. Neat. She drank it all. She simply couldn't stop crying until she had exhausted herself. In the middle of it all, he left. When she managed to ask where he was going he gave her the one word 'Work'. But he said it in a defeated tone which suggested that she had won, as perhaps she had. So she lay on the sofa and wept for her victory, her first over him, and wondered if things would ever be the same again. Crying gave her a worse headache than before and made her eyes ache and swell more than ever. The one he had hit felt as if it would burst. It was hours before she dared to look at herself, before curiosity triumphed over apprehension. The eye was swollen and discoloured. By tomorrow, no doubt, it would be blue, green, purple. It was enormous. It was obscene. She became hysterical at the sight of it.

But throughout the course of the day hysteria cooled into fear. Gavin had been violent – no, vicious – and she was pregnant. Nearly four months pregnant. That hadn't deterred him. She had had no way of knowing that he could behave like this, for they had never had a quarrel before, at least not one that could not be made up instantly by her giving in and him making love to her. She had never dreamt that she was tying herself for life to a man who was capable of hitting his pregnant wife. She resented, too, being made the living embodiment of a music-hall joke: it was such a

88

comic disability, to those not afflicted, like chilblains or a plaster-cast leg. It offered such unlimited opportunities for laughter. This worried her almost as much as the violence itself. But her mind returned to that with recurrent alarm. Had she really not suspected? Had there not perhaps been some current of violence in Gavin, unseen but clearly sensed, as in water-divining? Was this what she needed, was this why she had chosen him? (For he had certainly not chosen *her*.) She had never seen violence in her own home, beyond the most rudimentary taps on the twins' legs or bottoms in moments of stress. She herself could count on one hand the times she had been slapped, and at such an early age that she could not remember her reactions, though she now wondered if they had been significant. Was there something wrong with her perhaps? She became mildly excited at the very idea. It might be interesting to have something wrong with her. Did this explain why she tormented her father – did she want him to strike back? Perhaps Gavin's intractability had fascinated her so much because it offered unlimited opportunity for provocation, and the retaliation, when it came, would be so much greater – as indeed she had now proved. Was it something she needed and did it mean she was sick – or merely clever in finding out how to obtain the desired effect, like a cat eating grass? She didn't know.

She was still on the floor, in the dark, when Gavin returned. She shook all over at the sound of his key in the lock. He came in and switched on the light in one movement, then saw her.

'Christ! Have you seen your face?'

She burst out laughing. The relief was too great. 'Yes, of course I have. What d'you think I've been doing all day?'

'Baby, baby.' He was close to her, almost crooning over her. 'Did I do that? Was that me? Oh, precious baby ...' and he was kissing her all over her face. She put her arms round him and let her body go limp. She had never felt so relaxed. She was safe, they were suited. It would not be hard to provoke him again.

16

'There's someone to see you,' said Annabel when Sarah got in. She looked her up and down in a new, queer way before adding, 'He says he's your father.'

The frosty element of doubt in her voice confirmed all Sarah's worst fears about his appearance. She tried to be casual. 'Then he probably is. Thanks, Annabel.' She went into the sitting-room briskly, but suddenly feeling twice as tired as when she had left the office.

Her father was seated on the sofa and Connie was attempting to make conversation with him or rather to respond to his monologue. Sarah caught a quick flash of her childhood ('when she was a little girl') as she entered the room. Connie smiled gratefully at the sight of her. 'Oh, hello Sarah, I've been keeping your father company but I must wash my hair so will you excuse me?' She vanished before Sarah could answer.

'Well, Sally,' said her father, eyeing her critically. 'I've been waiting a while for you.'

Out it came, without thought or hesitation. 'Well, I do work, you know.'

He clicked his tongue. 'Now that wasn't kind. Aren't you pleased to see me? I thought if you weren't doing anything we might have a bite to eat together.'

Sarah sat down and said wearily, 'I'm going out.' She wasn't, but it looked as if she would have to. He wanted money, obviously: the question was how much.

'How did you find me, Dad?' She had purposely kept her new address from him with the idea of avoiding this very catastrophe.

'I had to ring up your mother.' He sounded indignant. '*She* knew, all right. You'd told *her.* I don't understand, Sally, it's not like you to be so secretive.'

Yes, it is, Sarah thought, very like me. But you wouldn't know. I've been keeping secrets from you all my life and you never noticed. She said, 'Can't you call me Sarah like everyone else?'

He looked at her in amazement as if the question had not arisen a few dozen times before. 'Why should I? Your name's Sally. Your mother and I, we've always called you Sally.'

'My name is Sarah,' said Sarah, persevering. 'You christened me Sarah, don't you remember?'

'But we called you Sally. We always called you Sally.'

'Oh, skip it.' He had infinite patience and time; he would argue all night if she let him. 'Look, Dad, I'm sorry but I have to go out and I want to have a bath and change first.' All the time they were speaking she wondered what Connie and, worse still, Annabel, had made of him : dirty bare feet in sandals, a matted beard, flowing black garments. The sort of thing she found mildly amusing in the street on someone of twenty. Oh God, it just couldn't be worse, in a new place, so soon after moving in. She would never live it down. It would give Annabel a permanent hold over her. 'I wish you'd phone instead of dropping in, Dad, then we could fix something. It's impossible like this.'

He eyed her sorrowfully : she thought he was probably high on something, either drugs or drink; she could not be sure which since she could always smell both on his clothes. 'You're hard, girl,' he said. 'You've got no heart. I didn't even have your number. But your mother did. And your address.' His speech rhythms were out, in some odd way : he seemed to be functioning at a different pace from the rest of the world.

'No, she didn't,' Sarah said truthfully. 'I gave them to Barbara. She must have passed them on.' And when I see her, she thought, I'll kill her. Typical Barbara : with John and the kids to fall back on she lands me right in it. Selfish bitch. All their childhood animosity flooded back.

'And why not?' he said indignantly. 'She's got some feeling in her, some natural feeling.'

'Then why not visit her instead of me, if I'm so hardhearted.' But she knew why. Barbara would claim she was broke and he would not dare approach John. Beyond patting the heads of the grandchildren there was not much to be gained there, maybe just egg and chips on a very good day.

'Can I help it if I want to see both of you? It wouldn't be natural if I didn't. My two little girls.'

He was getting maudlin. Sarah sat and waited for it to pass. It would not last long, she knew from experience, and never prevented him from appraising his surroundings. In a moment, predictably, he said, 'Nice place you've got here, Sally.'

It was at times like these that Sarah wished she smoked. She was sure it would be a comfort: it seemed to help other people. And at least it would have been something to do. She could not even have a drink without offering him one. She opened her handbag and began to repair her face. As if reading her mind, he started to eye the bottles on the trolley. 'How about a little drop of something?'

'Those are Annabel's.'

'But she's a friend of yours, she wouldn't mind. Surely one of your friends wouldn't grudge your father a drink.'

Sarah, snapping her compact shut, said, 'She's not one of my friends and she'd grudge anyone a drink. It's her flat and we're all sharing. Not friends. We pay rent to her and she pays the landlord. It's a nice place because it's expensive. So you see, we all have our problems, okay?'

'Sally.' He was looking at her with his shocked expression. How watery his eyes were becoming, now that she noticed, as if the blue, always pale, was leaking into the white, and the white itself was criss-crossed with red. God help me, she thought, I despise you, I'll never forgive you for being such a slob, and if I could afford it, I'd pay you to go away for ever.

'You're surely not thinking I'm after your money,' he said in outraged tones, as though she had blasphemed in church.

'Oh no,' Sarah said, letting full irony into her voice. 'Nothing like that. But since I can't have a meal with you, as I'm going out, maybe a pound would help?' And she took one out of her bag, after rapidly calculating what she had left to live on for the rest of the week.

He took it instantly: almost snatched it, in fact. Then, with it safely in his hand: 'Is that all you can spare?'

Sarah stood up. The crisis – for the time being – was over. 'Yes, Dad, I'm broke.'

He surveyed her clothes. 'You don't look broke.'

'No, I try not to.'

He shook his head sadly. 'You're very hard. I've always done my best for you and you turn out like this. I don't know.'

Sarah said, 'No, there's no justice, is there?' She thought if she heard once more about all he had allegedly done for her, she would do him a physical injury. A terrible nausea was rising in her throat, the recurrent sense of shame at their being related. Flesh and bone. He had made her. He and her mother, now mink-clad and chauffeur-driven and Riviera-brown. They had rolled around together one night and she had been the result. It was enough to put you off sex for life.

'But you've got a new job,' he went on, 'an important new job. You're getting more money. Barbara said so.'

Barbara, Sarah reflected, should fry in oil, slowly. 'That's right,' she said, 'and I pay tax on it. The remainder is there in your hand.'

His fingers clenched instinctively on the pound, as if she might try to take it away from her. 'Do you want me to go on my knees?'

'No, you're heartily welcome. If I had any more you could have it but I haven't, so there you are.'

His face crinkled up. Only the words got through to him, the tone meant nothing. 'You're a good girl, Sally.'

'Yes, good and hard.'

'Ah, I didn't mean that. You mustn't take too much notice of all I say. I don't always mean it.'

Then for God's sake why say it? Sarah thought. Her back

93

was stiff, she realized, and quite suddenly. That could only be tension. She must have been sitting so rigidly that she had made herself ache.

She walked with him to the door, feeling all the time the pointed non-presence of Connie and Annabel. They had not gone out. They were there somewhere, in their rooms, in the kitchen, in the bathroom. They were tactfully leaving her alone with her embarrassment.

'It's a fine big flat,' he said approvingly.

'Yes, for four people it's just right.'

He put on his hurt face, the one that long ago used to upset her. 'All right, child, all right. I'm not trying to move in.'

Not much, she thought, not much. But she couldn't say it. 'Have a nice dinner,' she said. 'Ring me up some time.'

He hesitated on the doorstep. 'And where will you be going?'

Sarah said, 'Out.'

'I know that, I know that. Out somewhere grand with a boyfriend, I suppose.'

'I don't know where. I won't be going anywhere if I don't have a bath.' She wondered when last he had had one, come to that. Now that she was close to him she could smell it, dirt and sweat, arising from socks and underwear mainly, she thought, and the terrible staleness of unclean old clothes.

'Boyfriends,' he said. 'You want to be careful with boyfriends. Remember, I've always brought you up to be respectable.'

'Oh yes,' said Sarah. 'Quite.'

He actually shook his fist at her, the one still containing her pound. 'Now then, my girl, none of that. After all I am your father.

'Yes.'

'Well, you remember that.'

'You don't allow me to forget it.'

His eyes narrowed, but he seemed to be looking past her. 'You're getting altogether too saucy for my liking.'

Sarah ached to close the door. Her whole body leaned

94

against it, her fingers trembled lovingly on the catch. 'I'm tired,' she said. Perhaps if she sounded pathetic enough he would let her go. 'I've had a long, hard day. Let me go and run my bath now, hmm, and we'll talk another time?' She was wheedling him and it sickened her, but there was no other way.

He said reluctantly, 'Well, all right,' and then to her horror leaned forward. 'Give us a kiss then.' So this was the price. She would have given five pounds to avoid it, ten if she had it, anything. But to refuse now would be to delay his departure – the greater evil. She inclined her cheek and held her breath as the furry chin and warm wet lips brushed against her face. She nearly retched. It was involuntary, like the times when a doctor or dentist pushed something down her throat. But he seemed not to notice. He said contentedly, 'Well, so long for now,' and trotted off down the corridor. Sarah closed the door before he had gone a yard. She went straight to the bathroom, locked herself in, and began to scrub at her cheek with soap and a flannel. She scrubbed till it was red and sore. In the middle of the scrubbing she began to cry. Once she had started she seemed not able to stop. She went on crying while she ran her bath full of green foaming water; she was still crying when she sat in it. She had filled it very full, wanting to immerse herself completely, and she thought how absurd it was to be wallowing in all this water and yet still producing more. She would have to go out. She could not stay in to be the object of sympathetic curiosity. No one must know there was anything wrong: that was rule number one. She must laugh it off or better still ignore the whole thing. Never show weakness. Never. There was not a person alive who would not take advantage of you if you did.

'Simon, can I come over? If you're not busy, that is.'

He was busy, she could tell. His sleepy voice meant he had been studying, curled up in a chair. But he sounded pleased and welcoming.

'I'll get a bus,' she said, meaning a taxi. She was feeling

reckless on her own account but she did not want to alarm him. At the off-licence on the corner she bought a bottle of wine as a gesture.

His room was in its usual mess and she did not mind. She pretended to be very gay but she did not want to talk so she got him talking and they played records and drank the wine. She got rather drunk rather quickly. He said he had already eaten so she pretended that she had, too. The time stretched out interminably, an agony of waiting. He never took her directly to bed, which normally did not matter, but tonight she needed the comfort of another human body, young, warm and clean, to heal her : needed it so much that her skin felt sore with waiting, as it did when she was getting flu. At last when they were in bed and making love she cried with relief and he thought he must have pleased her very much. He went to sleep like a puppy, curled up and happy, totally relaxed, and she lay awake protectively and wondered why she did not love him.

17

'Suppose I take the boys down to Salcombe,' said Cassie, 'and you join us at the weekend.' The twins were becoming restless now that the adjustment from school to home was complete, and they were not due to go abroad to visit friends until September. August yawned before Cassie as an unfillable void. Normally they made plans for it, went away somewhere together. She had never known her husband so irresolute. It was only since Prue's wedding, but a sort of blight seemed to have settled on him. He talked less, and when he did it was nearly always about Prue or the fact that he was middle-aged, which seemed to have only just occurred to him. She did not know how to make contact on any other subject, and she was becoming impatient at her own failure, and at him for causing it. He seemed indifferent to everything around him, and she felt that all her efforts at compensation had been disregarded. Inevitably, she attacked him through the children. 'We might as well go; they're not getting much attention from you.'

Manson looked up from a manuscript. She observed that he was bringing much more work home of late. 'What?'

She repeated what she had said with weary patience. She hated to be involved in a scene like this, not seeing herself as a complaining wife.

He said with his new detachment, 'That simply isn't true.'

'Well, my parents would like some time with them anyway and I don't suppose you want to invite them here.'

He gave her a small, tolerant smile which she resented. 'No.'

'Anyway, it'll be more fun for the boys by the sea. We owe them that much at least.'

He said, drawn, 'Don't make it sound as if we never do anything for them.'

She scented blood and perhaps, out of it, truth. 'Well, we don't do much. I think we rather take them for granted. We make far more fuss over Prue.' She hesitated, as if testing the ground before placing her foot on it. 'It's a case of the prodigal daughter, if you like.'

'Is it?' He stared at her coldly.

She thought they were becoming daily more separate and she did not know how to stop it. It was as if all the warmth of family life that she had devoted herself to generating all these years was now quite abruptly flowing out of the house, seeping through the walls, vanishing. They had lost some vital insulation.

'Well, she's away now, isn't she? So that's that.'

'Not really.' Cassie braced herself for another attempt at being calm and reasonable. When she caught sight of herself in a mirror these days she thought she looked worn out and much, much older. There was a tension in the house where before everything had been fluid and easy. 'She might as well be here. If you're not talking about her, you're thinking about her. The boys don't get a look-in. Oh, I know you play the odd game with them but that's not giving them your attention. God knows they're away enough. This is our one big chance per year to catch up on them. Find out what they're thinking; get to know them again.'

Manson, still holding his manuscript as a shield, said, 'I'm tired and I have a lot on my mind.'

'You have Prue on your mind.' It was out before she could check it. 'I simply can't understand a) why you're so worried about her and b) what makes you think you can do anything. She's on holiday with her husband and that is that. We've got our own lives to lead here.'

The words struck a chill in Manson. He visualized, and for the first time, although the words 'life to lead' were frequently thrown about, a man with a donkey haltered by a piece of string and bearing panniers on either side of its back. The man was leading the donkey but both were trudging slowly and pointlessly towards some unseen destination at the end of a long, muddy lane. No doubt it was a scene he had observed on some long-forgotten country holiday but it was none the less valid an image, and that it should come into his mind at that moment seemed meaningfully apt.

'Yes,' he said. 'So we have.'

'Well, we're not doing much about it.' She was distressed: the house and the home were her creation, their family life was all she had to show for *her* life, and in ordinary circumstances it was much more than enough. But conversely if it was threatened, the threat was much greater because it struck at all she had. There was nothing else. Frightened, she said, 'Please, darling, let's do something as a family soon and stop worrying about Prue.'

Manson looked at her. The straight thick ropes of blonde hair were mixed with grey, her skin tanned from gardening in the sun, her eyes vague and thoughtful as always, her mouth, unmade-up and incongruously voluptuous. She was wearing trousers and a shirt and looked comfortable rather than elegant, but if he went closer there would be the special faded-scent smell that he liked. She was his wife. Together they had discussed thousands of days' events over an evening drink, spent thousands of nights in the big double bed. The fabric of their life stretched back so far you could scarcely see the beginning any more, and forward, where you could not see the end. What was wrong with him, what more did he want? He loved Cassie; he knew she loved him. So why this restless urge for something more, what more could there be than work and love, a job and a wife and family, and a sufficiency with which to enjoy them?

But she did not look like Prue. Not at all. Prue was all him. And Prue was abroad with Gavin. He was sure something was wrong there. He could not believe all those tears had been for him. Something was wrong and he did not know what. He was powerless to help and his child might be suffering. Stemming from this, everything at home seemed colourless and purged of feeling. Prue was in a vortex of excitement or drama or pain somewhere and he could not reach her. The same force was around him in the street, everywhere he looked, young people involved with each other, feeling intensely; even that girl in his office had come in looking haggard the other day. But it was all for the young. There was some general current of feeling that they were all washed into, while he and Cassie, too old, were supposed to stand on the bank and watch without envy, or wander off along some sluggish tributary of their own. Envy. It was sheer envy. The realization shocked him.

He said, 'Meaning Prue isn't family?' and Cassie came back with it instantly: 'Well, she's practically got a family of her own.'

He said bitterly, 'Yes, I'm well aware of that.'

'Do you hate the idea of being a grandfather so much? I thought you'd be pleased when you got used to it.'

'Of course I don't hate the idea. But in due time – not like this, overnight. I don't understand you, Cassie. Prue's had no time to look around, she hasn't even finished her education.

God knows if she'll even get her degree now with a baby on her hands.'

Cassie said softly, 'There are worse reasons for not getting a degree.'

He stared at her. 'Well, now I've heard everything. And coming from you—'

'Why? What's so surprising? Oh, I know I was very academic but if I'd met you when I was Prue's age it might have been a very different story. And I never wanted to work after we were married. I surprised myself in fact – I never felt I was missing anything. Maybe Prue's like me – maybe all she needs is a husband and children. We may even have pushed her into going to college because we have this thing about education. It may not be right for her at all.'

Somehow he resented the idea of Prue being like Cassie, resented it very much. Now that he came to consider it, he realized that in all his fantasies about Prue's destiny he had always seen marriage as a long way off. He had been sure that she had a brilliant future ahead of her, and those were comfortingly vague terms in which to think. But perhaps if he analysed it he had really visualized that future in terms of academic achievement. Disappointed – yes, he had been – when she failed to get into Cambridge as a student, he had perhaps seen her ending up there as a don. But he had not been aware of it till now. Idiotic. What a deeply-buried, foolish dream. How absurd to plan another person's life. But in the case of a child – how tempting.

'No,' he said, 'I've been a fool.'

'Now I don't mean that.' Cassie was always gentle when she sensed agreement or victory.

'I do. I've been a fool to make plans for her. You're quite right. Just because she's capable of going to college doesn't mean she wants a career. Now that girl in my office—'

'You mean your new secretary?'

'Yes, the girl Monica found me. Now she's got no further education, she's just a damn good secretary. But she's ambitious, she wants to get on. There's something driving her.'

'What's her name again?'

'Sarah. She's an ordinary girl from a very ordinary background and she's not much older than Prue but she's realized that shorthand and typing can take her round the world.'

Cassie said tenderly, 'And is that what you wanted for Prue – a trip round the world? When you can hardly bear her out of your sight.'

He bristled at that. 'What d'you mean?'

'Well.' Cassie paused to pick her words carefully. 'You miss her now she's away. You worry when you don't see her for a while. Don't you?'

'Well, what's so abnormal about that?'

'I didn't say it was abnormal.' His use of the word puzzled her. 'It just doesn't fit in with round-the-world trips, that's all.'

'Oh, that was just an example. What I meant was – heavens, I'd have thought you would *know* this – I just wanted her to have freedom of choice, completely. The sky's the limit. That sort of thing. Surely you can understand that.'

Cassie, made flippant by the tension in the air and the aggression of his speech, said, 'Yes, she could have been an air stewardess.' She did not know what she hoped to gain from this – to annoy him or to make him laugh.

'Oh, for Christ's sake.'

'*Peter.*' It was unlike him to be so vehement.

'Well. You complain I'm too quiet and then when I try to talk to you, you come out with a damn fool remark like that.'

'I'm sorry.'

'Well, it's no wonder I don't talk to you about Prue if that's your reaction.'

Cassie was chilled. 'You've missed the point. I'm not asking you to talk about *Prue*, I'm just asking you to *talk*. About anything. About work or the boys or our holiday. Anything *but* Prue, if you like. Because I think we've done too much talking about her. It's pointless. You bring them up and let them go. You have to. Talking endlessly about things you can't change is pointless. And I think it's becoming a kind of obsession.'

The word was a bad mistake. She could see that as soon as she said it, as if she had struck him between the eyes with a dart that had penetrated at once to his brain. He said, 'Just what are you suggesting?'

'Nothing. Nothing. I'm not suggesting anything.'

'You said obsession. I'm concerned about Prue's welfare, as any father would be, and I think she's made a mess of her life and that worries me so I talk about it – and you call that an obsession.'

'Obsession was too strong a word. I'm sorry. I mean I think you're letting it get out of proportion.'

'You said obsession.'

'Yes, and I've said I'm sorry. I didn't mean it.'

'Since when have you ever said anything you didn't mean?'

Cassie panicked. She could feel the ground vanishing beneath her feet as if someone were rolling it up like a carpet. She said, 'Darling, please don't be so hostile. Do you realize we're actually quarrelling? And we never quarrel.'

It was true. And it was one of the things he had always liked most about her. Her tranquillity. Now he was shocked to find himself regarding it more as a placid acceptance of disaster. The fact that she was not even half as concerned about Prue as he was seemed to put a great distance between them. He felt alone, as if he was Prue's only parent, as if he had brought her up and lost her all by himself.

'No,' he said, 'that's right. We never quarrel.'

Cassie waited for peace moves but none came. She said helplessly, 'Maybe it's just as well I'm going away for a few days.'

18

The moment she had gone the house was unbearably empty without her. It reminded him how unfitted he was for bachelor life. He wandered round aimlessly, picking things up and putting them down, turning on the wireless and turning it off, opening books and closing them again. Marjorie and Alec had invited him to dinner and he went to be polite, because he could not decently get out of it, but he felt they had only done it to take pity on him and he resented their kindness. It was a good dinner, as Marjorie's dinners always were, and as he lived within walking distance he had rather a lot to drink. They talked desultorily about politics, television and money – they were renovating their house and obsessed with the subject – and he left early because Cassie was going to phone to let him know she had arrived safely. He had looked forward all evening to hearing her voice and yet when he did he was only conscious of the mileage between them : she sounded so far away, such a small voice, so distant. He knew it was not in her to bear him a grudge and yet he could not bring himself to refer to the quarrel, to apologize, to make it up, although he had intended to. To do so now, on the telephone, seemed to him to make altogether too much of it. So he said instead, 'I miss you,' and she said predictably, 'I miss you too,' sounding pleased and sad, but that was all, and then he talked for a moment or two to his in-laws and wondered yet again why he had never warmed to them. They were perfectly nice people who had always been charming to him, but he had never been able to feel that they were part of his family. When the phone call was over he wondered if it was his relationship with his own parents that was responsible: he had never been close to them either, though they had given him every possible advantage. He had wanted to love them – at times he had felt almost physically weighed down by the love he had for them – but he had been a shy child who needed time in which to express love, and there had never been any time. His mother on committees, with dressmakers, with hairdressers, at the theatre, on the telephone, lying down with a headache. And his father at the office, or abroad, or in his study surrounded by papers. And he himself playing games, or going to exhibitions, or studying, or away at school. And the house full of people, whether relatives, servants or guests: there never seemed a moment, looking back, when they were alone together, the three of them, with nothing to do except talk. It had made him all the keener to establish a proper relationship with his own children, to be an active father, to create a real family life, but he thought now that it had also stunted his emotional growth, made him capable of being a father but not a son.

The next day was sticky and warm. There was no news from Prue. He sat in his office as the afternoon petered out, trying to work but in reality preoccupied with dread at returning to the empty house. He had half-decided to ask Rupert to have a drink with him after work, maybe dinner; it was a long time since he had had an evening with Rupert and he was always an amusing companion. But about five o'clock Rupert looked in to say he was leaving early and was that all right? He still played the game of employee and boss, and his smile showed he knew it was a game, but Manson still enjoyed it as an amusing courtesy. He said yes of course, and laughed, and Rupert went off looking cheerful and arrogant, as if in expectation of a very good evening. Manson wondered idly if it was a man or a woman who was exercising Rupert's current attention, and then fell to considering his own changed plans. He could always go to his club, of course, but he did not want to; in fact he wanted to less and less often these days. Was it that he was getting old, he wondered, and too lazy to go anywhere after work, or was it the fear of finding himself becoming a club man, the least likely image he could ever assume. On an impulse, which he could never afterwards explain or justify, he said to Sarah, 'Why don't we knock off early and have a drink? Nobody can work in this heat.'

He could not see her face but there was only a second's hesitation before she answered, managing to sound pleased and non-committal at once, 'Thank you. I'd like that.'

He was somehow surprised that she accepted so readily: not that he had expected her to refuse. He did not know what he had expected: he had not thought beyond the actual invitation. He was not used to acting on impulse and did not know the rules.

'There's a place round the corner we can go,' he said, 'to save waiting till they open.'

Sarah smiled. 'A dive?'

'Yes. I suppose so. Do you mind?'

'Of course not. It sounds fun.'

He said apologetically, 'We can always surface at five-thirty and go somewhere decent.' For the first time he wondered what she felt: did she think he was making a pass? If so she gave no sign of it. He did not put the same question to himself.

It was dark and cool underground and the lights at the tables made it seem like the middle of the night. Sarah rested her elbows on the table and her chin on her clasped hands, looking at him with calm, friendly eyes like a colleague. He asked what she would have.

'Gin and tonic, I think, with lots of tonic and lots of ice.'

It sounded cool and saved him from having to think, so he ordered two. 'Well,' he said inevitably, while they were waiting, 'how do you like the job – as much as you thought you would?'

She shook her head but she was smiling. 'No. More. I really love it.'

'Good. I'm glad.'

'It's much more fun than Farrer's for a start. And I have

105

more to do. I like to be busy. And there seems more scope, somehow. I can't really explain but it's much more satisfying.'

He said, 'You seem to expect a lot out of your job. And you certainly put a lot into it.'

Their drinks arrived and she took a long draught of hers before answering. 'Well, there's no other way really, as far as I can see. It must be hell to spend eight hours a day wishing you were doing something else.'

'A lot of people do.'

'Yes. It's sad. I used to think about that at school when they were trying to find careers for us all; what hope had they got when at least half of us were bound to end up snarling behind a counter in Woolworth's. There was this one poor careers mistress and she was supposed to sort us all out, hundreds of us, and find the right little niche for each one. It was ridiculous.'

He smiled. 'But she succeeded with you.'

'Well, I was easy. If you say shorthand and typing they're happy. They've got you pegged. It's up to you what you do with it. If you say almost anything, in fact, they're happy. It's the don't-knows they can't stand — and that's about ninety per cent unfortunately.'

Manson said, 'Your parents must be very proud of you.'

'Oh yes, they are.'

'Do you see them very often now they're divorced?'

'Now and then.'

He sensed a sudden reticence: he must have put a foot wrong there. Perhaps she did not want to be reminded that she had confided in him about the divorce. Maybe she regretted speaking frankly the other day. There was only one way to deal with that.

'Rather like me and my daughter. Now she's married I only see her occasionally. It's funny, you can split a family as much by a marriage as by a divorce.'

She was listening as if she cared. 'I take it you don't get on with your son-in-law, is that it? Or is it just that you didn't want your daughter to get married so soon?'

'Both,' said Manson grimly.

Sarah turned her glass round and round. He noticed how slender her wrists were. Bony and fragile. Like Prue's. Golden skin over sharp little bones. 'Why did you let her if she was under age?'

'She was pregnant.'

'Oh.' She looked away for a moment then back, very direct. 'I'm sorry. It was rude of me to ask.'

'Not at all. I expect I'd have told you anyway. I don't seem to be able to talk about anything else. My wife says I'm becoming a bore on the subject.' He tried to make this sound light and trivial, as if he did not take it seriously.

Sarah said, 'That's how my sister got married, too. It's crazy, isn't it. Your whole life decided for you, just like that.'

'Yes, that's just how I feel about Prue.'

'I used to look at Barbara in amazement and wonder how she could be so stupid. I suppose that sounds very arrogant but I did.'

'Did you get on ... as sisters?'

Sarah smiled at the very idea. 'We fought like hell. Right from the start. As soon as we were old enough to lift our arms we were hitting each other. There was only a year between us so that made us pretty equal. My mother had to spend most of her time prising us apart – she was a kind of perpetual referee.'

Manson said, warmed by the description, 'You make it sound fun. But I speak as an only child.'

'You were lucky. No, really, I mean it. There's no fun in fighting.'

'But surely it wasn't really serious, was it?'

Sarah laughed. 'Oh yes, it was. Deadly serious. It was pure hatred, that's how serious it was.' She paused. 'The curious thing is, though, that it made a sort of bond. In later life, I mean. Now, for instance, if I move flats, Barbara's the first person I give my address to, though I know perfectly well she'll pass it on to some relative I don't want to see. But I have to keep in touch with her. I'm concerned about her and her horrid squalling kids. And I think she's concerned about me and my life. We have a sort of grudging respect for each other – perhaps you only get it between sworn enemies. We're sort of like – oh, I don't know – say, Saladin and Richard. We've been in so many fights we almost admire each other.'

Manson said, 'I was right. I *have* missed a lot. Are her children really horrid?'

'Yes, revolting.'

'Don't you like children?' What would Prue's baby be like?

'Some children, yes. But not Barbara's. They're so scruffy – it offends me. That sounds awful, I know, but I'm a terribly methodical person and I can't bear mess. My room is always tidy for instance – that was one of the things we used to fight about because Barbara likes to live in chaos and we had to share a room at home. I was for ever bashing her over the haed because she'd dropped her clothes on the floor instead of putting them away. God, what a prig that makes me sound.'

'Go on.'

'Oh you *can't* be interested.'

'Yes. I am. Really.' He found it all intensely soothing: the vitality of her description, the violence of the events, the clash of personalities – everything. He had noticed before the animation with which people speak of their past, their youth or their childhood.

'Well, now when I go to see her it's all completely chaotic, just the way she wanted to make our room. Everything stays where it falls – clothes, toys, bits of bread. And with three kids you can imagine how it mounts up. And they're *dirty*. Oh, I know you can't keep kids clean all the time, they have to play and get mucky or they'll grow up with psychological problems or something, but you *can* fling them all in the bath at night and get the worst of it off.'

He was laughing outright. 'Sarah, you *are* doing me good. How old are these monsters?'

'Seven, five and three. It's slightly better now with two of them at school, but before it was absolute bedlam and still is

108

in the holidays.' She grinned apologetically. 'Maybe that's what put me off marriage.'

Manson said, 'I have twin boys aged ten. But they're not quite like that. Have you really been put off marriage?'

She said seriously, 'I don't know. I've said that so often I believe my own propaganda.'

'Why? Is it a good line with boyfriends?'

She laughed a trifle guiltily, as though he had caught her out. 'Well, it helps; it makes them feel safe. But I think I probably do mean it, up to a point. After all, what are the main reasons for marriage? Children and financial security. Well, if you're not madly maternal that knocks out one reason. And unless you marry a millionaire, you're probably not much better off, in an average marriage, with two of you on forty pounds a week instead of one of you on twenty. Well, are you?'

He said wryly, 'You make it sound like a dying institution.'

'I'm sorry. I don't know much about it really. I'm sure it's lovely if it works.'

'But in your view it seldom does.'

'I don't know. My mother's happy enough now, in her way, but she's rich, she's an exception. When I think about marriage I think about shabby middle-aged women getting on buses with baskets of shopping. All varicose veins and pincurls. Getting excited over threepence off Daz.'

Her glass was empty. Manson said, 'Let me get you another drink.'

She glanced at her watch. 'I'd love one but I ought to be going.'

Something drained out of him, some bright growing hope of being amused and distracted like this for the rest of the evening. 'What a pity. I was going to ask you to have dinner with me. My wife is away with the boys and I hate my own company. I'm hardly ever alone and I'd no idea I was so bad at it.'

She hesitated. He could see she was thinking, weighing up the invitation. He wished he knew what was passing through her mind.

'Well...' Pause. 'If I could only just make a phone call. You see, we take it in turns to cook, at the flat.'

Was that all? 'Yes, of course.' He had thought to be ousted by a boyfriend at least.

Sarah stood up. 'I won't be a minute. But are you *sure*? I know I talk too much, are you sure you can stand it?'

He smiled. 'It's just what I need.'

The phone rang for ages. She was almost ready to give up when he answered. She said hullo in a weary voice.

'Oh, it's you. Sorry, love, I was in the bath.'

'Geoff, I'm sorry, could we call off this evening? Only I've got the curse and I feel lousy. I've only just left the office, I've been sitting in the loo for an hour, and I just want to go home and crawl into bed.'

'You poor old thing.' He hated illness. 'Well, okay then. What a shame.'

'Yes, I'm sorry.' She kept her voice low and pain-wracked. 'But I really feel rotten, and I'd be no good for anything.'

'Shall I ring you tomorrow?'

'Yes. That would be nice. I'll be better then.'

That night she could not sleep. She had, when she got home, the same elated sensation she had felt on walking off-stage from a school play, or latterly on parking a car after speeding. She was outside herself. For most of the evening she had behaved normally, alternating bright conversation with attentive listening as and when required. She had been, as usual, the expected person, until almost the very end. And now it was surprise that kept her awake. He was simply not the type. She had worked with a good many people and some of them had flirted with her: she reckoned she could tell within minutes of shaking hands if one was the type. And Manson was not. Or had not been. Over dinner, over wine, over coffee and brandy, making each other laugh, discussing books and authors, parents and children (she had been mildly astonished at the way he seemed to think all young people lived a life of riotous, almost orgiastic fun) – all that time, though she warmed to him as someone reliable, someone adult and dependable, they had been merely good companions, only one stage removed from an office relationship. She had been careful not to take advantage in any way, or even to give him grounds for thinking that she might take advantage in the future. She kept telling herself: he is lonely, at a loose end, and I remind him of his daughter. That's all. Why shouldn't he invite me to dinner? And tomorrow we ignore it. I can perfectly well play that game. Then, safe in this resolution, she had allowed herself to see him as a man instead of an employer. He was, she found, surprisingly attractive for his age; she assumed he must be nearing fifty. Normally she avoided married men, and since most older men were married, older men as well. This was less from conscience than convenience. Not having a place of her own she could not afford to date people who could not take her home. And it would be boring not to be able to telephone freely, boring to worry about who might see you together in the street, at the theatre, over dinner, boring not to be able to send cards, give birthday presents, mention names to your friends. And if they were family men, the children would worry her – little faces pressed up against the window waiting for Daddy to come home and kiss them goodnight, and Daddy working late at the office, making love to his fancy woman. It was like a Victorian melodrama, but that was how she had thought of it and so it had been easy to avoid. She did not want to get involved in anything so tiresome and so nearly ludicrous.

But with Manson these images did not occur to her. It was so obvious that nothing was intended, that it was simply the pleasant evening and the enjoyable dinner it appeared to be. She could afford to relax and enjoy herself. She kept thinking what a nice person he was – gentle, sympathetic, vulnerable. She even felt a little sorry for him. It was only when they were in the cab and he was taking her home that the atmosphere changed, the feeling tipped over into something else. She knew they were both aware of it. Suddenly they were close together in a small dark space and it was not at all like

111

being in the restaurant. They had both run out of conversation instantly and she had prayed for the taxi to get lost. It was suddenly unbearable to think that in a few minutes they would be separated; it seemed wrong that the evening should end so flatly and abruptly. She wanted something more.

She rebuked herself sternly for being so idiotic : sitting in a taxi with her boss and giving in to such adolescent ideas. But she knew she was not imagining the atmosphere, and he was as silent as she was. The silence gradually built up until it became so tense that she felt bound to say something, anything, to break it, and she had said in a voice that was meant to be prim and polite but came out disturbed and intense, 'I've enjoyed this evening very much.'

He looked at her then (for they had both been pointedly staring out of opposite windows) and the expression she saw made her want to take his face in her hands and stroke it. She was quite alarmed to feel such a wave of tenderness for him.

He said, 'So have I,' as if he meant it, and then went on quite casually and softly, so that she almost thought she had imagined the words, 'It's just as well I have to get the last train, it will spare you the embarrassment of fighting off my elderly advances.'

And she had said, 'Why should I fight?'

He kissed her then and she kissed him and there seemed for a while to be quite a little fight going on about whose turn it was next. She was aware that this was what she had wanted to happen all evening, and amazed that she could have deceived herself so efficiently. He said, 'You're very lovely,' and she said, 'So are you,' and they kissed some more until she felt distinctly uncomfortable and assumed that he did too. But they kept their arms round each other, their hands out of use.

Manson said, 'This won't do,' and drew back, and lit a cigarette. Sarah, shaking, said, 'Can I ask – do you want to make love?' and he said, almost angrily, 'What do you think? Of course I do.'

'So do I.'

The taxi drew up with a jolt and the driver demanded, 'This it?' Manson cursed softly and paid him and they both climbed out. As the taxi drew away Sarah said sadly, 'You should have kept him, there's nowhere we can go.'

'I know.' Manson drew her to him in a darkened doorway and held her closely and kissed her soundly. She could feel him pressing hard against her and she liked it very much except that it made her ache inside. 'Serve me right,' he said bitterly, in acknowledgement.

'Me too.'

He stroked her face. 'Do you really mean that? I can't imagine why you should.'

'Well, I do. You could tell, if you care to investigate.'

'No.' He shook his head. 'I'm no good at half-measures. And I seriously doubt if I could function in the street after all these years. Besides, can you see it? The policeman's torch, the bit in the paper: "Publisher and secretary on indecency charge." Not at all the beautiful experience I had in mind.'

They both laughed at that and the laughter was comforting and good. Sarah said, 'Some other time then,' out of the confidence the laughter had given her; she was shocked when he said soberly, 'No, I rather doubt that. Things are never the same in the morning. And just as well really. You don't want to get involved with an old married man; I don't want to lose a good secretary.'

She had said indignantly, 'Speak for yourself. And anyway, why should you lose me?'

'Sarah, these things never work out. I don't mean I'm experienced, I'm not; I'm as surprised as you are that we're both here now, like this – but it hasn't a prayer. You must know that. It's the old one about the boss and the secretary. You know what I mean.'

She said with surprising firmness, 'You're turning us into cliché and we're people. You're hiding behind it. I don't like that.'

He released her abruptly. 'No, you're right.'

'Now you're angry. I've offended you.'

'No. I just feel old and tired and rather foolish. And

113

tomorrow I think that's how you'll see me too. And that makes me sad, which is what I deserve.'

She said, 'Tomorrow I shall feel just the same but I won't let it affect my work. There, will that do?' She held her breath.

He burst out laughing. 'Oh Sarah, you're ridiculous and lovely.'

'Yes, I am, aren't I?'

They had parted on her doorstep without further kissing, but easily, like friends who know they will meet again.

Manson's time to think came on the train, which he nearly missed. Leaping from his taxi, which had been hard to find, dashing through the barrier and down the platform, flinging himself into a carriage and slamming the door just as the train began to move, he had no time to think, beyond registering that he was out of breath and out of condition. Somehow this made the scene he had just been involved in all the more unreal. If Sarah could see me now, he thought ruefully, surveying his fellow passengers, the usual crowd of late-night tired and late-night rowdy. Some boys, a little drunk, were playing cards and telling jokes, but with an eye on two girls sitting demurely in a corner and pretending not to notice. The older passengers sheltered behind newspapers or stared out of windows, though at this time of night it was easier to see a reflection of the carriage than the scenery outside.

He found he had a dual reaction. Part of him was appalled and amazed at having gone even this far. The words 'taking advantage' hammered in his head: poor girl, after all, what could she do? Wined and dined and then virtually pounced on by her boss: there was not a lot of leeway for resistance or repulsion or whatever she might have felt. He had put her in one hell of a spot. How would he ever know if her reaction had been genuine? At the same time, while despising himself heartily he felt an enormous sense of exhilaration, as if reborn. He had forgotten he could feel like that. The pressure of Sarah's body against his, the taste of her mouth, so different, so foreign, so unlike Cassie – another perfume, a smoother tongue and small sharp teeth – was it just the novelty he had found intoxicating or Sarah herself?

He had not been unfaithful to Cassie since she was pregnant with the twins and ill. He had felt badly about that, though he tried to convince himself that what she did not know could demonstrably not hurt her, and in reality he was doing her a favour, allowing himself to return to her relaxed and free of tension, better able to cope with the situation. But it had troubled him all the same. He was simply not cut out for that kind of thing; he never had been. Always out of his depth and vaguely distasteful – not disapproving (for after all other people's behaviour was their own affair) but, yes, repelled – in groups discussing masculine prowess. He could not regard any woman cheaply, as a conquest, did not want to boast of the few he had had, could not cope with the lies and evasions involved. Which made it all the more absurd to be even attempting to create such a situation now. It could not possibly lead anywhere; he did not want it to, anyway. It could not even be a pleasant interlude, if he were to be once again haunted by the complications of a double life, however slight; and to add to that an office situation, to risk losing a perfect secretary under embarrassing circumstances which he had himself created – he must be out of his mind. At the very least he had made a fool of himself. At worst he had ruined a professional relationship. What was the matter with him? Was he turning into the sort of middle-aged man who could not keep his hands off young girls? The image was unpleasant to him: he remembered publishing a novel on the subject once, and had only just let himself be swayed by the power of the writing and the insistence of Rupert's predecessor. All his instincts had clamoured to reject it. When the hero, if such a term was appropriate, had ended up in court, in the papers, under analysis, he had felt sickened at the humiliations that resulted from a few foolish, greedy actions. He had not understood how any man could be desperate enough to place himself so much at risk.

So why now did he not feel similar revulsion? Or rather

why, while feeling it, did he also have this amazingly light-hearted sensation of joy, a conviction not of folly terminated or disaster averted, but of something important just begun? He was surely not contemplating going on with it, even if Sarah were willing, which must be unlikely, however tactfully compliant she had been. But he felt so ridiculously sure that here was something he had been looking for without even knowing. It was the same sensation that he got on seeing a picture or a piece of furniture that would be ideal for his study – only wildly intensified, out of all proportion. He needed Sarah, as distinct from wanting her. In the taxi when he kissed her, despite all the strangeness of an unknown mouth, there had been an overwhelming sensation of recognition. He needed her as much because she was familiar as because she was new.

When he got off the train he collected the car from the station car park and drove slowly home, still mindful of his alcohol content. ('Publisher on drunken driving charge.') It was not till he got into the house and found a postcard from the South of France that he remembered there *was* somewhere he could have gone with Sarah.

19

The flat was cool and shuttered, but he was still hot with surprise at finding himself there. The chain of events was simple. Sarah had been as good as her word at the office: punctual, bright, unembarrassed. He had been grateful to her and felt that she deserved some acknowledgement of her attitude so he said, 'Sarah, you're marvellous and I owe you an apology.'

Sarah said matter-of-factly, 'No, you don't. I told you I'd feel the same today and I do. But I've no objection to being told I'm marvellous.' Then she had gone on calmly typing.

At eleven she brought his coffee without any sign of awkwardness and as she put it on his desk he said, 'Sarah, you really are making things very difficult for me.' Her eyes widened in surprise. 'A little outraged indignation would be much easier to take.'

She said, 'I'm sorry but I did warn you.'

He drank some of the coffee. 'I'm supposed to be driving down to Salcombe tomorrow to bring my wife back – she's taken the boys down there to stay with their grandparents.'

'And you're busy this evening?'

He looked up in surprise. 'No.' He saw tenderness and anxiety and hunger in her face and another look also – that suggested she was puzzled by her own behaviour. And that makes two of us, he thought.

She said, 'I can't bear to leave it like this.'

He said, feeling his blood begin to race, 'Sarah, you are either very kind or very foolish, tell me which,' and she said with a kind of desperation, 'Neither, neither.'

He got through the rest of the day in a daze.

About five, by arrangement, they left the office separately and met round the corner. Already they were starting to be careful. He hailed a taxi, trying not to look nervously round for spies, and when they were in it they sat and held hands, not daring to kiss, and smiled at each other.

He said presently, 'You're mad.'

'I hope it's catching.'

'I mean we're mad.'

'That's better. Isn't it lovely?'

The taxi crawled. He took in for the thousandth time every inch of the brown and gold flowered dress above golden-brown knees. Her hair was tied back with a piece of the same material. He said, 'I think you're a miracle.' An authentic feeling of insanity had swept over him : the situation was predestined and right, nothing could spoil it; he had complete trust in the madness of it all.

Sarah said, 'Where are we going?'

'Regent's Park. A flat near Regent's park.'

'Whose is it?'

'A friend's. They're away.'

He turned her hand over and over in his own. Small and square. Nails shiny-painted, uncoloured. The lines very firm and marked. He said, pretending to read them, 'Ah, a long and happy life.'

'I should hope so.' She smiled back. Her light-hearted lack of guilt reminded him of Prue ('Daddy, I'm going to have a baby.') Perhaps that was true innocence: if you did not see any harm in something, then for you it was harmless. Or was that rather the corrupt reasoning of the totally selfish, determined to have their own way? The first chill thought. He brushed it aside.

Sudden pressure on his hand. 'Don't be sad.'

'I'm not.'

'You were. I saw it in your face.'

'All right, I was. But it's gone.'

She shook her head. 'It hasn't really. But I'll make it go.' Now she held his hand in both hers. 'Look. This isn't going to make trouble for anyone – you, or your wife or me. I'm quite realistic and I don't expect anything. But I think this is something we need very much. Both of us. I think it would be worse not to do it. Really.'

'You're a witch.' It bothered him that both their minds should run upon the same lines of self-justification.

'No. Just realistic. *Please* don't be sad. Look – if you've changed your mind you can still stop the cab, throw me out. I'll quite understand.'

'Do you want me to?'

'No.'

'Neither do I.'

The taxi drew up before the curving row of white houses. She was impressed. He paid the driver and she said, 'God, they must be very rich, your friends.' Up the steps and inside across endless yards of carpet to the lift: up, purring almost silently. He became apprehensive. None of the neighbours knew him yet, he was safe there, but what if for some crazy reason – anything could have happened – they had returned home unexpectedly?

The flat was silent and empty. Very cool after the taxi and the street. They stood in the hall and looked at it.

Sarah said, 'It's lovely.'

'Yes, it's quite nice. Rather small but otherwise all right.'

'And to be so near the Park ...' But the chat petered out. 'Oh please – please kiss me or I shall run away.'

He put his arms round her. 'Sarah, Sarah.' He found he wanted to use her name more and more as if it expressed and held within itself all the words of love he could not (yet?) use. 'It's all right, it's all right, do you hear? You can't run away now, I want you so much, I need you. Sarah – beautiful Sarah.'

They kissed for a long time, until Sarah, drawing breath, said, '*Please* can we go to bed now or I shall fall over,' and indeed as he loosened his hold on her she swayed against the wall. The bedroom gave him an odd qualm, a sense of intrusion, of invitation almost, but strongly mixed with a sensation of triumph and justice. He watched her as they undressed and she was very beautiful; he said so. She said, 'Don't, you'll make me cry,' and he took her in his arms to lie down, saying, 'You're a funny girl,' and she said. 'It's no good pretending I don't do this often, because I do; but it's also no good pretending this isn't special, because it is.' And after that they did not talk much.

They took time to explore each other; he felt that he owed her a lot and must control his impatience. Her pleasure repaid him amply; she did not hide anything and her movements and the look on her face were enough to reward an eternity of effort. When he paused to take precautions (a lunch-hour visit to the chemist, the first in God knows how many years) she stopped him, saying, 'No, that's all taken care of,' and when he entered her they both groaned with delight and relief at achieving something so long delayed. He tried to make it last, tried to be controlled and expert, but it was soon too much for him and she seemed so nearly ready that he could not wait. It was not perfect, in the end, but for a first time it was remarkable. With her he felt free to let go, which amazed him; in the few extra-marital affairs of his life he had always felt a last veil of reticence, even in extremity. He had never known if this was a hard core of fidelity to Cassie or a buried resentment towards his partner of the moment. But he did not feel that with Sarah. Perhaps it was the confidence with which she entrusted herself to him. When he had regained his breath he kissed her all over her face and her shoulders and neck and said, 'Sorry, not perfect,' and she said, eyes closed and a rapturous smile on her face, quite sufficient to drive him out of his mind, 'No, but still *super*.' He laughed then with relief, and said, 'What a child you are.'

She made a face. 'Funny children you know,' and they both began to laugh hysterically, quite out of proportion to the joke. It was a long time since he had laughed so much after making love, and it brought it all back, the crazy hysterical well-being and goodwill. It was youth, or novelty, or love, or a blend of all three, but she had made him remember it and it was intoxicating. He played with her hair; he had never seen it all loose before. It made her look younger. They drew apart and admired each other. She was golden all over except for the pale bikini imprint; he said, enviously, 'You've had a holiday,' and she said, 'Yes, in May. In Italy.' He was suddenly quite sick with jealousy and said, knowing he had no right, no right in the world, 'Did you make love there?' and she said simply, 'Yes,' and he wished she had lied. It was a time when nothing could be concealed: not just that their eyes gave them away but their very skin seemed transparent and revealing. She said, 'I'm sorry you mind but I never pretended to be pure,' and he did not answer. He made a great thing of lighting a cigarette and lay there admiring her honesty and hating her for it. She said, 'Go on, say it,' and he pretended not to know what she meant. 'Go on, tell me that's why I'm here, call me names if you like,' and he pulled her to him, close and kissed her shoulder and said, 'Oh, Sarah, Sarah,' because it was at that moment the most beau-

tiful name in the world. She said in a muffled voice, 'I'm
terribly afraid I'm going to fall in love with you, but I won't
let it interfere with my work,' and suddenly they were laughing again and it was all right. He did not even mind that his
body next to hers was pale and there was a thickness round
the middle that he was ashamed of, whereas she was all
bones and correctly placed curves. Her breasts were more full
than he had expected and her waist curved in sharply; her
hip bones stuck out either side of a flat little stomach. He
looked all the way down and found beautiful legs and the
most tiny perfect feet, like the feet of a child who has never
worn shoes. Naked, he thought she was as neat and precise as
she was with her clothes on. He remembered her saying that
her room was always tidy and he thought that in some way
her body was tidy, too.

Sarah said, 'Shall I make coffee or get us a drink or something? Would your friends mind?' He was so silent that she
wondered if he had fallen asleep and as usual she was beginning to feel restless now the languid phase had passed. In
a little while she would be hungry. This was the unfailing,
predictable pattern and it was reassuring that this still remained, for there seemed little else to be sure of. She had not
expected anything to happen between them, not expected to
be here, most of all not expected to feel so much. She could
not remember such immediate involvement with anyone
since the boy in the sixth form (when she was in the fifth
form) who had touched her up pretty thoroughly behind the
science block one dark night at a school dance. She had
adored him after that, as a god (for surely anyone who could
produce such sensations must be a god?) and waited, trembling, scarcely breathing, for him to approach her again for a
date. But he never did. Term ended and he left and she never
knew if he was embarrassed, disgusted, indifferent, or merely
absent-minded. It had taught her a sharp lesson, intensified
by other later lessons, yet somehow perhaps the most important because it was the first, because she was only fifteen.
The glorious sensations behind the science block, her gratitude

to him for evoking them, her desperation to go out with
him – all this she had obviously failed to transmit; or, if
transmitted, it simply did not interest him. Perhaps he regarded her as cheap. Perhaps he laughed about her to his
friends. (This thought was too terrible to contemplate: that
he might be boasting of what she had 'let' him do, even now
while she was recalling the beauty of it all.) Lying awake at
night crying – but softly so as not to alert her parents – or
staring at him in Assembly, willing him to smile at her, writing his name on pieces of paper to admire the sheer poetry of
it (and then tearing them up), walking a discreet distance
behind him and his friends to admire what seemed to her the
easy grace of his movements, so casual, so self-possessed – all
this was clearly ridiculous and achieved no good at all. She
had made the mistake of caring. Not to care was the answer.
If you did not care they came running, all the people you did
not care about. They jostled each other to dance with you,
walk with you, buy you chocolates and take you to the
cinema – one had even left flowers on her doorstep and then
run away – and all you had to do was permit the occasional
kiss (or, later, make love). As long as you did not care, back
they came. So what was she doing now, letting all this feeling creep in? For it was not, she decided, what you *did* behind
the science block that counted, it was how you felt. If you
did not care, they could not hurt you; in fact they would not
even try. For eight years this policy had worked for her;
what on earth made her think it was safe to abandon it now?

She turned her head on the pillow to look at him and said
softly, 'Peter Eliot Manson.'

'What?'

'I thought you were asleep.' It was nice to speak as tenderly as she felt. She had forgotten how nice it was.

'No.' He opened his eyes and they gazed at each other.
'Why did you say my full name like that?'

'I don't know. Well, I've typed it often enough but I've
never said it.' And making love she had not called him anything: while the 'Sarah's' multiplied, she had not called him
Peter or darling, or anything.

'Well, now you have.'

'Yes.' She considered it. 'It's a lovely name. Very formal. Rather Victorian. I like it. But I don't feel it's mine to use.'

'You don't know me well enough, hm?'

They smiled.

'Well, in a way, no. And tomorrow it's Mr Manson again so I better not get in bad habits.'

Tomorrow was Cassie and Salcombe. Tomorrow was office. Tomorrow was reality, making now into only last night. 'Don't remind me,' he said.

She said easily, 'Oh, it will be all right, you'll see. Don't worry. And I love the way you say Sarah.'

'Sarah.'

'Yes.'

'You're a beautiful girl, Sarah.'

'Am I? Did I please you?'

'Yes. Very much.'

'You pleased me too. Very much.'

Somehow this exchange frightened them both: it was too absolute, it seemed final, marking the end of something. Sarah said, 'Well. Shall I get us a drink or some coffee? I asked you before but you didn't answer so I thought you were asleep.'

'No. I was thinking.'

'Not sad thoughts. Please. I promise you it's all quite all right.'

He said, 'No, not sad thoughts.' He chose his words carefully. 'I was thinking I care for you.'

'You don't have to say that, you know.'

'No. I know.' Strange how tenderness tipped into anger. 'But I care for you, too. That's the trouble. I've broken a rule.'

'What rule?'

'My own rule.' She stroked his shoulder. It was funny seeing him naked and tousled, and remembering his office suit, his hair immaculately brushed. She was glad he had plenty of hair. 'My rule not to care.'

'What kind of a rule is that?'

She smiled, feeling sad. 'The first law of survival. Don't you know it?'

'It sounds like death to me.'

'Does it?' She sat up. She suddenly felt much older than he, and protective. 'Then you must be very brave.'

He put a hand on her arm. 'Don't be cynical, Sarah, it doesn't suit you.'

'Doesn't it?'

'No.'

'Why, because I'm so *young*? That's got nothing to do with it. I know about me. If I care I get hurt and behave badly.'

'I'm not going to hurt you.'

'No, of course not.'

'I mean that.'

'I know you do.'

'And I can't imagine that you could ever behave badly.'

She sighed. 'Why do you think I'm so nice? You don't know me at all.'

He said seriously, 'Are you wishing we hadn't done this?'

'Oh no. No.'

'Then why all the sadness?' He pulled her back, down to him and wrapped his arms round her. She buried her head in his shoulder, wanting to hide. He said, 'Darling, listen,' and she stiffened, ever so slightly, at the word. 'You're lovely and precious and you've made me so happy I can never repay you. *Please* don't be sad, or I shall feel I've taken advantage and behaved like an old-fashioned cad. Last night I called myself names all the way home. If I can't make you happy all the names will be true.'

She said, 'Oh, you can make me happy, you have. You do,' her voice muffled against his skin. 'It's just – I never imagined this happening.'

'Neither did I. But now that it has we must make it work. We mustn't make anyone unhappy, even ourselves. That's my rule, if you like, though I've only just thought of it. Heads everyone wins and tails nobody loses. Isn't that a good rule?'

'That's the best kind of rule.'

They kissed. Sarah said, 'By the way, you still haven't told me whose flat this is.'

He hesitated. The temptation to tell the truth was strong, perhaps to set a seal on their relationship. But the temptation to lie was stronger, representing safety and self-preservation. 'Just friends of mine. No one you know.'

'A couple? Married and all that?' She sat up.

'Yes.'

'But they don't mind? Us in their bed and everything?'

'Well, we're not exactly *in* it.' They were lying on top of the bedspread and he had been careful to spread a towel.

'No, but the principle's the same. The married are generally on the side of the married, aren't they?'

He wondered how she knew that. 'They're my friends, not Cassie's.' Deeper and deeper in. It felt odd to speak her name in these circumstances. Unlucky.

'And you're sure they won't mind?'

He felt irritated by her questioning and his own thoughts. 'I told you. Why go on about it?'

'Sorry.' She sounded very innocent. 'But it's odd to be in their flat, in their bed, and not know anything about them. It makes me feel strange. I feel I *ought* to know more. For instance are they young or old, happy or unhappy?'

'Young and happy.'

She studied his face. 'You sounded bitter when you said that. Do you envy them?'

'Yes, I suppose I do.' He had been mad to bring her here and mad, having brought her, not to lie properly and make a thorough job of it.

She got up, wandered over to the dressing-table, smoothed her reflected hair and opened a drawer. 'Don't,' he said sharply, a reflex.

She stared at him in the mirror. 'Why not?'

'I'd rather you didn't, that's all.'

She said slowly, 'It's your daughter's flat, isn't it? I think I knew all the time.'

20

Prue lay in the sun. She had pictured herself on a crowded beach, flaunting her stomach, which was developing a most gratifying curve. But Gavin had neglected to tell her that the cottage was not by the sea and she had not thought to consult a map. So she lay in the garden instead, on a small patch of ground they had cleared of long grass, and watched herself turning brown and glistening with oil. There seemed to her something inexpressibly voluptuous about sunbathing while pregnant. She even chose to lie on the ground, with a cushion under her back, rather than in a deckchair. She wanted contact with the earth. When she closed her eyes and the bright colours chased across her eyelids, she felt at peace on the ground, as if she and the child had come home. Earth Mother – Mother Earth, she chanted softly to herself when Gavin was out of earshot. She felt she was doing herself positive good, just as much as by absorbing vitamins, but she did not want to appear ridiculous.

Gavin was very brown, too. It had not taken long, given their honeymoon tan, for they both had tough skins and could spend most of their time in the sun. She thought she had never seen him so attractive. He even waited on her a little now that her pregnancy was actually visible. And rushed to put his hand on her stomach when the baby kicked. She loved him.

All the same, she was restless. It was a perfect existence: sun, food, wine, sleep, love. She could not have improved on it. Yet something was lacking. She felt she had opted out: that somewhere the real world continued without her. She was afraid that when she got back to it, it might have

changed unrecognizably, away from her influence. She liked
to remain in touch with things; she did not believe that
everything would continue properly, lacking her supervision.

There were insects in the long grass near her, bigger or
brighter, or both, than the ones in England. She squinted at
them through half-closed eyes, feeling like Gulliver. Occasionally one would alight on her or run across her, which she
rather liked, although she worried a bit that the sun-oil might
have an adverse effect on its feet. Gavin admired her: to her
amazement he thought she was very brave not to make a
fuss. Apparently his aunt had always screamed if an insect of
any description came near her. And he admitted once having
placed a beetle on the pillow of a girlfriend he had wanted
to get rid of: it was easier than telling her to go. Prue had
felt a strange thrill at this story, the simple cruelty of it, and
the logic. But she thought it unfair that he should admire her
courage in the garden. She did not disillusion him, but no
courage was required to accept what did not worry you. She
had noticed before that often you were given credit for things
that took no effort at all; the really difficult things passed
unnoticed and unpraised. He had been overly impressed by
her forgiveness over the black-eye incident, too. She thought
this proved that she knew him better than he knew her,
which rather pleased her. It was fun to keep a secret self,
dark and mysterious, tucked away inside her; it made her feel
powerful and important. Doubly pregnant, in fact.

He came towards her now, out of the house, naked and
carrying a tray. They both sunbathed naked in the private
little garden, though sometimes she felt the need of a bra as
her breasts were growing heavy. She laughed now, at the
sight of him: the image of a nude waiter was irresistible. He
had two tall yellow drinks on the tray in long thin glasses
clinking with ice. They were making their own *citrons
pressés*. In fact they hardly went out: every day to the village for fruit and vegetables, cheese and eggs, bread and fresh
milk, but never to a restaurant. They had no inclination, they
could not afford it and there was nowhere to go. They had
brought all they could in their luggage: hardly any clothes

but packets of soup, coffee, tea, tins of fish, and cartons of cereal. They had more or less stopped eating meat, and their cigarette consumption had dwindled: it was too hot to smoke. But they drank gallons of wine bought locally and stored in the larder. She had never felt so healthy in her life. And in the night, when she woke, it was always to thoughts of the baby, growing firm and strong inside her. She tried to remember the diagrams she had seen and wondered which stage it was at. It would be all hers. Her child. Hers and Gavin's.

She sat up and took the tall lemon glass and sipped it gratefully. Rivulets of sweat, having collected in the crease, now ran down her arm. Her knees if she pressed them together left little damp patches. Her head swam with the sudden movement of sitting up. She was dazed with heat.

Gavin sat beside her with his glass in his hand and they both stared idly at the cottage, blindingly white in the sun. She said, 'Fancy living here all the year round.'

'They don't; they rent it out.'

'Well, you know what I mean. Fancy *owning* it.'

He shrugged. 'Why own when you can borrow?'

The lemon was very cold and sharp. The sourness made her mouth contract. 'You've got some useful friends.'

'Yeah.'

She studied him. Black hair and black eyebrows; curly black hair from shoulders to navel and a sprinkling on his back; tough black hairy legs. And the whole of him so brown. He was more like a monkey than ever. An ape. Or a gorilla. A beautiful monkey. (She wished she knew more about monkeys.) She began to laugh.

'What's the joke?'

She said the first thing that came into her head. 'I was thinking I'd like to telephone home.'

'What the hell for?'

'Oh, not parents. *Our* home. The flat. Just to see if it's still there. I'd like to hear our phone ringing and know it still exists, it seems so far away.' She wondered if he would make love to her soon. It was really too hot, though; they usually

128

waited till evening. But she liked to do it in the garden. She almost wished there were other houses nearby – not too near, but with just the possibility, no more, just the uncertainty of being overlooked and never knowing for sure. That would have done something to her, she decided.

She finished her drink and lay down, smiling at Gavin. She said, 'I hope Sue remembers to water the plants.'

21

Cassie said, 'I tried to phone you, but you'd already left.'

'Yes, I left early and came straight from the office. How bad is she?'

They both spoke in low voices, instinctively. The whole atmosphere of the house was hospitalized: it even smelt different, and there was an institution air of routine and expectancy about it.

'Well, it's not good at her age, of course. (Poor Dad, he's worn out, he's been with her for hours.) But the doctor seems to think she has a fair chance. Only I never know whether to believe them when they're being cheerful. Funny, isn't it? If he was gloomy I'd believe him like a shot.' She squeezed his hand. 'It's marvellous to have you here. I've felt so alone trying to cheer Dad up and keep the boys out of the way.'

'How are they taking it?'

'Oh, they're a bit subdued. It's rather awful – they keep saying to me, "Granny's not going to die, is she?" and I have to say, "I don't know, I don't think so." I can't say I'm sure she won't because then it would be so much worse for them if she does – oh, Peter.'

Tears. He put his arms round her and let her cry against

his jacket. He was deathly tired. Driving home and sleeping badly after Sarah's abrupt exit, going to the office full of trepidation and finding no Sarah but a message 'Miss Francis phoned to say she won't be in today, she has a sore throat,' then a day full of phone calls and no one to syphon them off, irritatingly punctuated by Rupert ('Where's your Miss Thing, playing hookey already?'). He had left early, deeply dispirited by the past twenty-four hours and set out on the long drive to Devon. How quickly it all turned to – what was it called? – wormwood and gall. Was this what 'they' meant by retribution? And now to find Cassie so distraught, so much in need of his comfort, was the final ironic straw. Illness was the last thing he had expected; with so much upturned in his own life he had not left room for drama in anyone else's.

'Poor love,' he said to Cassie. 'Poor love.' He kissed the top of her head. All the guilt and exhilaration of yesterday had faded into a kind of weary tenderness. 'You've been very brave. I'm sorry you had to be alone with it all this time.'

She looked up and smiled. He was moved and alarmed to see how much his presence comforted her; he felt undeserving. 'Well, there was Dad.'

'Yes, so you had to be strong for two; and cope with the boys. Shall I go up and see if they're asleep? If they're not I could make reassuring noises.'

She looked grateful. 'Oh yes, would you? They'd love that. I went up half an hour ago and they were still awake then.'

He poured her a drink. 'First things first.'

'You are good to me.'

'Is Granny going to die?'

Manson sat on a chair between their beds. 'We don't know for sure. But the doctor thinks she'll *probably* get better, so you mustn't worry too much, all right?'

They nodded solemnly. He saw in their bright, sleepy eyes the typically childish mixture of genuine concern and a certain ghoulish enjoyment.

'If we pray will it help?' School religion was strong at this age, he noted.

'It might.' He never knew how far to communicate his own doubts to them: as wrong surely to indoctrinate doubt as certainty. He compromised. 'But if it doesn't it will be because she's too ill, and we wouldn't want her to live if she couldn't get better, would we?' Strange how this fraud must be perpetrated on the young, that everything happens for the best, as if they could grow up in a different world and never learn the truth.

One twin shook his head obediently. The other, already a free thinker, said, 'I would.'

His brother turned on him. 'Oh, you wouldn't.'

'Yes, I would.'

'But that's not *fair*. She wouldn't *enjoy* herself any more.'

'She doesn't enjoy herself much anyway.'

'She does when *we're* here.'

Manson admired their self-confidence. He said, 'Well, the odds are she's going to get better, so you'll just have to be quiet in the house for a day or two, and let her get plenty of rest. All right?' He wanted to go now. His stomach was aching for a drink and the back of his neck, after such a long drive, felt ridged with cement.

The more ghoulish one of the two said, 'If Granny dies will Grandad come to live with us?'

Manson froze: this was out of the mouths of babes with a vengeance. He had not looked ahead at all and here he was, presented with it. He wondered if it had occurred to Cassie.

The other twin said obstinately, 'But she's not going to die.'

'She might.'

'If she dies will she go to Heaven?'

'Of course she will.'

'No, she won't.'

'Well, she won't go to Hell, will she? She's *good*.'

'She'll go to Purgatory like everyone else. My friend Sullivan says everyone goes to Purgatory before they go to

Heaven because no one's *quite* good enough to go straight there. He's a Catholic.'

The other twin, the disbeliever, roared with laughter. 'He's silly.'

'No, he isn't.'

'Yes, he is.'

'He's my friend and he's not silly.'

He longed to leave them to it but he couldn't; he was obliged to say, 'Do you want to wake Granny up and make her worse?' They sobered instantly.

'No.'

'Oh, no.'

'Well, then, you'll have to keep quiet. Try and go to sleep now and tomorrow you can make all the noise you like on the beach.'

He tucked them up; he did the goodnight-and-a-glass-of-water routine. Walking down the passage, so tired he felt he might fall down at any moment, he found himself suddenly and unaccountably thinking of Sarah. Her face flashed on the screen of his mind, all dark eyes and pale hair and sharp bones and that look of concern, and he said to himself, 'Oh, my love, where are you?' There was no place for her here, and being here illustrated the insanity of what he had done more clearly than anything else. Turning the corner of the passage, he almost bumped into his father-in-law coming out of the sickroom. He had been so far away in his thoughts that this really startled him but the old man noticed nothing. His eyes were glazed and red; Manson even thought he might have been crying. The old people were what was popularly called a devoted couple.

The old man said absently, 'Ah, there you are, my boy. Good to see you.' He put his hand on Manson's arm. Contact was rare between them, reserved for occasions of great emotion. Manson's and Cassie's wedding, the births of the children, Prue's wedding. Similarly the words 'my boy'. As always they moved Manson strongly, coming as they did, so seldom, from a man he hardly knew, whose daughter he had long ago taken away. He gripped the hand and felt the veins sticking up like soft string.

He said, 'I'm so terribly sorry, is there anything I can do?'

The old man appeared to consider, as if there actually might be. Then he said, 'No. No, I don't think there is. Except – just hold the fort for a moment, I don't like to leave her alone.' He shuffled off into the lavatory.

Manson entered the room reluctantly. He looked at the woman in the bed, ugly and pathetic with illness, and was too much reminded of his own mother dying and himself, aged seventeen, desperate, because the magic, unspeakable words, 'I love you' had never been said. He had shouted them over and over again, in a frenzy, till his father, out of very private grief, said curtly, 'It's no good, she can't hear you,' and that seemed like the judgement of God. He had wasted seventeen years of opportunity. He should have *made* the occasion, forced it if necessary, dragged the impossible words past his lips and *made* her hear them. She could not have been *that* busy. Useless, afterwards, to be told by well-meaning relatives that she knew, all the time, that she would understand. He had missed all his chances. He had let her die without being *told*.

His mother had died with a face like white marble. Perfectly white and beautiful, and so smoothed out that it could not be skin. He would never forget it. She was already one of the statues they placed over graves. It was like her to die so elegantly; it was in keeping with her life.

The old man came back and stood regarding his wife. 'She looks peaceful, doesn't she?' he said, as if she were already dead.

Manson shivered. 'Yes, very.' He made an effort. 'Now you mustn't worry too much. You heard what the doctor said – he's most optimistic.'

'Yes, yes.' The old man resumed his seat and picked up the paper. Manson wondered if he even heard the words of comfort, or needed them. Perhaps he too, like the twins, was caught up in the drama of life, and death, the uncertainty, the long vigil. 'You run along, you'll want to talk to Cass.

She's a good girl. It's been wonderful to have her here. Providential.'

Manson went downstairs. Cassie was waiting for him, her feet up, on the sofa. She said, 'I poured you a drink.'

'Thanks.' He sat down beside her and drank it: lovely healing fire trickled to every limb. 'This is *just* what I needed.'

'Are you hungry? I could cook ...'

'No. I ate on the way, in a pub.'

Already the journey seemed remote, to say nothing of the life he had left behind. He held her hand without knowing whether the compassion he felt was for Cassie his wife, whom he loved, or another human being, anyone who happened to be in distress.

'How do you think she looks?'

'Well ... a bit strange. But she's bound to—'

'Yes. Dad's been marvellous.' A long sigh. 'Did you settle the boys down?'

'More or less. All the drama's gone to their heads a bit.' He wondered if he should say it; hesitated; said it. 'They wanted to know if Grandad would come to live with us if Granny died.'

'Oh God.' Cassie closed her eyes. 'You'd hate that, wouldn't you?'

'We can talk about it.' He tried to sound easy-going and relaxed. 'But I don't think the situation will arise. I think she'll get better.'

'Do you? Really?'

'Yes, really. Don't you?'

'Maybe. This time.'

'Well, of course, *eventually* ...'

'Yes.'

22

'Well,' said her mother, opening the door, 'long time no see.'

Sarah winced. The greeting never varied, perhaps because her visits were always infrequent. But this time it was a refuge, it was somewhere to go, however unlikely, where she was safe – and officially safe – from Simon and Geoff, and where she could *think* against a social background, just as some people might choose to study in a reference library rather than alone in a room.

'How are you?' she said, ignoring the greeting and kissing the presented cheek. It was heavily scented and satiny with cosmetics. Her mother wore a white linen dress with white embroidered flowers on it, and lots of gold jewellery on her very brown skin. She had actually overdone the suntan, Sarah thought. The skin on her arms and neck was beginning to look tough and dried up.

'Oh, I'm very well. We had a marvellous holiday. Well, come in, sit down; you're staying, aren't you?' She moved edgily around the stiffly furnished room.

Sarah said, 'Is he out?'

Her mother paused in the act of pouring herself a drink: gold bracelets dangling from the hand that held the bottle, ice clinking in the glass. 'I wish you'd find some other way of referring to Bob than that; you make him sound like some kind of ogre and he's been kindness itself to you.'

Sarah sat down. 'All right. Is Bob out? Is my stepfather out? Is your husband out? Take your pick. Now it sounds like three different men.'

'There's no need to be offensive. I don't know why you

come if you're in this kind of mood.' But bickering was so much second nature that she let it pass. 'Do you want a drink?'

'No, thanks.' Sarah could not explain how frugal – even puritanical – her mother's *ménage* made her feel. In it she always ate and drank sparingly, feeling she might choke, refused presents, looked with disapproval at the trappings of wealth and thought of the deserving poor as if she had a social conscience.

'Hmm. Up to you. But you look as if you could do with one – you're looking a bit peaky. Been seeing your father?'

'No. Why?'

'Oh, he generally makes you look peaky when he's around. I've noticed it before.'

'He was round the other evening – just called in. That's all. I haven't seen him since.'

'Hmm. On the scrounge, was he?'

Sarah didn't answer.

'He'll never change,' said her mother with satisfaction. 'He's got no initiative. He doesn't even want to better himself. I suppose he got at least a quid out of you.'

Sarah didn't answer but smiled faintly.

'Aren't you ever going to learn? He goes straight in the boozer with it, you know. If you think you're putting a hot dinner inside him by throwing your money about you're very much mistaken. The only way you'll ever do that is to cook it yourself and watch him eat it. You're soft. I don't mind betting Barbara never lets him have a quid.'

'John wouldn't let her.'

'Oh, John, John. That's a lovely way out. Barbara wouldn't give you a quid if you were dying. And good luck to her, why should she? That comes of having a hard life. She's learnt her lesson. Now *you've* had it too easy. Why can't you learn from her mistakes? Get yourself a rich husband.' She lit a cigarette, diamonds flashing, Sarah thought, almost self-consciously. Shivering in the light.

'Like you,' she said.

'Well, why not? I haven't done so badly, have I, and I'm

no chicken. You've got youth on your side, you can take your pick, but you don't want to work in an office all your life, do you, and you've seen what happened to Barbara. Now there's no need for it. It's just as easy to fall in love with a rich man as a poor one, if you're set on falling in love.'

'So you said,' Sarah replied. Often. Her mother was the sort of woman who would recommend any discovery – a rich husband, a new deodorant, a cure for piles – as enthusiastically as though her life depended upon it, or she were a major shareholder in the company.

'Well, it's true. I'd be dishonest if I pretended otherwise.'

Oh, Peter Eliot Manson, Sarah thought suddenly, conjuring his name to herself like an incantation, where are you? Walk in and rescue me, no, better still ride in, arrive on a white charger like the chap in that advertisement, all tossing mane and shining armour, and trample her beige Wilton under your hooves. Carry me off to marshmallow land where I needn't be tough any more. What rubbish, she thought bitterly.

A key turned. A door slammed. Her mother's face froze in the alert position and switched on a welcoming smile.

'Well, well, well.' Footsteps. It was the giant, it was Fee-Fo-Fum, and the child's reaction was to hide. 'Both my beautiful girls.'

Her mother got up as he came in the room. She made various small sounds, like purring and cooing, and exchanged kisses. Sarah sat stiff where she was. He came over and patted her on the head. 'Hullo.' She said hullo back. He was careful these days and did not try to kiss her, not since the time when, alone with her, he had stuck his tongue in her ear and she had kicked him smartly on the shin. His bad leg too. *Good.* And Barbara swore he had once put his hand up her skirt but that could just be Barbara. One thing was certain, though, she thought, he wouldn't have bothered with Mum if he could have got either of us. And at night he takes his teeth out and puts them in a glass in the bathroom. I saw them once. My mother sleeps with a man who does *that*.

She suddenly felt, if not actually light-hearted, a little

drunk with contempt. At least my teeth are my own and I haven't fried my skin into leather, and nobody buys me, I do what I like when I like, and I'm *young*. If I make a mistake, the odds are I can put it right (I made a mistake on Friday, not going to work); there'll be another time. But they're on their last chance and lucky to get it, I suppose.

Her stepfather sat down beside her; she felt the thud of his weight in the springs of the sofa beneath her and thought, Christ, when he takes his clothes off it must be *obscene*. She glanced at him furtively, with horrid fascination, as at something diseased or rotting, and observed the vast overhang of his stomach as it strained against his leather belt. He had hair sticking out of his nose and ears. She felt sick but there was a kind of satisfaction in feeling sick, and it led on to pride in Manson and all his lovely elegance. The two men were not even far apart in years. She thought, I am lucky. I am lucky, oh God, if only I haven't ruined everything. I was silly to mind. It just gave me a funny feeling, using her flat. But I shouldn't have minded.

She had let her stare become fixed and her stepfather caught her staring. He winked. 'And how are all the boy-friends then?' Her mother put a glass in his hand, fussing round him as if he were a child or an invalid – in other words behaving, Sarah supposed, like a good wife.

'Fine,' she said. 'Just fine.' She knew the way to avoid cross-examination would be to produce a monologue of her own, but she could not manage it.

He leered at her; at least she could not see the look on his face as anything other than a leer. 'How many are there of them now?'

Sarah shrugged. 'Oh, I've lost count.'

He appeared delighted; he did not seem to know she was being rude, telling him to shut up, leave her alone, stop asking her stupid questions. 'Make them jealous and keep them guessing, is that it?'

'Something like that,' said Sarah, nauseated. Her mother in the chair opposite was gazing at him with a rapt expression, as the fountain of wisdom and wit.

'That's right,' he said. 'Like mother, like daughter.'

Her mother fell about on her chair, giggled, protested, became kittenish. She forgot to keep her knees together and Sarah glimpsed the bulging flesh above. The rest of her had been rigorously health-farmed but her thighs, always a weak point, had either resisted treatment or reverted promptly to type. Now I am being catty, she thought without shame, as a fact. Time to go. Not that it was ever really time to come. Not *here*.

She stood up, saying resolutely, 'I must be going.'

They both protested, but her mother only mildly. She knows he fancies me, Sarah thought; she'll never leave us alone again if she can avoid it. Well, that suits me. But why does he think it necessary to make all this bright chat, to be so *silly* with me, when he must be a clever man in business to have made so much money? She tried to be fair, to think how it could have gone. Hullo, Sarah, how are you? Yes, fine. You look well (or not). How's your new job going? Good. And the new flat? What about the other girls? Oh, there was masses of stuff, especially at the moment. But instead he had to be coy, leaving her nothing to say. And to make it worse, he probably thought he was being clever.

I am intolerant, she thought. I am intolerant and I don't care; that's how intolerant I am. When she got out of the house she ran and ran, along street after street of smug, silent white houses in the full gloss paint, till she was past the boundaries of Belgravia (where she was sure his neighbours must despise him) and into Knightsbridge where she caught a Nineteen to the embankment. She enjoyed moving out of salubrity, watching each row of houses, each line of shops grow less exclusive and select, enjoyed seeing the litter and the dirt increase, and the people grow shabby. I'm sure there's a way to be rich and real, she thought, but those two haven't found it, and it's all the worse because they started with nothing; it ought to be such fun to have made it that they'd be realler than anyone.

Down by the embankment she wished she had told them she was coming here instead of pretending to have a date. At

139

the time it had been easier but now she wished she had stood up and said, 'I have to go and walk by the river and look at water and ships and houseboats and swans and mud.'

Lorry drivers and men in cars and boys on bicycles whistled at her as they passed, and she smiled. She knew she looked good. Good, and tidy. Some girls could look good and messy but she had never learned how. She even admired the messy look on others, but it was not for her. Everything attractive about her – and she had studied herself like a textbook, for on herself depended everything – was based on neatness. Daily bath, twice-weekly shampoo, teeth cleaned after every meal. Nails immaculate and make-up meticulous. What began as effort became simple routine and attention to detail. It was the same with her clothes: whether cheap or expensive they were always clean and pressed. Everything she had looked new because she kept it in mint condition. She set aside evenings for buttons and zips and recalcitrant hooks and eyes; her hems were always level and adjusted to her version of the fashionable length. She had learned what suited her; she knew which magazines to read for guidance, which colours to wear and which to avoid, how to make her own clothes, adapting the more freakish fashions to flatter her; when to pay a lot (and what for) and when to economize, how to get an expensive effect from something cheap. She had learned because she had to, but she had also wanted to. Now, though neither clever nor beautiful, she could make herself appear both. She had to make the best of herself because she had nothing else to offer.

The same attitude applied to her job. She hated to make a mistake but aimed at speed *and* accuracy because she also could not bear to be slow; she was punctual because it was part of her image and gave her satisfaction (not least because it didn't come easily). All in all, it was a textbook image, an impossible ideal, viewed from outside, maddening to others who were tempted to retaliate by hinting that anyone so methodical must be a born spinster. But since no one could look at her and do that, she had won. Except that she had few friends. She drove them all mad, and alienated most, with her competence. But it was not done just to impress. Sometimes she thought she only did it to hide the mess inside. At other times she thought it was simply a compulsion. And sometimes it made her cry.

23

He said, 'So there it is. My wife is staying on for at least a fortnight and the boys are staying with her. There's no point in disrupting their holiday, after all, and there's no one to look after them here all day.'

'No.' She put her hand over his and felt the strange thrill of contact that comes from touching someone on whom you have projected the love image. 'I'm sorry. You've had a rotten time.'

'It was a rough weekend certainly. But it's worse for Cassie. She's stuck with it. Still, the old lady seems to be rallying.'

'How old is she?'

'Oh ...' Manson had to think. 'About seventy-five, I suppose. Something like that.'

Sarah said, 'I missed you.'

'Did you?'

'Yes. Are you glad?'

'I suppose I am. Yes, I am.'

'Are you still angry with me?'

'Angry? No. Do you want another drink?'

'No. I was lying on Friday. I didn't have a sore throat. I just wanted time to think.'

'I knew that.'

'Do you want to dock my pay? You're perfectly entitled.'

'After what I did? You were right, it was a shabby trick.'

141

'No, no, I was wrong about that. I don't know what I felt. I was upset. It seemed such a risky thing to do and so ...'

He said carefully, 'Unnatural?'

'No, no.'

'It doesn't matter.'

'Oh, but it does.' She looked and sounded desperate. He gazed at her, so neat and elegant in the burnt-orange suit of linen and the flowered shirt, crossing and uncrossing her shiny black shoes, opening and closing her shiny black hand-bag, her huge dark eyes staring at him out of a pale, pale face. She looked as if she hadn't slept and yet somehow made it suit her. The young, he thought, have such resilience, such capacity for drama. They can feel so intensely, and stay up all night, and still have huge appetites and not look run down. They thrive on emotion. Whereas I just feel tired. And look it.

She said, 'Please don't write me off. I'll be so good from now on if you'll let me.'

It was ridiculous. To be offering a second chance and begged for one in return. He knew what he ought to do, of course, and he had no intention of doing it.

He said, 'Sarah, you're beautiful but all I want to do right now is sleep.'

She said urgently, 'Can I be there?'

He woke about six, in the unfamiliar hotel room, and expended a few seconds wondering where he was. Then his brain cleared. He felt wonderfully refreshed. They had dined early; he must have been asleep by nine. He felt a twinge of guilt about that: he had really taken her at her word. He looked down at her, marvelling at how neatly and quietly she – perhaps all the young – slept. He remembered watching Prue sometimes as a child or an adolescent and she had scarcely moved. He had even had difficulty in hearing her breathe. Whereas he knew that both he and Cassie had developed, over the years, a habit of threshing about in bed, of snoring or grinding their teeth. (The first one to fall asleep

142

was the lucky one.) He hoped to God he had not done any of that with Sarah.

With a sense of privilege as well as making amends he woke her up and made love to her. They were both very gentle, perhaps through being so recently asleep, until the end when it became explosive. He had intended to be experimental and different, to challenge her experience, but when it came to the point there seemed no need; after all they were not running a competition. He had the uneasy feeling all the same that she was probably more experienced, in variety, if not in frequency, than he was.

He said afterwards, still holding her, 'That's the only time you ever lose control, isn't it? The only time you aren't neat and tidy and well ordered. It's beautiful to see you like that.'

She smiled. Her face was damp with sweat. 'It's my thing. My one liberating thing.'

He thought about it. 'Towards the end you're like an aeroplane preparing to take off. You stop taxi-ing and you rev your engines and then you make your run.'

'And then I take off.' She liked the analogy.

'If you're lucky.'

'I'm lucky with you.'

'Well.' She was being too generous. 'Not so lucky the first time.'

'Well, first times never are.' She amended: 'Hardly ever.'

He thought, now that's something I must never ask: how many men, how often, how much better? Cassie said Prue had two before Gavin. Could that be a lie? and if it is, which way would she lie, more or less? Would Sarah lie if I asked her? But I can't, mustn't ask her. What does it matter, after all? (I don't have a yen for virgins.) Enough that she's here. That makes me lucky enough. He was struck by his own lack of guilt; such a feeling of lightness in an affair was a novelty to him, an even greater novelty than the affair itself.

'You make me feel good,' he said to Sarah, in gratitude.

'And you make me want to tell you all my secrets.'

'I'm listening.'

'No. They're grubby little secrets.'

143

'Nothing of yours could be grubby.'

'Well, boring then. They really are. Anyway, I don't really need to tell them. It's enough to feel I could.'

He hugged her. 'You're a funny girl.'

'Do I make you happy?'

'Yes.'

'That's good. You weren't very happy when I met you, were you?'

'No.'

'You mustn't worry about her, you know. She'll be all right.'

'Yes, of course.'

'Oh, don't be cross. Aren't I allowed to mention her?'

'Surely. After all, I took you to her flat.'

'And I was silly about it. I'm sorry. Are you going to forgive me?'

'Don't be absurd.'

'No, really. I nearly ruined everything. And I don't want it to be ruined.'

He said seriously, 'Well, it isn't, so stop worrying. What I can't understand is, why you should care. I can see exactly why I need you but I can't for the life of me imagine why you bother with me, and that's the truth.'

She said, 'One day I'll tell you.'

They took to meeting at the flat again, perhaps to prove to each other that all was well, two or three times a week. They made love, talked, dined, and departed early for their separate homes, for the look of the thing. In between Sarah saw Geoff and Simon, for she was afraid to give them up; she had no confidence that the affair with Manson would extend beyond his wife's return and yet she hugged it to herself like a golden bale of cloth that could unroll and stretch out for ever, as in a fairy tale. Her physical sensations with Geoff and Simon were undimmed, but emotionally she found it hard to continue. She was both pleased, at this unexpected evidence of fastidiousness, and alarmed, at the unprecedented loss of freedom. He had made her cease to enjoy her normal

144

way of life. She tried to analyse it, for her own satisfaction; she needed to know. It was not that he was exceptional in bed – most of her boyfriends had been as good or better. Not that he took her to nicer places – he had to be discreet, and in any case Geoff, for example, probably had more money. Not that he was especially gentle and understanding – he was, but Simon was more so. On the face of it there seemed nothing she could not obtain elsewhere. She found herself listening more and more to pop songs (which must mean she was in love, that was how she always knew) and there was one that seemed to echo her thoughts. 'It's the way you make me *feel* . . .' it said, not this or that, all the reasons she had dismissed, and she thought it was indeed the way he made her feel, and the way he made her feel was safe. She felt in the hands of an adult, protected, cradled almost, and this was incongruous since she so often comforted him. But the fact remained that he made her feel safe and cherished; logically she knew that she had probably never been less so in her life.

He said, 'You see, when she was a child, she used to depend on me entirely. It was an extraordinary sensation: I felt like God. She'd come to me if she grazed her knee or lost a pencil or couldn't do her homework. She was so trusting, so sure I could fix whatever it was. When all that stops, almost overnight, it's a terrible jolt. She was so beautiful – well, she still is – but I mean I used to look at her and think how vulnerable she was, as if she might snap in the wind, and somehow I could always protect her. She was very thin, like you, and I thought she might break, so I had to be there.' He was rather drunk. 'It's uncanny to look at someone and know you've produced them, you're responsible for their existence. You *have* to make everything right for them, or the whole thing's a mockery. I used to think I'd be had up in some heavenly court and they'd say, 'Well, and what have you done for your daughter? She's actually been crying. Why didn't you prevent it?' And I'd have no defence. Wanting to work miracles just isn't good enough, you have to actually do it.' And he had failed. When it came to the point you could not provide the one thing your children needed, which was luck. You could only give them love, and a good dentist, and music lessons, he thought bitterly to himself.

They had been looking at wedding pictures, sitting on the floor of Prue's flat. He had his arm round Sarah as he turned the pages. She thought, he doesn't love me, not the way I love him, but it doesn't matter. She had never thought to accept so little gratefully. She looked at the dark, pretty girl in the photographs, the blank face, the thin pussy-cat features, the look of mystery and self-containment, and searched lovingly in Manson's face for the original. She felt the bitterest envy; she could almost taste it, like lipstick. This girl had every atom of love and care that she had been denied. Each moment of her life had been hedged round with concern. The boy in the photographs, the husband, long-haired and patently self-conscious in the formal clothes, was as nothing to her: anyone from off a street corner. She could have said to Prue, 'Why him? Why not another? Why anybody, in fact?' She looked at the pictures of Cassie without guilt, even without connexion: she was not seeing a woman whose husband she was leading astray, her own position was too precarious for such clichés to be valid. But a nice woman, a kind woman, that was evident, not at ease in smart clothes, with a homely hair-do and marks of age and involvement on her face. She obviously did not care about money or status; her identification was with her family. She thought, no wonder he loves her and no wonder they can't really talk about Prue. She even thought that she and Cassie could have been friends, had they met, had it all been otherwise. She looked at the unpainted mouth and thought, yes, you'd be easy to hug, easy to talk to. She was consumed with envy and she could not tell him. Besides, what was there to tell? Only that her life had been different.

She began to call him Eliot, when they were alone. She could not get her tongue round Peter, and the entire name was clearly absurd for general use. The more he talked, the more he confided in her, the more desperately she made love

146

to him, in an effort to prove something. She felt it was the only talent she had, and she used it like one under sentence of death.

Weekends he spent with Cassie in Devon, and she hoped they made love. She was not jealous, she was never jealous, and besides it would help to redress the balance. But she did not ask him and he did not tell her. Instead he would mention that Cassie was tired or the mother-in-law was rallying or the boys were getting restless. Safe information. Weekends she spent with Geoff or Simon, or divided between them, and spoke vaguely to Manson about girlfriends and sewing. She thought how funny it was that, in so far as there were rules for adultery, the rules would say that it was (of course) all right for him to continue sleeping with his wife but all wrong for her, Sarah, to continue sleeping with her boyfriends. But she was afraid to let them go and could think of no adequate reason to give ('I am having an affair with a married man who is sure to ditch me presently,') that would neither sound ridiculous nor hurt their feelings. It had its funny side, too, and it was good sometimes to be cynical and laugh at herself and the whole situation. She now realized that three was the maximum she could cope with unless each knew about the other two. Although Geoff knew about Simon she decided not to burden him with Manson, as she was not sure how much her image could stand, even in Geoff's eyes Simon and Manson had no grounds for thinking she was not exclusive to each of them: the subject was never mentioned and they could assume what they liked. Meanwhile she juggled frantically with her diary and hoped that they would never all meet head-on in a restaurant.

With Manson she soon became extremely self-conscious and furtive in public, prepared at a second's notice to disappear under the table or on to the floor of the cab, although he repeatedly assured her that, firstly, they were unlikely to meet anyone he knew (she found this most unconvincing) and secondly, if they did, it would not mean All was Discovered, merely that he had to admit to taking his secretary out on

147

that one occasion. But Sarah, having once become jumpy, could never relax completely again. So sometimes she would cook for him at the flat, being careful to replace everything exactly as found. She became very fond of it and sometimes wondered if this was how it would feel if they were married.

'How long is Prue away for?' she asked one evening when they were lying on the bed, too lazy to dress, and she was watching him smoke just one more cigarette.

'I'm not sure. I've had two postcards in three weeks, and originally they said they'd be away for a month or two, so I really can't say.'

Sarah shivered. 'We'd better be careful then.'

'Oh, we're all right for another week at least.' He felt extraordinarily relaxed. All his anxiety about Prue had been dispersed: she was simply enjoying herself in the sun. His mother-in-law was not dying: there was no judgement of God there. He felt like a schoolboy on holiday, knowing that the time would pass and term begin again, but not yet. There was another week at least before Cassie's return, before Prue's return. A golden week of freedom.

Sarah said anxiously, 'What will we do then?'

'There are always hotels.' He stroked her shoulder. But he did not really want to think, to make plans. It was too soon to face up to the real, cold world outside.

Sarah was thinking that this would not do. She had not liked the hotel very much – she had in fact felt surprisingly self-conscious – and if it was only for a few hours instead of the whole night that feeling would surely be much, much worse. She blamed herself for being unsophisticated but could not change. She made wild plans for a place of her own, as a last resort, and yet she more than half-believed that the affair would soon be over anyway. She wondered if she would have to look for another job. How did you go on working for someone who had stopped making love to you? Would her feeling of safety remain, like a legacy, or would it vanish with him, and would she be worse off than before? She looked tenderly round the room, where she had been happy, trying to imprint it on her memory, in case, as seemed likely, after another week she never saw it again.

'You never told me,' she said as the point struck her, 'how you came to have a key to this place. Did Prue leave it with you?'

'No.' He was a little shamefaced. 'When I took out the lease I had duplicates made. Wasn't that reprehensible of me?'

'And she doesn't know?'

'No, of course not.'

'But *why*? I mean – you didn't plan to do this, did you?'

'Good God, no. Now you *know* I didn't.'

'Then why?' She thought how she would feel if anyone did such a thing to her; and here she was benefiting from something she deplored.

'I suppose I wanted to feel still in charge. Able to walk in – if anything happened.'

'Such as?'

'Oh, I don't know. Trouble.'

'What sort of trouble?'

'Anything.'

'You mean you expected it?'

'No. I'm just making excuses. I had to have a key because I wanted to feel I could still walk in like a father. I never meant to use the key, actually. Just having it helped.'

Footsteps passed in the corridor all the time and they were used to them. These stopped, on the word key, outside the front door. Sarah stiffened.

'Ssh.'

'What?'

Immediately it was every farce that had ever been written. And also pure terror.

'There's someone outside.'

'It can't be them.'

She knew she should be doing something – dressing, hiding. She couldn't move. A key was inserted in the lock and carefully turned.

'No.'

149

The door opened and closed. The feet in the hall hesitated. Sarah lay frozen, too frightened to move.

'Get dressed,' Manson said in a quick, urgent whisper. 'Get dressed *quickly*.' He slid off the bed and began flinging on his clothes. His speech made her capable of action. She too got up, shaking all over, and started to climb into her dress, shoving her underwear into her handbag for speed.

A tap ran for a while in the kitchen. The footsteps moved about the living-room.

'Our coats,' Sarah whispered in agony, suddenly remembering. 'They're in there.'

Manson didn't answer but merely gave a sigh of despair. They were partly dressed but barefoot and extremely dishevelled, standing on either side of the rumpled bed with its rumpled towel in full view, when the bedroom door opened. The moment of classic horror. They froze, as if by remaining motionless they could become invisible. A girl with long red hair and a jug in her hand appeared, saw them, and gasped; her eyes grew quite round while the rest of her face managed to register no expression at all, but slowly turned scarlet.

'Oh,' she said, retreating. 'Excuse me.'

They both remained in their attitudes of frozen shock as they heard the door bang behind her and her footsteps going away, rather fast, down the passage. Sarah was the first to move. She sat down out of sheer weakness, looked at Manson, still quite motionless with one sock in his hand, and said, 'Oh *Christ* ...'

He said automatically, mechanically reassuring, 'It's all right, it's all right,' as if to a child, the parental reflex.

'But it *isn't*.' She burst into tears of anger and misery. 'It couldn't be worse. Oh, *God*.' She wept savagely. He was thinking hard but getting nowhere, like a vehicle spinning its wheels in sand. He put out a hand to comfort her but she flinched away, and he felt suddenly alone. Of all the insane, unlucky ways to ruin something ... Then he heard the sound change, emerging from the first sound as if struggling for supremacy. She was actually laughing. He turned and looked at her in amazement as she rolled on the bed, her knees tucked up to her chin and howled with laughter, tears streaming from her eyes, until she nearly choked and had to pant for breath. It was at that moment that he found himself thinking quite calmly and matter-of-factly, And now I have fallen in love with her. That was the only way he knew it had not happened before: it dated from that moment. If she had not laughed perhaps he would not have fallen in love. It seemed as simple as that.

'Oh God,' she said finally, still spluttering with laughter, 'what a thing to happen. She looked so *shocked* – didn't she? That *look* on her face.' But just as suddenly she sobered. 'Who d'you suppose she was?'

He shrugged. 'A friend of Prue's. Come in to water the plants, I imagine.'

Sarah was silent, retrieving her underwear from her hand-bag and slowly putting it on. He was surprised to find he wanted to make love to her again but in the circumstances did not like to suggest it. 'Let's get out of here,' she said.

'There's no hurry. She's hardly likely to come back, after all.'

'She might. And anyway – I just don't feel comfortable here any more.'

He said sadly, 'You never did really, did you?'

'Yes, I did. In a way. Maybe too comfortable.' She was brushing her hair, repairing her face, all with a terrible brisk coldness. 'We started taking it for granted, didn't we?'

'Well, we haven't done any harm.'

'Who knows? She might talk, mightn't she?'

'Talk?' He had not considered this: the shock of the discovery, and the aftermath, had numbed his brain. 'You mean – to *Prue*?'

'Who else?'

'Oh, surely not.' A vast chill spread over his body. He could even feel gooseflesh rising on his arms. He put on his jacket slowly, and the remaining sock, feeling numb all over.

'Why not? It would be perfectly natural. She doesn't know who we are – she finds us here – why shouldn't she say to

151

Prue – oh, God, it doesn't bear thinking about. I shouldn't have laughed. It just isn't funny.'

He said, 'I liked you laughing.'

She looked at him without comprehension. 'You must be crazy. Come on, let's go; I can't bear to be here another minute.'

He did the usual tidying up while she watched him; for once she did not help. When they were outside the door she said, 'Well, that's that,' and walked rather fast to the lift. He followed her. They travelled down in silence and left separately, as usual.

Outside on the pavement he said, 'Let me buy you a drink; I'm sure we both need one.' She was very white and he thought she was trembling slightly. 'We've had quite a shock, after all. Come and have a brandy or something.'

She shook her head. 'I don't want one.'

'Maybe not, but you need one all the same.'

She began walking energetically. 'I want to go home.'

'No.'

'What d'you mean, no?' He had never heard her speak so coldly. 'Why shouldn't I go home?'

He temporized, soothed, terrified that if he let her out of his sight she would disappear for ever, as if she had never existed, like some fairy-tale creature, both magical and doomed. 'Darling, of course you can go home, you can do whatever you like, I'm only asking you to come and have a drink first, just for half an hour, and let's talk about it. After all, I'm as worried as you are.'

'No. You're not worried at all. I can't understand you.' She marched on, at such a pace that he could hardly keep up with her. They were heading in no particular direction.

'Of course I'm worried,' he said, as she seemed to want him to be. 'That's why I want you to stay, so we can talk. After all, I've got much more to lose than you have, if she talks.'

That was a mistake. She tightened her lips and said sharply, 'Yes, your wife and your daughter and your reputation. And what about me? I only lose you. That's nothing, I

152

suppose. Oh, I feel so shoddy. So bloody *cheap*. No one's ever made me feel cheap before. Well, that proves it, doesn't it? It's not what you do that counts, it's who knows about it. It's all idyllic till someone finds out. Then it's cheap. You keep telling yourself it's all beautiful and harmless but it isn't. It stinks.'

He grabbed her arm. 'Now stop it. Listen to me. First of all it isn't like that at all. Nothing's any different. We've been unlucky, that's all. But if you just think about it for a moment – that girl may say nothing. She may think it's too embarrassing to mention. Or she may think Prue gave keys to someone else – why not? But even if she does mention it – yes, all right, let's face it, suppose she does – she still doesn't know who we are. She can only describe us and Prue's never seen you. Why should she jump to the conclusion that the man was me? In fact what could be less likely?'

Sarah said morosely – but, he thought, with a faint note of hope – 'Then what *will* she think?'

He couldn't answer that. Instead he said, 'Come and have that drink.'

In the pub she downed two brandies rather fast and he watched the colour come back to her cheeks. He chain-smoked, but only sipped his drink, wanting to keep a clear head. They were silent at first, but the warmth of the room and the presence of other people was soothing, pushing back the nightmare quality which had pervaded the street. Presently she said, 'I'm sorry I got so worked up.'

'Darling.'

'I was scared.'

'I know. And I love you.' Somehow it was important at this point to say it. He knew it was valid, though he felt a twinge of disloyalty without knowing to whom.

She stared at him in amazement. 'You don't mean that, and you don't have to say it. I don't expect it. You know I don't.'

'I mean it. I love you and I want to protect you. I don't

153

want you to be worried and upset. That's why I was so happy when you laughed.'

She looked at him gravely. 'I don't think I understand you.'

'It doesn't matter. I just don't want you to have problems, that's all.'

She smiled. 'Well, I have. We have. We've just been caught in the act. Or had you forgotten?'

'All right. So let's sort it out. Even if the worst happens and that girl describes me to Prue, the description could fit almost anyone. Remember, Prue won't be thinking of me. She doesn't know I've got a key, for a start. How could it be me? Why should it be?'

Sarah drank some more brandy and gave a half-hearted smile. 'What then? Burglars?'

He laughed. 'Possibly.'

'Burglars making love?'

'Well ... sexy burglars then.'

She shook her head. 'It doesn't work. And how did they get in? Three floors up, no broken glass, no locks forced. No.'

'Previous tenants who kept their keys. Came back for a final fling.'

'Oh yes.'

'I'm sorry, I'm not doing very well, am I? I just want you to stop worrying about it. After all it's my problem, not yours.'

'That doesn't say much for togetherness, does it?'

'Darling, there are some things it's better not to share.'

'Perhaps. But there's so much of your life I don't share already.'

'That cuts both ways, you know.'

She ignored that, but it registered as the first vaguely possessive remark he had ever made. 'There's another point. If that girl tells Prue, she's bound to tell you. Even as a "guess what happened, isn't it extraordinary?" story. And then what will you say?'

He considered. 'I shall be amazed and horrified and advise her to change the locks.'

'And that's all?'

'What else can I say?'

'Are you sure you won't give yourself away?'

'Yes.' But he wasn't.

She shrugged. 'Well, I hope to God you're right.'

They tried to talk of other things after that, but it did not work. He could still feel the tension in her like an electric charge, even after four brandies. Finally she got up, rather unsteadily and said with a kind of nervous politeness, 'I should like to go home now.'

'All right, I'll take you.'

In the cab he put his arm round her and after a little momentary stiffness she leaned against him and rested her head on his shoulder. He kissed her hair. Once again he was amazed, after all that had happened, how strongly he wanted her. It made all that had gone before seem like mere flirtation. He said, 'Promise me you won't worry. Get a good night's sleep and don't worry about a thing.'

She said vaguely, 'All right.'

'There's a good girl.'

She was silent after that for a long time, so silent that he thought she was asleep. Many years ago Prue had fallen asleep in his arms many times and he had carried her to bed, being careful not to wake her. Now he wished he could do the same for Sarah.

As they neared the flat she suddenly stirred and said, 'I don't know what we expected; something like this was bound to happen. We were asking for trouble.'

He turned her face to him and kissed her, saying, 'Do you wish we'd never begun?' and saying it safely because he could feel from her response that she did not.

'No. I'll never wish that. But even when you say you love me, what does that mean? You love me and Prue and your wife' – he noticed she never used Cassie's name – 'and there just isn't room for us all.'

'But that *is* how people love.'

'I know.' She looked at him anxiously. He thought the anxiety was a new look he had put in her eyes and he was

155

not proud of himself. 'But I get so muddled. That's why I half don't want you to say it, even though it's beautiful. I'm not used to people saying they love me and it muddles me. It can mean so many different things and you remember them all and you don't know where you are.'

The taxi had stopped at her door. He asked it to wait and go on to Victoria. He kissed her forehead and held her face between his hands. 'Please don't be sad. I know how you feel but I'll make it up to you, I promise.'

She smiled, as though partnering him in some complicity. 'Yes. But don't you remember what you said before we started, before you believed I wanted to? You said we hadn't got a prayer. And we haven't. You were right.'

24

Cassie pulled the rug over her knees. The weather had changed and already there was an autumn chill in the air. August was nearly over. But he liked to drive with the window open, and to have the heater full on made him sleepy. The boys were at last asleep in the back seat, curled up together like puppies.

'I can't believe it,' Cassie said in a low voice. 'I was beginning to think I'd never get away. That nurse seems a bit of a dragon, don't you think?'

'Oh, I expect they're all like that.' He did not know what to say: you should have stayed, she's better off with professional care, it's about time you came back, by the way I'm in love?

'I suppose so.' She sighed. 'Well, we've had a lucky escape, haven't we?'

'How do you mean?' He heard himself being deliberately

obtuse again and pangs of guilt seized him, not so much for Sarah as for the last few months which seemed to have established a pattern of evasion whereas before there seemed – perhaps by contrast – to have been total *rapport* between them. He glanced at her smooth, blunt profile and thought how much he loved her. The steady warmth of that love, sustaining him as it had for so many years, and the painful thrill of being in love with Sarah, so tightly pressed between discomfort and joy, made him aware as never before of the difference between the two states. Some people made much of this distinction and others ignored it, and for years he had been publishing novels that dealt with the subject or at least touched on it, but all without any sense of relevance to his own life. This seemed to him to make nonsense of work, of professionalism, of involvement. Was nothing real until it actually happened to you?

'Well.' Cassie sighed; he had forgotten he had asked her a question. 'She's pulled through this time and we don't have Dad on our hands. That's a lot to be thankful for.'

'We'd have managed.' He spoke easily; it was simple to be magnanimous when the threat had passed.

'Would we? You weren't very keen when the boys mentioned it.'

'Oh, that. I was taken aback, that's all. I hadn't considered it.'

'Well, we'll have to consider it. Another little do like this and it could be the end. Funny how you always expect your parents to live for ever.'

'Don't think about it now,' he said soothingly. 'You've had a rough time. Just take it easy for a while.'

'It's been the longest month of my life.' She spoke resentfully and he was surprised: her behaviour in Devon had been so perfect that he had never doubted she was willing to be there. 'But you've been marvellous coming down every weekend.' She touched his arm. 'I really appreciated that.'

He felt undeserving and guilty. 'That was the least I could do. You had all the hard work; I just had to drive.'

'Yes, but it's a long way. You've been looking tired; it must have taken it out of you.'

Her compassion was more than he could bear; it made him long to confess and be abused as he deserved to be; or absolved. 'I'm all right,' he said tetchily.

Cassie lit cigarettes and passed one to him; she was trained by years of experience to do this and now could anticipate his needs almost perfectly so that he seldom had to ask. 'Well, at least the boys have had a good holiday. Almost too good. I think they were actually beginning to get sick of the beach but of course they wouldn't admit it. They look well, don't you think?'

'Marvellous.'

'We were lucky with the weather, of course. They're as brown as berries.'

The expression irritated him: it stuck out like a thorn and impaled his sensibilities. It was meaningless. He doubted he had even seen a brown berry. He grunted agreement.

'Suppose Prue is, too,' Cassie went on.

'What?'

'Brown. Rested. Sated with holiday. When's she due back?'

'I don't know. You saw the last postcard. Five words of conventional greeting.' He spoke offhandedly but felt a lurch of the heart at the realization of how little he had thought of her lately.

Cassie liked the offhand tone. She blessed Prue's absence, thinking, maybe he's getting over it, maybe he's accepted it at last. She trembled inside: it was as though she had not realized the extent of the danger until it was nearly past. She said, 'That only leaves us then.'

'What?'

'Who haven't had a holiday.' She waited, holding her breath. 'Peter, couldn't we? When the boys have gone, I mean. Just take off somewhere, just the two of us. The last two weeks in September, say. We could go to Scotland and take the car. We've never done that. Or Paris maybe. Or somewhere hot if you like.' She was a fiend for heat herself, and Prue had inherited this, but she knew he was not quite as keen and tempered her requests accordingly. 'It's a good time to go – not too late but the rush would be over. Couldn't we?'

He felt a great flood of affection for her, even while registering that he did not want to go anywhere. London already held too much attraction for him. But he thought how much he *liked* her, what a nice person she was, what a good woman. He approved of her; he found her thoroughly admirable. She spoke her mind without nagging, and stood up for her rights without making unreasonable demands. He pulled himself up with a shock, noticing that he was virtually giving her a reference. And he had no idea what kind of holiday Sarah would like. In fact he hardly knew anything about Sarah at all.

'All right, love,' he said, with a vague sense of making up for something, however inadequately, even something unknown. 'We'll go somewhere. You deserve a holiday.'

'And you,' she said. 'What about you?'

When they got home, tired as she was, she wanted to make love. He was flattered and rather pleased. She was as warm and responsive as ever and there seemed a sense of extra freedom and release that had been missing in Devon. The presence of the old people, the atmosphere of illness, had inhibited them both as much as Cassie's exhaustion. Even after all these years they could not relax in her parents' house with only thin walls to separate room from room. He wondered briefly if Gavin and Prue had felt the same in this house – and then lost himself in giving pleasure to Cassie. She was so easy to please: he knew her so well. Whereas Sarah – well, of course, Sarah was marvellous and exciting and new but – there was always a sense of trying to excel, of being on trial. He was sure it was of his own making, not hers. Something to do with the age gap perhaps, or even the fact that she worked for him, or some hidden element he had not divined. But it was there. However loving she might be, he felt they were involved in a battle for sexual supremacy. This made him want her again almost as soon as he had had her, long before he was physically capable of doing anything about it, because in some way he felt he had not had her, that she always eluded him. She could look at him with all the sincerity in the world but he did not know her.

Cassie said afterwards, long afterwards, when he was nearly asleep and thought she was too, 'God, it's good to be home.'

25

'Well, I've found you a genius at last.' Rupert flung the manuscript on his desk and raised an imaginary trumpet to his lips. He was clad in various shades of pink and mauve, which, Manson imagined, were intended to tone, and probably did, if you knew about such things; he could not tell. Then lowering his voice – or perhaps raising it, the effect was the same – to a piercing stage whisper, 'What's up with Miss Thing? She looks somewhat doleful, methinks.'

'How should I know?' Manson said, curtly. Since Cassie's return the atmosphere of uncertainty and sexual frustration in the office had been so tense as to be almost unbearable. There was nowhere they could be alone; she refused to consider hotels, and anyway after so much complaining to Cassie about endless eating out he had to rush home on the dot to home-cooked dinners. He saw young men waiting for Sarah as he went; he recognized them from the early days. She talked briefly and sadly about him wanting to end it, or being obliged to, it was all the same thing to her, and how she would make it easy for him. This drove him nearly mad. Sometimes he thought that was the effect she intended,

160

sometimes that she acted innocently. It hardly mattered, the effect was the same. 'Is it really good?' he said to Rupert, touching the tattered wodge of manuscript.

Rupert sat down, put his feet, very elegantly shod, on the desk and lit a cigar. 'It is. Perhaps genius was too strong a word, perhaps I was a fraction over-exuberant there, but he can *write*, thank God, and apart from that it's commercial. *Extremely* commercial. I can just *see* the movie. When I close my eyes I am dazzled by dollars. We must be *madly* careful with this contract.'

'Well, that's your department – with the usual cautions.' Pointless to interfere with Rupert if it could be avoided. Manson thought sadly, I know why I hired Rupert, because he is a wide boy, perhaps the original, the prototype, and I am as narrow as they come. 'What's it about?' he asked.

'Prison. Now don't groan: there aren't *that* many of them around and this one's red hot. Besides he can *write*; it isn't your usual sob story.'

Manson said affectionately, 'You're really impressed, aren't you?' Though Rupert never recommended anything insincerely, this degree of enthusiasm was rare.

Rupert smiled. 'That was the impression I intended to give. No, really Peter, this time I'm serious. And he's halfway into the next, which is really something.'

Manson flicked the pages, tea-stained and dog-eared. 'Okay, I'll read it. Been around a bit, though, hasn't it?'

Rupert rose, shedding ash on the carpet with splendid nonchalance. 'The world is full of fools, alas, and some of them come to rest in publishing. Just as well for us, of course, or else where should we be? Well, I'll leave you with it. Make a start now and I guarantee you'll miss your train.'

In the outer office Manson heard him saying to Sarah in the same light but resonant tones that he must have used on the stage, 'Cheer up, my chicken, it's not the end of the world, or is it? You tell me.' And Sarah's laugh, and the cool way she said, 'Well, rumour has it, it just might be, this time.' And Rupert's laugh as he banged the door. Rupert, he thought, made everything into theatre when he was around, but he alone had a script: the rest had to improvise as best they could. I have surrounded myself with charm, he thought; with easy fluent people like Rupert, and Cassie, Sarah and Prue. They warm me and enchant me, but I envy them too because I cannot be like them, because of the difference between us. No wonder I wanted to stay at Cambridge, what a lovely cocoon, what a chance in a million to hide from the world. And now I'm getting old, and bitter: it really won't do.

He opened the manuscript and knew at once that Rupert was right. Not that he had had any serious doubts; Rupert was always right. It was good. It was simple and stylish and real, with something about it to set it apart from the others. He read without noticing time; he was fully absorbed. When Sarah came in with his tea he looked up with a start. She said, 'Can I ask you a favour?'

'Yes, of course.' He wondered in which capacity, as lover or boss. Already, in the office, it was becoming confusing.

'Could I leave early tonight – about five?' She had great blue marks like bruises under her eyes as though she had not slept.

'Yes, I should think so.'

She hesitated. 'It's only shopping. I mean I could pretend it's the dentist or something but it *is* only shopping.'

'That's all right. Would you like to go now?' There was a curious pain arising from the conversation as if it was about something else.

She shook her head. 'No. Five will do. It's late-night closing.'

'All right.'

She turned away. He said, suddenly moved by an odd sort of desperation arising from nothing he could pinpoint, nothing more tangible than the general atmosphere, 'Look, I'm sorry this week's been so bloody but things will get better, I promise; I'll organize something.' He had no idea what but he had to say something, anything, to take that look of resigned disillusionment off her face. She looked like a

162

disappointed child. (No, we cannot go to the Zoo.—But you *promised*.) He had let her down.

She said coolly, 'It's all right. I quite understand,' hitting back with a touch of adult dignity.

'I can't help it,' he said, somewhat indignantly, defending himself.

'I said I understand.' She walked to the door.

'Sarah.'

She stopped, still with her back to him.

'Sarah, will you please turn round and look at me.'

She turned obediently like a puppet, blank-faced. He tried pleading with her.

'Darling, it's bound to be like this for a little while, till I get something sorted out.'

'Yes, of course.' She was unmoved.

'You're not making allowances,' he said, suddenly furious.

She looked at him with cold, stubborn patience. 'Yes, I am. What do you want me to do? Cry? Make a scene?'

'What's the *matter* with you?'

'Nothing. I knew it would be like this. I said so.'

It was impossible to get through to her. He lowered his head to the manuscript and heard the door close. But this time the writer, good as he was, could not hold him. He kept looking at his watch and reading the same paragraph again. He forgot about his tea and when he came to drink it, it was cold. At five precisely he found himself, much against his will, at the window, in time to see Sarah climb into a red Jaguar, which he had seen before, and be enthusiastically greeted by an elegant young man whom he also recognized.

26

Sarah had not meant to behave badly. In fact she was surprised and shocked to find herself doing so, but she seemed to have no control over her behaviour. It was so uncalculated and instinctive that she did not even know what it was meant to achieve. She was ridiculously glad to see Geoff; Simon had gone away for a month's hitch-hiking in Europe, and Geoff she now saw as her last link with the old way of life which had worked so well until Manson disrupted it. Though in fact she blamed herself entirely for this, since she had brought it about by breaking her own rule. If you did not care, no one could hurt you.

'You look tired, love. Been burning the midnight oil?'

She said no and then yes and he laughed and drew his own conclusions. He was taking her back to his flat for drinks and a snack before the theatre, and to make love, if they had time. After the theatre there would be more drinks and dinner, then back to his flat for the night. She liked the nights at Geoff's flat because it was beautiful and reminded her of how she wanted to live. But now she found herself wanting to ask his advice, to say, 'Geoff, what shall I do?' and tell him the whole story, such as it was. He had probably guessed there was someone new on the scene; that would not matter. But making an appeal to him would. It would be dangerous, breaking the rules. It was not what she was there for, to be pathetic or uncertain, in need of comfort and guidance. That was not why he kept her in his life. At least, so she assumed; she had never given him the chance to prove otherwise.

They had a good evening. Fortunately she was able to

switch off her office mood and sparkle for him. The play was amusing and they laughed a lot. Over dinner she drank more wine than usual and said, 'Don't we have a good arrangement? It's so uncomplicated. I do like it.' And looking down at her plate she reflected that her life was really just a series of meals and beds with different people.

He looked at her over his glass and said, 'Yes, I couldn't agree more. That's why I shall miss you.'

'Miss me?' She was suddenly cold, in the warm restaurant, full of food and wine; she shivered.

'Yes. Oh, only for a while. The old man is sending me to Frankfurt for six weeks. He seems to think I should get a look at how they run things at that end. Absorb a bit of German efficiency before he kicks the bucket and I take over.'

She said, 'Oh,' very small.

He was smiling at her. 'Will you miss me?'

She looked at him fondly, thinking how brash he was, how handsome and vulgar and arrogant, so uncomplicated, so fond of living. She thought he was the only person she knew who really enjoyed himself all the time, whose whole life was dedicated to the pursuit of enjoyment. She admired that. It was as if he was a particularly devout member of a minority religion. 'Yes, I shall miss you. Very much.'

He grinned at her. 'Good. But cheer up, sweetie, it's only six weeks.'

'When do you go?' With Simon away she would be entirely alone.

'In about ten days. We can still whoop it up for a bit. If your other commitments allow.' He smiled, and she thought, he likes me like this, I mustn't disappoint him.

She said, 'Oh, I expect I can fit you in.'

'Well, try to fit me in a bit better than lately 'cos my days are numbered, as it were. Who's the new man by the way?'

She was startled but in a sense relieved. She thought quickly. 'Oh, very middle-aged and square. An aberration really.'

'The father image.' He was laughing.

She said, 'Something like that.'

In bed that night, after they had made love and were having a final drink and he his post-coital cigarette, he said, 'Do you want to borrow the car?'

She was startled. 'What?'

'The car. While I'm away. It's a bit pointless garaging it and if I leave it at home I know what will happen. My dear brother will take it on a joy-ride and like as not smash it up. He's itching to get his hands on it.'

She was awed. She knew what the car meant to him and she loved the feud with his brother because it reminded her of hers with Barbara: it seemed to make a bond. 'God, Geoff, do you mean it?'

'Sure I mean it. You're the best woman driver I know.'

'Now don't spoil it.' She liked the way he teased her. As she recalled, this was not something Manson did.

'Well, I'd like you to have it. You would use it, wouldn't you?'

'Would I? !'

'Well, I don't want it standing around. Bad for its innards. And I'd like to think of you dashing around in it. You make a good pair.'

'Geoff, you are sweet.' She snuggled against him, feeling immensely comforted. It was such a little thing to do and yet it was enormous. She felt he had helped her as much as if she had told him her troubles – only without risk.

'Well, I like you, that's all.'

She was very moved. Suddenly this seemed more important than all the love and declarations of love in the world, that people should like one another and say so. 'I like you too.'

'Well, that's fine. So you'll have it; I'll give you the keys before I go. Only don't let *him* drive it, that's all. Okay?'

27

'Mummy, I'm back.'

'Darling! Where are you – at the airport? Shall I come and fetch you?'

'No, back in the flat. We just got in. How's Granny?'

'Oh, much much better, darling. I told you I'd let you know if there was any need for you to interrupt your holiday, and thank God there wasn't. She's got a nurse now: I came back about ten days ago.'

'You must have had an awful time.'

'Well, it was tiring. Anyway, all over now. What about your holiday? We enjoyed your postcards.'

'Oh, it was great. Fantastic. I'm practically black. If I could have the baby now, no one'd believe it was mine.'

'In other words it was hot.' Cassie smiled at the pleasure in Prue's voice.

'You could say that, yes. How was Devon? Did you manage to get out at all?'

'Not much really. But the boys enjoyed themselves. They were on the beach every day and the weather was quite good. Not up to the South of France though.'

'Can I talk to them?'

'They're not here, darling. They went off to Sweden yesterday – don't you remember? – to stay with that family. You know, the Swedish twins at school.'

'Oh yes. Aren't they lucky? That never happened to me when I was at school. So you're all alone again. Aren't you and Daddy going to get away at *all*? You really ought to, you know.'

'It's all right, darling, we *are* going. No need to sound so anxious.' Somehow Cassie sensed an implicit criticism of Manson in Prue's inquiry. 'Later this month. We're going to take the car on the train to Scotland and drive round looking at mountains and lochs.'

'Lovely.'

'Yes, it will be nice.' Cassie knew it sounded tame to Prue. 'Have you spoken to Daddy yet?'

'No, not yet.'

'Well, give him a ring, darling. I'm sure he'd like to know you're back.'

'I thought I might call in instead and give him a surprise.'

Prue walked up unannounced, telling the girl in reception that she wanted to surprise her father. She had dressed carefully for the occasion in a white linen maternity dress the length he approved of, and wore plenty of scent but very little make-up, letting the colour of her skin speak for itself, and her dark, sun-streaked hair hang loose. It was actually not quite sunny enough for this image and in the street she developed gooseflesh; she was glad to reach the warm office.

A girl with golden hair scraped back and an air of charm and efficiency which Prue instantly disliked opened the door to her and said, 'Can I help you?' For a split second Prue fancied there was something like recognition in her eyes, although they had never met, but it was so immediately damped down that she thought she must have imagined it.

'I'm looking for my father,' she said. So this was the new secretary. A far cry from Monica.

'I'm afraid Mr Manson is out of his office at the moment. Would you like to wait?'

'Yes, I would.' Prue walked past her and pushed open Manson's door. 'I'll wait in here.'

Sarah resumed typing. Prue sat on Manson's desk, swinging her legs, smoothing her dress over the baby bulge, poking about amongst her father's papers and watching Sarah out of the corner of her eye. Presently she said, 'Where is he, by the way?'

'Only in Mr Warner's office.'

168

Prue slid off the desk. 'Oh, I'll go up then.'

Sarah put on a secretarial face and said doubtfully, 'Well, they *are* in conference and I don't think they'll be long.'

Prue laughed. There was something about this girl that annoyed her intensely and she could not pinpoint it. 'Uncle Rupert and Dad in conference! They'll be gabbing away for hours if I don't interrupt them.'

Sarah picked up the phone. 'Then I'll tell them you're here.' Prue, transfixed by her coolness, simply stood and watched, heard her say, 'Mrs Sorenson is here, Mr Warner; could you tell Mr Manson? Thank you.' Then she turned to Prue. 'Can I get you some coffee, Mrs Sorenson?'

'No thanks,' said Prue, sulking, and aware she was sulking. 'It's too hot.'

'Lemon barley then,' said Sarah brightly.

'All right.'

Sarah brought the glass of lemon barley, very cold and clinking with ice.

'Thanks.' Prue knew she ought to enthuse – Sarah had made an effort – but she could not. She stood by the window and watched the traffic. The typing started again. Suddenly she could not bear it. She swung round and said, 'What's your name?'

'Sarah Francis,' said Sarah, still typing.

Prue digested this. The continuing noise infuriated her, making her feel deliberately excluded from the busy life of the office. Surely they were not all so occupied that they could not even spare five minutes to be polite. She said, raising her voice, 'Can't you stop typing a minute?'

Sarah stopped, smiled beautifully and said, 'Well, I do have rather a lot to get through.'

Prue thought of the job she had left and the infinite tedium of it. This one could not be much better. And here was this girl, hardly older than she was, pretending to be too busy to talk.

'I suppose you took over from Monica,' she said.

'That's right.' Sarah began licking stamps and sticking them on envelopes. Prue watched her.

169

'Good heavens,' she said, 'did they tell you you'd get the sack if you stop to breathe?'

Sarah smiled. 'It's not very arduous,' she said, 'and I like to be busy.'

The door opened and Manson came in. He was smiling a welcome but Prue thought he looked flushed and agitated. Surely stairs were not getting too much for him already?

They hugged and kissed. He stood back and admired her. 'Well,' he said, 'that's quite a colour.'

Prue slowly revolved in front of him. Sarah had started typing again. 'And it's all over,' she said. 'Even the bulge is brown. It was that sort of garden where you could do everything naked. I've never worn so few clothes on a holiday in my life before.'

'Good for you,' said Manson shortly. He went to his desk.

'Well, I suppose it was a sort of second honeymoon really.'

'Yes, I suppose it was. Look, Prue, it's lovely to see you, darling, but I do have a lot of work—'

'You, too. Your new secretary won't stop for a minute either. What's the matter with you all? Is it Back Britain week or are they running a competition for England's busiest publisher?' She laughed to take the sting out of the words.

'All right,' said Manson, lighting a cigarette. 'My time is yours. What can I do for you?'

Prue smiled. 'I was hoping to cadge some lunch. We only came back 'cos we'd run out of money and I'm really quite hungry.'

Manson hesitated; Prue thought he looked evasive. He called out, 'Sarah, aren't I busy for lunch today?'

There was a pause. Then: 'Nothing I can't get you out of.'

'Oh,' Manson said. 'Then I seem to be free.'

He said furiously, 'Now why did you do that?'

'What?'

'You *know* what. Cancel our lunch so I could eat with Prue.'

'I thought you ought to eat with Prue.'

'Since when do you judge what I ought to do? I can eat with Prue any day.'

'You can eat with me any day. But surely Prue takes priority.'

'Dammit, Sarah, *whoever* takes priority, it's for me to say. Not you.'

'Yes, you're right. I'm sorry. I interfered.'

'And it isn't good for Prue to get her own way all the time.'

'No.'

'Walking in here and upsetting all my arrangements . . .'

'Yes.'

'Are you laughing at me?'

'No.'

'Then come here.' He held out his arms.

'No, I can't. Anyone might walk in.'

'You're right. Christ, why are you always right?'

'It's something they taught me at commercial school.'

He laughed. 'At least you still make me laugh. That's about all you get a chance to do, these days. God, I want you so much – if this goes on much longer I'll be walking around the office with a permanent erection and that won't be good for my image – or will it?'

She said, 'Oh, darling,' and then, 'this thing seems to get madder and madder; I don't know where I am. I don't think Prue liked me; there was a terrible atmosphere between us.'

He said, to his own amazement, 'Damn Prue.'

'You don't mean that.'

'Yes, I do. Don't tell me what I mean.'

She said lovingly, 'Darling, you're awfully stroppy these days.'

'I know.'

'I love you for it though.'

'Do you? I thought you'd gone off me.'

'Did you? I wish I had.'

'Do you really? Don't say that.'

'Well, you make me unhappy, that's all. And nobody's ever done that before. I'm not used to it.'

'Aren't you really? What a happy, lucky life you must have led.'

'Yes, I have. That's me, to a T.'

She sounded so bitter that he said, suddenly concerned, 'Sarah, what's the matter?'

'Nothing. You just don't know anything about me, that's all.'

'I'm sorry. I'd like to.'

'Yes, I know. But you don't get the chance, do you? It's all wives and daughters and work and trains. Oh, nothing to complain about and I'm not complaining.'

'Aren't you?' he said.

'Well.' She considered. 'Okay, so it's great in bed and we make jokes and you take me out to dinner. But so what? That doesn't tell you what makes me cry in the night.'

'I'm sorry,' he said. 'Do you cry in the night?'

She smiled. 'You wouldn't know, would you?' She thought of Geoff, and the car, and his arm round her as she fell asleep.

'I'm sorry,' he said, 'it's not my fault.'

'No,' she said, 'of course not.'

'Look, I will do something about this. I promise. Just give me time.'

28

Gavin was actually laughing as he came through the door. 'Boy, do I have something to tell you. I had lunch with Sue and Victor – you should have come – it was great.'

Prue was curled up in a chair. She said moodily, 'I had lunch with Dad.'

'So why aren't you radiant? Didn't you get the full Mira-belle bit?'

'Oh yes.'

'So?'

'I don't know. He was in a funny mood. Not himself somehow. I don't know what it was. As if – he didn't want to be with me.' She felt her eyes pricking again as they had done all afternoon, and blinked rapidly.

Gavin laughed again. 'Well, maybe he didn't at that.'

She stared at him. 'What d'you mean?'

'Honey, you're not listening. I said I had something to tell you.'

'What?' She spoke sulkily.

'Okay, be like that. I guarantee this will make you sit up. Sue wasn't the only person with a key to this flat in our absence.'

'What d'you mean?'

'Ah, I knew that'd get you.'

'Gavin, what do you mean?'

Gavin flopped into a chair opposite her and laughed at her consternation. 'I said you'd sit up, didn't I?'

'Oh, for Christ's sake. *What d'you mean?* Someone else was here? Who? Was anything taken? Who *could* have a key?'

'Relax, honey, it wasn't burglars. Just a couple of people using the bed. Sue walked right in on them when she came to water the plants. Gave her quite a shock but gave them a bigger one. Scrambling into their clothes, she said, guilty as hell. Middle-aged man and a young girl.'

Prue said slowly, 'I don't understand. How could anyone but us have a key?'

'Put it another way. Who but us is likely to have a key?'

Prue frowned. 'The porter? The previous tenants? The cops?'

'You're not concentrating, hon. Let me spell it out for you. Who is the person most likely to have a key to our flat? Who would want to feel free to walk in at any time? Who would want to feel it doesn't really belong to us – and Christ knows it doesn't, we never paid for the lease – that's right, now you've got it.'

'Gavin, *no.*'

'Gavin, yes. I think. Sorry about that, baby. But don't look so shocked. The poor old guy's only human after all. What's so terrible about that? Did you think he wasn't?'

Prue uncoiled her legs from the chair very slowly and placed them on the ground so that she was sitting stiff and square, facing Gavin, her hands around the bulge as if to protect it. She said, 'Look, have I got this straight? You're saying . . . my father was here with a girl. You're saying he's had a key to this flat all along and when we went away he brought a girl here and—'

'Screwed her on our bed, yes, that's what I'm saying. And Sue caught them at it – or damn nearly.'

Prue said, 'No.'

'What d'you mean no?'

'It could have been anyone.'

'Oh yes. Like the porter – have you taken a look at him lately? Like the cops – very likely – bet it happens all the time. Like the previous tenants – well, we met them didn't we? Sure, it could have been anyone.'

'You *want* to believe it was him, don't you?'

'Well, it's a great new angle on a dreary subject.'

'You hate him.'

'I don't hate him, honey, he just bores the ass off me, that's all. I'm full up to here with his sanctimonious shit about your spotless purity and my filthy lust, when you were the randiest thing this side of L.A. and practically tore my pants off. Not that I objected, that I grant you. But he sure got a screwed-up version of our courtship, as it were, that's for sure. I don't hate him. In fact this makes me like him better. Shows the old guy's got some life left in him after all; I thought maybe he was jealous 'cos his balls had dropped off. Only thing I wish is he wasn't such a bloody hypocrite. He bawls me out all over the place and then he comes screwing in my bed.' He began to laugh again. 'Say I bet that gave him quite a kick. I bet he thought about me screwing you the whole time. Or pretended that girl was you. Yeah.'

Prue put her hands over her ears. 'I don't want to hear

174

any more.' Tears were burning her eyes and yet at the same time she felt so unbearably stimulated that she could hardly keep still.

'Baby, have I upset you?' Gavin came across and put his hand on her knee. She trembled violently. 'Oh, like that, is it? Too much talk. Too many dirty words. Well, now, what shall we do about that?'

He undressed her slowly while she moaned softly but did not help him. 'Well, you *are* randy, aren't you? Bet your dad'd like to see you now.' He stroked her. 'Oh yes. He'd love that.'

She went berserk, clutching and clawing at him, and both to control and heighten her pleasure he gave her as much pain as she wanted, being careful to remember the baby and not to hurt her there. The floor became a battle ground. When they had finished they were both soaked in sweat. They had left the electric fire full on.

'Wow,' said Gavin presently, rolling over and switching it off, 'let's keep it a secret or they'll all want some. Cigarette, hon?'

'No.'

He lit one for himself.

Prue waited till the baby, disturbed by all the activity, had stopped moving. She was still not used to the sensation and found it hard to speak while concentrating on it. 'Gavin, you weren't kidding, were you, just now? About somebody being here.'

'No. Sue really did see them.'

'What did they look like?'

'Well, she said the guy was tall, middle-aged, grey hair. Quite good-looking she said. Left his jacket in here with an Eliot and Manson catalogue sticking out of the pocket. No, really. Corny but true.'

Prue said slowly, 'What was the girl like?'

'Why? Don't tell me you know her? Or are you just curious about your rival?' He tapped ash in the grate.

'Did Sue describe her?'

'Yeah, well, she said she was small and pretty with blonde

175

hair, that's all. And a startled expression, but I guess that's not permanent. Not much to go on.'

'It's enough.'

'You *do* know her.'

'I met her this morning.'

'*What?*'

Prue eased herself into a sitting position and leaned against the chair; she began putting on her clothes again. 'She's his secretary.'

For about ten seconds Gavin's face was a superb study of amazement and shock. Even his mouth formed a perfect round which Prue viewed with the same detached pleasure as a successful smoke ring. Then he burst out laughing. 'Oh *no*. But I thought his secretary was a dog.'

'That was Monica. She left. This is the new one. Sarah Francis. We disliked each other on sight; now I know why.'

Gavin ground out his unfinished cigarette. 'Boy, oh boy, what a gas. What a pity we can't share the joke. Isn't that always the way – the best stories are always the ones you can't spread around.'

Prue got up carefully and finished dressing. She opened her bag and started to comb her hair. 'Why not?'

He stared at her. 'Why not? Do you want a story like that all over school – well, do you? I swore Sue and Victor to secrecy and they haven't told anyone. It's got to stop there.'

Prue said coolly, 'I didn't mean college. Of course not; I quite agree. There's only one person who ought to be told.'

'Oh, now honey . . .'

'I mean it.'

'You mean – your *mother?*'

'Yes. That's who I mean.'

'You *are* joking, aren't you?'

'No.'

They faced each other, very cold and still.

'You want to tell your mother. Have I got that right?'

'Yes.'

Silence. 'Do you have a reason? Or are you just plain out of your mind?'

Prue shook her head. 'I think she ought to know.'

'Why?' She didn't answer. 'Why? Go on, tell me. Just to be bloody-minded, that's all, isn't it? Hell, what's the matter with you? You've caught your old man with his pants down – okay – isn't that enough for you? So what did your mother ever do to you that you have to rub her nose in it too? Huh? Tell me that. You'd actually do a thing like that to get back at your dad because he objected to me knocking you up. Christ, honey, you must be sick.'

'It's not that at all.' Prue's mouth made a thin little line.

'Then what is it? Go on, tell me; I'm interested. This more than makes up for that psych course I missed. So it's not revenge – then what is it?'

Prue said tightly, 'Justice.'

He laughed. 'Oh yeah? And just who are you to start dispensing that doubtful commodity? And how does it differ from revenge, tell me that? And even if it's justice for your dad, which I question, how come it's justice for your mother too? You can't have it both ways, that's for sure.'

'He should have thought of that before.'

'*He* should! Oh, that's great. Who are you to sling mud at your dad?'

'He slung mud at me fast enough.'

'Sure. He's your father. That's kind of a right parents have. Like we'll sling mud at Junior if he steps out of line. It's kind of to compensate for buying the food and paying the rent. It's like the balance of nature. And it just doesn't work both ways.'

Prue stared at him, narrowing her eyes. 'You're on his side. Just because he's a man you stick up for him.'

Gavin slammed his hand on the table, making it shake. 'Christ Almighty! I'm sticking up for your mother as well. More, if anything, because she's the one you'd be hurting most. Look, have you thought about this at all? Either she doesn't know and you'll be telling her and *hurting* her, *badly*, (are you listening?) or she does know and she's trying to ignore it and you'll be humiliating her by saying you know as well. Now, do you *want* to do either of those things? Do you really think that's justice? If you're out to punish your dad tell him, not your mother. That's quite sick enough. You don't need to punish her too.'

'I'm not trying to punish anyone.'

'Not much you aren't. Christ, I don't get it. What's so terrible if your dad has a girlfriend? It happens all the time. And it's just not your business.'

Suddenly Prue started to cry. 'He's supposed to be faithful.'

'Who to – you or your mother? Look, you can't have it both ways. You nearly throw up when I say he'd like to screw you, but the moment he screws someone else, wham, you're after his blood.'

Prue was sobbing freely. 'He's got Mummy. She's lovely. He doesn't need . . . he doesn't have to . . .'

Gavin lit a cigarette and tossed the match on the floor. 'Balls. Don't give me that eyewash. He's done it before and he'll do it again. Every man does. Plenty of women too. Maybe your mother even. Why should she be a saint? And we'll do it, too. Oh, not now, not yet, maybe not for years. But we will. You can't seriously think we're going to be faithful to each other till the day we die.'

She said in a small voice, choking through sobs, 'We promised we would.'

'Oh, Prue. Promises are for kids.'

'No.'

'Yes, they are. Promises like that anyway. Like swearing blood brothers with the kid next door. No adult can look at another adult and guarantee to feel the same for ever and ever. It's just not possible. And no adult would ever expect it, either.'

'But we did. We said it. When we got married—'

'Yeah, I know. But that was kind of emotional. Like it's something you feel at the time, not something you *know* as a fact. Like I might say you're the most beautiful girl in the world—'

'But you never have.'

'Well, like I might say Beethoven was my favourite com-

178

poser. Sure I'd mean it. Only next week it could be Mozart. What do I know? You say it and you mean it, sure, at the time, but people change. Come on, Prue. You know they do. What about those guys you had before me?'

'I wasn't in love with them. And stop trying to change the subject.'

'What subject? That's all settled. You're not going to tell your mother, that's all. What you say to your father is up to you but you're not going to tell your mother because if you do I'll knock your head off, that's all.' He smiled very amiably. 'So you see? The subject is closed.'

29

Manson said, 'Well, this is it. What d'you think? Go on, have a look round.' He lit a cigarette; he was surprised to find himself actually nervous. If she did not like the flat ... if she should resent his acting without consulting her ...

Sarah walked from room to room. It did not take long: the flat was tiny. Two inter-communicating rooms, kitchen and bath. But it was very white and well furnished, and high up, in a quiet street with a view of trees and roof-tops. She liked it at once but she was too surprised – and somehow also alarmed – to speak. So she just went on walking round the rooms, saying nothing and looking at things. Lots of things were so nice she might have chosen them herself. But she had not.

'It's five minutes from the office,' he said. 'I timed it. So you'll save on fares.'

'Enough to pay the increase in rent?' she asked lightly, finding her voice.

He felt himself flushing. What was the matter with her?

Wasn't this what she had been angling for? 'Of course not. That's all taken care of.'

She turned her back on him to look out of the window. She said, 'You're setting me up.'

There was unmistakable hostility, even suspicion, in the words which he forced himself to ignore, saying, 'That's one way of putting it. I thought I was just making it easier for us to meet.'

Silence. She gazed out of the window with absorbed attention.

'Look, you don't even have to live in it,' he went on. 'We can just . . . come here. But I thought a single room would be sordid, that's all.'

She said, 'But you can't pay all this rent if I don't live here.'

'That's not the point. Would you *like* to live here?'

She turned round, frowning. 'You mean money's no object all of a sudden? Business is booming, I'm getting a raise?'

He stubbed out his cigarette in a clean ashtray and sat down. He felt tired. The whole thing was misfiring badly. He said, 'I thought you'd be pleased. I'm sorry. I made a mistake.'

All at once she rushed over to him and hugged him, hard. It was actually quite painful, his ear pressed against the buckle of her dress. 'No, you didn't, it's lovely. I love it.' She kissed the top of his head. Familiar gesture, Prue or his mother, maybe both; not Cassie though.

'Are you sure?' he said, disentangling himself.

'Yes. It just gave me a shock. It seemed so Victorian, somehow – or professional – being set up in a flat. No one's ever done that for me before.'

'I should hope not indeed,' he said with mock severity. But he thought at the same time how true it was that he knew very little about her, and he was chilled by the thought. 'It's vacant – you can move in any time you like,' he added quickly to stop her picking up wavelengths. 'I've only got to sign the lease.'

'*You* have?'

'Well ...' He hesitated, not knowing how to put it.

'Oh yes, of course. Because you'll be paying the rent.'

'I'm sorry,' he said. 'It's just how these things are done. Don't let it bother you.'

She smiled an odd little smile. 'How long is the lease?'

He wished he did not have to answer that. 'Six months.'

'Oh.'

'Well, initially six months that is, then automatically renewable if you don't set the place on fire.'

'I see.'

He said, 'It doesn't mean anything. It's just a formality.'

'Yes.' But she could not help thinking that it meant a limit to their relationship, that he had had to think in terms of time. To cover the unworthiness of this thought she said, 'It's funny, d'you know, I'd actually started looking at bedsitters. Only you don't get much for four pounds which is all I pay for my share of the flat. I wasn't joking. It'd be cheaper to give me a rise. Anyway, here's what I'd like to do. If I move in here I'll pay you four pounds a week towards the rent.'

He wanted to say, 'Oh, don't be ridiculous,' but she wasn't, she had sudden dignity and he was embarrassed to argue with her. He said, 'Is that what you really want to do?'

'Yes.' She turned away, fiddling with a lampshade. 'That's the only way I can do it. It wouldn't work for me otherwise. Every Friday I shall pretend you're my landlord, okay?'

'You really are extraordinarily independent, aren't you?'

'Yes, I shall never get on in the world, my mother's often told me.'

'What?'

'Nothing.'

When she got back to the office she cried in the lavatory. Part of her was elated, excited, yet she felt the need to cry. She felt the first stage was over; they had either to part or to embark on the second stage, and this they had done. But it had a finality about it. It would lead nowhere. And she was angry that her first home alone would not be all hers,

181

completely paid for and answerable to no one. She resented his kindness and yet the thrill that she got from thinking of the visits, the phone calls, the sense of possession, ran right from her neck to the soles of her feet, making her shiver with delight.

She cried more at home in the bathroom getting ready to go out, and in the car Geoff noticed her red eyes at once and said they matched the paint. He was excessively jovial with nerves at his imminent departure: once, rather drunk, he had told her he hated, was terrified of, flying. She wanted to say she would pray for him and although she was not even sure about God she said it anyway and felt better for it. He squeezed her hand.

'Crazy, isn't it?'

'Not a bit. I'm frightened of moths, that's far crazier.'

They had nothing to say. They sat in the lounge and drank drinks they did not want and looked at each other. They had met every week for six months and never been separated. Suddenly she became aware that she was thinking of him as her brother, like Simon. Their images, once so distinct, had merged.

When his flight was called she went with him to the barrier and the tears started again. He looked at her in amazement, touched, and said, 'Are all those for me?'

She said yes. In a way it was true. They kissed and hugged, very hard, and she noticed he was white with fear. She felt a sharp pain that she could not protect him from the flight and wondered if that was some deep-buried maternal instinct. He left without looking back and she said out loud to herself, 'Everyone goes out of my life.' A man passing by said 'Pardon?' She shook her head and walked quickly away to where the car was parked, hers for six weeks; she could not bear to watch the aircraft take off. Driving home she was still crying and switched on the wireless to cheer herself up. She had the feeling that she had lost a friend, and no one could afford to do that.

30

She moved in haste that weekend, with her things in a hired mini-van. She was sure she detected relief in Annabel and some regret in the others; but she had never really fitted. All the same, she felt oddly desolate leaving the flat and the rows of big white South Kensington houses with their steps and pillars and balconies. She had always lived in South Ken, ever since she left home. South Ken *was* home.

The new flat was so absurdly central that she felt the mini-van driver must think her a call-girl, at least, and newly promoted. She would not have found the description too incongruous either. The proximity of the flat to the office no doubt meant lunchtime sessions to make up for the even-ings – most evenings – when he could not stay late. She thought it was very like the Hollywood drama she had always imagined and avoided : the stolen hours, the secrecy, the isolation. Not like her life at all. Despite deceiving people when necessary, she had always thought of her life as very open. She had not had to be furtive, merely evasive. It had been she who kept moving, set the pace. Now she felt that she was being put in storage, for use as and when required. She would be in a safe place, where no harm could come to her, but where she would be immediately accessible to him, as she had not been while sharing a flat. And he would be paying part of the rent. The greater part, she felt sure. Would that entitle him to walk in at any moment, unan-nounced? Would he expect to have a key? Or would he telephone first? Would she be free to invite her friends here in his absence? In fact, would it really be her home?

All these qualms chilled her profoundly. She could not

understand herself. Nothing would have persuaded her to turn down the flat: it solved everything. And yet she could not rejoice in it wholeheartedly. There were the prickings of excitement, but distantly, in secret, as if under her skin or in her veins. On the surface she was very much disturbed. After the driver had moved her stuff in and left, having made a few admiring and faintly suggestive remarks, she was actually shivering and had to switch on all the fires. She unpacked as quickly as possible, to have her own things around her; nothing already in the flat felt as if it belonged to her. She found when she unpacked that she handled quite unimportant objects, like a rather ugly vase Barbara had once given her, with a new tenderness. They seemed more valuable. They made up the fabric of her life, her past. She placed them carefully, in prominent positions, to establish her identity.

She shopped, for weekend things, and put them away in the strange new kitchen. It was *well planned*, and disconcerted her. She felt she was standing in a shop, in a showroom, and half expected to see people looking in the window, regarding her. She went in the bedroom and made up the bed and thought about him, but with affection, without desire. She felt in a dream, that she was going through the motions in some preordained role.

In the afternoon flowers arrived, roses, with his name on the card. She was thrilled as she unwrapped them, she felt special, but at the same time there was a shaft of panic, a sense of ownership. She had been labelled. His secretary, his mistress, in his flat, receiving his flowers. She felt he had invaded her. Suddenly frantic, she rushed to the window to see the car far below where she had parked it in the tree-lined street. There seemed no problem attached to it. A simple loan, an act of friendship, fun. Geoff had not put his brand on her; he never would. Nor Simon, drifting easily round Europe, raising his thumb at passing cars. They were her brothers, providing sex and jokes, comfort and freedom.

She cried a little. And told herself it was only the anticlimax, the aftermath of moving. Someone should have been

184

coming for a drink, to admire the flat (if it had been really hers), to take her out. But there was no one to come. Even a girlfriend, to watch television, which he had thoughtfully installed. She switched it on and stood looking at it, thinking, my God, this is Saturday night. What a popular girl I must be. She could not remember when last she had spent such a fruitless evening. But she could not even summon up the energy to go out to a film. She ate some cheese and watched television and thought vaguely about washing her hair.

About nine he phoned from a call-box. She shook at the sound of his voice, which seemed an incongruous reaction in view of her earlier chilly resentment. He asked if she had got his flowers and she enthused, but guiltily, wishing she had mentioned them first. His voice and her shaking had distracted her. She wanted to say that, in case he was disappointed, but did not think it would sound convincing. Although it was true there seemed to be an artificiality about it. She asked instead how he had managed to get out to phone her, which she at once thought was quite the wrong thing to ask, and he said he had gone out for cigarettes. He sounded reluctant to give her the information. She thought desperately that the flat had made them both self-conscious, aware of the need for gestures, like flowers and phone calls, and she wanted him to be with her so she could reassure him that these things were not necessary. She said she wished he was there and he took this to mean desire and his voice became more cheerful and he said so did he, but perhaps they could lunch at the flat on Monday. She liked the use of the word lunch. But the image of him leaving the call-box and going home for the rest of the weekend disturbed her, not so much because it was apart from her as because it seemed unglamorous. Just like her image of herself shut in her new flat all weekend, admiring the roses and waiting for her lover to phone. Both seemed such old-fashioned things for them to be doing. She became frightened. Was it all slipping through their fingers, and at what a moment, when he had just signed a lease? What could they do to preserve it? But they should not *have* to do anything. She felt that they had

made some fatal error somewhere, for which they were now
paying, but which they were not allowed to correct. She said
a lot of nice things to him, quickly, to counteract this impression, and when she was sure that he sounded happier she
asked what he was doing on Sunday, tomorrow, so she could
think of him doing it. He said Prue and Gavin were coming
to lunch to show off their suntan. It was also Prue's birthday
and he had bought the gold bracelet they had once discussed,
did she remember? Meanwhile, he missed her, and wished he
had bought the gold bracelet for her instead, because there
was no fun in it as it was, he did not know why.

3 1

Cassie was happy. Not content, not run-of-the-mill happy,
but mindlessly euphoric. It was years since the prospect of a
holiday had affected her so, and she wondered why. She was
tired from Devon, from anxiety and nursing, yes; it was also
the year in which concern over Prue had taken priority over
all else. But it was still more than all that. She felt that they
had passed some dangerous corner, narrowly averted catastrophe, faced some unnamed peril, and now it was over. She
deserved a holiday. *They* deserved a holiday. Over the last
few weeks she had sensed Manson coming gradually to terms
with Prue and the situation : he was closer now, she thought,
than he had ever been to acceptance. Their family life was
nearly restored to normal, and this mattered more to her than
anything, since there was nothing else to matter. And now
she wanted to be creative about it; she was tired of being
helpless. She wanted to put the final gloss on it, as if icing a
cake, to restore it to all its former splendour, and she did not
know how to do it other than by creating a loving atmos-

phere, making the house warm, cooking delicious food, and filling the rooms with flowers.

She admired Prue's present and wrapped it carefully, asking him to write the card, but he said, 'No, you do it,' in a casual tone that gladdened her heart and also made her feel guilty. (Was it possible she had actually been resentful – jealous – of her own daughter?) So she wrote 'Happy Birthday, darling, with all our love, Daddy and Mummy,' and smiled at Manson, feeling secure and loved. 'It's beautiful,' she said, with an overspill of generosity. 'She'll adore it.' He smiled absently. 'It's pretty,' he said. 'And it certainly cost enough.'

'Cynic.' She tied red ribbon round the box, as much to amuse herself as to do the thing properly. She felt festive. (Why not holiday decorations, as well as Christmas? She could have festooned the house with garlands and tinsel and brightly coloured paper, and instead of Happy Christmas a message announcing 'We are going away'. The holiday – this holiday – seemed to belong to her, just as Prue's baby belonged to Prue, and she hugged it to herself in the same way. She could not even speak about it much. Once he agreed to go, once he actually said, 'All right, we'll go to Scotland at the end of the month,' she became almost totally silent on the subject. It was too exciting. She would be childish if she spoke about it. Or it would go wrong. As a child she had never spoken about things that mattered to her. It was too dangerous: if you put your feelings into words people could injure them. The things she loved had been physically hidden, too, in drawers, cupboards, envelopes, to spare them damage from parents, brothers, dailies, dogs, even from the air itself, from contact with something as insubstantial as reality. She did not know what she meant by that, but she knew it was dangerous. The times she felt closest to Prue were when she detected the same emotional reticence, the same instinct for privacy and secrecy, in her.

They were coming for lunch and staying to dinner, an entire day of birthday celebrations. She said, 'Will you meet them or shall I? Only I do have a lot to do in the kitchen.'

She was doing complicated things with fish for lunch, and roasting a duck for dinner, because Prue loved duck, reversing the traditional Sunday order. She had made Quiche Lorraine and lemon meringue pie and a huge birthday cake, and was experiencing a warm, all-pervasive glow only slightly inferior to the aftermath of orgasm.

'Yes, I'll fetch them. Do you know which train they're getting?'

'No. They said they'd phone from the station.'

'Here or there?'

'Here. Victoria's impossible; all the boxes are either full or broken.'

He considered this. 'Well, it's twelve already,' he said, and poured them both a glass of sherry. Cassie looked out on the lawn. It was a bright, crisp day, curling at the edges, turning into autumn before her eyes. She said lightly, 'What a pity we can't have fireworks.'

He looked amazed, then smiled at her indulgently. She thought he was being very gentle and tolerant these days. 'For Prue's birthday,' she explained. 'It would be fun. Like a kind of royal salute. We should have thought of it before.'

'Never mind,' he said. 'It's too late now.'

Prue sat in the train and put her feet up on the opposite seat. She felt that this must surely be against some dim regulation and so it gave her pleasure, and she gazed defiantly at passing porters, daring them to challenge her, protected as she was by pregnancy.

She felt huge, and *suddenly* huge, at that. As if someone had secretly doubled her load in the night and left her to get on with it. She remembered similar days before, when you became abruptly aware of your size and weight, as if you had not noticed it before, but this was the worst.

'Only two months to go,' she announced to Gavin, who grunted but did not reply. He had brought the Sunday paper with him and was reading it.

'I feel enormous,' she said more loudly. A man across the carriage sank deeper beneath his hat; a pink-faced woman

188

quivered. Gavin momentarily raised his eyes and gave her a fractional glance.

'Yeah,' he said briefly. 'You look it.'

'Gee, thanks.'

'Uh-huh.'

She stared at him coldly. He had not made love to her last night when she wanted him to, and that was rare. Nor this morning. Was she getting at last too fat, too unattractive?

'You might at least give me the colour supplement,' she said.

He did not look up. 'I'm reading it.'

'No, you're not. That's the review.'

Silently and, she thought, a trifle sullenly, he pulled out the magazine and tossed it onto the seat beside her. Just throwing it at me, she thought. As if I didn't count at all. What's the matter with him?

'Thank you,' she said pointedly, exaggeratedly polite.

'You're welcome.'

There was a feature on babies. Blue-veined embryos and shiny, blood-stained new-born. She felt sick and shut the magazine in a rush. It was too much. Didn't she have enough to contend with, being so ugly and bloated, without looking at pictures like that? She did not want to think of her baby looking so messy, so subhuman, being dragged out of her. She knew enough facts of birth without having to study technicolor pictures. It was obscene. They were going to hurt her, and all to produce an object like that. It was unfair. It was out of all proportion.

She had never felt frightened before.

'I feel sick.'

'Uh-huh.'

She repeated more loudly, 'I feel sick.'

'No, you don't, honey.' Keeping his eyes on the paper. 'You're probably hungry.'

'I tell you I feel sick.' She raised her voice, noticing the other passengers quivering with attention and gazing, steadfast and unconvincing, out of the windows. 'Christ, I should know how I feel. What do *you* know about it? *I feel sick.*

You don't know what it's like carrying this great lump around.'

'Well,' he said, 'you should have been more careful.' The ears of the woman across the aisle turned slowly pink.

'Should I?' Prue said, with all the venom she could muster. 'Should I indeed? Well, I didn't do it all by myself, now did I?'

'No,' he said equably, 'but you were in charge, remember? And there's no point feeling sick. This is a non-corridor train.'

She felt fury rising like bile in her throat. Perhaps she was going to be sick with sheer temper. 'You think I feel sick for *fun*? You think I *want* to feel sick?'

'You want attention,' he said. 'That's all you ever want. And mostly you get it. But right now I'm reading the paper.'

Her stockinged feet were very close to him on the opposite seat: the temptation was too great. She kicked, catching him unawares, flipping the paper up towards his face with her toe. It was most effective. He looked surprised, annoyed, and ... silly. Yes, she had actually made him look silly. She laughed. Gavin showed no emotion. He folded the paper into four and calmly hit her across the face with it. Prue let out a small, startled cry and the man across the aisle half rose from his seat, murmuring, 'I say—' while the woman quickly pretended to be asleep. Gavin snapped, 'Keep out,' and the man sank back at once as though attached to the seat by elastic that would only allow him to stretch so far. Film dialogue flashed through Prue's mind ('Keep out of this, stranger, if you know what's good for you. This is between me and her'). Her heart was beating very fast and she felt slightly hysterical. She put her hands over her face and started to cry. Gavin unfolded the paper as if nothing had happened and went on reading. The train pulled into a station and both their fellow passengers got out, the woman staring straight ahead, the man with a backward glance of concern and distaste. No one else got in. Prue went on sobbing. Doors slammed and the train moved on.

'Cut it out,' said Gavin evenly, still reading. 'You got what you wanted.'

Barbara inspected everything with an appraising eye, like a dealer. Sarah felt that she could price everything, both new and second-hand, to within a pound of its market value. 'Not bad,' she kept saying, 'not bad. So you're a kept woman at last. Good for you. That's what I should have been before I got too run down. Who'd want me now?'

Sarah studied her sister. Peroxided hair, dark-rooted and without lustre. Bitten fingernails, nicotine-stained. An old skirt and sweater, the wool tight-shrunken over her body, which now curved rather too much since the last child. Laddered tights, scuffed shoes, smeared lipstick and sooty eye make-up. Yet she remembered, and so could still see underneath, the trim, slick, smartly obvious go-getter of seven years ago. My sister. My favourite sparring-partner. My devoted, unconcerned, loving, hostile, down-at-heel, reliable, untrustworthy sister. And she pondered the peculiar quality of the love between them, for she could find no other name for it.

'Presumably John still wants you,' she said lightly.

Barbara lit a fresh cigarette from the one that was dying. 'Oh yes,' she agreed, 'but who wants him? He's not much of a catch, now is he?'

'You thought so once.' She did not mean to sound reproving, merely could not bear to believe that Barbara felt as sour as she sounded.

'Yes, like I thought babies were fun and money was elastic.' She sighed. 'Oh well. It's up to you to retrieve the family fortunes. What's he like?'

Sarah hesitated. 'Nice.'

Barbara snorted. 'Well, I gathered that. Married, of course.'

'Yes.'

'Kids?'

'Yes.'

'They're all alike.'

'Are you disapproving?'

191

'Not of you, him. And envious. They get everything their own way. God, if I'd been born a man ...'

And if you had, Sarah thought, what would you have done? Got yourself some crummy job, because you couldn't be bothered to train for anything worthwhile. Got married young, just as you did, and for just the same reason, in reverse. It would all have been exactly the same, because you never meant to try, you never believed it could be different, you had no faith in yourself. She squeezed her own arms, tight, as if to make sure that she was still there, Sarah, her own person.

'Well, anyway,' Barbara resumed, 'he'll feel good and guilty about it, you ought to get some decent presents out of him, to say nothing of living rent free. You should come out of it quite well if you're clever.'

Unreasoning resentment swept over Sarah. It was one thing for her to look ahead to the inevitable conclusion, quite another for Barbara to take it for granted and talk about it. 'I've only just got into it,' she said sharply, 'and I don't want to be clever, and anyway I'm paying part of the rent myself.'

Barbara stared at her. 'You're having me on.' Pause. 'No, you're not, are you? God, you must be mad. You get an offer like that on a plate and you turn it down. What's the matter with you?'

Sarah got up and began to pace around. She felt very restless and wanted Barbara out of the flat. She would have liked to snap her fingers and magic her sister away. At the same time she felt a sharp little pain of disappointment. 'I wanted you to understand,' she said.

Barbara said, 'Oh, I do, I do.'

'No, you don't. You're being just like Mum, hurray, rich man, let's take him for all we can get, and serve him right for being a dirty old man, yippee.' She felt her face growing hot with indignation.

Barbara was unmoved. It might have been one of their childhood rows all over again, for it followed the same pattern: Sarah losing her temper over the latest damaged toy, the untidy room, the spilt paint; Barbara shrugging it off as nothing. She had always been able to get under Sarah's skin and provoke her as no one else could. Now she said calmly, 'Why all the fuss? He wants something he's not entitled to, why shouldn't he pay for it? That's perfectly fair. You're the one who has to be tucked away, waiting for visits, hiding in corners. He's not offering you anything permanent, he's just wasting your time while he gets the best of both worlds. Well, the best of both worlds is expensive. He knows that, he *expects* to pay for it. *You're* the one who's not being realistic. You're doing *him* a favour, not the other way round. Can't you get that into your head?'

Sarah said stubbornly, 'I don't see it like that.' But she wasn't sure how she *did* see it; Barbara's words were too close to the truth. She felt uncomfortable, and Manson, surrounded by family, seemed far away. Already he wasn't here when she needed him, and for the first time in her life she had no one else.

Barbara, with uncanny precision, went on, 'Well, how about the others? That student's no use, he's penniless, but the other one, the rich one, what's his name, Geoff. How come you let him lend you the car? Now that's really something, but you don't mind accepting that.'

'That's different,' said Sarah mechanically, but meaning it.

'Is it? Well, this little affair could mess it all up, have you thought about that? You could actually marry Geoff, you know. My God, that family of his, they're rolling in it, aren't they? If you throw all that over to have an affair with your boss, at least you deserve a bit of compensation. That's all I'm getting at and it's just common sense.'

Sarah said, 'There's no question of marrying Geoff. We've never discussed it.'

Barbara laughed. 'Well, if you ask me, a man who'll lend you his car is more than halfway there. He only needs a little nudge. And I bet you haven't even tried.'

'That's right, I haven't. Oh, do drop it, Barbara. We're not even in love. It just isn't like that.'

Barbara opened her eyes wide. 'Love? What's that got to do with it?'

'They're at the station.' Cassie put the phone down, and Manson got up, a shade reluctantly, she thought.

'All right. I'll go and fetch them.'

She watched him go down the drive to the car. She felt suddenly uneasy. Gavin's voice on the phone, the oddly chosen words : 'Prue's not feeling too well, ma'am. And she's acting up a bit, too. So if you could make allowances, I'd be obliged.' She liked the 'ma'am', though he had never used it before, and it sounded as if he were copying someone in a film. And she liked the blend of ancient and modern in his speech. But the meaning alarmed her. There was something about his voice and the words he selected that made her think she was being warned – even alerted – more for her own good than out of conjugal consideration for Prue. A sudden attack of nerves made her shiver; she poured another glass of sherry and drank it slowly, trying to calm herself. She had always thought that he saw Prue in a very clear light; in fact it seemed a marriage remarkably without illusion on both sides. But it was still unnerving to have this brought out in the open, and so abruptly, in the form of a warning. She knew Prue's faults : that she was selfish and greedy and spoilt, that she liked her own way. To some extent she and Peter must accept responsibility for all that. But she was also tough and independent and honest, and for these more attractive qualities they could also take credit. Cassie felt very detached about her daughter, observing her as another woman whom she happened to have studied at close quarters. Yet there was also an element of self-identification which she would have found hard to explain. She was not even sure if it showed. The boys were more her sons than Prue was her daughter, but Prue could have been herself-when-young, and for that she felt special affection. She remembered that when she was pregnant for the first time she had wanted a daughter and the miracle of getting what she wanted had quite eclipsed the miracle of birth.

She checked that all was well in the kitchen and returned to the window, wanting to see the actual arrival of the car : it was part of the ceremony of the day. When it came she watched them all get out : Peter, grey-haired and slightly stooping (should she tell him about that?); Gavin, dark and dramatic in eccentric clothes (she pushed away the memories – and, Oh, Prue, did I ever tell you I understand? No, I didn't, but I do, so well); and Prue, the last, and slow, weighed down with the child. She moved heavily; she seemed to Cassie to have put on an astonishing amount of weight. She felt the weight of her own body; the identification was so acute that she even glanced down at her own ankles to see if they had swelled. It feels awful, she thought, bloody awful, but it's worth it; did I ever tell you? Had there ever been a chance, had there ever been time to talk, to form the close, warm conspiracy of pregnant women? No, and with Prue's reserve there probably never would be. It was unfair. My child, and we have so much in common. The one time I can be some help to you, if only you would let me. She was at the door.

'Darling. Happy birthday.'

'Hullo, Mummy.'

Kisses. Pale, drawn face. The child pressing between them. 'Hullo, Gavin.'

'Hi.'

He looked so familiar it was ridiculous. Peter followed, face blank, in retreat. She nearly greeted him too, as if he had been away a long time.

'Sherry?' she said brightly.

'Thanks.'

'Yeah, thanks.'

'Or would you rather have Scotch?'

'No, it's okay.'

'Mummy, can I have tomato juice or something?'

Manson poured the drinks, taking over. Cassie sat and watched her daughter, her son-in-law. She reached out a hand to the parcel, wrapped and beautiful, on a shelf.

'Darling. Do you want your present now?'

'All right.' Prue was languid. Cassie felt a stab of anxiety. She was so shuttered, so enclosed, such an interior person.

'You can have it later if you like.'

'No. I'll have it now.' She took it and began tearing at the wrapping, casually, not appreciating the care that had gone into it, but also without eagerness, as if presents happened every day, as if they were a chore. Manson handed drinks, saying, 'Hope you like it,' but without conviction. What was wrong with him? Cassie felt waves of uneasiness; all Gavin's words flooded back; the whole scene was odd, out of gear. Unreal, as if they were all drunk.

Prue had got through to the box. She opened it. 'Oh God. Look at this.' She showed it to Gavin.

'Wow.'

'It's beautiful,' Prue said, in a funny, repressed little voice. She took out the card, read it, and put it back. 'Thank you.'

'Christ, aren't you lucky,' Gavin said, oddly hearty.

'Yes.' She looked slowly from one parent to the other. 'Thank you. Thank you very much.'

Cassie said, unable to stop herself, 'Aren't you going to put it on?'

'What? Oh yes, yes of course.' Slowly, almost clumsily, Prue fastened the bracelet on her wrist and turned it in the light. 'It's beautiful,' she said again. 'But it must have cost the earth.' She looked at her father. 'You really shouldn't have done it, you know.'

Manson drank instead of replying; Cassie said, 'But you like it?'

'I can't help liking it.'

'Well, then. That's splendid.'

Prue turned the bracelet round and round. 'Must be my lucky day,' she said.

It was dark in the lane on the way to the station and there was no one about. He hit her systematically, holding her by the wrist and slapping her across the face, to and fro, over and over again, as he had done before, only this time his full weight was behind the blow. She shut her eyes tight and screamed -- not loudly, for help, but almost against her will. His fist caught her mouth and a tooth loosened sickeningly. She stopped screaming. The night was very still and then the only sounds she could hear were his blows to her face and his tortured breathing, curiously similar to making love. She was panting in exactly the same way.

There was a sharp, blinding pain as he caught the bone of her nose, and she felt, or heard, it crack. The divisions between her senses were becoming blurred. Tears of pain began to flow down her cheeks without effort and she felt sick: she sagged at the knees and could not stand up. She drooped till she was almost hanging bodily from the hand he had locked round her wrist. She had expected him to call her names as well but he did not and his silence terrified her more than anything, making the blows seem more methodical and deadly than ever before. She suddenly wondered if he meant to kill her and started to struggle with what strength she had left. The next moment she was lying on the ground and he was kicking her. Too weak to scream any more she could only fold her hands over her stomach, saying faintly, 'Not my baby.' Her last conscious awareness of anything beyond the red hot circle of pain that seemed to enclose her, in which she seemed to be endlessly revolving, was of car headlamps moving on the main road a hundred yards away and gently touching the tops of the bushes above her head.

'So I came to you.' He walked up and down; he could not keep still. 'I couldn't think of anything else to do.' Then as if to amend his tactlessness: 'I had to see you. There's no one else I can talk to.' He promptly went through the story again, incredulously, in a state of shock, as if he even did not realize he was repeating himself.

Listening, even a second time, did not make Sarah understand. 'All day there was something in the air ... you could tell something was wrong ... she wasn't herself ... ghastly ... dropping little hints ... looking at me to see if I was frightened, playing with me. She saved it up till dinner. Oh, she was drunk, of course, she'd had too much wine but oh, God . . .'

Sarah got up, put her arms round him, said, 'Come and sit down.' He slumped on the sofa and she poured him another drink and held his hand while he drank it. She could not drink herself. She felt she was on duty, a nurse, obliged to remain soberly in charge of the patient. Her time would come later, perhaps.

He let out a groan. 'God, Cassie's face.'

'Should you have left her? I mean should you really be here, not with her?' She thought her own sense of responsibility, her bitter acceptance of total personal blame was the most heavily adult feeling she had ever had. She did not need to say, 'It's all my fault'; a statement usually made to elicit denial, in any case. She picked up her burden voluntarily and in silence.

'Oh yes. She wanted to be alone, to think. She said so. She said if I stayed we'd only spend the night talking and there was plenty of time for that. So I left.' He leaned back and closed his eyes.

Sarah thought she could not bear the feeling of pity that swamped her. Was this how mothers were supposed to feel? A dreadful engulfing sensation of concern and responsibility, that no one else could help their actions and she must rescue them all or have the pain transferred to herself : she breathed it in the air like gas. Pity for Prue, to be hurt that she wanted to hurt, pity for Cassie who deserved none of it, pity for Manson, sitting spent and grey-faced in her living-room, caught in a situation he had never meant to create and which had accelerated rapidly out of control. But she had not wanted to feel pity for him.

'Why don't you go to bed?' she said softly. 'You're worn out. It won't look so bad in the morning.'

He opened his eyes, said alarmingly, 'Maybe it's all for the best. A fresh start . . .'

'You know you don't mean that.' She found herself trembling. 'Now come on. Come to bed. You need a good night's sleep.'

198

'Who says I don't mean it?' He sounded suddenly belligerent, reached for his glass, found it empty again. 'Oh Sarah,
Sarah.' He buried his face against her. 'You're so good to me.
I need you. Don't leave me, Sarah.' He was suddenly very
drunk.

She held him and stroked his hair; she felt about a hundred years old. 'Where would I go?' she said gently.

After he had gone Cassie thought that it might not have
happened at all. She could be still waiting for them all to
arrive, or it might have been a play she had watched on TV.
She wandered over to the mirror and looked at herself,
touching her face. She looked the same. She felt the same.
Maybe she *was* the same. Maybe in the morning it would not
have happened : with Peter beside her, yawning, waiting for
tea and the paper, she would never have heard the ugly
words because Prue would not have said them, would not
have denounced her father to her mother and been dragged
away screaming and crying by Gavin, who looked as if he
wanted to murder her. There wouldn't be much sleep in that
household tonight, Cassie thought, almost with detachment.
Not that she expected much herself. For Peter she wasn't
sure; the girl might soothe him. No, Sarah. Already she was
falling into the humiliating trap, the classic way other people
said *the girl, that woman*, the anonymous venom. She did not
want to be like that. Sarah Francis : she had a name. She
was not *the girl*. She had feelings and friends and presumably
parents; she was a person who could cry or have a headache
or feel cold waiting for a bus. And she was probably in love
with Peter, for what other motive could she have? He was
not a rich man and, though attractive, far from glamorous.
So she must care for him. The world was not divided into
loving wives and evil mistresses; the divine plan or whatever
it might be was not nearly so simple. And she herself was the
last person who could afford to feel smug.

Thus she reasoned. But reasoning could not go any further,
could not accompany her into the dark places of her mind
where she pictured them together, touching, talking,

laughing, making love. She had not known she could feel jealousy like this. Previously she had never known for sure if he was ever unfaithful so it was easy to gratify herself and imagine him faithful. Now she saw her husband for the first time positively contaminated by another woman. It was that which had made her ask him to leave, no matter how she disguised it in civilized words about talk and sleep and solitude. She did not want to look at him and see what she saw. To shut out the images she must shut out the object on whom they were projected.

She was shocked by the violence of her feelings and the strength of her sense of property. She felt ashamed. He was a person like any other with a choice of action – a life of his own to do as he pleased with. She could not own him, except by courtesy; it was reprehensible that she should even want to, and unfair. My home, my husband, my children – was she really so possessive? Had she completely sunk her own identity into theirs all those years ago and was this why she now felt so primitive? There were reasons for everything, or so she believed.

Irresolute, she stood in the middle of the room with a drink and a cigarette and said aloud, 'I am being ridiculous.' She dimly caught sight of herself in the mirror where she had examined her face and thought she looked older than she remembered as if she were a past acquaintance not met for some time. She had aged. And she looked foolish. Drama and suffering did not sit kindly on the middle-aged, did not flatter their features. Whereas Prue, going off with Gavin under sufferance, sobbing, struggling, had through all her blotched make-up and swollen eyes the beauty of youth, of even the plainest young creature (which she was far from being), the beauty of skin and hair.

The telephone rang and she answered it, but so automatically that at first the words meant nothing, might have been scrambled for security reasons or spoken in a foreign language. She had to get the voice at the other end to repeat everything, and she thought how odd that it managed to sound calm and urgent both at once. Then she made out that it was saying something about an accident and she must hurry.

32

'I don't understand,' she said. The doctor was patient. He began telling her all over again. A nurse brought them both cups of tea, very hot and sweet and strong. Cassie tried to drink hers but it burned her lips and she put it down.

'Your daughter is going to be all right, Mrs Manson,' the doctor said with frightening compassion. 'And probably the baby, too; we can't be sure yet. But we're doing everything we can and you must try not to worry. It's very important for you to be calm when you see your daughter. At the moment she's asleep, of course.'

The room was white and dark hospital green, with a funny smell. There were papers on the doctor's desk and filing cabinets around the walls. People passed continually in the corridor, quiet brisk footsteps. Cassie shut her eyes to stop everything spinning round but immediately opened them again, afraid she was going to faint.

'Are you all right?' the doctor asked with concern.

'Yes.' She took a deep breath and forced herself to gulp some of the hot tea, hoping it would shock her back to normal. 'Yes. I'm all right. Really.'

'Good.' He looked pleased with her, as if she had passed some kind of test. 'You're being very brave.'

She shook her head. 'But I don't understand. Where's Gavin – my son-in-law? Wasn't he with her? They left the house together. What happened?'

The doctor said, 'That's what I was trying to tell you before. It's ... very difficult, but apparently there was some kind of argument and your daughter was, um, rather badly assaulted by er, her husband.'

The room spun like a roundabout. Cassie put her hands on the desk as if that would steady it. The doctor leaned forward and offered her a cigarette. He seemed embarrassed, she thought. Details like this were terribly clear while words made no impression, like balls bouncing off a wall.

'Could you light it for me?' she said, unable to leave go of the desk. She was very conscious of the feel of the wood beneath her fingers; abnormally conscious, the way she imagined she might feel if drugged. The wood seemed the only real thing in the room.

The doctor lit two cigarettes and put one in her mouth. He began to speak rather rapidly. 'I'm sorry, Mrs Manson, I know how difficult this must be for you, but it seems your daughter and her husband had some kind of argument on their way home and he hit her and went on hitting her. Then he carried her in here unconscious, with a threatened miscarriage. But as I've told you we think we can avert that and your daughter is certainly going to be all right. It's only fair to add that your son-in-law is extremely upset – in fact he arrived here in a state of shock. On the other hand we only have his account of what happened, as your daughter hasn't been able to talk yet.'

He paused. Cassie, nearly blinded by smoke, forced herself to take the half-smoked cigarette from her mouth. She said, 'Gavin beat her up?'

'So he says.' The doctor cleared his throat. 'But he's completely overwrought. Quite frankly I don't know what to make of it. If his story is true then of course you could inform the police, but as it's a family matter you may not wish ...' He paused again, adding hesitantly, 'May I ask if there is any, er, history of violence?'

'What?'

'Do you know if he has ever struck your daughter before?'

'No. I mean I don't know.' Gavin hit Prue. It was unbelievable. They might as well have told her that the world had come to an end and she was in hell.

'Never mind. Drink your tea,' the doctor said soothingly. She drank. How quickly it cooled. He pushed the phone towards her. 'I expect you'd like to contact your husband.'

She looked at the phone and shook her head, noticing that her cheeks were wet. Without being aware of starting to cry she found everything in the room had blurred and tears were falling on her coat. She searched in her bag for a handkerchief and blew her nose.

'I'm sorry.' The doctor shook his head, exonerating her. 'I don't know where my husband is. He ... had to go out.' She wiped her eyes: this was not a time to break down. She could not afford such a luxury when she had to go through the whole thing alone. But it was getting worse because she was beginning to believe it. 'Can I see my daughter?'

The doctor hesitated. 'Well, you won't be able to talk to her; she's asleep. Of course you can see her if you wish but you must be prepared for rather a shock. Now don't be alarmed; I assure you that her injuries are largely superficial. It's just that her face ... well, she looks much worse than she really is.'

Cassie began to tremble. Terror and shame swept over her. My child. I'm afraid to look at my own child. 'Yes, I understand,' she said calmly. 'I'd still like to see her.'

She was sick, and a nurse even younger than Prue held her head. She felt she had disorganized the whole hospital, that everyone's valuable time was being expended on her family. And it was humiliating being sick. The tea and the drinks back home and the lovely meal she had cooked and half-eaten before Prue really began to talk. She felt she was regurgitating the whole hideous evening.

'That's better,' said the nurse, pleased with her, producing a glass of water. 'Now drink this. You'll soon feel better.'

Cassie drank the lovely cold water. She couldn't even say thank you. She couldn't speak at all. She had never seen anyone's face in such a condition, except perhaps boxers on television being helped out of the ring. But it was Prue. Prue's face smashed and discoloured and bandaged. She felt herself beginning to heave again and quickly drank more water and tried to breathe deeply. The nurse disposed of the bowl and returned.

'She really is going to be all right, you know,' she said. 'She looks a lot worse than she is, honestly.'

Cassie stared at her. A pale freckled face of a child with incongruous dark shadows under the eyes. They were all understaffed and overworked, so people said. She found her voice. 'Are you going to look after her?'

'Part of the time, yes. I'm on night duty in this ward.'

'What's your name?'

'Jones.'

'Nurse Jones. I'll remember.'

The girl smiled. She didn't know what to say.

'And the doctor I was talking to just now?'

'Doctor Carter.'

Cassie repeated the name. She had no idea why she wanted this information, but it seemed something to hang on to. If these two people had names they must be real and they were taking care of Prue. She couldn't take care of Prue. Her own child and she couldn't even look at her without being sick. What kind of a mother was she? And without Peter there was no one she could call on to help her. Unthinkable to inform her parents; they had troubles enough. The shock might kill her mother, even. But it meant in effect they were as useless to her as she was to Prue. And she had no friends. What had she done with her life that she had no friends, now, when she needed them? She began to cry again, pure tears of self-pity and helplessness, not tears for Prue. She was ashamed. But she had never felt more alone in her life.

'Oh, please,' said Nurse Jones, patting her shoulder in a motherly way. 'Please, Mrs Manson. She is going to be all right, honestly. You've had a bad shock; would you like to lie down for a bit?'

There were new arrivals as she walked through Casualty, more people who had injured themselves or been injured. It was a busy road. She had to wait to see Dr Carter and while she waited she phoned home in case Peter had changed his mind and returned. But he had not, and indeed she had not thought it likely. She let the phone ring for a bit – there was always a chance he was there and asleep – and listened to the strangely disquieting sound of her own telephone ringing in her own house. Then she put it down, suddenly chilled. There was no one to help her through this. She was on her own. Then she wondered if perhaps Peter was with Rupert, not with Sarah, or in an hotel, but she saw it was nearly midnight so she did not like to ring Rupert, and in any case, if Peter was not there, what could she say?

Dr Carter said briskly, 'How are you feeling now, Mrs Manson? I thought you were lying down for a bit.'

'I was.' She had dozed for ten minutes in a chair. 'I feel much better now.' After all, what was the point in saying she did not think she would feel better ever, in her life? 'I'd like to see my son-in-law. Gavin. Could I?'

The doctor looked at her doubtfully.

'I'm quite calm now,' she said, trying to sound convincing.

Dr Carter said, 'Well, from our point of view he's a patient too, although we expect to discharge him in the morning. Could it wait till then? We had to give him a sedative so he's probably asleep in any case. I'd really rather you didn't disturb him.'

'You don't trust me,' she said, smiling.

'Well.' He paused, selecting tactful words, or so she felt. 'It's not that, of course. But I do feel that a confrontation at this stage might be rather too much. For both of you, I mean.'

They were protecting Gavin from her maternal wrath. They were afraid of what she might do. 'You're quite right,' she said matter-of-factly. 'I have to admit I'd rather like to kill him. It must be what they say about violence breeding violence, do you think?'

'Something like that.' Dr Carter was beginning to look anxious, as though she might actually be dangerous. 'You don't mean it, of course, but I quite understand your feelings. If it was my daughter I'd feel exactly the same, I'm sure.'

He was trying to reassure her. Trying to make her feel better by telling her that they were all barbarians under the skin. She thought how abruptly her whole world had turned over. Nothing was as it had seemed: Prue's marriage, even her own character. It was all quite hideous. And somehow it suspended all moral judgements. If she could feel so savagely she was just like the others and not entitled to blame any of them. She said aloud, 'It's a very ugly world, isn't it? I didn't realize before.'

33

Sarah slept badly. Manson, exhausted with drink and emotion, fell asleep immediately while she still had her arms round him, and she lay awake, listening to him breathing rather heavily and feeling the arm that was under him grow gradually numb. The scene he had described revolved in her mind until it became so vivid she could hardly bear it and switched her attention to the morning and how tired they would both feel, and how unfit for work. The thought of work then instantly reminded her that he had come as he was, with nothing, and while he was welcome to use her toothbrush and tiny razor, she could hardly provide him with a shirt. She was quite appalled at the idea of him going to the office in a dirty shirt and spent about five minutes gingerly extricating her arm, now painful with pins and needles, so that she could get up and go to the bathroom to wash the shirt. It seemed vital to do this, quite disproportionately vital (since he could have bought one and in any case did not have superiors to impress with a smart appearance), probably because it was something practical that she could do to help.

It was the first shirt she had ever washed and while she

was doing it she thought, would I like to do this for ever? and looked at her pale, smudgy-eyed reflection in the bath-room mirror with a sense of isolation, as if she were the only person in the world awake. It was half past two. She wrung out the shirt in a towel and hung it up, leaving the bathroom heater on all night to ensure that it would be dry by morn-ing. By the time she went back to bed she felt so alone that she was quite startled to see him lying there in her bed (or was it his?), and he had moved so that he was lying almost diagonally and there was hardly room for her to get in. She squeezed herself into a tiny space beside him and he flung his arm across her body without waking and began to snore.

34

Cassie saw him coming up the drive. Although he was alone, it made her feel the drama of the previous day was being replayed : time had turned back. She had slept heavily and absolutely, to her own amazement, for about three hours, then wakened at six, far from her usual time. She was in the kitchen by half-past, boiling a kettle and looking blearily out of the window, when she saw the familiar figure in flowered jeans and sweater, with tousled black hair, and a scarf floating around his neck. She thought quite calmly, well, that takes guts, and waited for the bell to ring.

She opened the door. He did not seem surprised to see her up and dressed, merely relieved. 'I hope I'm not too early,' he said, and waited.

She looked at him. Far too dark and angular and attrac-tive, he was the other son she might have had, but had not. He was unbearably familiar, and yet only last night she had wanted, really wanted, to kill him. She said, 'Come in,

Gavin,' and held the door open for him. The past flooded back and suddenly it did not matter that she had a daughter in hospital because of him: she understood. She did not know if it was the effect of too little sleep, or the drinks of the night before, or what, but he was suddenly a person in distress and she knew him.

He came in. He looked around, as if the hall, the whole house, was strange to him, and said, 'Mrs Manson, I guess you hate my guts but I had to see you.'

She had a feeling that he was offering himself, freely, as a victim, that she could do anything. If she should scream abuse or attack him with a knife he would not defend himself. She wanted, illogically, to hold out her arms, but that would be too much. She said, 'No, that was last night. I've been expecting you.' And as she said it she realized that it was true.

He followed her into the kitchen. She said, 'I've got the kettle on. Would you like tea or coffee?'

'Coffee, please. Black.' He slumped against the wall and watched her make it. She realized in that moment that she had never been alone with him before, and knew at the same moment, understood exactly, why Prue had married him. All the old clichés about animal magnetism, sheer vitality, dangerous unleashed power swarmed in her brain. And yet he seemed defenceless, like a child. He said, 'You must think I'm the all-time shit and you're right, but I owe you an explanation. No, that's the wrong word. Christ, you can't explain these things, but I had to come.'

She said, 'I know,' and actually smiled at him. She put the coffee things on a tray and said, 'Come in the sitting-room; you must be worn out.'

He followed her, saying nervously, 'Is your husband awake yet?'

She shook her head. 'He left last night. We ... needed a breathing space.'

He nodded. 'Yeah. I understand that. But about Prue ... D'you want to get the cops? Maybe you have already. I shan't blame you.'

'No.' She poured his coffee and handed it to him. 'I've done nothing. I think I was waiting to hear from you.'

He drank the coffee, hot as it was, wiped his lips, and lit a cigarette, offering her one. She accepted, and he lit it for her. 'Christ,' he said, 'I think you understand. I think you're the most together person I've ever met. I wish we'd talked before.'

She smiled, to her own surprise. 'We haven't talked yet. Don't stop.'

He made a wry face. 'You're right; I haven't even begun. Look, it's pointless to say I'm sorry. You can't *apologize* for beating up your wife, especially to her mother. What *can* you say?' He took a long drag on his cigarette. 'Look, I'm not here to make excuses for myself, that's not my scene, and no one, but no one, could make excuses for what I did. I'm responsible for Prue being in that hospital, no one but me. And I've got to live with that. Believe me, it won't be easy. But there are reasons. Not excuses. Just reasons.'

She said gently, 'Tell me.'

There was a long silence. He drank more coffee, dragged on the cigarette. She felt her life was suspended by a thread. Eventually he said, 'I don't know where to start.'

'Just start. Anywhere you like.' She was amazed at her own tolerance. Perhaps it was partly due to the early morning light. She felt they were alone in the world.

He said, 'In a *way* it's all my fault. I mean I told Prue. That girlfriend of hers who walked in when your husband and his secretary were in our flat, she told her boyfriend and he told me. Then I told Prue. As a joke. Now you're going to think that pretty sick; bear with me, please. I knew Prue had a thing about her father, I guess I was jealous, well, not jealous exactly, but it got me on the raw. I couldn't resist telling her when I had something on him. I didn't even think of you at the time: can you forgive that? I guess I thought it was just between Prue and me.' He wiped his forehead. 'I must have a pretty simple mind. I mean, I knew it wasn't important, these things happen all the time, but I had to tell her, I simply couldn't keep my mouth shut. Now you can

209

say what you like and I won't blame you, but believe me, I didn't mean any harm, it was private, it was a family matter.'

She said, 'Go on.'

'I don't know what I expected. To fix things between us, I guess. Oh, not that they weren't okay before, but – oh, I'll come to that. Anyway, I told her and she flipped. She went out of her mind. I tell you I was scared. It had *literally*' – he stressed the word – 'never struck me she might want to tell you. But never. Not in my wildest dreams. She said she did. She went mad. We both hit the roof. She was very upset and I argued with her, and when that didn't do any good I said if she told you I'd knock her head off. Those were the actual words I used.'

He paused and she was transported years, to a studio, to wood shavings and slabs of bronze, and broken plaster. She was young again, young for the last time, and the memories that came flooding back made her reel. She said to herself, I thought I was over all this, and here it is. She said aloud to him, 'And?'

He poured himself another cup of coffee. 'I forgot all about it. I honestly did. Then yesterday on the train she was kind of funny. In a crazy mood. I knew something was brewing. We had a kind of crazy argument in the train, about the Goddamned colour supplement. I didn't want to give it to her because it had pictures in it, you know, babies before they're born, that kind of stuff. I thought it might upset her. But she insisted. Then I knew we were in for trouble; that's why I called you the way I did. But I still didn't know what. I still couldn't believe she'd actually ... blow her top.'

He was silent. Finally he said, 'Anyway she did. I don't need to tell you the rest. I still haven't explained the rest; I don't know that I can, I don't know that you'll accept it. But I have to try.' He lit another cigarette. 'Look, I love Prue, I really do. She's ... fantastic. But she has this thing – this need, I don't know, this urge for violence. Now you're not going to believe this, you're going to say I'm just making shitty excuses for beating her up, but I'm not. Honest to God.

210

I'm talking now about months ago. Look, you can blame me as much as you like, I'm not trying to get off the hook. I know I should never have hit her. But *way* back, before any of this jazz about your husband and his secretary, she made me hit her. She wanted me to.' He buried his face in his hands and the words came out muffled. 'Oh, you're not going to believe this. But it was as if it wasn't enough that we did the usual things, made love, you know. She wanted something more. She'd pick arguments. I didn't understand at first, I thought it was just a game. But she went on and on. Finally, one row we had, I hit her. I blacked her eye. Now I don't know how to explain this. It was before we went away. We had a row about her job; she wanted to quit. But she made me hit her. She went on and on till I did.'

Cassie said, 'How did you feel?'

'I don't know. God, you're fantastic. Do you actually understand any of this? You're acting as if you did. What I want to make clear is, I'm not blaming Prue, she can't help the way she is. It was up to me not to play along. But I did. So that's my fault. The point is ...' he paused, frowning. 'I've thought a lot about this, I've tried to get it clear. But I've never discussed it with Prue. Maybe I should've. But I think *she's* got it all clear, she doesn't mind. Oh, I don't mean last night, that went too far, but before. I think it's all part of some crazy scheme in her head. Whereas to me, afterwards, it's ridiculous; I can't believe I've done what I've done. If it's in me, and God knows it seems to be and she brings it out, then Christ, it's something I'd rather repress. I don't want to know. You just can't imagine how hideous it is.'

Cassie said, 'What you're saying is, Prue is a masochist and she makes you into a sadist, only you're not really one. Or if you are you'd rather not be. Is that about it?'

He frowned; he seemed suddenly embarrassed. 'I guess so.'

'Can't you just accept her the way she is?' She felt she was making a fervent personal plea, but of course he did not know that.

'What? So I buy this whole crazy set-up and one day I kill

211

her. I nearly did last night. Is that what you want? Good God, you're her mother, are you out of your mind?'

Cassie said gently, 'I'm sorry; of course I don't want that. I'm just trying to understand.'

'Yeah.' He brooded. 'Well, maybe you understand too well. Honestly, I don't get this whole scene – you mean you actually want me to beat up your daughter?'

Cassie felt the weight of years as she had never done before. There was a bitter taste in her mouth, as tangible as lipstick. She said, 'These things aren't simple. Of *course* I don't want you to beat up Prue; last night I wanted to kill you for what you did. But that doesn't mean I can't understand. There's' – she hesitated, but knew she had to go on – 'a bit of this thing in me too; maybe Prue's got it from me.'

The sun rose palely over distant trees. A little warm light began to fill the garden. Gavin said, very young, the authentic note of horror, 'You mean your old man beats you up?'

Cassie almost laughed at the horror and the ludicrously improbable picture; she also wanted to cry. 'No – I don't mean that. That's the last thing he would ever do. But there was a time when I would have liked him to be ... well, more aggressive. Look, it's really very simple. Most women like a man to be masterful. Maybe even a little bit rough. You only have to push this a stage further and you've got real pain, real violence. The problem is where to stop it. How to provide enough to satisfy the person's needs without letting it all get out of control, like last night.'

He stared at her. 'Yeah. But that shouldn't be too difficult, not if it's a sex thing. This thing with Prue, oh, it started with sex, that was fine, but I think it's gone beyond that now. I kind of feel she wants me to punish her for something; like it's not a game any more.' He frowned. 'D'you think – gee, I don't know how to put this – but this thing between her and her father, well, they feel pretty strongly about each other, don't they? D'you think maybe Prue feels guilty about that and that's why she wants me to punish her? Say, if I'm right, that's pretty sick, isn't it? But I guess we'll never know; it's not something I could ask Prue and I don't

212

think she knows herself. If it's true then it's buried. It has to be.'

Cassie, depressed by the plausibility of his argument, said as much to convince herself as him, 'It could also be that we just didn't give her enough discipline as a child. Have you ever thought about that?'

He brooded for a moment, then looked up, suddenly flashing her the wide, candid smile of a child. 'Yeah, let's believe that.'

35

Sarah said, 'Do you want to telephone her?'

He looked up; he looked guilty. Caught. 'No. No. You mean Cassie?'

'Yes.'

'No, I don't want to phone. That's up to her, when she feels ready to talk. She's the injured party after all.' He held out his arms. 'Apart from you. You're having a rotten time, aren't you? Shut up with me all day at the office and all night here and I'm as miserable as sin. It's not much fun for you, is it?'

Sarah managed a smile. 'It's just ironic. Wishing for time together and now we've got it, only we can't enjoy it because of *how* we got it.' She held his hand, not wanting his arm round her. It was not that she loved him less but that she had never felt so alone as now, when he was with her. Far more thoroughly alone than when she had waited for him. She felt that she was a refuge, not a person; all the feeling of security she had built up was flowing away, like bath water, when someone pulls out the plug. She said, 'Why do you think Prue did it?'

'God knows. I've been asking myself that all day.' He had done virtually no work, while Sarah sought refuge in typing and had got through enough to occupy two normal days, by five o'clock being reduced to tidying the filing cabinet. At this point, in a rage of guilt and helplessness he had telephoned Prue's flat to demand explanation, justification, redress; but there was no reply. 'I suppose she was shocked and when she started drinking it all came out. She must have wanted to punish me for letting her down.'

'And punish her mother too?'

'I don't know. Maybe it was the only way she *could* punish me. Properly. Maybe she didn't think it would be enough to tell me in private that she despised me.'

Sarah thought this over. 'And would it have been?'

'What do you mean?'

'Well, how much do you value her good opinion?'

His face darkened; he said, 'About as much as she values mine. Or as little. That's not the point.'

'Isn't it?' She felt so sad; she looked round the smart white room and thought what a waste of paint it all was. Someone had tried so hard to make it nice and they were not appreciating it. 'You love her; of *course* it matters what she thinks. And your wife. You love her too.'

'And I love *you*,' he said, seriously, intensely, holding tight to her hand. He looked as if he meant it. But she did not believe him. She said, 'Yes, you love all three of us, you said so before, but it doesn't work, does it? You've always loved them best; there's never been a place for me. Maybe Prue was only trying to bring you to your senses; maybe she did you a favour.'

He said sharply, 'Now you're being ridiculous.' But he had never felt more involved and alive than when Prue said those fatal words, 'Do you know Daddy's been fucking his secretary in our flat while we were away?' The words in all their cruelty dropping one by one into the social atmosphere of a family party, Cassie's face turning as white as her plate, Prue trembling with spite; he himself and Gavin quite immobile, and for a moment silent, with horror. It was as if all

214

the drama he had perpetually been on the fringe of had finally washed over him, like a wave that you stand and wait for. It was not the monopoly of the young after all. But it hurt and he did not know how to deal with it, any more than he had known how to deal with Prue's hysterical sobs as Gavin dragged her from the house, or Cassie's silence when they were left alone. Finally she had said, 'Was all that true?' and he had said, 'Yes.' And really it had all been said, though they analysed the details for an hour or more, using words like jealousy and incest and revenge as if they did not belong in an Elizabethan drama but in everyday life, and discussing youth and middle age as if they were actually not afraid to face their implications. It was all very fine and brave but it left them empty and wanting to be alone, apart from each other. They had admitted too much.

He started to make love to Sarah, as much to comfort and reassure her as to give himself pleasure, but when she said, 'Do you mind if we don't? I'm awfully tired,' he was more relieved than disappointed and stopped at once.

36

Cassie wrote, 'Darling, I've had a lot of time to think since you left yesterday. It isn't easy to write this but I think it would be even harder to say, on the phone, or face to face.

First of all, I wasn't quite honest with you yesterday when you were blaming yourself for everything. In fact one of the reasons I asked you to go was I couldn't bear to hear you take any more blame but I wasn't brave enough to share it. I hope I am now. Also I wanted to keep certain things private but now I think that was selfish of me and, in the circumstances, unjustified.

I'm trying to be very calm. Forgive me if I sound pompous. I think there are three reasons why we are in this situation: the normal attraction between you and Sarah, the stress of Prue's marriage which you've found hard to cope with, and a very natural longing for excitement and change after being married for so many years. It's the last reason I want to write about. Five years ago I had to face the fact that I would never have another child, and we had been married a long time. Do you remember, it was about that time Prue was sculpted by Sven? I never wanted to tell you this, I wanted to keep it private, but now I think I should tell you. I had an affair with him. It lasted for nearly two years, until he went away, and it was very humiliating and painful because he did not care for me at all, except in bed, and I was in love with him. It was also, in a sense, the happiest time in my life. That isn't meant to hurt you, just to prove that I can understand how you feel about Sarah. I have never felt more alive than when I was with him; in fact the more he despised me the more I adored him. I even wanted to have a child by him, before it was too late, but in the end that was something I couldn't do to you. It was a very difficult affair to manage because of you and the children – sometimes when he phoned I couldn't go to him because you or they were there, and then I really wished you all dead. I think I was a little out of my mind. At others times I would phone him and he'd say, "Not now, I'm working." Or I would go round there, if I was quite desperate, without phoning, to his house, to the studio, and he might make love to me if I was lucky, but sometimes he just said, "Go away, I don't want you today, I've got someone else coming." He knew there'd always be another time because I just couldn't stay away from him. And when he finally left he didn't even tell me he was going, or anyone else – I was just as surprised as the whole village was. One day the house was empty and the next day the agent's board went up and that was the first I knew of it. That was when I was so ill for months and you put it down to the menopause and the doctor kept giving me those pills – do you remember? I

216

thought it was a kind of judgement on me because I had been praying that one of us would die, you, me, or him, to solve everything, and then he solved it by simply going away, which was the one thing I had never considered, and much worse than death. So I thought it was God punishing me.

I'm telling you this now for two reasons. One to prove I understand the need for excitement, even misery, after years of contentment. As one gets older, it seems to get stronger, this longing to be reminded of the distinction between loving and being in love. You know which is better, just as you know it is better to be sober than drunk as a permanent state, but sometimes it is so wonderful to be drunk that you simply can't stop yourself drinking and you don't even want to try.

The other reason is about Prue. Now don't get alarmed, she's perfectly all right. But she's in hospital because Gavin hit her rather badly on their way home. He was very upset by her behaviour and he lost control. They think the baby will be all right too, so you *must not worry*. I've talked to Gavin and I'm certain he loves her and is terribly ashamed of what he did. But the point is that from what he said I gather they have always had a very violent relationship, instigated and encouraged by Prue, and leading up to the other night when it got completely out of hand. My relationship with Sven was also violent, although it never went as far as this, obviously, but I expect you remember the time I was always getting bruised or cut and again I had to blame it on the menopause : I said it was making me clumsy so I kept having accidents. I don't say this to hurt you – at least not consciously – but to explain that I know how Prue feels and that what happened last night is not entirely Gavin's fault. You remember how we tried to cope with this problem (in a much more minor way) when we were first married and we solved it, if that's the word, by ignoring it. This was an area where you couldn't meet me, you were always so gentle and sweet, so I tried to suppress this side of me because everything else was so good. But it came out again when I met Sven.

Anyway, that's all in the past. It's been painful to write

217

about and I hope we won't have to discuss it, though of course we can if you want to. I just wanted to stop you feeling that you were the unfaithful husband of a faithful wife – we have both been in the same boat, though at different times. And I wanted to tell you about Prue's accident without making you want to kill Gavin, which was my instant reaction and I don't even dislike him. He is staying here at present so as to be near the hospital for visits. Because of the circumstances they asked my permission to let him see her. I wasn't sure but I saw her today and all she could say was it was all her fault and please could she see Gavin. So I let him go and he's with her now.

He reminds me of Sven. Perhaps I shouldn't say that – don't misunderstand me, please – but he always has and I think that's why I never objected to him as a husband for Prue. It seemed like fate. In fact it used to amaze me that you didn't notice the resemblance, until I realized that you had no reason to remember Sven or even think of him, and besides when we met him he was already forty and going bald. But when you are in love with someone you can picture them at all ages, I think; your eyes get some kind of extra power, and you can see into their past and their future because you want their whole life.

Your feelings for Prue and your feelings for Sarah are your own affair and I don't want to pry. I still love you and would like you to come home but obviously not before you are ready to do so because that would accomplish nothing. Perhaps I should not assume you will ever be ready.

I hope you will agree with me that we should keep the whole incident quiet about Prue and not involve the police. Legally, of course, we could take action but I think this could only do harm. At the same time I am very worried about the future of their marriage because I don't see what course it can possibly take – I don't see how they can work out a solution that will satisfy both of them. Still, that is up to them.

There is one more point. I don't suppose Prue could have inherited this tendency from me but I wonder how much we may have encouraged it in the way we brought her up, whether she had too much love and not enough discipline. It was the other way round for us so maybe we tried too hard to compensate. We were so anxious not to spoil her materially, maybe we spoilt her emotionally and she needed Gavin to make her feel there was some power she could kick against that would always be too strong for her. Or maybe she felt guilty about always getting her own way – after all she always has twisted you round her little finger, hasn't she? – and wanted to be punished for that. Am I making any kind of sense?

Anyway, I know you'll want to visit her. Please be tactful. And if you want to see me you know where I am. But only if you want to. I love you anyway. Cassie.'

37

He kissed her hand, squeezed it, and sat down on a chair at the foot of the bed. He had meant to kiss her cheek and hug her but the sight of the swelling, the technicoloured bruises, the half-closed eye, repelled him. He felt himself tremble at the sight of his daughter like this; and he trembled more because he could not approach her as if it made no difference.

She said, 'Hullo, Daddy,' and smiled. He saw that one of her teeth was chipped and the sight made him shiver, as if another person were masquerading as Prue.

He said, 'Hullo, darling, how are you?' He felt unspeakably alienated and prayed that it did not show.

She said, 'Are you very angry with me?' and he was surprised at the inadequacy, even irrelevance, of the word. His daughter had chosen a husband who beat her and his wife had had a lover years ago without his even suspecting. Apparently these two women, the two he had loved most in the world, were both raging masochists and deceitful into the bargain. Cassie had betrayed him long ago without conscience, Prue had stored up evidence against him and revealed it to hurt Cassie and discredit him in her eyes. Whereas he had loved them both devotedly all his life, worked hard to provide for them, suffered guilt over his own rare and tiny infidelities. He felt they had both become strangers who yet still expected him to understand their points of view. He thought of Sarah, thought of her with longing and gratitude, wanted to be with her, to make amends for all he had failed to give her or had inflicted upon her.

Prue said, 'I shouldn't have told Mummy. I was wrong. I'm sorry.'

He registered her apology and knew it must have cost her a lot. He wanted to respond to it, out of human justice if nothing more, but he could not. She was apologizing for betraying him to Cassie, but Cassie had herself betrayed him years before and she was not sorry. She had preferred a man who ill-treated her. And he would not be here, in this hospital, visiting his daughter, if she too did not prefer to be ill-treated. He had been totally inadequate for the women he loved, apparently : had he been able to beat them they might both have adored him.

He said, 'You had your reasons.'

'No. No, I didn't. It was just spite. Beastly rotten jealousy. Oh, I kidded myself it was justice, that Mummy ought to know and it would serve you right, but really Gavin was on to it at once, he knew it was just spite.' She wiped a tear from the swollen, discoloured eye, and he winced for her. He found the whole scene offensive and disgusting, and would have given anything to avoid it. To his horror the tears gathered momentum; she went on, 'Oh, I'm too much for him, I know I am, he came to see me and he was all quiet and guilty. He doesn't understand, I can't make him understand. I think he's afraid of me now. He sits very quiet and then he says things like "This must never happen again", as

220

if it was the end of the world.' The tears oozed out, seeming to flow with difficulty past the bright, swollen flesh, and he wanted to turn his head away. Yet this was the daughter he had anguished over and loved too much, this was his child, part of his body and part of his life. He patted her hand and gave her his handkerchief; but more he was unable to do, and he did not even feel ashamed, merely numb.

She said, weeping, 'You see I love him very much and I need him.' He nodded but for all the comprehension that he felt they might have been discussing some strange addiction. The picture of Gavin swung before his mind, untidy, bizarre, dramatic, and suddenly crossed as on a double exposure with another, older face with receding hair and short thick body, middle-aged, kindly agreeing to sculpt Prue for her devoted parents, and even to do it a little cheaper because they were so nearly neighbours. He felt sick. And Cassie was not sorry. Prue was not sorry. They wanted to wallow in it, both of them.

Prue said urgently, 'Have you made it up with Mummy? Is it all right? She's been marvellous to me, so understanding. She's fantastic, isn't she?'

He said, 'Yes. Fantastic.'

'It will be all right between you, won't it?'

He hesitated. 'Don't push it, Prue; it's our affair.'

She burst out, 'Oh, but I'm sure she'll forgive you, I think she has already. I know I'd forgive Gavin, anything. You must make it up, I can't bear it.'

Sudden anger flamed up in him and he lost control, in so far as he ever could. 'You can't bear it,' he said. 'You. Always you. You had to tell her. Now you want it all smoothed over, you've had your fun.' He saw her look shocked, saw her lips, pale and puffy, move to frame a denial. He went on: 'And Gavin. He has to jump when you say jump, too. You want all three of us on the end of a string. Then you only have to tug on the string and say, "Hit me, love me, forgive me," whichever it is, and hey presto we do it. Well, if Gavin wants to play that game, let him; it's about all he's fit for. What do you know about your mother and

221

me? We must make it up, you say, because *you* can't bear it.
Well, what can't you bear? You're not at home with us, you
don't have to bear anything except responsibility for your
own actions, and we all have that. You can't bear to see what
you've done : well, you don't have to look. But kindly don't
imagine that Gavin beating you up makes the whole thing
all right; the odd black eye and it's all cancelled out. You
talk of your mother forgiving me ... Why should she forgive
me? Why should I forgive her? What do you know of your
mother and me, what's between us, whether it's good or bad?
I walked out on Sunday night, if you really want to know,
and I haven't been back since.'

Her lips moved again : she said almost inaudibly, 'Oh no,
not to *her*. You didn't go to *her*,' and he thought he could
actually see her move away from him, as far as the bed
allowed her. He stood up.

'What the hell does it matter,' he said, 'if I went to *her* or
not? And her name is Sarah. You know that perfectly well.
You've met her, for God's sake; you've been introduced. Of
course I went to Sarah, where else would I go? And it has
nothing to do with you what I do. You've made it plain
enough this past year that I don't affect your actions, so why
in God's name should you affect mine?'

A nurse put her head round the door and seemed surprised
to see him. She glanced at Prue and back to him. 'I'm
afraid,' she said, mildly reproving, 'you're disturbing the
other patients. And anyway, your daughter needs absolute
quiet. We can't have you upsetting her.'

Prue somehow managed a smile. 'He's not,' she said,
defensive.

'Well.' The nurse examined their faces with professional
concern. 'Better not stay too long; she gets tired easily,' she
said to Manson.

Alone again he said to Prue, 'I didn't realize I was shouting.'

She smiled again. 'You were rather splendid, I think you
frightened her.'

He felt sick. Everything was violence, noise, cruelty, loss of

222

control. That was what counted. No one had any respect left for old-fashioned virtues like peace and consideration. He said, 'I'll have to go now.'

'Why? They haven't rung the bell yet. And anyway, I'm a special case.'

'Oh yes,' he said, 'you're that all right.'

38

'Daddy came to see me today.'

'Oh good, darling. I thought he would.'

Prue was frowning. 'He was a bit peculiar. He got very angry when I asked if you were going to make it up. You *are* going to make it up with him, aren't you?'

Cassie hesitated: she felt extreme reluctance to discuss this with Prue. 'I've written to him, darling. The next move is up to him.'

Prue clasped her hands over her stomach; she had to reassure herself constantly that the baby was still there. It still seemed too much of a miracle to believe without frequent confirmation. 'But he's with *her* – that girl. He's *living* with her. Don't you mind?'

As Prue's recovery grew more certain, Cassie's urge to slap her returned. She said very gently, 'I'd really rather not discuss it with you, darling. I think you've said enough on the subject, don't you?'

The easy tears spilled out. 'Oh God. I'm so sorry. I truly am. Don't you believe me?'

'Yes, but I'd rather you proved it by not saying any more. That's fair, isn't it?' She was reminded irresistibly of childhood bargains. Prue had always been swift to promise, slow to fulfil.

'That's more than fair. I don't even deserve to have you here at all.' Instant retreat. The pattern was familiar.

She said brightly, 'Let's talk about cheerful things. Isn't it wonderful to know the baby's all right?'

Prue said mournfully, 'Poor baby.'

'Why?'

'Having me for a mother.'

'Darling, you really mustn't *wallow*.'

'I know. Or you'll lose patience with me.'

'I didn't say that.'

'But it's true. Oh, I know I shouldn't, I really do. But I'm so scared. I want this baby so much but I've never felt sure I'd be a good mother, the way you were. I'm too selfish. And I can't cope with Gavin either; he's too much for me. He won't go the way I want him to go.'

Cassie said gently, 'Can't he go his own way? Why won't you let him?'

'I can't stop him. That's what's so terrifying.'

'Cassie.'

She turned her head, startled, and there he was, his head out of the window, calling to her. She should have noticed the car but had been too wrapped in her own thoughts to be aware of her surroundings. She walked over to him and said, 'Hullo,' thinking how pointless and inadequate the word sounded.

He said, 'I want to talk to you.' Hesitated. 'Can you sit in the car for a minute? I don't want to come to the house.'

She got in, wondering idly if his reluctance was due to the state of their marriage or the temporary presence of Gavin. She said to break the silence, 'I'm glad you've seen her.'

She thought he actually shuddered. 'Yes.'

'Oh, I know she looks terrible.' Automatic soothing. When it came to the crunch she was stronger than he was, she thought regretfully, not for the first time. 'But she's going to be all right. They both are, please God.'

He shook his head. 'I don't understand any of this.'

'I know, it's a shock. But I tried to explain in my letter—'

224

He cut her short. 'Oh yes, your letter. You wrote that to punish me, didn't you?'

She was shocked, then wondered guiltily if that had indeed been her subconscious intention. Retaliation for the night of anxiety and revelation that she had endured alone? 'Not on purpose,' she said.

'You could have phoned me at the office,' he said furiously. 'You made me wait twenty-four hours for news. I suppose you thought it served me right; I'd forfeited my rights as a father, was that it?'

'No.' She tried to be honest. 'I just didn't feel I could explain on the phone.'

'About Prue or *Sven*?' He nearly spat the name at her. 'You put that first, I notice. Prue was an afterthought. Oh, by the way, she's in hospital. But don't worry, it's fun to be beaten up. I suppose you thought I wouldn't bother reading your true confessions if you put Prue first. Well, you were right, I wouldn't have. Not that it matters. There's not much to choose between you as it turns out.' He put his head in his hands. 'My God, and to think you made me feel guilty. I actually felt guilty for loving my own daughter and being unfaithful to you. God. You'd never have told me about him, would you? But when you did, my God you did it thoroughly. You must have wanted to make me feel I'd been there.'

Cassie wondered if she had. She had not re-read the letter before posting it but she knew once she started writing it a kind of total recall had come over her. Maybe she had said too much, but if so surely more to remind herself, to re-live some of the buried memories, than to punish him. 'I wanted you to understand,' she said. 'I thought that was all. But perhaps I was self-indulgent.'

'Perhaps!' He laughed, a bitter, theatrical laugh.

'Oh, Peter.' She was embarrassed. 'You're making too much of it.'

He shook his head. 'I don't feel I know you any more.'

'Oh, that's ridiculous.'

'Is it?'

She said nothing, hating his new way of talking: heavy, melodramatic. He went on, 'You're strangers, both of you. You and Prue. But you obviously understand each other perfectly.'

'That's not fair. I was trying to help you understand, and make you feel less guilty. That's all. Honestly.'

He turned to look at her and she was shocked by his remote, accusing expression. 'You *honestly* thought that now was the time to favour me with all the squalid details of your revolting affair – with Prue in hospital? He could have killed her, have you thought about that? You're sheltering a homicidal maniac. I hope you know what you're doing, that's all.'

Cassie said evenly, 'That's nonsense, and you know it.'

'Oh, is it? Well, of course you're the expert. I'm too old-fashioned to appreciate the finer points of sadism.'

'It's not like you to be so pompous.' She was angry. 'Can't you see it's more important to *understand* people than to worry about wounded feelings?'

'I didn't notice you being particularly understanding on Sunday night.'

'No, maybe not. But I've had time to think and I'm trying to make up for it.'

'You mean you're trying to get even.'

Cassie's depression increased. 'Peter, we're not children. Do we have to have a slanging match? Do you really think it will help?'

'I don't think anything will help. If you really want to know, I think we've all got in one hell of a mess and I can't see any way out of it.'

Cassie had regained her calm, although she wondered if it owed more to exhaustion than generosity. 'In time you will. You'll know eventually if you want to be with me or Sarah. Prue and Gavin have to work out their own answers. We only have to accept them.'

He was silent. Presently he said, 'Does that mean you want me back?'

'If you want to come.'

'How very welcoming.'

226

Cassie shook her head as if shaking off flies in the summer. His words and his tone of voice were an irritant, flitting round her head and disturbing her. 'I'm sorry, I'm too tired for emotion.'

He said suddenly, abruptly, 'But you wished me dead.'

She was shocked. 'No.'

'Yes, you did. In your letter. Do you want me to show it to you? You wished me dead when you were grovelling to him. You didn't care about me or the children or anyone.'

She was sobered. 'Did I write that? I can't remember. I . . . wanted a way out, that's all. It was a long time ago.'

'You wanted me dead.' He repeated the words with a kind of grim satisfaction. 'And you wanted his child.'

Cassie gathered her failing strength. 'Look, I wrote that letter in a kind of dream. I'd been up most of the night, I'd had you and Sarah to think about, then Prue in hospital, then Gavin telling me his side of it. I was in such a state I can't even remember what I wrote. I just felt we all had to put our cards on the table.'

'Well, you did that all right.' He paused, then added slowly and deliberately, 'I just can't tell you how indescribably dirty I think the whole thing is.'

Cassie, stung, hesitated, then said, 'I could say the same about you and Sarah using Prue's flat.'

He said as if he had conditioned himself to believe it, 'There was nowhere else we could go.'

'Oh, really. All the hotels had closed down.' She heard the barely repressed savagery in her own voice and pondered again the nature of sexual jealousy.

'You know what I mean.'

'Yes, I certainly do. It was the only place you wanted to go. Well, I expect you had your reasons.'

There was a long pause. Finally he said, 'I don't think there's any point in continuing this conversation.'

Cassie shrugged. 'I suppose not, now you're not winning. As long as you were telling me how disgusting I was it was all worthwhile.' She felt herself trembling. (I was right not to tell him before. *This* is why I was so reluctant. I must have known he'd trample all over it.) They had never had a row like this before.

He said, 'All right, I'm sorry I used that word.'

'But you meant it.' She marvelled that she could not let it alone. After years of pacifism she suddenly could not even accept an apology.

Her mood must have reached him for he said, 'Well, you're not ashamed of anything, are you?'

'You mean it would be better if I was?'

He didn't answer.

'You think I ought to be? Why? Are you ashamed? Does being ashamed make everything all right? I must tell Gavin; he certainly feels ashamed. It's ironic, really, when he had more provocation than any of us, but there it is.'

He said heavily, 'I don't even want to hear his name.'

'Well, I don't see how you'll avoid it, with Prue and the baby and everything. Or are you planning to cut us all out of your life?'

He sank into his seat. She thought he looked suddenly old; she was even moved to pity in the midst of her anger.

'I don't know what I'm planning. I'm incapable of planning.'

'You'll know in time,' she said soothingly.

'You mean if Sarah lets me down I'll come back to you. Is that what you mean? That's why you stayed with me, isn't it, because he went away?'

'There was never any question of leaving you.'

'But only because he didn't want you. You told me. You wanted his child and everything. You wished us all dead.'

She burst out violently, 'God, I wish you'd stop saying that.'

'Well, isn't it true? You put it in your letter.'

She lit a cigarette. It tasted awful. Since Sunday she had smoked almost constantly. 'I was out of my mind.'

'What, when you wrote the letter? Or when you were with him? Which?'

'Both. Oh, I don't know. I never thought about leaving you.'

228

'But you would have if he'd asked you.'

She shook her head. 'I knew it would never arise.'

'So you put up with me. How very generous of you.'

'Oh, don't. It ... wasn't the same. Surely you can understand that. You can find room for me and Sarah – you must know what I'm talking about. Don't make me wish I hadn't told you.'

There was a long silence before he said, 'I'm sorry. I've taken it very badly, haven't I? And it means a lot to you, doesn't it?'

She was silent. In her mind she saw Sven, retreating, stubby and hostile, and she thought, I've betrayed you, oh, forgive me. At the same time the rational part of her reflected, I am going mad. How very alarming. This whole thing has turned my brain. She said, 'It was like a dream. I'd never have told you because I didn't think you needed dreams, I thought it was a weakness peculiar to me. But ... this thing with Prue brought it all back. It seemed relevant.'

He said almost resentfully, 'I can't get over how alike you must be. I'd never realized. This whole business of violence ...' She thought she felt him shudder. 'I just don't understand it. It makes me feel quite inadequate. When I looked at you just now ... you were a stranger. When I went to see Prue, I couldn't get it out of my head. I didn't know what to say. Have ... have you discussed it with her?'

'No. No, I couldn't. Besides, it's none of my business really. It's between the two of them. Whatever I said would only be irrelevant.'

He said in a low voice, embarrassed, 'You must both think me very unsophisticated. I was shocked. I mean your letter shocked me. I know it's very old-fashioned to be shocked but I was.'

She said gently, 'And you still are.'

'I can't help it.'

'I know.'

Another long silence. 'Well, I suppose I better be getting back.'

'Yes.' She picked up her bag, her gloves.

'Shall I run you back? ...'

'No. I'm parked over there.' She pointed.

'Oh yes.'

They both sat still and surveyed the windscreen.

'Well, you can contact me at the office if you want to.'

'Yes.'

'I mean—'

'Yes, I don't want the other address.' She was surprised how strongly she still felt about that.

'No, I meant ... well, I don't think I'll be coming to see Prue again.'

'Oh.' She was chilled. Intellectually, she understood but emotionally she was chilled just the same.

'Unless ... there's any change, I mean. Will you let me know?'

'Oh yes. Of course.'

'You blame me,' he said, suddenly harsh.

She shook her head, shrugged, weary with emotion expressed and restrained.

'I can feel it.' He was hostile, defeated.

'I'm tired,' she said, meaning it. 'I've no energy left to blame anyone.'

39

He said to her, 'I feel the world's gone completely mad and you're the only sane thing in it.' She did not know how to answer this, being only too conscious of the burden it imposed upon her. She could only think of things impossible to say ('But I wanted to depend on *you*') and so she became very silent and much more affectionate in order to fill up the silence. At the office it was easy to survive: she was shielded by routine and distance and the merciful presence of other people, but each evening in the flat she was at the mercy of his need. He talked endlessly about Cassie and Prue, how they had both let him down, how they were not as he had imagined them to be, how his whole life was based on fraud. 'What would I do without you?' he said fondly at intervals, and she kissed him to avoid answering. She began to feel pure terror, like a trapped animal. There was nowhere she could go. No one would take her in. The flat was supposed to be her home but he was in it day and night; she was never alone. She did not dare to drive the Jaguar in case he questioned her about it, so it sat in a side street, permanently parked, red and streamlined, mutely reproaching her. And at any moment Simon was expected back: the telephone might ring. She dreaded this and the explanations that must follow and yet she also longed for it, as for deliverance. She had left her new number with Annabel for anyone who might phone, except her parents. But the phone did not ring and she felt alone in the world. She sat with him, eating dinner or watching television, and wondered how it was possible for her to feel so alone with someone in the room, and for him not to notice. He said, 'I feel so comfortable with you,' and squeezed her hand, and she thought, 'No one has ever loved me before and now I don't like it. What's wrong with me?' She could not even tell how she felt about him because she could not get back far enough to find out: there was no perspective to guide her. Sometimes she thought that if only he knew more about her it would be all right, but whenever she started to tell him, something would remind him of Cassie or Prue and he would be off again, talking for hours. He had given up visiting and merely telephoned the hospital asking for news. He seemed particularly incensed that Gavin was still staying at the house with Cassie and they both saw Prue every day.

40

'Gee, you've been good to me,' Gavin said on their last night.

Cassie merely smiled. It had been easy: he had been the most accommodating of guests. Up early and out for a walk, then studying in his room; cooking either lunch or dinner for her and refusing to let her wait on him, dividing visiting hours scrupulously with her and in the evenings playing cards or listening to music. He was the ideal guest and sometimes when she caught his face at a certain angle the memories were so sharp, the similarity so acute that she felt she had never looked at him before. It's just a reaction, she told herself, a mad reaction to shock and strain. I am not quite myself. Or was it that she was now herself for the first time in years? She was scared, and it was rather delightful.

Gavin went on, 'I don't know if I should say this but do you think your husband will be back soon? I mean I hate to think of you here all alone.'

'He'll be back when he's ready, I suppose.' She smiled. 'You mustn't worry about me, really. I'll be all right.'

'I don't know. I don't think you're so good at looking after yourself.' He was quite serious and her heart turned over.

'Maybe I haven't had much practice. But I can learn.'

He frowned. 'Would you like us to stay here for a bit? Prue needs to convalesce anyway and we could just as easily ...'

'No. You said you wanted to get her home and you're right. That will do her more good than anything, I'm sure.'

'Well, term will be starting soon. But ... you could always come and stay with us. Hey, that's a good idea, how about that? Why don't you?'

She shook her head; she was surprised how much she

wanted to agree. 'No. You need to be alone. You really do. I'll be all right.'

He leaned forward, clasping his hands: something on his mind. 'Look, can I ask you something? Do you mind a lot, about him and his secretary? Because I always think these things aren't important. Even if Prue ... well, I mean I'd be sore, of course, but it wouldn't be the end of the world.'

She said slowly, 'No, it's not the end of the world.'

'I'm glad you feel like that. I mean it's a shock and all that but it doesn't really matter, it's what's between you that counts.'

'Yes.'

'He'll be back,' he said confidently. 'I just know he will. He'd be such a fool not to come back.'

She smiled. 'It's nice of you to say so. But it's a bit more complicated than that. We'll see. You mustn't worry about me, please.'

'If I want to I will.' He looked at her hard: the moment was peculiarly intense.

'You've got enough to worry about with Prue,' she said, retreating against her will.

'Prue doesn't need it. She's tougher than all of us.' He got up, began to pace about. 'She scares me. I think she's great but I don't really know her and I don't think she needs me.'

'Oh yes, she does.' Panic. 'You mustn't think that. I'm sure she needs you. I *know* she does.'

'Oh, I think I have a function to perform in her life – though I'm not too clear what it is and that scares me. But the real me, me as a person, not a function, I don't think she needs. I don't think she knows who I am. She just takes what she needs and leaves the rest lying around. She doesn't wait to be offered what you want to give. She makes her own selection and that's it.' He shivered. 'And that sure scares the hell out of me.'

Although Cassie had not thought in these terms before she found the analysis strangely penetrating. 'Maybe we spoilt her,' she said. 'Maybe she just needs a firm hand.'

'Yeah. That's just what I mean. I'm a *person*. I shouldn't

233

be around to provide a firm hand – or to spoil her either, if it comes to that. She's got to grow up.'

'So have I. So has everyone.'

'Oh, you,' he said, stopping in front of her. 'You're grown up all right. I guess you always were. D'you know, it's funny, I don't know what to call you. I know I always called you Mrs Manson but I can't any more, it's too formal. I haven't had parents since I was a nine-year-old kid. I just rolled around from one aunt to another till I was fourteen, then I quit and took care of myself. That was eight years ago. You can grow up a lot in eight years.'

'Yes, you can.' Or a day. The estate agent's board in the garden.

'So what do I call you?' He squatted in front of her chair so their eyes were on a level; clasped his hands and stared at her.

'I suppose you call me Cassie.' There was a pain in her chest where she had forgotten to breathe.

He grinned. 'Do I? Gee, that's nice; I thought you'd never say it.'

'Well, I did. Now suppose you get me a drink.' She did not want a drink but she needed one, and in any case, anything to get him to move.

He did not move. 'Are we friends, Cassie?'

'Of course we are.'

'Really friends?'

'Yes.'

'That's good.' He held out his hand. 'Shake, friend.' She put her hand in his, hesitating, and he pulled her towards him, quite slowly, giving her time to resist, and kissed her on the mouth. At first she was quite still with shock, then she found herself kissing him back and hanging on to him as if she were drowning. He gathered her into his arms.

'Poor baby,' he said presently, rocking her, and she found she had started to cry. 'Poor baby, never mind, it's all right.' He held her very tight with her face pressed against his shirt so she could hardly breathe and she sobbed like a lunatic for about two minutes: she did not even know what she was crying about. He kept murmuring above her head with soothing monotony like a litany, 'There, baby, it's all right, cry it out, I've got you, let go,' mesmerizing her, letting her wash it all away, whatever it was. When she had finished crying she felt wonderful, pure and drained and peaceful; she smiled at him with real friendship and said, 'Thank you. Now will you get me that drink?' feeling the danger had passed, but he still held her, both hands on her arms quite tight, and said simply, 'Cassie.' She began to tremble again; she said, 'We're not going to do this, you know.'

'Aren't we?' His eyes were very dark and fixed on her face as if to hypnotize her.

'No. Of course not. After all—'

'If you say you're old enough to be my mother I shall hit you.'

'Gavin, you're being ridiculous. And taking advantage. Have you forgotten—'

'Prue and your husband? No. Will you stop telling me things I know. Come here ...' and he pulled her down on the floor beside him. 'There's only one relevant thing you can say and I'll stop right away. Say you don't want to and mean it. That's all.'

They stared at each other for a long time. She could feel his whole body trembling through the hands that held her.

'We're not going to do this,' she said again, but presently, quite soon, she found she was wrong.

'Don't get dressed yet.' He put up a hand to stop her and shifted position so he could look at her. 'You have such a beautiful body.'

'I've had three children.' Moved and incredulous.

'I know.'

'And I've put on weight.'

'Don't argue with me. I think you're beautiful.'

'I'm forty-eight.'

'So? I don't care if you're sixty-eight, you look great to me.' He put his head in her lap, closed his eyes. 'Cassie,

Cassie.' Opened them again. 'Wow,' raising his head to kiss her breasts. 'Are you really Cassandra?'

'Yes, of course.'

'How did that happen?'

'My parents in a mad moment. Most uncharacteristic.'

'I like it. I hope you don't have her gloomy gifts, though.'

'No. I don't think so.'

'That's good. Can I call you Cassandra?'

She didn't answer for a long time.

'Can I?'

'When?'

'In future.'

'I suppose so. But it may sound a little odd; nobody uses it.'

'That's why I want to. Beautiful Cassandra, will you kiss me please.'

She bent her head with considerable discomfort and kissed him. He made purring noises, remarkably authentic. She said slowly, 'I don't believe this.'

'Why not? It's the here and now. What else can you believe? Didn't I make you happy?'

'Yes,' she said. 'You know you did.' She had forgotten what the vigour of youth was like, but even more astonishing had been the tenderness.

'Good,' he said. 'I thought so. I've been wanting to for ages.'

'Have you? I couldn't be more surprised.'

'Then you must have very little imagination. For months I've been thinking, my God, this woman, she's so attractive. But that wasn't enough. Then over the past ten days when I found we actually liked one another, we were friends, we were close, I thought, wow, this is too good to be true.'

She smiled at the dark, sleepy head in her lap, hair tousled and damp with sweat. 'No pangs of conscience?'

He looked surprised. 'No. And you're not to have any either. It's a beautiful thing to make love to someone you love. Now I know and you know we're not in love the way Prue and I are, but I *love* you, you as a person, and that has nothing to do with Prue or your husband, it's just between us. When you think what we've been through together, you

236

and me, the hospital and all that stuff and being here together all this time getting on so well, it would have been terribly wrong not to make love.'

Cassie smiled. 'The complete amoralist.'

'I don't know what that means.'

'Yes, you do. But never mind, it doesn't matter.'

'Yes, it does.' He sat up, taking both her hands in his own. 'I'm not making excuses for anything, I don't have to. To say I love you if it isn't true is wrong. To make love when you don't even like someone is wrong. I'm very old-fashioned. I have my own rules and I don't do things I know to be wrong. The only wrong things I've done in years have been hurting Prue. That was wrong, that's why I felt so bad. If a thing is wrong you feel bad about it, that's how you know.'

Cassie said gently, 'Then if Hitler didn't feel bad you mean he was justified?'

'I don't know about Hitler. I only know about me.'

'No, you must know. Murder is wrong, and persecution.'

'Sure. Sure I know. But Hitler was nuts. Say, how did Hitler ever get into this conversation? Cassandra, you're cheating. I was talking about us and you drag in a lousy guy like that to put me down.'

'No.' She felt herself irresistibly smiling again. 'Not to put you down. What a lovely expression.'

'Don't change the subject. You're always changing the subject. Now listen to me. I'm not going to let you feel bad; you've done nothing wrong, do you hear? What's worrying you, Prue or your old man?'

Cassie hesitated. 'Both. But mostly Prue. And ... well, the fact that I'm your mother-in-law, doesn't that bother you at all?'

'No, not a bit. Should it? I don't go around putting lousy labels on people. Okay, let's take it step by step. Your old man's busy. Oh, he'll be back but right now he's busy. Prue's in hospital. We've not done anything together that we could have done with either of them. If you don't tell them they won't ever know. I'm not a blabbermouth like Prue. As for the family bit, I just don't see it. I don't feel related to you

237

and even if I did, what of it, what could be nicer? Prue's dad kind of fancies her, doesn't he? Well, that doesn't shock me. Oh, I know it shocks him and it shocks her, maybe it shocks you too, I don't know. But my mom ran off when I was three, I don't even remember her. And Dad died when I was nine. Now if my mom's alive somewhere she may have remarried, she could have a different name, anything; she wouldn't know me and I wouldn't know her. We could meet and make love, what's the difference? Maybe we already have.'

'Oh, Gavin, *really*.'

'It's the truth. My aunt even changed my name, so how would my mother know? But that's not the point. The point's how you feel, not who you are. And making people happy not sad. That's all there is to it.'

In the morning she watched as he helped Prue down the path and into the car she had lent them. Images of the night swam in her brain across her line of vision when she saw the two of them together. Making love again when they finally got to bed, his saying, 'Now we can sleep. I've always wanted to *sleep* with you,' and holding her as if he were the mother and she were the child. He was holding Prue in the same way now, she noticed, protectively, and she could not decide what she felt, if it were jealousy or relief. Certainly there was a feeling that she had had what she was not entitled to and now it was restored to its rightful owner; but the restoration hurt nevertheless. No matter what he had said in the night ('You can count on me always, I mean that. Just pick up the phone any time') there was no getting round the facts. It shocked her that she seemed to see people in terms of ownership, of property. She knew it would have shocked him even more. She envied him his sloppy, free, young outlook on sexuality and pitied him too; it would not last long, she thought, when brought up against nappies and teething and wind. He was young; he had not yet had time to learn the emotional laws of cause and effect, that actions produce results, whether in terms of babies or trauma. He still imagined, as if rooted in a charmed circle, that immunity was his right, that he could say with certainty, nothing bad will follow from this act of mine, whereas this could only be accurately said in retrospect, in the past tense, and even then how many years did it take to be sure? Yet it was easy to believe the worst, for suddenly with a flash of premonition such as she had never experienced before, she thought, Prue is going to have trouble with that baby. She simply could not *see* it going well: it was as if she really had vision and saw darkness and trouble. She blamed him at once, lovingly but fiercely, as she had blamed him (as well as herself) for making it hard for the first time to look Prue straight in the eye. This time it was all his fault. He had called her Cassandra, and now that was who she was.

41

The flat seemed strange to Prue, as if she had been away for a very long time. She moved around it slowly, awkward with the child, like a dog sniffing at the furniture of home after a spell in kennels. Suddenly it wasn't home any more, just a place she used to live in.

Gavin said, 'Sit down, honey. Take it easy,' which was so unlike him that she wanted to laugh.

'I'm okay,' she said. 'I just want to mooch around.'

He followed her into the bedroom where she stood staring at the bed. He misinterpreted her look and said, 'Yeah, good idea, why not lie down for a bit?'

She shook her head violently. 'It's funny, I keep seeing them there. Can we sleep in the other room?'

'What, on the floor?'

'No, on the sofa.'

'It isn't big enough.'

'It is if we snuggle up.'

'With you in that shape. Can you imagine it?'

'Yes, I am pretty big.' She surveyed herself in the mirror: she looked tired, untidy and huge. 'Do you think it's all right?'

'What?'

'The baby, of course.' She looked at him in amazement. 'Our baby.'

'Yes, of course it is. They said it was.'

'I know.' She looked back at herself, doubtfully. 'Pity we can't take it out, have a look to make sure, and then pop it back in the oven like a cake.'

'Why pop it back?'

'What d'you mean?'

'Well, if it's okay let's keep it out and get back to normal.'

'You said if.'

'What?' He was vague, starting to unpack her things.

'You said if it's okay.'

'So what?'

'Don't you think it is?'

'Honey, how should I know? They said it was, so it is. Why don't you lie down, huh? You look all-in.'

'I don't like this bed.'

'Oh, Prue, come on. That's old history.'

'No. It's here, all round us. And I don't think the baby's all right. I'm worried.' She stared at her bulging stomach as if she could X-ray it with her eyes. 'Oh, I wish I could see it.'

'They said it was okay,' he repeated patiently.

'I know. But it's *my* baby. They don't know enough about it.'

'Honey, they're doctors, for God's sake. If they don't know, who does?'

She wandered back into the sitting-room and he followed her as if it were unsafe to leave her alone.

'Gavin, you do want this baby, don't you?'

'Well, I don't want any other baby, that's for sure.'

'What kind of answer is that?'

He said very slowly. 'I was joking.'

'Oh.'

'You know. A joke. Funny. People laugh.'

She went on as if she had not heard him. 'Because I want this baby more than anything in the world. And ... that night ... you ... you hit my baby.'

The colour came up in his face. 'Now look, you know how I feel about that night. A lot of things happened I'm ashamed of. I hit you all over. I can never make it up to you. I know you asked for it but I still shouldn't have done it.'

She shook her head. 'No I deserved every bit, you were right, after what I did. But the baby didn't deserve it. Not my baby.' She remembered saying these words to him at the time, before she blacked out, and she thought from the look on his face that the echo had reached him too.

'I was out of my mind. You know I didn't mean any of it. Hell, I've told you often enough.'

She sat down on the sofa and he sat at once opposite her as though relieved she had come to rest. She said, 'Gavin, did I trap you into marrying me?'

'Trap me?'

'Mm. With the baby.'

He thought about it. 'Well, I guess we'd've gotten married anyway eventually. The baby just gave us a nudge. I mean it was a shock you getting pregnant like that when we thought we were safe. But I guess these things happen all the time.'

How thoroughly she had deceived him. And he her, as it now appeared. She said, 'I thought you wanted to marry me. I thought we were in love.'

'Sure we were. We are. But that didn't mean we had to get married so fast. That's all I'm saying.'

'So if I hadn't got pregnant you wouldn't have married me.'

'Honey, now look here. We were in love, we'd have gone on just as we were till we both finished school, then maybe we'd have travelled a bit, I don't know. Maybe got jobs or gone back to the States, I don't know. You're talking about two or three years. If we'd still felt the same after two or three years then I guess that's when we'd have gotten married. Hell, we're not *old*.'

She said, 'But I wanted a baby. As soon as we fell in love I wanted a baby; I wanted *your* baby, I wanted to be married. Not play about, not going steady, not having a silly affair, but grown up, and married and pregnant, I wanted real life.'

'Are you telling me you did it on purpose?' He was staring at her as if she had said something really awful.

'Yes. Of course I did. I was careful at first, then I stopped, and even then it took ages. I thought you'd guess but you didn't.'

He wiped his face with the back of his hand. 'No, I certainly didn't.'

'Well, there you are.' She clasped her hands round her stomach in the way that had become second nature.

He burst out, 'But it's so *irresponsible*. What if we'd had a row or you'd met someone else or I'd got run over, what then?'

'What d'you mean, what then?'

'Well, you'd have been stuck with a baby.'

She repeated simply, amazed at his obtuseness, 'But I wanted real life.'

42

She became convinced of impending disaster and wrote letters to carry around in her bag. The one to her parents said, 'Dearest Mummy and Daddy, I'm sorry I've been such a bad daughter to you but I couldn't wait to grow up. Everything was always so easy and soft for me but it wasn't for you. I thought if only I could have some trouble and problems I'd be grown up like you. I wanted to stop receiving and start giving. I wanted to be involved in something frightening that would be too much for me, and when I met Gavin I knew he was it. Do you remember that dream I used to have when I was small, the one I could never describe properly? Everything in it was brighter and bigger and louder than normal, and all the textures of things were rougher. It was more real than real. I don't have it any more, there's no need. But I seem to have overdone it, I think. It's all burnt up. The trouble is, it's so hard to get the dosage right, like scientists with a new drug. But don't worry, it's all been worth it. And I do love you both. Prue.'

To Gavin she wrote, 'Darling, I don't blame you at all. No one could love anyone as much as I love you and survive.'

43

Gavin phoned almost every day. Cassie had never believed he would; she had tried to put the whole thing out of her mind either from shame it had happened at all or misery that it would never be repeated. But the phone calls came, so regularly that she found herself waiting for them, and if he missed a day she did not know how to occupy herself till the next. She wrote longer letters to the twins, feeling that this was the one area left in which she could still behave dutifully.

'Cassandra, how are you?' He always said the same things.

'I'm all right. How's Prue?' She talked to Prue, occasionally, on the phone, but always when he was out, hating her own calculation. And he always phoned her from college.

'She's okay. A bit odd. Kind of dreamy. I don't know.'

'She's retreating,' said Cassie. (How it all flooded back.) 'She'll be all right when the baby's here.'

'I hope so.' He sighed. She pictured him shaking his head. 'I don't know.'

'Oh yes. Lots of women get a bit funny about this time. It's natural. Don't worry.'

'I wish I could see you.'

'No.' Too quick. Was she really so scared?

'No, I guess not. Is your old man back yet?'

'No?'

'Hmm. I hate to think of you there all alone.'

'I'm all right.' She caught herself smiling at the concern in his voice.

'I love you, Cassandra.'

She couldn't reply.

'Oh, don't get alarmed. I love Prue as well, it's just like I said, I'm in love with her but I don't understand her, I don't know what we're meant to be doing, either of us. But I really do love you.'

And you know nothing about me, she thought in a panic. Nothing at all. The kind of person I am you might not even like. And I love you too, whatever that means.

'You can't say it, I know,' he said calmly, shattering her. 'That's your kind of loyalty. It doesn't matter, I quite understand. I've got mine too, only it's different. Okay?'

'Okay,' she said, her eyes closed, the phone wet in the palm of her hand.

'Call you tomorrow. Take care of yourself, Cassandra.'

44

Sarah said one night when she could no longer restrain herself, 'What are you going to do?'

He seemed surprised; he said, 'What d'you mean? About what?'

'About Prue. About your wife. I mean you can't just leave things the way they are, can you?'

'Can't I?' He looked at her longingly. 'That's all I want to do. What more do I need if you're here?' But her face must have betrayed her, for he went on quickly, 'It's not enough for you, though, is it? Do you want to go out, see your friends? You must do whatever you like. Don't let your life come to a standstill because of me.'

'I haven't got many friends. Not really. It's just ... that I've never lived with anyone before. I don't know how it goes.'

He took her hand, saying quite tenderly, 'You're bored, aren't you? That's quite natural. Would you like to go out more? I'll take you anywhere you want to go, just tell me. I'm a bit of a stick-in-the-mud, I'm afraid, but I only need prodding.'

She shied away, frightened: he was at once too near and yet not near enough. 'It's not that. I'm worried. There are other people in your life, surely you should be attending to them, not sitting here with me all the time.'

He smiled. 'It seems we're both telling the other to go out and neither of us wants to go.'

Sarah said stubbornly, 'I'm worried about your wife and daughter. I can't help it.'

His face darkened. 'They're perfectly all right. Prue's out of hospital and back with her husband where she belongs. If she wants to live with someone who ill-treats her, that's her affair. And Cassie ... well, I showed you the letter.'

'That hurt you very much, didn't it?'

'Is that so unreasonable? It was a shock. She's not the person I knew. All these years and I had no idea how she felt, what she'd done. I've been living with a stranger.'

And you still are, she thought, terrified. Am I supposed to make up for both of them? I can't do it; there isn't enough inside me. And you never gave me a chance to tell you things, you were always in trouble yourself and I had to be strong. Just loving you isn't enough. She said, 'I think she

245

was only trying to make you feel better – more equal, if you like.'

'I'm sorry, I don't see it like that. Tit for tat and that makes it all right?'

She said desperately, 'No, but when you saw her, you must have felt something.'

'Yes, chilled.'

'But she's your wife, she must be terribly upset.'

'I don't think so,' he said equably. 'But you obviously are. Do you want me to go, is that it?'

'No,' she said. 'No.' And was not even sure if she meant yes.

'Look,' he said, 'you were the one who was upset when we had nowhere to go. When I had to go home all the time and we couldn't meet. That's why I took this place. If you don't like it, say so.'

'Oh, you're so *absolute*.' She looked around wildly for help. The room had become a prison. The meals and the bed and the television, all the routine, and always his presence and the knowledge that he was the one with problems and therefore entitled to be difficult. She even thought it might have been all right if only they had not been together all the time.

'Sarah, I need you.' He took hold of both her hands and she wanted to pull away and scream. 'My life is in pieces. Nothing, absolutely nothing, is the way I believed it was. I love you, you're all I have left. But if it's all too much for you, you've only to say so.'

His tone made it clear that saying any such thing was out of the question. She said, 'No, no, it's just ... well, it's just rather like winning the pools, you don't know what to do with the money. And you go on doing the coupon in a kind of daze.'

She felt him relax. 'What do you want to do?'

She hesitated. 'Would it ... would it be all right if I went to see my sister?'

'Good heavens, is that all? Yes, of course. I'll drive you ... where does she live?'

246

'No.' Too prompt. 'No, really, there's no need for that. It's sweet of you but—'

'You don't want me to meet her. She doesn't know—'

'Yes, she does. I just—'

'You want to go by yourself.'

'Yes.' God, was it such a crime?

'Well, of course you must go.' He let go of her hands.

'I won't be very long.'

'Darling, it doesn't matter how long you are. I've got plenty to do.'

'It's just ... that I haven't seen her for a while.'

'Of course. I understand perfectly.'

The atmosphere was unmistakable. She mooched around, doing her face, getting her coat, being much too slow because she was afraid to be too quick. He read the paper. She felt him observantly behind it all the time.

'Do you want to phone her before you go?'

'She's not on the phone.'

She went round the corner and phoned Simon. The number rang for a long time. Finally he answered, sounding sleepy.

'Simon, it's me.'

'Oh, Sarah.' There was a long pause. 'How are you?' He sounded different but she could not pinpoint the difference.

'When did you get back?'

'Oh ... a few days ago.'

'Did you have a good time?'

'Yes. Yes, it was nice.'

'Are you brown?'

'Yes, quite.'

'Well.' Really he was being extraordinary. 'Didn't Annabel give you my new number?'

'No. That is—'

'You didn't ring.' Suddenly it was all clear. 'Simon, I'm sorry, I'm being stupid. You've got someone there. Shall I call back another time?'

Another long pause. 'Well, it might be better if I ring you.'

'No. Better not.'

'Oh, I see. You're in the same boat.' He sounded relieved.

She wanted to shout, 'Help me, Simon. I need help,' but she choked on the words and turned them into a cough.

'Are you all right?' he said with all the old concern.

'Yes, I'm fine.'

'Well, give me your address and I'll write.'

She gave it to him, knowing it would be no good, and he whistled softly as he took it down. 'That's rather grand, isn't it?'

She laughed.

'Well, I'll write then. Look, I'm sorry about this.' He sounded embarrassed.

She thought what a fool she had been not to know. No postcards, that should have been enough to tell her. He had met some girl and she was there now. It had been bound to happen some day. Was she so conceited that she had imagined he would always be there when she needed him? Lovely Simon, brother and friend, I wouldn't mind sharing you. But losing you hurts.

She said, 'Don't give it a thought.'

She went back to the car and got in. She had never intended to visit Barbara; she knew exactly what Barbara would say. So she headed for the M4 and when she got on it put her foot down hard.

Speed was soothing. She got in the fast lane and stayed there, doing about eighty. She personalized the car, making it glad to see her, like a long-neglected dog being taken for a walk. That was what they both needed. Fresh air and exercise. She switched on the radio and accelerated with the music, shutting out everything else. Don't think, just go with it. Music and speed. Trouble is, eventually you have to go back.

For about ten minutes, perfect euphoria. Then on one of her routine glances in the mirror the blue bulb on the Jaguar behind her. Oh God. And she was doing ninety, more. Christ, what luck. She could not even hear over the radio if the siren

248

was blowing or not. She slowed down, pulled over, and over again; they drew alongside and signalled her to stop.

They were young and very formal. She gave them all the relevant papers, Geoff's and her own, and answered their questions. Halfway through she began to cry, not on purpose but because she couldn't help it. They were very embarrassed.

'You do realize, miss, that we shall have to report this.'

'Yes. Yes, of course.'

'But you may be lucky.' They wanted her to stop crying. 'You never know. So cheer up.'

She howled. Lucky? She would never be lucky again in a million years. She said something to this effect quite inaudibly through the howls and one of them leaned in the window, looking concerned.

'Are you all right?'

She nodded miserably, untruthful.

'You're not in any kind of trouble, are you?'

'No.' Not much.

'Because if there's anything we can do—'

'No.' Just arrest me, please. A nice quiet cell would be lovely. 'Thank you.' It was good to know someone cared, even officially.

'Where were you making for?'

'Nowhere. I was just ... driving.'

'Well, you can drive on. Only not so fast this time, all right? Goodnight.'

She watched them go. She was quite exhausted and wanted to stay parked for ever. Pulling herself together briefly, she drove slowly to the next exit road and soon found a quiet lay-by where she could rest. Promising herself just ten minutes, she curled up uncomfortably in the passenger seat, imagining Geoff at the wheel, and fell asleep.

He was very angry. As soon as she walked in the door anxiety gave way to relief and relief to rage. Then coldness. She had seen it once or twice at the office, but always directed towards other people.

'I suppose you have an explanation.'

The sight of anyone so ready for a scene always unnerved her. She went limp, as if the energy he had summoned up had been drained out of her. 'I'm sorry.'

'Is that all you have to say?'

She had prepared her lies in the car, with miserable efficiency, after the first shock of discovering the time had worn off but left her thoroughly awake.

'I'm very sorry. Barbara's husband went out and she wanted me to stay till he got back.' She had heard or read somewhere that it was best to keep lies simple and short. But she hated the act of lying, and hated the necessity even more.

'It's ten to two.'

'Yes, I know. I'm sorry.' She wondered how many times he wanted her to say it.

He poured himself a drink. She looked at the bottle and thought he must have had quite a few already. 'And you couldn't even phone?'

'I told you, she's not on the phone.'

'Don't they have call-boxes where she lives?'

'I'm sorry,' she said again, monotonously. 'I couldn't leave her. She gets frightened on her own with the children at night. And anyway – ' the lies were beginning to stick in her throat – 'I didn't think.'

'No. That's obvious.' He drank his drink, glaring at her. 'It never occurred to you I might be worried. Christ—' and he suddenly let fly, 'I thought you'd had an accident, I thought you were dead, I didn't know what to think. You stay out half the night and you don't let me know, what the hell am I expected to think?'

'But you knew where I was.'

'Did I? You might have been anywhere.'

'I told you—'

'Yes. I know what you told me.'

They were both silent. She made a final effort. 'Look, I've said I'm sorry and I've explained. I didn't mean to worry you. What more can I say?' She was shaking inside.

He said, tight and hard, 'It just isn't good enough, Sarah.'

Everything suddenly broke loose. 'No, it bloody well isn't. For Christ's sake, I haven't left you for a minute in weeks and I go out one night and you make a big scene about the time. The hell with the time. It's *my* time, not yours. It's not office hours and you're not married to me and I'm not your daughter either—' She stopped. The look on his face was enough. 'And that's what it's all about, isn't it?' She felt very tired but relieved, as if they had suddenly reached the end of a journey. She walked past him to pour herself a drink and he grabbed her by the shoulder and shook her. She said quite calmly, 'No, I'm not Prue. She likes that, I don't. You save it for her.'

His hand fell away. 'I don't think you know what you're saying.'

She went on and poured the drink. She was amazed at her own calm. 'Yes, I know what I'm saying. I've just never dared say it before. You're in love with Prue. Not me, or your wife, just Prue. You can't bear her being married, you can't bear her being pregnant. You don't want me as a person, you just want someone to take your mind off her. But nobody can because you're obsessed with her. As long as she lives you'll be thinking about her and wanting her back. You're going to ruin her life. What chance has her marriage got with you breathing down her neck all the time? Or your marriage, for that matter. Or my future. I can't sit around being a second-rate substitute for Prue all the time.'

He was white and silent. Finally he said, 'I've never heard such disgusting, ridiculous rubbish in my life. I love my daughter, I want the best for her, and that's *all*. You can't mean what you're saying.'

Sarah sat down heavily. 'But it's true. Oh, why can't you admit it? It might be easier if you could. Easier to bear or easier to cure, I don't know. But we can't go on telling lies like this and pretending all the time. That way nothing works – it can't. Oh, why can't you see it?'

He said, tight-lipped, 'I'll leave in the morning. Or would you rather I leave tonight?'

She shook her head, smiling, wanting to cry. 'But it's *your* flat. I should be the one to leave.'

'No, it's yours. I got it for you.'

'But I can't pay the rent.' She started to cry. 'You got Prue a flat too, didn't you? Can she pay the rent or do you help her as well? Oh, why do you want us all to be so *beholden*? How can anything work if we all have to keep saying thank you?'

'But you don't,' he said. 'That's not what I want.'

Sarah said, 'If you want to be loved just let people go. Then they'll love you. Just let them be free.'

'Really? Do you guarantee it? And how free do you want to be?'

She shook her head. 'I don't know. Just ... not a prisoner.'

'And you're a prisoner here?'

'No. Yes. Well, it's just ... claustrophobic somehow. I'm not me any more, I'm just part of the scenery. I'm beginning not to exist. One day I'll go to the mirror and there won't be any reflection.'

He was startled. 'What? Why do you say that? It's horrible.'

'I know. It's a nightmare I used to have. I wanted to tell you about it but you never gave me the chance. You were always talking about Prue.'

'That's not fair,' he said. 'You could have told me anything.'

'Not really. At least I didn't feel I could. There was always so much on your mind. Oh, I thought because you were older you could help me. But you never let me ask.' She blew her nose loudly on a tissue.

There was a long silence. Then he said, 'Someone rang up for you tonight.'

She froze. 'Who?'

'A man. He said, "Sarah, I'm back." When I spoke he got very confused, asked the number and said sorry, it was wrong, he'd made a mistake, and hung up. Who was he?'

'I don't know.' Why were lies so automatic?

'Yes, you do.'

252

'Just a boy I used to know.'

'Used to, or still do?'

She said desperately, 'He went abroad—'

'Were you sleeping with him? Well, were you?'

'Yes. Oh, why not? What does it matter?'

'Were you in love with him?'

'I don't know. No. Oh, why all these questions?'

He said, 'Look, Sarah. No one has ever loved me. I thought Cassie did but it turns out she cared far more about some crazy artist. My mother I never got through to. And Prue ... well, you've said your piece about her.'

'I'm sorry.'

'No. Maybe you're right. I can't tell. But all the people I've loved have ... evaded me somehow. I've disappointed them all, I haven't been ... enough. I thought you were the one real thing in my life. Are you saying I've let you down too?'

'No. I'm just saying ... well, I had a life before I met you, that's all.'

'And you want to hang on to it. So if I asked you to marry me you'd say no. Is that it?'

'You mean you want a divorce?' Shock.

'I want a new life, Sarah. That's all. Is that so bad?'

She said, appalled, 'But how can you? You haven't let go of the old one.'

45

She sneaked out to meet Geoff at lunchtime, feeling guilty and furtive. Even the phone call had been difficult to organize with Manson in the next office. She was a little late and

Geoff was already in the restaurant. He got up to greet her and settle her into her seat.

'I ordered you a drink,' he said. 'You look as if you need one.'

'Oh God, do I look a mess? It's been a bit of a rush.' She sank down and sipped gin and tonic gratefully.

'No, you look marvellous as usual. Just a bit harassed, that's all.' He held her hand under the table and the waiter pretended not to notice. 'Look, no names, no packdrill, but I'm sorry I rang at the wrong time last night. Was it all right?'

She felt a great rush of affection for him, for looking the same and being so uncomplicated. 'Yes, it was. Well, no, actually it wasn't, but nothing to do with you, not your fault. I'm sorry I was out.'

'Out?' he said, surprised. 'I thought you were probably in bed.'

'Oh no, *no*.' She surprised herself with her own vehemence and remembered at the same moment that she had something else to confess. 'I was out in the car. Geoff—'

'Yes, now d'you think I could borrow the keys? I'm only here for a week and I'd like to get around a bit.'

'Oh, *Geoff*.' She heard herself almost wailing. 'You're not back to stay.'

'No, I told you. I've got to be there for six weeks. But something cropped up and I had to come over so I thought, not bad, I'll see my girl and see my car, and all on expenses.'

The waiters hovered. Geoff began to say, 'We're not ready—' but Sarah shook her head and ordered steak and salad in a rush. Geoff did the same, made a brisk decision on the wine, and leaned towards her rather anxiously. 'Are you all right?'

'Oh, Geoff.' She wondered if he had any idea how pleased she was to see him. 'No, I'm not all right. I must talk to you.'

'Talk away.' He lit a cigarette. 'But you don't have to tell me anything you don't want to, you know that.'

'Oh yes, I know. You're lovely. Well, first of all, they pinched me for speeding last night. That's where I was when

254

you rang. I went for a ... sort of burn-up, I suppose, on the M4, and they caught me. Oh, it's all right, the car's fine, I didn't have an accident or anything—'

'I should think not,' he said quite calmly. 'I'd never have lent it to you if I'd thought you'd be careless. What were you doing when they got you?'

She flushed. 'Oh, about ninety-five. It *was* silly, I'm sorry, but I just wanted to get away.'

He raised his eyebrows. 'What, from *him*?'

'Yes. (Oh, I do wish I smoked.) Oh Geoff, I've got myself in such a mess. I don't know how it happened, it's sort of crept up on me. Oh dear.' She finished her drink with a despairing gulp and thought, if it wasn't so serious it would be really funny.

'Now, just a minute. Keep it simple and start at the beginning. We'll soon get it straight.'

Oh, you're nice, she thought. I *like* you. I didn't know you were so strong.

He said, 'Is this the same chap who was around when I left?' She nodded. 'Is it your flat or his?'

'I don't know.'

His expression was comic. 'But you *must* ... Oh, I see. You're living together. After all you said about never—'

'I didn't mean to. He's my boss. Oh, please don't be shocked—'

'Shocked?' he said. 'Me?'

She heaved a great sigh. 'Oh, when it started I thought it was just an affair, *you* know, and his wife was away ... oh, I don't know what made me begin ... And then she came back and we had nowhere to meet and he ... just took this flat, just for me, and I pay some of the rent, as much as I can—'

'That sounds like you.'

'Yes, only I hate not being able to pay it all, I just don't feel right. Then ... oh, it got so awful, his daughter found out and she told his wife, and there was a scene and the daughter's husband beat her up so she ended up in hospital, and she's pregnant, and he left his wife and moved in with me.'

255

She paused for breath. The waiters brought food and wine while she watched Geoff absorbing the story. When they were alone again he grinned and said, 'Well, I don't know, it's not safe to leave you for a minute, is it?'

She began to cry with relief. 'Oh, Geoff, I'm so glad you've come back.'

'Hey, what's all this? You'll ruin your lunch. Come on, eat it, don't wash it.'

'I can't eat.'

'Yes, you can. It's easy. Just cut a bit off and put it in your mouth. Your teeth will do the rest.'

She began to laugh, choked, blew her nose. 'You must think I'm an idiot.'

'No more than I am. I've only been gone three weeks and already there's a girl in Frankfurt who thinks I'm going to marry her.' He paused. 'But I'm not. Now tell me how I got into that one.'

'It's your compulsive charm.' She began to eat, anything to be busy, to cover up the shock he had given her. (But we were never in love. Why do I feel like this?)

'Sarah.' Serious voice. 'Come back with me. I mean it. I could use a good secretary, in more ways than one. If you're in a mess, if you're not happy, just cut the job and the flat, and get out. Come to Frankfurt. I can wangle it all on expenses.'

'For three weeks?' she said doubtfully, tempted.

'Why not? Call it a working holiday. It'll be fun, Sarah, try it. If you're not in love with this chap ...'

'Oh, I'm not.' It was out: she inspected the words with appalled relief. 'But I thought I was. I really did.' She shivered.

'Well, we all make mistakes.'

'Geoff, why should you rescue me like this?'

'Why not? We're old friends.'

'Yes, we are, aren't we?' The words warmed her.

'So old friends must stick together. After all, we do have an E-type in common.'

'Yes.'

He lowered his voice. 'I've missed you, Sarah. I really have.'

'I've missed you too. But that doesn't mean—'

'It means what it says. We've missed each other. That's all. But it's a start.'

'Yes.'

'Look, we're not big on commitment, either of us. We're not loyal, we're not exclusive. Maybe we're scared. But let's not knock what we have. I like you more than any girl I've ever known. I even trust you with my car. What more do you want?'

'What more indeed?' She was smiling.

The waiter, hovering, seized his chance. 'Is everything all right, sir?'

'Yes,' Geoff said decisively. 'Everything's fine.'

46

She climbed a spiral of pain. When it was more than she could encompass, like drowning because you could not swallow enough, she blacked out. Coming to, there was a blissful moment of relief, of no-pain that felt like well-being, before it sliced into her again and screwed her up, making her twist into its own pattern. Mixed with it were dreams like memories of dreams, textures and sounds and emotions all mixed, so that she did not know where or when she was. But of *who* she was, she was quite certain. She said her own name aloud, 'Prue. I'm Prue,' and the knowledge comforted her. It seemed that she must hang on to it, because it was too late to tell anyone else. She thought, vaguely, that she was dying, and there was the satisfaction of being right, mixed with bitterness, when she thought, more precisely, how much there was that she had not had time to do. She had not thought so clearly before in terms of her own contribution to the world, and even now it was not specific: she felt that she could contribute more remarkably by simply being herself, than by positive action. She remembered herself as a child, on the swing in her parents' garden, and again as an adult in the South of France, brown and oily and close to the earth. She saw herself playing netball at school, cutting her knee on a walk, at table eating stew and saying, 'More please.' The tears that came in her eyes were for her own remembered self far more than for the pain. The pain, although it was taking her over, was irrelevant. She saw her own existence as something separate: Prue, free and young, walking apart from the pain. She knew she was valuable; yet she felt she had never been valued, except by herself. The images she saw of Prue were like clips from an old film, so that she thought, that was me, that was my life. How unfinished, and how beautiful. No one had ever really appreciated it. They did not know the infinitely complex, messy texture she had tried to create. The Prue-person roamed about, through the past and the present, calm and gleaming, and capable of anything. And yet she knew she would not survive to do it, any of it; she would not make a mark of any kind. I am dying, she thought, of over-ambition, no matter what they put on the certificate; and my baby, too. She wanted to think that the child would go on, would continue the Prue-person in disguise, surreptitiously, under another name, but the fantasy lacked conviction. She stared upwards, over the huge curve of the child, saying goodbye to it, just in case there was nothing beyond; and when Gavin came in and rushed to her, appalled, she saw him but she could not speak his name.

47

'Well? Have you told him?' Geoff's voice was crisp as ever but intensified by the phone. She had jumped, when it rang, almost literally out of her skin, as the saying had it, so great was the shock of breaking such an extreme silence. She felt uneasy in her skin, in any case, as if it did not adequately cover her: she felt her nerves were exposed.

'Sarah? Are you packed?' More decisive still.

'They're at the nursing home,' she said.

'What nursing home? Who?'

She felt angry with him for not knowing at once. 'Prue's ill,' she said helplessly and looked at the clock. Too much time had passed: it could not be good news.

'Who?'

'His daughter,' she said, and started to cry.

'Sarah. Are you all right?'

She went on crying, having no choice. A great storm of tears forced its way out and erupted over the phone.

'I'm coming round. Tell me the address again.'

'It's all my fault,' she said, howling. The receiver was damp in her hand.

'The address,' he repeated. 'Where are you?'

She told him; it took her a minute to remember it.

'I'll be there in ten minutes.'

'Oh Geoff, I can't bear it.'

'Get a hold of yourself. Have a cigarette.'

'I don't smoke,' she said miserably, hysterical.

'Well, try.' The phone went dead.

She walked round and round the room. Then she walked round the flat. She wanted a drink but she had already had two and she did not want to be uselessly drunk when news came. She kept thinking, or hoping, that they might need her, that all was not lost, that she might be allowed to make amends. When the bell rang she ran to the door, convinced that this was her chance. She had forgotten about Geoff.

'Oh. It's you.'

'I said I'd be here in ten minutes.' He came in, looking at her anxiously.

'I forgot.'

'Come and sit down.' He put his arm round her but it felt strange, alien. She thought bitterly, enviously, you're outside all this. It's not your trouble.

'Drink this.' He had poured her a large Scotch.

She shook her head. 'I've already had two. I want to keep sober.'

'Whatever for? That's the last thing you want to be. Drink it.' He poured one for himself.

'Oh, Geoff.' She sipped the drink – he had made it too strong as usual – and began to cry again.

'Now tell me.' He shook her gently. 'What happened? Come on, Sarah. You'll feel better if you tell me.'

'She ... I think she's dying. And it ought to be me. I'm her and she's me. But they've got it the wrong way round.' She was still holding her drink to her lips and tears actually splashed into it. Salt Scotch.

He took hold of her free hand in a tight grip. 'You're not making sense. His daughter is in hospital, that's all you've told me so far. Come on, darling, I want to know so I can help you.'

She looked at him, puzzled, as if she had never seen him before. Who are you to help me? Stranger. Or perhaps it was always so, one stranger or another, a hand to clutch, a body to lean against, a face to show concern. The endless charade of finding someone in whom to hide.

'She's having her baby. But it's too soon. There must be something wrong. They rang him at the office this afternoon and he went straight away. He said he'd phone but he hasn't.' She wound her handkerchief round her hands. It was wet

260

and bit into her fingers, leaving a mark. Perhaps if she could hurt herself enough Prue would be all right.

'Well, it's just taking a long time. Why all the fuss? People take ages having babies, don't they? My mother never got tired of telling us what hours of agony she endured to produce the two of us. What are you in such a state about?'

She got up, wanting to free her hand, feeling guilty to have even that much comforting contact with another human being. (This is something I must bear alone.) If she had known any magic spells she would have done them.

'I was a substitute,' she said. 'But they're killing her.'

48

'Champagne,' said Prue rapturously. 'Oh, I wanted champagne more than anything else in the world and you knew. You've brought it.' She started to raise herself up in bed, pulled a face and subsided. 'Ouch, I forgot. Stitches. God, I'm a wreck. Mummy, you never told me it was so painful – no, good job you didn't. And I thought I liked pain – ooh, sorry—' as she caught the look, simultaneous and identical, on all their faces. 'Well, you know what I mean. But I think I'm cured, if anyone's interested. God, it was *awful*: right now I hope I never even prick my finger again. Sorry I'm a bit woozy, it's that wretched stuff. But it helped. Not enough, though. God, they do pull you about. I felt like a horse or something, everyone tugging at me. Ugh. But I did it. D'you realize, I actually did it. Not alone and not unaided but I did it. I produced!'

Manson struggled with the cork, watched by Cassie and Gavin. He felt Gavin restraining himself from offers of help. He grew hot, felt the veins on his forehead, the tension in his fingers and the start of sweat. Excitement, relief, old age?

'Careful,' said Prue, and the cork popped. They all laughed nervously and he started to pour. Cassie handed Prue the first glass. 'Well done, darling,' she said. 'I'm sure this is very unethical but never mind.'

Prue laughed. 'They can't say a word, you're paying. Oh, you were clever to get me in here. Imagine if I'd been in a stuffy old hospital where you couldn't all come, and no alcohol. Imagine.'

They all had their glasses. Manson cleared his throat, glanced at Gavin and Cassie, and then turned to Prue. 'To both of you,' he said. There were sudden tears in his eyes.

Prue drank to herself. 'Isn't she beautiful? Oh, don't you think she's just the most beautiful thing you've ever seen?'

Gavin sat on the edge of the bed. He sipped his drink awkwardly, as if he wished it was something else. 'Yeah, she's great. I guess we're prejudiced but she looks great to me.'

Cassie drank with concentration, her eyes fixed on Prue. She didn't look at Manson or Gavin. Mingled with light-headed relief was the purest envy. Prue had her baby. Everything was all right. It was over. 'She's beautiful, darling,' she said.

Prue looked at Manson. 'Daddy. You're not saying anything. Don't you like your grand-daughter?'

'I love her.' Prue's face blurred as he looked at her.

'So do I.' Prue sighed with total contentment. 'God, I can't believe it. It's over and I've got her. Eve. Do you like the name Eve? I only thought of it the other day. Eve Sorensen. It's terribly good, don't you think? And wasn't she clever to come early? I was so sick of being huge and Gavin was sick of me *being* huge, weren't you? (Oh, don't look like that, don't be silly.) And now look at me. All gone. You wouldn't think such a tiny baby could make such a mound, now would you? I thought she'd be a monster. Huge. But it must have been all the padding. I wish she didn't have to be in that incubator, I want her with me, all the time. But I s'pose it's all right. It won't be for long, will it? Oh, she's so pretty. I thought she'd be hideous, I really did. That is when I wasn't thinking she'd be dead. Oh, I didn't tell you, did I? I thought we'd both die, I really did. Wasn't that silly? I even wrote you all letters. Now I'll have to tear them up.'

Manson said, 'Excuse me a minute.' He put his glass down and went out of the room to the phone down the passage.

Prue frowned. 'Where's he gone? What did I say?'

'Nothing, darling, I expect he's just gone to the loo.'

Prue laughed. 'Poor Daddy. His eyes are quite misty, did you notice?'

'Oh, honey, give him a break.'

'Well. It's not like him, that's all. I'm flattered. D'you think he approves of Eve? Oh, I know I could have called her Petra or Cassandra, or Gavina come to that (wonder why "a" is so feminine in all languages) but I like Eve. It's like a fresh start and that's what I want. Oh, I know I've been bloody to everyone but I'll make up for it, promise. And I'll be such a model mum you won't recognize me. Honestly. I'm going to be the greatest mum who ever lived. Well, maybe the second greatest. God, I just can't stop talking, have you noticed? Do you think it's the champagne or the stuff they gave me, or just having *had* her? I feel so elated I could burst.'

Cassie said gently, 'It's everything, darling. That's what it's like.' She had the strangest sensation of loving them both, Prue and Gavin, with separate passion, as if she were physically split down the middle. And Manson must surely be telephoning Sarah, but it did not matter, there was no jealous pain. It seemed trivial, faced with the enormity of birth.

'I don't think I'll bother going back to college,' said Prue. 'It's so unimportant, with Eve to look after. And Gavin's clever enough for two ... aren't you?'

'I don't know. Guess I'll have to be.'

'You're not sorry she isn't a son?'

'She's Eve – how could she be a son?'

Prue grabbed his hand. 'Oh, I do love you. Mummy, isn't he lovely?'

'Yes.'

'Oh, I'm so lucky.'

Manson came back into the room. Cassie, watching, thought she saw him switch from one mood to another by merely adjusting the muscles of his face.

'Daddy, you've been ages. Is there any more champagne?'

Manson gave them all a little more. Prue held up her glass. 'Now then, come on. I want to see you shake hands, you and Gavin. And put your arm round Mummy. Oh, come on, Daddy, please. Let bygones be bygones, all of you. It's not much to ask and surely I'm entitled. After all, just think how you'd feel if I'd died.'

49

'He must have hated that,' said Gavin as Manson drove away.

'What?'

'That kiss and make-up bit. God, that was pure Prue, wasn't it?'

'Meaning you hated it too?' She was smiling.

'Meaning it was typical of Prue. But yeah, I did hate it. Not that I mind shaking hands, I've got nothing against him, but it wasn't spontaneous so what does it mean? Just Prue, getting her own way again.'

'Get in the car,' Cassie said. 'I'll drive you home.'

In the car he stretched out his not very long length and sighed, 'Jesus, I can't believe it. I had – not like me a bit but wow – the wildest premonitions.'

'So did I.'

'*Cassandra.*'

'No, really I did. And Prue did as well, it seems.'

'Oh, she's probably making it up. Anything for drama. God, the relief. I can't believe it's all over.'

'I know.'

They drove for a while in silence. Then: 'I thought he'd stay, though. I thought you'd drive off together in a cloud of marital bliss for the Technicolor finale with choirs and a sunset.'

'Sunrise, you mean.' Already the sharp, pale dawn was rising as they drove towards Regents Park.

'Were you disappointed?'

'I didn't consider it. You can't . . . do things like that just because you feel emotional.'

'What other reason is there?'

'We're too old to be hasty.'

'Oh, come on. Don't give me that.'

'We're grandparents, have you forgotten?' She was light-headed with relief. Prue was all right. The baby was all right. No one had been punished. To have escaped scot-free seemed to her the purest good fortune, a gift from the gods, and made her frivolous.

'So what? I still love you, Cassandra. Do you love him?'

'Yes, of course I do.'

'Well, that's all right. That gives us two each.' He sighed contentedly.

'You have a very simple mind.'

'Why? What's the problem?'

'Doesn't it ever occur to you there's an element of choice about this. That people can't just . . . love each other all over the place.'

'Why not? Why can't they?' He sounded genuinely surprised.

'Well, for one thing you're married to Prue and I'm married to Peter. And you and I are legally related.'

'So what?'

'Well, it makes a difference. Surely—'

'Oh, balls. If you mean you don't love me just say so, don't fence.'

She was silent. They had reached the door of the flat and she drew up at the kerb. 'Ah, you can't say it,' he exclaimed in triumph.

'I can't say I do either.'

'That's different. If you can't say you don't then you do, even if you can't say you do.'

'That's too much for me.' She was trying to be flippant.

'Don't laugh it off. It's too important.'

'You're home,' she said gently. 'We've arrived.'

He ignored that. 'Look, Cassandra, I'll tell you something. I used to think about going back to the States with Prue. When I'm through with school.' He shook his head. 'Not any more. You're in England, so that's where we'll be. I don't just fuck and run away. I mean it. You've altered my life. Now do you believe I love you? Oh, I'll be a good husband to Prue, there's no problem, but I love you as well. I mean it.'

She made a huge effort. 'You're just saying you can cope with two women. Well, lots of men can. Or more.'

'Meaning you can't cope with two men?'

She didn't answer.

'Well, can you or can't you?'

'Gavin, you're bullying me.'

'All right, and you like it. Have you ever tried to cope with two men?'

'Yes.' Why was it so hard, such anathema, to lie?

'And?'

'It was tricky.' She closed her eyes; she did not even want to be reminded. And yet it had worked: she had not gone off Peter at all, merely loved him and pitied him.

'But you managed it, yes?'

'Yes.' She did not know if the image in her head or the image beside her were the stronger.

'Well, then, what's the problem?'

'No problem. Look, you better go in. I've a long way to drive and I'm tired. It's terribly late.'

'It's early.'

'Yes, that's what I mean.'

'So come in.'

She was amazed, tempted, disappointed. 'No, I can't. You must know I can't.'

266

'This night of all nights we should be together. Who's closer to Prue than the two of us?'

'That's lovely incestuous reasoning.' She wondered how long she could hold out. Exhaustion beat in her brain.

'Well?'

'No, I can't, Gavin.'

'He's got his secretary, you know, all tucked up and warm.'

'Yes, I know. Thank you for reminding me.'

'Yeah. I'm mean enough to do that. Amazing, isn't it? I want you so much, Cassandra.'

'That's a frustrated husband talking.'

'No. I just love you. I really do. You want to know what that means? I like you, I respect you, I want to take care of you, see you never catch cold or get tired, and I want to fuck you blind. What more can I say?'

She had screwed up her face in an effort not to cry. 'No more, please.'

He leaned across. 'Is it too much?'

'Yes, it's too much.'

'So you will come in?'

'No.'

50

They made love to celebrate. Sarah thought she had never seen him so happy, and despite all her own joy and relief she felt a twinge of resentment that she had not been able to do that much for him: inevitably it had taken Prue and her baby to restore him to life. Afterwards she was tranquil but empty, as if they had reached the end of something. Their lovemaking had had a goodbye taste: did he already know what she had to say? She opened her mouth to begin and closed it again. Geoff would call this an ideal opportunity, no doubt, but Geoff did not have to find the right words. She was relieved when Manson spoke instead.

'Sarah.'

'Yes.' Anything to postpone the moment.

'Darling, I don't think we can go on.' He took hold of her hand. 'I've been thinking about it all night. At one point I was even making bargains with God : if You let Prue be all right I'll even give up Sarah – you know what it's like when you're desperate.' He sounded apologetic; she squeezed his hand. Surprise, relief, even disappointment : all combined to keep her silent. He went on, 'But it's more than that. You were right when you said I hadn't let go of my old life. I haven't, and I don't think I can, because Prue is the only reality for me. You've been wonderful. I'll always be grateful to you, but tonight I'd have died, gladly, not just to save her life, that goes without saying, but even to spare her a minute's pain. I'd cut off my arm to save her a headache. Does that sound ridiculous?'

He's embarrassed, she thought, to be telling me how he feels. Was I ever real for him? What did we have, did we imagine it? Was I just Prue, her hair, her skin, when he shut his eyes? Was I ever a person for him, Sarah, myself? But that was selfish. She said, 'No, of course not, I understand. You want to go back. I thought you would.'

'Well, I haven't talked to Cassie yet, but I think she'll agree. I don't see that we have any choice. If we're going to function as a family again, if I'm going to visit Prue and the baby without any tension, well, Cassie and I will have to be together.'

Sarah thought how unloving it sounded, how functional. 'Yes, of course,' she said.

'Prue was right,' he added. 'Tonight she – oh, we had a lot of champagne – she made us all make it up in front of her. She even made me shake hands with Gavin. But she was right. I'll have to accept him or I'll lose her and the baby. I'll

268

always be an outsider. I'm sorry, Sarah, but I can't do it any other way.'

'No, of course you can't.'

He turned his head on the pillow to look at her. 'You'll be all right, won't you? You're so independent. You'll have a life of your own again, remember? Of course you must stay here as long as you like, that's understood, but I think I must move out tomorrow. I'll find an hotel or something. But I can't talk to Cassie from here.'

She felt her eyes prickle. This is terrible, she thought; I'm not used to goodbyes. 'Well, actually,' she said, 'there's no need. I've been waiting to talk to you about that.'

51

'She's leaving tomorrow,' he said to Cassie on the phone. 'Apparently some old boyfriend has offered her a job in Frankfurt. It's ironic, isn't it? Aren't you amused? I made such a big effort to tell her I was moving out and it turned out she'd been trying to say the same thing. So of course I said never mind about notice or references, I'd fix all that.'

Cassie was silent. He said anxiously after a moment, 'Cass, are you there?'

'Yes. I'm here.'

'Well, what do you think? Can we try again? I truly did tell her before she told me. I knew before I left the nursing home that it couldn't go on.'

It's Prue, she thought. You're doing this for Prue.

'I was wrong to be so upset by your letter,' he said. 'You were right to tell me everything. It's the only way it can work, if we're both totally honest.'

But it's too late, Cassie thought wildly. I can never be

totally honest with you again. I've simply exchanged one deceit for another.

'I really did tell her first,' he repeated.

Cassie said, 'I don't see that it matters who said it first.'

'Of course it matters. Surely ...' He stopped; she could feel him thinking how to put it. 'It means I'm not asking you to try again *because* she's going. It means I really want to ... I really want us all to be a family again.'

You are too honest, she thought, and not honest enough. Prue broke us up and now Prue brings us back together. That's all.

He said urgently, 'I don't think I ever meant to stay away. And now ... well, the other night somehow put everything back in perspective. It's so much more important than who slept with whom – don't you agree?'

Cassie thought dully, of course he's right. It's the only thing to do. Restore the *status quo*, go on as before, only better, please God. And we do love each other, after all. But he hasn't said that; he's said everything else. What's the matter with me? I'm too old to be dreaming mad dreams. She said, 'Yes, you're right.'

He sounded relieved. 'Take your time, there's no hurry. I'll see you tomorrow at the nursing home, won't I? We can talk about it then.'

Cassie put down the phone and looked in the mirror. You're old, she told herself. You have no choice. You'll never have the strength to go on saying no if you're alone. But you won't be alone. People don't break up marriages like this. It's too trivial. Marriage and children and stability. That's what counts. Continuity. Family life. Not the insanity of believing you can fashion the future out of a scrap of the past.

52

'Well, see you in a couple of days then.' Geoff was angry that she was not going with him.

'Yes, of course. It's all fixed.' She smiled to soften him.

'Pity you couldn't fix it sooner. You know how I feel about flying alone.'

'Yes, I know. I'm sorry. But I've got packing to do and people to tell.'

'Like parents.' He laughed. 'Well, if yours are anything like mine, which I suspect they are from the way you don't talk about them, get out first, tell them later. The same goes for him. Don't let him change your mind.'

'He won't. I've told you. He's going back to his wife. Well his daughter really. He's doing what she wants.'

Geoff smiled. 'Yes, and he'd have done it anyway. Have you thought about that? If I'd never come back he'd have still left you flat.'

She was shocked by the truth of his hard common sense, yet also relieved that there was someone around to be tough. Perversely it strengthened her confidence in him. She thought that perhaps the people she wanted were not and never could be the people she needed : they were too much like herself. Together they would all sink in a terrifying swamp of emotion. So her mother and Barbara were right, she had been looking all along for security, not love? Or were they the same thing, and the rest just human weakness?

'So stop feeling guilty,' Geoff went on. 'You did them all a favour. They've all survived, they're all older and wiser and no harm done. You're the one who could have got hurt.

'Oh no.' She smiled. 'I'm tough.'

He shook his head. 'I don't think you are. I'm a lot tougher than you and even I don't feel tough. It's a jungle, Sarah. Everyone grabs for themselves. No one cares, we're all out there alone. I want to hold your hand when the hyenas start howling. Don't you want to hold mine?'

She hesitated, feeling an enormous weight of disloyalty. 'Yes.' She could not explain why it felt so wrong: not just leaving Manson (even though he had suggested it) but joining Geoff, offering her parents and Barbara such hideous satisfaction in his money, his looks, his car. He was just what they wanted for her. She thought, if I go away with you we'll maybe live together, perhaps even get married, but what will that prove? Just that we're scared, both of us. It won't change anything. The next time I meet someone in need I'll be off, with a sense of vocation, and I'll live to regret it, again. She felt exhausted, defeated, by the impossibility of trying to change human nature.

He said, laughing, 'Who knows, we may even get married,' and her heart rose and sank as she thought, God, I knew it. Yet when his flight was called she kissed him goodbye with real affection and a surge of panic that if anything happened to him she would not know, as they said, where to turn. Going back to the office for her last half-day, she felt her spirits lift, in spite of the lunch-hour traffic. (Manson had kindly allowed her the morning off.) The sun had come out, the car moved like music, and the next plane she saw would be hers. Geoff was right: they had all emerged unscathed and she ought to give thanks. She stopped for lunch then drove on, a little braced for farewells but otherwise calm and relaxed until she reached the door of her office, finding not Manson but Rupert, who informed her with clinical precision, despite reddened eyes, that Prue had collapsed that morning with a pulmonary embolism, and died within hours.

53

'Rupert told me,' she said when he phoned.

'Yes.'

'I can't believe it . . . she was so well.' She understood now about wanting to beat your head against a wall. 'Oh God, poor you, oh God, how will you bear it?'

'It's not real,' he answered after a long time. 'I've . . . seen her and I don't believe it. It makes nonsense of everything.'

'Can I . . . do anything? Shall I stay? Is there anything . . .'

'No.' He relapsed into silence. Only his breathing assured her he was still there.

'I'm so sorry.' Useless, inadequate words. He didn't answer. She cast around in her dazed mind for something to comfort, anything to maintain contact: found herself instead suddenly and childishly helpless, kicking at fate. 'It's not fair, we'd split up, we'd done the right thing,' as if Prue had died out of sheer perversity and broken her side of the bargain. 'Oh God, it's not *fair*.'

'I know.' He was silent for a long time until finally with a great effort he produced the words, 'I loved her so much,' and began to weep.

'It's like a judgement on me.' Cassie sat quite still and dry-eyed.

Gavin, now calm after becoming hysterical at the nursing home, said, 'You mean on both of us.'

'No. I was her mother. That makes me responsible.'

'I don't accept that.'

'That doesn't matter. It's how I see it.'

'Then how d'you think I feel about beating her up? You

can't share my guilt for that. If I hadn't done that maybe she'd be alive . . .' He choked.

'No. They told you, they assured you it had nothing to do with that. You've got to believe them.' She wanted to comfort him but all she could think of was, over and over again, this morning I had a daughter. This morning Prue was alive.

'Oh yes.' He faintly smiled, with irony. 'The same way you believe me when I tell you that sleeping with me wasn't a crime so this isn't a punishment. Oh yes.'

Cassie said after a long pause. 'We've got to help each other. I don't think I can bear it alone.'

'You won't be alone, you'll have him. I shall have no one. It serves me right.'

'I meant we must *all* help each other.'

Gavin put his head in his hands. 'I loved her, I really did. Do you believe me?'

Manson came back from the phone, looking old and red-eyed and ill. 'Where is he?'

'Being sick, I think.' She poured further drinks without asking. 'How's Sarah?'

'Very shocked.'

'Yes, of course. Did she know?'

'Rupert told her.'

'Oh yes.' Cassie lit a cigarette and passed him the packet. 'Is she still going away?'

'She offered to stay, I said no.' He sat hunched in his chair, a sudden old man, reminding Cassie of her father at her mother's bedside. 'There's nothing . . . I mean it's a family matter now.'

'Poor Sarah.'

'You were always forgiving.'

'Oh, that. I just meant it must be terrible for her to feel involved and yet be excluded. And . . . she's only a child really.' She thought of the boy upstairs, younger even than Sarah, being sick because he had loved his wife and now she was dead. She envied him his emotion: she herself was totally numb, her feelings locked away, fastened down, like

274

somebody screaming behind sound-proof glass. 'We've all got to help each other, Peter. I can't bear it if we don't.' He put his arm round her but she still could not cry. Gavin came back in the room, ghastly white, and she got up. 'I'll make some tea.'

He could find nothing to say to Gavin. Alone with him for the first time in months, and at such a time, he knew with certainty that now was the moment for words, for reconciliation, for all Prue had wanted and all he had intended to do for her. It would be his last gift. But the words would not come, nor could he stretch out his hand. Despite his own guilt and remorse the one festering thought remained and would not be quelled. My daughter would be alive if she'd never met you. But for you, Prue would be alive.

54

Geoff was waiting just beyond Customs. He flung his arms round her and hugged her, then stood back for inspection. 'You look good,' he said. 'I've missed you. God, I really have.'

Sarah was numb with travel and the strangeness of the airport and the language all around her. On the plane grief for Prue had combined with the guilty past and the uncertain future to create quite unreal isolation, and a selfish terror that shamed her. She said stiffly, 'What about the girl who thinks you're going to marry her?'

'Oh, that.' He seized her suitcases. 'Oh, I've got out of that. Come on. I've got a car waiting.'

There was a driver in the car to whom he gave orders in his business voice, rather brusque. Then he slid back the partition and put his arm round her.

'I've got you a room,' he said. 'It's nice and quite cheap. And not far from my flat, so you'll be independent but accessible. How's that? Of course you can look around for yourself if you'd rather.'

Sarah said faintly, 'Is it worth it for such a short time?'

'Oh.' He glanced at her sideways. 'I forgot to tell you. Dad phoned. I'll be here for six months at least. Maybe even a year. Be worth bringing the car over perhaps.'

She wondered if he had rigged it, and could not ask. The lights of this strange foreign city that was to be her home flashed across their faces in the dark of the car. She looked at him (stranger, friend?) and wondered if he was an end in himself, the answer, or merely a stepping-stone to something as yet unknown. She did not even know which she hoped he would be.

She said, 'Geoff, I'm scared.'

'Yes, I know, so am I. Hold my hand.'

She took told of it, hard. 'Let me tell you what happened.'

55

The funeral was unspeakable. Afterwards, numb with the obscenity of necessary ritual, the three of them gathered again at the house. They had scarcely been apart for three days, three days of tears and disconnected speech, alcohol, arrangements, and silence. Despite the mourners, even those close and genuine in their grief, like Rupert, they felt isolated together, set apart. They had decided to spare Cassie's parents and the twins such an ordeal, so there remained just the three of them, enclosed in their separate loss. The letter, which they had found when Gavin went through Prue's handbag, echoed in Manson's head, setting out her life apart from him, a whole new dimension. He had tried so hard to hang on to her and she had released herself, perhaps in the only way possible. And yet the baby remained, a part of her, thriving, and biding her time to come to them.

Gavin, looking white and ill, vanished into the bathroom, leaving Manson and Cassie alone. They chain-smoked in silence. He found himself searching her face for signs of Prue, as he had even searched the baby's as she lay incredibly small in her incubator, because it seemed unbearable that he could no longer physically see his daughter. The image of her cold, dead face battled with memories of her living one, animated or sulky or serene, became confused with the cherished marble of his mother. He shook his head as if to clear the picture.

Cassie said, 'Are you all right?'

'I can't see her properly.' He put his head in his hand and began to weep.

'I know.' She touched him lightly on the shoulder. 'I can't either. But we will.'

'It's ... such a waste.' He tried to stop weeping: it was unfair to solicit sympathy and force Cassie to be strong. Her calm frightened him: he wondered what storms would break later.

'Try to think of the letter. It was a happy letter.'

'I didn't understand it.' But it had only confirmed that Prue, while resembling him (though he could no longer see any trace of her in the mirror) was Cassie's child inside. 'I suppose you did.' He was envious.

'Up to a point. Yes.'

He blew his nose, poured another drink. Cassie, smoking furiously, had hardly touched hers. 'I wonder what she wrote to him.' The exclusion had tortured him even while he saw it as just. 'Where is he, by the way?'

'I think he's being sick again. Poor Gavin.' It was like her to have sympathy for everyone, Manson thought bitterly. 'He really loved her, you know.'

'In his way I suppose he did.'

'Oh, Peter. Be generous.'

Defensively he changed the subject. 'Do you think we should have let your parents come?'

'No. It would have been too much for them.' She looked vaguely surprised. 'I thought we agreed all that.'

'Yes.' But he had felt a sudden pang of isolation, a longing to gather the clan, however pathetically small. 'And the boys.'

'Oh, they'd have been so upset.' She shook her head. 'No. It was something for the three of us. Surely.'

'I suppose you're right.' He lit another cigarette, hesitated, braced himself. It had to be said. 'Cass, what do you want to do?'

There was a long silence. Then: 'Well, I shall be here with the baby, when she comes out.'

'Do you want me back?' It sounded crude, abrupt: aggressive even.

'If you want to come.'

'I . . .' He stopped and cleared his throat, embarrassed, at a loss. 'I do want to come but . . . I don't know if I can. I'm no help, I can't comfort you. I ought to be able to, I want to, but . . . these last few days, and now, all I want is to be alone. I want to be with her, hang on . . . I can't let her go. It . . . doesn't seem to be something I can share.'

She touched his hand. 'I know. Don't worry about it. Whenever you're ready, I'm here. But Gavin will have to visit the baby. Can you stand that, d'you think? I mean later, eventually. There's no way round that.'

He shook his head. 'I don't know. Not yet. It's too much. You and the baby and Gavin. It's too soon.'

Cassie said softly, 'She's very like Prue.'

'Is she? I can't see it yet, I wish to God I could. I just see him when I look at her.'

'You mustn't go on hating him, you know. Or nothing will work.'

'I know. I just . . .' But the words wouldn't come. Deadlock.

'He was what she wanted. I think that's why I can't cry.

She had what she wanted. Many people never have that, in a whole lifetime.'

'Including you.' The bitterness was too strong for him; it forced its way out.

'Including both of us.' She was so forthright she terrified him. 'The sooner we face that the better our chances.'

He didn't answer; he did not want to face the implications. There were footsteps on the stairs and Gavin came back in the room. He was so white that he had clearly been sick. He paced about, refusing drinks, coffee, cigarettes, sat down abruptly on the sofa facing them and said, 'Look. I've got to say this. It may not be the moment but I can't put it off. You're not ... I mean I appreciate what you're going to do, about Eve, I know I can't cope on my own, with school and all, I wish to God I could, I even thought of quitting but that's stupid, of course, only ... well, I do have to say this.' And stopped.

Cassie said gently, 'It's all right, go on. She's *your* daughter.' And Manson's heart turned over at the words.

'Cassandra.' He clasped bony hands between his knees, frowned, unclasped them, waved them in helpless emphasis. 'I'm not ... I'm not accusing you. Or you, sir' – turning to Manson. 'I mean, I don't know what your plans are, if you'll be around or not. But I have to say ... I just can't let you bring up Eve like Prue. She's my daughter and I don't want her all mixed up and crazy. I don't mean you did anything bad but whatever you did – oh, I guess you meant well, I mean I know you did – we all know how she turned out and I don't want that for Eve. She'll never be happy that way. I want her to be simple and normal and happy. No hang-ups.'

Manson couldn't speak. Cassie said, 'Yes, I understand. But they're not the same person, remember. Eve is half you.'

'Yeah. Well, I'm taking no chances. She's all I've got and I'm responsible. Okay, she has to be here with you to begin with, I know that, but as soon as she's old enough I want her with me, and meantime I'll visit her during the week, and I want her all weekend, every weekend, I'm sorry but I do. I have to say it. And another thing. I'm moving out of that apartment. It isn't mine, it never was, it was something you gave Prue, like a gold bracelet. I'll get a room or a small apartment of my own, whatever I can find, you won't subsidize me *and* look after Eve or I won't have the right to open my mouth. And I have to; I have to be in control. Even if I'm wrong.'

Manson said, 'But you don't think you are, do you?'

'Oh, for God's sake.' Cassie jumped up. 'Today of all days, do you have to *quarrel*? Of course he's right, she's his daughter. Whatever we did with Prue, if we loved her too much or gave her too much, whatever it was that made her the way she is' – her eyes suddenly filled – 'the way she was, we've no right to do it with Eve. We're only guardians. And very temporary guardians.'

Manson said bitterly, amazed at her vehemence, 'Suddenly he knows all about children, is that it?'

Cassie turned on him. 'He's her *father*, for God's sake. You've *had* your chance. We both have.' She started to cry in real earnest.

Gavin said, 'Cassandra, I'm sorry. I had to say it but I didn't mean to make trouble.'

Manson said slowly, not quite alerted but disquieted somewhat, '*Cassandra?*'

Gavin said, defensive and aggressive. 'Should I call her *Mother?*'

'Mrs Manson would do.'

'When you're hospital visiting for a fortnight you get beyond that. But *you* wouldn't know.'

'And who *put* her in hospital?'

Cassie screamed, 'Christ.' She put her hands over her ears 'Stop it. Both of you, stop it. I don't want to *hear*. We're all guilty, we're all to blame, and she's *dead*. Now shut up, can't you? We all helped to kill her and you fight about *names*.' She collapsed into sobs and they both stared at her horrified, relieved and helpless.

Presently Gavin said to Manson, as if they were friends. 'That's good. That's better. She needs to cry.'

56

For Manson, total unreality took over. He ate, he slept, he lived at the flat. He even went to the office, like a ghost, an office now run by Rupert, attired in theatrical black, who had touched his arm, saying, 'You poor bastard. Our lovely Prue,' and thereafter left him alone. He expected to be left alone, because he did not exist. Sometimes he wondered if his life had ended with Prue's, so detached did he feel. He thought of Sarah occasionally as a distant image of beauty, but it was Prue's face that haunted him in dreams. Sometimes he woke crying for her, for himself, and the pillow was wet and he was alone. He worked in a vacuum and went home alone, to dream. Sometimes, so lost was he in his mind that he nearly stepped out in the path of a wildly blaring taxi. He had forgotten how to cross the road. He felt victimized, as if by loving people too much you lost them, and that this was a rule of life which, unfairly, had not been explained to him. But he hoped, and he lived on dreams, undefined. London looked unreal to him, as if seen through mist or frosted glass, and the people he met spoke remotely, from a long way off, and the responses he made came from another agency. At times he almost enjoyed it, this total dissociation from life. It was Cambridge again, it was youth. He was detached from the real world, where people made demands and suffered. But still he missed it; it had been his home for so long.

Living like this, it was a shock to find a letter from Monica. She knew nothing, she was writing to ask him a favour. Did he know of anyone needing a secretary? Her marriage was over and she urgently needed a job. Could he help? She didn't want to be a nuisance but she was desperate. Manson read the letter twice, all his earlier premonitions about the marriage haunting him as if he had made this happen, had willed it and brought it about for his own ends, to put back the unforgiving clock.

57

Cassie had forgotten what a small baby was like. She was nervous at first handling Eve: even Gavin seemed more confident, having no expertise to forget. They were together a lot, inevitably, with the baby, and glancing from father to child she saw Sven and the child they might have had till she felt dizzy with the fusion of past and present. It was all in her mind, she told herself, but that did not make it less real. The resemblance was more in essence than in feature, the generation gap huge, and yet there it was, the danger, the threat, the culmination of her life in all its delicious terror. She did not know if she wanted to run towards it or away from it. Everything that was functional in her life, the contact with Gavin, the caring for Eve, seemed to force her automatically into Prue's role. She felt sometimes that she was being transfigured by events, by a force beyond her control. And they were inexorably allied, she and Gavin, by their love and their guilt; whereas Peter had chosen to grieve all alone. When they talked on the phone he was so remote that she marvelled they had ever been married.

Gavin came down most evenings, straight from college, but always caught the last train back. This was something they did not discuss. He did not touch her. Not once since Prue's death, not a kiss on the cheek, not a hand on her shoulder. Even passing the baby to each other they did not make contact. But they loved her together, unself-consciously.

And they ate and talked and watched television; they even began to make jokes again. She did not know whether to be ashamed or relieved at the resilience of human nature, or indeed how much of it was due to Eve. But they were endlessly compatible, and she was grateful and amazed.

One night in December it was foggy and she was worried about his train yet did not know how to ask him to stay or even if she should. They hovered at the gate, one on each side of it, saying goodbye but not going.

'Don't stay,' he said, 'you'll get cold.'

'I'm all right.' She smiled at him to be reassuring. Their faces were dim, the mist damp on their hair, in their mouths.

'You're fantastic with Eve,' he said.

'I love her.'

'Yeah, so do I.'

I'm forty-eight and he's twenty-two, she told herself. Those are facts. And it's facts that matter, not feelings. We're related by marriage. I must be out of my mind.

'You'll miss your train,' she said.

'Yeah, I must go.' And he did not move. Then suddenly he leaned across the gate and kissed her hard on the mouth. 'Cassandra.'

'Yes.'

'Is he going to come back?'

'I don't know.' This was the truth.

'Do you want him to?'

'I don't know.' This was also true.

'I'd so much rather he didn't.'

58

They met in the park. She had refused lunch, feeling that food would choke her; it was so long since they had eaten together that it seemed an unnatural act. Besides, the social ambience of a restaurant was alien to her now, so enmeshed was she in domestic life. She realized now that this was what she had missed all these years, since the boys went to school. She marvelled that she had ever let them go away, to board; marvelled too that she had ever played with the idea of work, a career, of using her qualifications. She was obviously not cut out for it. Her academic brain was a red-herring, completely irrelevant. Emotionally she wanted only the home and a child, the only true creation for her. She thought she had not been so happy since Prue was born. It had been a wrench just to come up to town for this meeting; Marjorie was baby-sitting, gladly, but she envied and resented every second.

Manson said, after the usual greetings, 'I'd like to see the baby.'

'Well. You can any time.'

'I don't know. It feels awkward, visiting you while we're . . . like this. And *he's* always there.'

She didn't answer. Perversely she thought, why should I make things easy for him? And she was tired of speeches emphasizing Gavin's parental rights.

'Monica wants to come back,' he said, breaking a long silence.

'Oh? But I thought—'

'Yes. But her marriage has folded up. She needs a job.'

'Oh dear. Poor Monica.' A nice girl. She dimly remembered her kind, plain face. 'That's rather convenient though, isn't it, from your point of view.'

'Yes it is. I hate it to happen this way but since it has, well, I couldn't be more relieved to have Monica back.'

She saw at once how good it would be for him: a healing touch of the past. She said hopefully, 'And have you heard from Sarah?'

'No. But I didn't expect to.' No emotion.

She watched the ducks on the pond, and the people feeding them. How simple to be a duck. Quack, dive, little forays below the surface, bread on the water, all that. But perhaps they had their problems too. Duck problems, unknown to man. She felt herself smiling and wanted to tell Gavin the joke. The realization pulled her up short.

He was saying, 'Cass, what are we going to do?'

'I don't know.' She shied away from decision. Decision was final, was endstopped, when life should be open.

'I thought ... I'd feel better but ... she's with me always, I can't relate to anyone else, not yet ...' His voice petered out.

'There's plenty of time.' She still loved him, she realized, but it was no longer a choice. Gavin was right, or else she was mad. You *could* love all over the place: it was not a question of choice.

He tried again. 'Perhaps by Christmas. When the boys come home. If ... I feel like a human being again by then, I don't know ... I do love you, believe me.'

'I believe you.' She wanted him to be happy. She would have done anything to spare him the wretched isolation he was inevitably imposing on himself. But in a sense it was irrelevant, whether he came back or not. She loved him, he was her husband, she wanted him to be happy. But there would always be Gavin and Eve. Whatever he decided, and she would not influence him, that much was fixed. Her life, full of richness and complexity. She realized now that the whole must be accepted, no matter how messy, how unorthodox, how impossible. It had to be attempted. What she had always believed and then crushed had emerged like green shoots, forcing their way through the frost-iron earth. She kissed him on the cheek. 'Take your time,' she said. 'I'll always be there.'

In the taxi, on the way to college (for there was just enough time to catch him after his last lecture), she thought of herself for the first time in years. Herself and Eve and the person who called her Cassandra. Then she focused her mind on Peter, on Sven's distant shadow, on Prue in happier days. They were all part of her life; there was no division. Whatever so-called decisions were made, there was no choice. She was open to everything; she had accepted. Arriving at the college she paid off the taxi and walked through the gates; students were pouring out of the building. She screwed up her eyes to pick out the one; in a jumble of bodies she suddenly saw Gavin emerging at the top of the steps, smiling broadly, hair tousled, scarf flying in the wind, his arm round the girl looking up at him – the image was seized, extended and fixed, as in a frozen frame.